Fighters, Bombers, Tanks, Wolves

GITCHIGUMI

William Myers

ISBN – 10: 1511668598
ISBN-13: 978 - 1511668590

CONTENTS

ACKNOWLEDGMENTS

Your humble author slouches in the shadow of giants like Len Deighton, Leo McKinstry, Patrick Bishop, David Isby, Richard Overy, and Mark Zuehlke. In addition, I highly recommend the excellent works on World War Two by Max Hastings, Anthony Beevor, Martin Gilbert, and John Keegan, who have likewise informed this writer. I must also express my profound gratitude to the good friends and relatives who generously took time to read my manuscript and provide suggestions which greatly improved the work.

For Trooper Jack Myers and Gunner Steven Renault

The Rim – World

The sulfurous fumes burned his nostrils and he clawed at the restraints to escape the flames rising all around him. His hands and feet were on fire as he struggled over the edge into a howling gale which carried him away...

September 1944. Belgium

Major Peter Schmidt's eyes flicked down to the altimeter, confirming that he was at 9,000 metres, then instantly resumed their perpetual scan of the skies westward. Every few seconds, he glanced through the Plexiglas canopy above him and into the rear-view mirror affixed to the top of his bulletproof windscreen, searching for the tiny specks that could suddenly materialize, and then rapidly expand into enemy fighters seeking to shoot him out of the air.

At the briefing this morning, he had been advised that *Major* Roland Schwartz's *Gruppe* of new *Me262* jet fighters would be up. Hopefully this would improve their chances against the unrelenting allied advance, aided as it was by a seemingly endless supply of new aircraft and skilled pilots. Although there was a fair degree of personal animosity between himself and Schwartz, he was grateful for the additional German fighter support that might result in one less Mustang or Spitfire trying to climb onto his tail.

Today's assignment was to intercept a group of American P-51 fighter escorts before they could link up with a stream of B-17s over the coast of Belgium. Regardless of feelings he secretly held against the Nazis and this damned war, any action that resulted in one less bomber unleashing its lethal cargo on a German target could save innocent lives. Poorly aimed or errant bombs inevitably, and often, fell on civilian homes or shelters – in addition to the ones deliberately aimed at them.

A knot formed in his stomach as he thought about his parents and younger sister who were in constant danger from the Americans by day and the British at night, as long as the bombers got through.

The deep roar of the *Jumo* 213A-1 engine reassured him that his *Focke-Wulf* 190D-9, with its improved horsepower, was equal to the best allied fighters he would meet in the skies today. He and his fellow pilots affectionately called it *Langnassen-Dora* ~ Long-nosed Dora, because of its extended length in front of the cockpit. This accommodated an in-line, liquid-cooled V-12, instead of the as originally designed and stubbier air-cooled radial. Peter appreciated that improved surge of power every time he passed above the older engine's performance ceiling of 6,000 metres.

If it was possible to love something that was not flesh and bone, then Peter was in love with this aircraft. Not only did it handle and perform like a dream, but as a young man, perhaps not destined to grow old, he also recognized its similarity to some of the women attracted to his fighter pilot mystique…in that her elegant appearance was a joy to behold.

Alternating asymmetric patterns of dark green and olive camouflaged the upper surfaces of its slender 'stretched' fuselage and wings. Further down, a pale bluish grey colouring similarly disguised the plane's undersides, while mottled irregular spots of olive green speckled the transitional area along the sides and the rudder.

From above, to an inattentive eye, the camouflage scheme blended almost contiguously into the topographical colours of Northern Europe. While viewed from below, it disappeared with equal effectiveness, into either clear or overcast skies.

Being nearly invisible was an incalculable advantage to a fighter pilot. Contrary to popular belief, most dogfights did not consist of long aerobatic contests involving all the twists or turns and expert flying skills possessed by experienced veteran pilots. In actuality, most kills resulted when an attacker could bounce an unsuspecting enemy pilot and squeeze a burst into his aircraft before he ever knew that he had been stalked.

One generally flew away unscathed from a successful first pass, whereas an extended dogfight could, for many different reasons - including pilot skill or experience, aircraft performance, and fuel remaining - result in you being the victim.

Peter appreciated the fact that it had been his good fortune to fly high performance, well-camouflaged aircraft that complimented his excellent skills, and which cumulatively allowed him to prevail over his opponents during these many years of aerial combat. Each of the sixty-four black bars adorning the rudder of his aircraft attested to a victory, and ultimately his survival.

On the Eastern front, the victories had come more easily, particularly in the early years. Although the Russians flew some excellent fighters like the deadly *Lavochkin* La-5, and agile *Yakolev* Yak-3, he had always felt that as a pilot he held a qualitative edge over most of the Soviet fliers.

This was not the case against pilots from the British Empire and America whom he was facing now. They too had excellent aircraft, and he had fought victoriously against all of them. 'Spitfires' and 'Tempests', P-51 'Mustangs', and the huge, but equally potent P-47 'Thunderbolts', had all fallen before his guns. However, these allied pilots on the Western front were often the equal of veteran German pilots, and in several cases his victories had resulted as much from luck as they had from his superb flying skills.

In the back of his mind he reflected upon the composition of his current squadron. It was a motley collection of *Bf*109G and H variants, *Fw*190As, and faster 190Ds like his own. The 190D with its superior performance was his fighter of choice because of the way it evened the odds against the latest allied machines. While the *Bf*109H possessed similar performance to the *Fw*190D, at 182 cm and 90 kilos he found the cockpit cramped compared to the more spacious *Focke-Wulf*.

Unfortunately, the *Fw*190D was still a relatively rare bird, and because of the incessant allied bombing raids on German production facilities it was not appearing on the replacement manifest of his squadron as often as he'd have liked.

His more pressing concern was pilot attrition. The new pilots did not yet have the veterans' skill levels, and regardless of which aircraft they flew, most quickly fell prey to the more experienced and numerous allied fliers.

As leader, he was out in front of his *schwarm*, and was the first to spot the flashes of sunlight reflecting off the shiny aluminum skins of the P-51s as they bored in from the west, still climbing about 2,000 metres below them. The Americans had grown so confident in their numbers and skill, that aside from a bit of anti-reflective olive drab paint on top of the engine cowlings, they were no longer applying camouflage patterns on most of their fighters and bombers. They were in effect inviting the dwindling remains of the *Luftwaffe* to find them easily and to mix it up, knowing that the Germans had the most to lose in this battle of attrition.

Less than five seconds after they had started to dive on the unsuspecting Americans, he saw the mass of small dark shapes that quickly grew into another squadron of P-51 Mustangs diving down on him from the right.

It had been a classic set up. The P-51s that were now on the Germans' tails had taken a more northerly tack eastward. Then, at a higher altitude, the Mustangs had circled around behind them. Meanwhile, the American group below had been alerted by radio that he was diving on them and had all begun to scatter or turn into him.

He shouted a warning into the radio. "Mustangs are diving on us from four o'clock! Fly through the Americans below, and follow me into the clouds under them!"

"Stay close to me Heinz!" He called to his young wingman as he rolled right and dove through a torrent of American 50 cal. tracer fire.

Some of the enemy shells found their mark. He saw Heinz's rudder fly off, and the entire tail of the *Fw*190 disintegrated under the hail of bullets from a P-51. That fighter then skidded under Peter, as it overshot the already doomed German.

He briefly saw the canopy detach as his wingman jumped out of the *Focke-Wulf*, but he had no time to observe whether Heinz's parachute had opened as he slid his aircraft in behind the Mustang.

The American was unable to shake him, but he was a skilled pilot. Banking into a series of diving turns the racing fighter always managed to jerk out of his sights every time he tried to squeeze off a few rounds. He finally managed to fire a short burst of 20mm cannon shells. Most of them flew over the P-51, but at least one round went into the American's engine. A mixture of glycol and engine oil began to stream out of it directly onto the windscreen and canopy of the fighter, completely obscuring the pilot's view.

The American slid his canopy back and jumped clear, before pulling the ripcord of his parachute.

Peter banked left and briefly scanned below for Heinz. There was no sign of his wingman, but as he levelled off he suddenly saw Roland Schwartz's *Me*262 - distinctive because of its nose art depicting a black boar's head - dive below him and fire a burst of cannon at the parachuting American.

In horror, he saw the man literally explode into a tattered mass of blood and viscera as one of the huge 30mm rounds passed through him. Then, with a massive surge of power the jet accelerated eastward to circle around in search of another victim.

"You bastard!" he screamed, but swivelling his head to the right he was shocked to realize that during the few seconds when he had been focusing on Schwartz, a Mk XIV Spitfire had flanked him. He was now lined up by the allied pilot in a perfect deflection shot. Reflexively, he stomped the left rudder pedal while slamming the stick forward and to the left, which would put his fighter into a spinning dive away from the British aircraft.

Time seemed to slow down as he saw the Spitfire drift over, and past him. Then nearly blacking out from the 'G' forces unleashed by the violence of his manoeuvre, he was suddenly enveloped in an impenetrable mist as he plunged into the cloudbank. He desperately struggled to correct the aircraft's spin by reversing the rudder and stick positions, but when he suddenly emerged from the bottom of the overcast he was flying upside down. Luckily, the aircraft was traveling in a relatively straight line, so after only a moment of disorientation he righted the fighter.

A quick glance at the instrument panel, confirmed that Peter had less than a quarter tank remaining - barely enough to get him home - so tacking east toward the airbase and maintaining his present altitude, he began to reflect upon what had just happened.

His breathing steadied and his pulse normalized, and there came a dawning realization that he should not now be alive. The allied pilot had possessed the second or two required to shoot him at relatively point blank range...but had hesitated. He thought he knew why however, and it seemed incredible.

As his eyes had swept over the long cowling of the Spitfire, he saw the red Canadian maple leaf in the small white circle below the cockpit windscreen, but there had also been a more distinctive piece of nose art further forward, just behind the spinner. It was an image of Lake Superior fashioned into a wolf's head...exactly like the one on his own aircraft. However, it was more than just that. For like him, when their eyes had met, there had been the flashing shock of recognition on what he could see of the enemy pilot's face. It was fantastic, unbelievable luck. In that situation, no one but Jason would have spared his life!

Major Roland Schwartz eased the throttle of his *Me262* jet fighter forward and felt a rush of smooth acceleration as the two *Jumo* 004 engines - each hanging from one of the fighter's swept wings - responded to the increased fuel supply with a surge of power.

Messerschmitt had finally designed the perfect aircraft, he told himself. Responsive to its flight controls and lethally armed with 30mm cannons, the jet most importantly enjoyed an advantage in speed of at least 150 kilometres per hour over any enemy fighter. Whereas the *Bf*109 had been intolerably cramped, with poor rearward vision, the raised bubble canopy of the *Me262* provided an excellent view in all directions, and ample room in the cockpit for even his beefy torso.

Having cruised effortlessly at 11,000 metres around the top of the cumulus tower, Schwartz banked left and dove toward the dogfight unfolding below. It was then that he saw the two Spitfires also diving into the periphery of the melee about 2,000 metres under him. With his airspeed indicator registering over nine hundred kilometres per hour, he closed on the two aircraft. In seconds he had the nearer aircraft in his sights. Just before he depressed the firing button, the lead Spitfire did a snap roll to the left and dove away. The wingman was a fraction of a second slower and was just beginning to dip into a snap roll to the right as the first 30mm rounds from Roland's four nose cannons passed over the fighter. However, the rest of his burst tore into the aircraft causing it to explode.

As the speed of his dive carried him below the fight, he pulled back on the stick and applied enough rudder pressure to bring the jet into a climbing right turn. At the outer edge of his vision he saw an American P-51. Its canopy was open, and the pilotless aircraft was on fire, trailing black smoke as it spiralled downward out of control. Continuing through the turn, Roland saw the parachute about a kilometre in the distance, slightly above him.

The memories of a year and a half earlier came flooding back to him. 12.7 mm rounds from the Russian *La* 5 on his tail had torn through the right wing of his *Bf*109. Searing flames had ignited everything around him, while the skin on his hands bubbled and cracked as he struggled to open the canopy and free his oversized body from the cockpit. Finally, there had been the blood-curdling fear and disorientation of tumbling through the air before his parachute opened.

Now, with his body suddenly bathed in a cold sweat, the pace of his breathing began to increase. A visceral hatred rose from deep in his guts as he pointed the jet's nose toward the pilot dangling in his harness directly ahead of him.

It would have been a simple matter to fly just above the parachute and collapse its canopy with the vortex from his passage, but by now the beads of perspiration had turned to tiny rivulets on his forehead, and his breath was quickening even more in anticipation of another kill. The idiot American must have known what was coming, for the tiny figure began to claw at the holstered firearm on its hip as if there was even the slightest chance that the puny weapon could do any harm to Schwartz's aircraft.

At this range he couldn't miss, and Roland thumbed the firing button for the tiniest fraction of a second, unleashing about four rounds. He grunted in satisfaction as the first 30mm cannon shell passed through the centre of the American's chest and he literally exploded into a red mist while the parachute simultaneously collapsed, to begin its fluttering journey earthward.

Suddenly, something glinted in the rear-view mirror atop his windscreen. Twisting his head around, Roland saw the Spitfire turning onto his tail. Simultaneously, he could see an *Fw*190D traveling in the opposite direction as it disappeared eastward into a cloudbank. The other German pilot could not have failed to see him, but the gutless bastard was cutting and running, leaving him at the mercy of the enemy fighter.

The Spitfire was the least of his problems though, as three P-51s were already diving directly down upon him and about to open fire. He rammed the throttle forward, and at the same time rolled the jet over on its back. Diving into a reversed loop, he arrived in an upright position at the bottom, traveling in the opposite direction. The Mustangs had flown past his previous position, and the Spitfire was trying in vain to follow him through the manoeuvre, but the *Me*262 with its tremendous speed advantage pulled further away and rocketed into the same cloudbank as the *Fw*190D.

When he had climbed up through the cloud into the brilliant sunshine above, there were no other aircraft to be seen. However, Roland now had his mind on other things. He'd recognized the wolf's head insignia on the *Fw*190's cowling. For a fraction of a second, he had glimpsed an identical image on the engine cowling of the attacking Spitfire.

The cousin! One way or another, that bastard Schmidt was going to pay!

August 1938. Storm Clouds

The lake was calm this morning.

David Hunter dug his paddle into its smooth surface and felt the canoe glide forward as he pulled the shaft back along the gunwale. At the last second, just before lifting his paddle out of the water near the stern, he gave it a turn, rotating his wrist to compensate for his partner's stroke, and thus kept the craft's movement steady and straight.

In the front of the canoe, confident that his friend David would make the necessary adjustments to keep their heading, Jason McMurchy dug his paddle in again, maintaining a steady rhythm of long powerful strokes which caused the craft to surge smoothly ahead.

On both sides of the canoe's prow David had painted the outline of Lake Superior, altering it slightly to create a stylized version of a wolf's head. His grandfather had smiled and called it *Myeegun*. However, the reaction of his three friends had been rather more boyish and less reflective. Regardless, he had been only mildly chagrined when upon first viewing, this had caused them to jokingly refer to him as "the paddling Picasso."

The day before, they had started at the mouth of the *Michipicoten* River and were now making their way east along the Lake Superior shoreline. They hugged the water's edge to ensure they did not fall victim to one of the fearsome storms which could suddenly rise with awesome power upon the lake. The furious winds and huge waves were capable of sinking the largest of ships, much less their relatively tiny canoes.

Today the lake's glassy surface reflected the shapes and grey-green colours of the trees and rocks that stood silently along the shoreline. The water stretched in various gradients of blue, until it formed a thin indistinct line at the limits of vision both south and west, still hundreds of miles from the opposite shores.

The great lake existed near the centre of the continent, imbedded in the impervious pre-Cambrian geology as a vast freshwater inland sea. A remnant of the ice age, its cold depths were replenished with every spring's snow melt, and its overflow through the St. Mary's River fed the four other Great Lakes before finally exiting down the St. Laurence River, and eventually into the Atlantic Ocean.

David's grandfather, an Ojibwa Tribal Elder, had told him their name for the lake was *Gitchigumi*, which meant Great Lake Spirit. The lake had borne this name before the arrival of Europeans, but although David too was Ojibwa, he normally tended to think of it by the name he had learned in his geography classes at school. He understood that to the Europeans' geometrical way of thinking, with their tendency to measure and classify, "Superior" connoted the lake's relative size and status, whereas his people's name focused more upon the lake's spiritual presence, and how its innate properties related to the larger wholeness of the natural world. This included an undeniable influence on the immediate surroundings, which his geography teacher would have described as a "microclimate".

Still, as he looked out on the lake's great expanse, David did have to acknowledge that *Gitchigumi* possessed all the characteristics of what the shaman of his tribe would call a shape-shifter. Though often wreathed in rising tendrils of morning mist, or conversely, sparkling diamond-bright to a distant azure horizon, its skies could suddenly darken, and the surface morph into shrieking wind-driven havoc. Its level could also change, rising or dropping with the seasons, while transforming both the contours and nature of the shoreline.

Additionally, the lake's surface experienced a seasonal alteration of state, as it froze solid every winter. Whether due to the effect of lunar gravity on the waters beneath, or perhaps variation in the wind and temperature, the ice sometimes moved, driving up huge crystalline ridges along the rocky beaches. Here, the jagged and prism-like forms randomly shattered the cold slanted rays of light that shone through them, to reveal their previously invisible, but now luminous, spectral patterns.

In its way, the lake also seemed to audibly breathe, and David knew the sounds. Not only the lapping of water on rocky promontories, or the steady crash of waves upon the shore, but also the repetitive hiss of water advancing and retreating over the slopes of beaches comprised of mineral-hued pebbles worn smooth by wave action over many thousands of years. During the spring melt, these same inexorable undulations bore a myriad of small ice shards, rhythmically washing over the shoreline in a rippling curtain of delicate high-pitched and glass-like notes.

Resting the paddle across his knees, David reached for the much-dented tin cup in his pack, dipped it into the cool water, and took a long thirst-quenching draught. Jason too, had stopped paddling, and as he twisted around, David cried, "catch," then tossed him the empty cup. His friend caught it effortlessly, only slightly rocking the canoe.

David and he had been pals from the age of five, and their many years of paddling together had forged an almost seamless balance between the two of them in the precariously tippy craft.

After filling the cup and drinking its contents, he tossed it back to David. "Thanks."

Nodding at a point behind David, he winked. "I see our erstwhile companions are doing a pretty good job of keeping up."

"Yeah", David observed. "Their style lacks a certain degree of elegance, but Peter seems to have really got the hang of it, and Jack, well he could probably keep up even if he were paddling a coal barge".

Jack was Jason's younger brother, while Peter Schmidt, was their cousin, visiting from Germany. Their mothers, from Oslo, were sisters. The two women had met their respective Canadian and German husbands - both mining engineers - in 1919 when the men had been studying new hard-rock blasting techniques in Norway.

Jason and Peter, both eighteen, were nearly mirror images of each other, and as six-footers were about two inches taller than David though perhaps not as wide through the shoulders. David possessed the straight black hair and soft brown almond-shaped eyes of his people, while all the cousins were identically square faced and blond. However, while both Jason and Peter had similar blue-green eyes, Jack's eyes were the pale blue colour of the sky.

Jack was a year younger than the other three boys but was clearly the more robust. He was two inches taller than either Jason or Peter and was at least twenty pounds heavier. A natural athlete, he excelled at any sport he chose to take up, but hockey and boxing - not necessarily mutually exclusive activities - were his favourites.

Peter had taken to calling him "Max", in reference to Max Schmeling, after seeing Jack enter an impromptu boxing tournament and knock out two grown men over the course of a single day.

The four of them were stripped down to their canvas shorts and wore grey wide-brimmed felt hats to shade their necks and faces. Their lean muscled bodies had been bronzed by more than a month of practicing their skills on the water, where the sun's rays were additionally intensified by reflection from the lake's surface.

The boys pulled their paddles from the water as the two canoes slid silently into the lea of a cliff face on the eastern side of Old Woman Bay. The rock wall rose straight up out of the lake, towering above them for nearly six hundred feet. From a distance under certain light conditions, the various seams and crevices on the looming formation could bear a striking resemblance to the countenance of an old native woman, hence its name.

Peter had his head tilted back while he stared at something on the cliff face.

"Careful you don't get sun-burnt on the roof of your mouth," David joked.

Peter smiled, but kept staring, and soon they were all gazing at the spot that had attracted his interest.

"How high up would you say that ledge is?" He asked David.

"About forty-five, fifty feet maybe," he replied.

"That's about what, maybe fifteen metres?"

"Yeah, about that."

Peter shifted his gaze to the base of the cliff then peered into the dark green depths. "How deep is it here?"

"Plenty deep." David replied. "You wouldn't be able to hold your breath long enough to swim to the bottom."

Peter grinned. "That's all I wanted to hear."

He then kicked off his shoes, tossed his hat into the bottom of the canoe, and clambered out onto the adjacent rocky wall, where, with remarkable agility, he began to climb up toward the ledge. Using the wider cracks and small outcrops for purchase, he gingerly pulled himself upward as the others stared with disbelief at his ascent.

"What the hell are you up to!" Jason cried. "For Christ sakes, be careful!"

"It's okay. I know what I'm doing!" Peter shouted down at them.

The three boys' eyes met. David and Jason shook their heads, but Jack, whose face had borne a momentary look of puzzlement, suddenly grinned as he explained. "We'd better move out of his way. That crazy bastard is going to jump!"

David shot Jason a worried glance. "Is your cousin nuts? That's a hell of a long way up."

A note of apprehension had crept into Jason's voice as he yelled up to his cousin, who had just scrambled onto the ledge. "Peter, don't do it! You're too high up! At least come down a bit before you jump!"

Peter now stood on the edge of the outcrop, arms raised at his sides to shoulder height, beaming exultantly. "Don't worry guys, I'm not going to jump!"

Then, as his face broke into a wide grin, he shouted. "I'm going to dive!"

With that, he swung his arms around in front and launched himself outward from the ledge. At the top of his arc Peter rolled into a forward somersault and then straightened out to plunge unerringly down through the remaining distance. With hardly a splash, he knifed soundlessly into the water.

David expelled his breath in a long whistle of appreciation.

Jack nodded his head in admiration and murmured. "I'd say that guy has had a diving lesson or two."

Jason sat silently, a growing look of concern on his face as he stared toward the centre of the expanding circular ripples where Peter had disappeared beneath the surface at least thirty seconds before. He looked at the others. "He's been under too long!"

Having thrown off his hat, Jason had one leg out of the canoe when Peter's head burst out of the water beside where David sat.

"Whew!" David gasped. "It's nice of you to rejoin us. We were getting a little worried. What took you so long?"

Peter looked at his cousins and grinned conspiratorially. "I met a beautiful mermaid down there who told me that you had captured her heart. She asked me to give you this."

With that, he raised his hand out of the water and handed David a small green weed. "I watched her pick it from the bottom of the lake."

This time it was both Jason and Jack's turn to whistle appreciatively.

David turned the small plant over in his hand, and with an amused chuckle reached over with his other to push Peter's head under the water. Smiling at the brothers, he shook his head. "The bull-shitter pulled this off the bottom of the canoe!"

When allowed after a few seconds to resurface, Peter admitted to the joke, and suggested that they pull the canoes up on the nearby beach so they could have a swim. Soon, they were all cavorting in the lake and practicing different strokes, but the greatest pleasure lay in holding their breath while swimming under water. The lake was so clear, that when they opened their eyes, visibility beneath the surface nearly equalled that above.

Because of the frigid water temperature, there was a limit to the amount of time they could spend in the lake, and a half hour later the four were warming themselves on a large flat slab of granite. Like much of the rocky shoreline, it was shot through with crystalline veins of white quartz and worn smooth by thousands of years of wave abrasion.

They had changed into dry shorts, while the ones they had swum in were hung nearby on the prows of the canoes and slowly drying in the afternoon sun.

In the vast quietude of this place, every tiny sound seemed to gain both magnitude and clarity. The buzz of an insect, the calling of crows, seagulls, or warblers, the lap of the lake's swell on the shoreline, and the hissing rush of a rising breeze as it passed through the leaves, all resonated as they lay silently contemplating this immense beauty.

The movement of air had wrinkled the lake's surface, and now it was dappled to the distant horizon with a million tiny glints of golden sunlight. In this natural idyll, they each reflected upon the transitions occurring in their lives. The three eldest had all finished high school, or in Peter's case, *Gymnasium*, the German equivalent.

Jack still had a year to go, but his spirit had grown restless these past months, and other urges were beginning to stir his wanderlust with an almost irresistible incitement to travel. One thing he did know for certain, was that over the next year he would acutely miss the camaraderie of his three companions.

Their father, Collin McMurchy, had long been a friend of David's grandfather. In an effort to help David avoid the government warders of the despised residential school system, their dad had pretended to adopt him, and thus he was able to attend the local public school with his friends.

The ruse had been successful, allowing David to continue living with his mother and grandfather, rather than being boarded for months at a time in distant Thunder Bay. In return, quarters of moose meat and buckets of fish would sometimes appear mysteriously at Mrs. McMurchy's back door, out of season, when only those on the native reserves where legally allowed to hunt and fish.

Because the school system in the relatively isolated *Michipicoten* township district only provided the first eight years of education, Jason, David, and Jack had all boarded together and attended high school classes in Sault Ste Marie, more than a hundred and twenty miles from their homes and families.

Jason had decided to go to university, and Peter would return to Germany in September, where he would try to study aeronautical engineering. David had the academic credentials, and would have liked to join Jason at university, but his family lacked the financial resources to assist him. He had decided to work a few years to save money, and then perhaps he would go. In the meantime, he would hedge his bets with an electrician's apprenticeship at the local iron mine.

Jack, on the other hand, was thinking impatiently about completing his final year. He had been dating Henriette Lafrance, oldest daughter of the local doctor, and they had secretly begun sleeping together a month earlier. They attended the same grade in high school, and Jack now closed his eyes to fantasize about her long black hair, and lithe olive-skinned body. These days he longed for the opportunity to spend more time with her during the upcoming school year, when they would both be away from the prying eyes of family or neighbours.

Peter was sitting up on the smooth granite slab with both arms wrapped around his knees, gazing out at the endless expanse of shimmering water.

Jason turned his eyes toward Peter. "That was one hell of a dive pardner." He mispronounced the word intentionally, cowboy-like.

"It sure was!" Jack chimed in.

"Why weren't you on the German team in the Berlin Olympics two years ago?" David asked, only half-joking.

"I don't know if I'd ever have been that good." Peter replied seriously. "I was always the best at my sports club when I was a kid, but when they passed the Nuremburg Laws, my father pulled me off the team."

"Nuremburg Laws?" Jack looked puzzled.

Peter grunted. "Yeah. In 1935, the Nazis passed a series of laws designed to restrict Jewish activity in almost every area of society."

"But you're not Jewish!" Jason interjected.

"I know, but a couple of the boys on the team were, and the authorities forced them to quit. Father said that on principle, he would not allow me to be part of such an organization. I'd have probably quit on my own anyway. The two Jewish guys weren't really close friends of mine, but right after they left, the coaches started trying to fill us with that master race shit. I saw one of the cretins last spring. He was strutting around in a uniform and giving the Hitler salute. It made me want to puke!"

"You mean like when you drank that whole bottle of whiskey last week?" Jack piped up.

"Something similar to that." He replied, cringing.

Peter's mood was picking up as a result of Jack's prodding. "But the vomit would have looked much better all over that arse licker's boots!"

Jason's voice took on a serious tone. "Peter, from what I'm reading in the papers about Europe, things look like they will get a lot worse there before they get any better. Why don't you stay in Canada and go to university here?"

Peter looked wistfully out over the water. "When I was up on the ledge looking toward the horizon, I thought about how beautiful and fresh everything here is. There are hardly any people, and nobody is trying to force their ideas down your throat. Yeah, it would be great to stay here forever, but I'm the only son my parents have got, and then, there is my little sister…"

His voice trailed off, but then his gloomy face brightened. "Besides, I really must find out what Willy Messerschmitt is up to!"

He looked beyond the beach and spied an Osprey spiralling on a thermal current that was rising up the rock face. "Last year I joined a soaring club and learned how to pilot a glider. It's amazing how you feel up there. Like that hawk," he said, pointing.

"At first my father was against it. He really hates these youth clubs because of all the political indoctrination that goes on, but I convinced him that it was a necessary prerequisite to becoming an aeronautical engineer, and he relented. When you are up there alone in the glider, it is very peaceful. No one is yapping about their idiotic political ideas, or any other kind of nonsense. You should try it when you get to university. They are sure to have a soaring club, and I can promise you won't be sorry."

They watched the Osprey, its wings still rigid, leveling off to drift lazily for several seconds along the face of the cliff. Without warning, it dropped like a bolt to the water, dug its claws beneath the surface, and then shrieked, as it flapped its powerful wings to rise into the air with a wriggling silver trout flashing in its talons.

"You won't need to twist my arm on that one Peter. I've always wanted to fly, and the next time you visit us here, you'll mistake me for that hawk."

"Really?" Peter was grinning. "Then you had better start practicing how to hold a fish in your toes!"

David and Jack chortled, then shook their heads disparagingly while pretending to examine Jason's feet.

Peter liked his cousins. It was as if they were the brothers he never had. His uncle Collin and aunt Brigit had welcomed him warmly, and perhaps it was because his aunt resembled his own mother so much in both appearance and mannerisms – even the sound of her voice - that he felt completely at home.

Their friend David had known his cousins since they were small boys, and in all his life, Peter had never met anyone like him, but in some strange way they both seemed to be on the same wavelength and had quickly become fast friends.

The banter continued for several more minutes until David finally stood up and motioned to the canoes, before he jibed. "Well, before the sight of my magnificent physique makes all you round eyes turn queer, I'm going to put my shirt on and climb into my 'man-of-war'. We'll have to paddle hard if we want to reach *Agawa* this afternoon."

Jack rose to the challenge. "Yes, but that's because you can hardly paddle Davey!"

David deadpanned, and shook his head sadly as there was more hooting all around.

Eventually, the four canoeists were paddling their way along the shoreline, with the occasional hilarious exclamations or vehement denials echoing along the lake's surface, where they went otherwise unheard, except perhaps by the distant mute topography.

David wondered again, if it was a good idea to show his friends the pictographs. He knew they had promised not to tell anyone about them, or to ever give away their location. However, it was only after his friends had convinced his grandfather, and he had given his consent, that David had agreed to take them.

The existence and nature of the pictographs had been rumoured for more than a hundred years - possibly generated in previous centuries by passing Voyageurs. However, his friends might still be among the first non-natives to lay eyes on them. His people in *Batchawana* and *Michipicoten* knew of them, but to his knowledge, no one else understood precisely where they were.

His grandfather had been impressed over the years by the boys' genuine interest in Ojibwa culture, and their desire to understand his interpretation of natural phenomena. Their inclination to take everything he said very seriously was quite unusual in his experience when dealing with 'white' people, and to some degree he found it amusing. However, he interpreted their earnestness as a positive sign, and winked at David when he nodded his assent.

The pictographs were ancient, and as far as David knew, they had been there as long as his people. Apparently, they had been painted by some long-dead shaman and depicted beasts that were unlike those his tribe were now familiar with. Had the beasts disappeared he wondered, or were they the symbolic products of an artist's fantasies and imagination?

There were other images too, including snakes and canoeists.

Some of David's people speculated that the pictographs were similar to creation myths in that they somehow reflected the original balance of nature, and the relationship of his people with the world - both organic and spiritual. Maybe they also had some kind of connection with a primal force within the lake that exerted its influence on everything...

Much of this puzzled David, although some of it made sense to him, for he understood the balance and cycles of nature, but other elements, including many of the images, seemed to elude him. His grandfather and the tribal shaman on the other hand, appeared to instinctively grasp the significance of the images, calling the creature with serrated ridges *Mishi Peshu*. However, when he queried either of them more deeply, their response was usually an ambiguous shrug of the shoulders, and the admonition that he would understand more when he had lived more.

He had been five years old when his father, during one of those rare weeks that he'd been sober, took him to see the pictographs for the first time. Even now, he could remember watching him place his large palm on each of the symbols as if trying to draw some kind of strength from them. Then, shaking his head slowly, while slumping his broad shoulders in resignation, and looking back at David, shamefaced.

At one point, tears had begun running down his father's cheeks, and between sobs he spoke to the uncomprehending boy. "My son, there are some things you can never undo. Some things so terrible they change your spirit and release a *Wendigo* stronger than anything you can fight. When that happens, you can feel it coming for you. Nothing can stop it, and it will pursue you relentlessly until it has dragged you into your grave."

Less than a year later, he was dead.

David's father Joseph had been orphaned during one of the periodic influenza epidemics which sometimes swept through the isolated native communities after visits by prospectors, fishermen, government people, or relatives. He'd been raised by an aunt and uncle on the *Batchewana* reserve and had grown into a strapping and assured young man, highly-skilled as a hunter, fisherman, and fur trapper, in addition to being well regarded as a carpenter. On one of his visits to the *Michipicoten* reserve, he had met David's mother Anne. He moved there to marry her shortly afterward, and for a time they lived happily, until the autumn of 1914.

On an impulse, and a dare from some of his friends, he had gone with them, joining the Canadian Army to fight the Hun in France. During the next four years he saw action in all the big battles including Vimy Ridge and Paschendale. On those bloody battlefields he had seen all of his friends and hundreds of his comrades gunned down, gutted on bayonets, decapitated, or ripped apart by white hot shrapnel. Some disappeared, literally vapourized by the explosion of artillery shells. Through all of this he fought, hardly sustaining a scratch, seemingly invincible and protected by some invisible aura of luck or good fortune. At the end of a battle his uniform would often be soaked through with blood and viscera, but none of it his.

This did not go unnoticed by the more observant of his brothers in arms, and some would try to befriend him, or gravitate near him in battle to share in his good fortune or survival skills. They called him 'the chief', or 'lucky Joe', each hoping beyond reason that somehow at the end of it, they too would walk out of the smoke and fire unscathed, as he had on countless occasions. Their hope inevitably withered in the merciless fusillade of lead and exploded shell fragments, as one by one, without fail, they all fell to the bullets, or were scythed down by the shards of jagged shrapnel.

Joseph became a fearsome killer of men. He didn't take prisoners, and with his uncannily accurate aim, almost no bullet was wasted. When he ran out of these he was equally lethal in the enemy trenches with his bayonet, running the long blade viciously through heart or throat. He was known on more than one occasion to strangle a terrified German with his bare hands. Although he never mutilated any of his kills, it wasn't long before the men began to bet on how many 'scalps' the chief would take in the next big show.

His picture sometimes appeared in the local papers, and he was always written up as a 'brave warrior' or 'hero'. David's mother had saved the clippings and when he looked at his father's faded sepia photos, he saw a man rigid and uncomfortable in his uniform, staring straight ahead, seemingly at something in the distance beyond the camera.

By the time he returned home, Joseph had retreated somewhere deep inside of himself. At night his dreams were haunted by the faces of his dead friends, or the men he had killed with his bayonet and bare hands. He couldn't shake the sounds of their screams, or the looks of disbelief on their faces when they realized they were about to die. Worst of all were the recollections of their whimpering as he withdrew the blade, and their lives slowly seeped out of them. Somehow, he could clearly remember all of their faces – dozens of them.

His previously gregarious nature was subsumed by a general indifference to friendship, and a sullen unwillingness to engage in any but the most rudimentary of conversations. The only time that he had been capable of making love to his wife Anne, David had been conceived.

He began to drink heavily. The oblivion of alcohol seemed to be the only way to make the dreams go away as he sank into unconsciousness. One January night while taking a shortcut home across the harbour ice, he fell through.

David could still remember the scene where they had found him next morning. His father's large leather mitts with their thick wool liners were frozen to the snowy edge of a darker shiny area. A new layer of clear ice about two inches thick had frozen over the exposed water of the break, and through this, David could see his father lying on the bottom about ten feet down. There, his body appeared to be resting peacefully on its back in a relaxed, almost comfortable position. His eyes were open, and he seemed to be staring with resignation through the fresh window of ice at something far above them.

Instinctively, David had glanced upward, but saw nothing there.

The men began to hack through the fresh ice with their axes, and using a logger's pike pole, they were able to retrieve the body. However, as David and his mother turned for home, a large shadow flickered briefly across the white snow. Looking up, he saw a Great Horned Owl glide silently across the sky, then quietly alight in a tall pine tree on the edge of the encroaching forest. From there, it continued to observe them through dispassionate, unblinking eyes.

David realized Jason was calling to him. "There's a bank of clouds starting to build on the western horizon!"

He turned to look behind and was amazed, as the towering mass advanced rapidly across the sky toward them. A westerly breeze had risen while the surface of the lake took on a light chop.

Jason had also called to Peter and Jack in the other canoe, who were now paddling in earnest to catch up as David pointed to a narrow section of beach between two rocky projections and motioned that they should head in to shore.

In the few minutes of strained paddling required for the boys to near the beach, the surface of the lake had transformed. The clouds were nearly overhead, and in their shadow the water had changed to a dark slate colour. Driven by a wind that had strengthened considerably, large curling waves, topped in white, rose in long diagonals around them. As these breakers reached the shallower waters near the shore, they surged up suddenly and broke in great hissing explosions of foam on the sand.

They timed their landings, so that as soon as their craft beached on the shore, both paddlers leapt out to drag their canoe further up the sands, thus avoiding the chance of another looming whitecap rising up to crash over the stern. This was a crucial manoeuvre, as a flooded canoe would be too heavy to pull up the sloping beach to safety.

The eastern peninsula was 'L' shaped, and about a hundred feet up the shore they dragged their gear into its lea, where protected from the gale tearing at them off the lake, they hastily pitched their tents.

When a grey curtain of rain advanced across the waves toward them, the boys retreated into one of the tents. Jack then pulled a deck of cards from his pack and they proceeded to while away the hours playing rummy and snacking on some of their biscuits as the tempest roared outside.

By nightfall the rain had stopped, and they emerged from the tent to build a small cooking fire on the beach. They heated two large cans of pork and beans, and then took turns spooning the contents into their hungry mouths. With blankets wrapped around their shoulders, the boys sat on an old driftwood log, and watched the clouds moving off to the horizon. The ghostly shapes were occasionally illuminated by internal flashes of lightening as they drifted east, leaving a clear, star-speckled sky behind them.

The Boar

June 1938, high above the baking plains of Valencia, *Leutnant* Roland Schwartz of *Jagdgruppe 88*, banked his *Bf*109D to dive down on the struggling *Polikarpov* I-16 monoplane. With its open cockpit and stubby, less streamlined fuselage, fronted by a massive radial engine, the Russian-supplied aircraft, while originally a revolutionary design when conceived in 1933, now looked like a throwback compared to the sleek aerodynamic lines of Schwartz's fighter.

The German pilots called them *Rata* - Rats, but its slower speed and faster roll rate made it very agile in the twisting turns of a dogfight. In the hands of an experienced fighter pilot, it could sometimes win against the faster and more modern German aircraft.

Today they were flying in the recently introduced four aircraft *schwarm* formation. It was comprised of two *rottes*, each containing a pilot and his wingman. They flew in a pattern that roughly resembled the four fingertips of a hand, and in slightly descending altitudes starting from the aircraft in the small finger position. Schwartz led from the index fingertip position.

When Molders had first outlined the new formation one month ago during a squadron briefing, Schwartz had immediately seen the wisdom in it. The four members of the *schwarm* had a greater field of vision and could also observe a greater depth in three dimensions from their staggered altitudes.

By diligently practicing their crossover turn, they also developed the ability to put the full-frontal firepower of all four aircraft on any enemy attempting to attack their flank.

Perhaps best of all, compared to the three-plane formation, it solved the problem of two wingmen spending half of their energies trying not to collide with each other when protecting a leader who had engaged the enemy. In such situations, one of the two wingmen would inevitably fall further out of formation with the leader, and as a straggler, became easier prey for other enemy fighters. Once again, superior German martial intelligence had resulted in another battle-winning innovation.

Schwartz first noticed the Republican plane because of the black smoke trailing behind it, most likely from a damaged cylinder. If he could shoot this one down he would finally have that fifth kill, conferring upon him the elite status of fighter Ace.

"This one is mine!" He barked to his wingman. "Follow me down!"

The enemy pilot, struggling with his controls, did not notice Schwartz diving upon him. Flames were now licking voraciously around the cowling behind the smoking engine. Having released his harness, the pilot was standing in the open cockpit preparing to bail out of the burning aircraft.

As Schwartz lined up on the tail of the I-16, he realized with some alarm that if the pilot abandoned the aircraft, it would in turn fall out of control and then crash to earth before he could rightfully claim it as a victory.

At the last second, the pilot turned to see the German plane lining up into position. Before the pilot had time to move, Schwartz pressed his thumb down on the firing button, sending a stream of bullets into the cockpit and tearing the man to pieces. Other rounds continued forward into the engine causing the aircraft to explode.

He banked sharply right to avoid the spinning debris and shouted exultantly into the microphone at his wingman. "You saw it! I got the victory! That's number five! You must confirm it!"

"*Ja...*" came the laconic reply.

Schwartz turned south to lead his wingman home. They were quickly joined by the other two aircraft which had circled above during the attack. He squinted as the sun reflected from the smooth silver skin of the sleek Messerschmitt fighters, emblazoned with their black roundels and the superimposed white *X* of the *Condor Legion*. On the engine cowling of his own fighter, Roland had painted the head of a powerful wild boar. He was finally an ace, and now people would have to genuinely respect him.

Later, as they began their landing approach to the airfield, he began to reflect on how far he had come since those bleak days in 1925...

At age 15, Roland Schwartz was already as big as most men, having grown hugely strong from years of delivering coal on weekends and nearly every night after school. Matted black hair poked out unevenly from beneath the soft wool cap he had pulled down tightly above his ears, while periodically, he would place a grimy forefinger against one of the large nostrils in his wide pushed-up nose, and blow hard to expel a wad of dust-impregnated mucus out of the other.

The irritating coal dust also aggravated the pustules that had begun to erupt upon his cheeks over the past year or so. These he compulsively scratched, sometimes causing them to burst, or grow to carbuncular proportions. After rupturing, they often left the skin on his face and neck permanently pitted.

Because of his size, and the layer of black grit - which despite repeated scrubbings regularly accumulated under his fingernails - people often assumed he was an oaf. This was far from true, for Roland excelled in his mathematics and physics classes at the *Gymnasium*. In fact, if he had not needed to spend most of his free time working, he might easily have qualified to go to any of the elite universities that the more affluent Jewish boys in his classes were planning to soon attend.

Roland was descended from a long line of honest and hard-working men. Like many, they had abandoned their agrarian roots to rise by merit in the state bureaucracy created during the Bismarck years. In fact, his father had retired at the age of sixty-five in 1919, after an entire career toiling in the Customs Department of the National Finance Ministry, and with a well-earned pension as a result.

After 1921, the fixed pension soon became worthless, as over the next three years the Weimar Republic was afflicted with hyperinflation, and the old man soon fell into long, raucous bouts of drinking. These were punctuated by episodes of physical abuse in which he regularly inflicted beatings upon Roland and his mother.

Through his old connections, Roland's father had access to ample supplies of cheap alcohol. During his drunken rages he would often rave loudly about the injustices that had been meted out to the German people because of the duplicity of international Jewry, and the Treaty of Versailles.

"How was it possible that Germany had lost the war? At the armistice on November 11, 1918, the German army was still in Belgium and France. Not a single enemy soldier had set foot in Germany. Not a single building or piece of property in Germany was ever damaged by enemy action. The High Seas Fleet was completely intact!"

For the embittered old man, the answer was clear. "No! Germany did not lose the war. We were stabbed in the back by the Jews. They took advantage of our preoccupation with the war to corner the market on agricultural commodities and drove the prices for Germans up to levels that brought starvation to the land. The Rothschilds controlled the bond market, and they had manipulated the rates on German bonds up to a level that had bankrupted the Fatherland!"

"Germans fought well, and did not lose the war on the battlefield. They were betrayed by the Jews! You just have to look at the Jews who are running the banks in Germany. They are the only ones who are not suffering! They are getting richer every day and living lives of obscene luxury and debauchery, while they exploit every true German. They're sucking the blood out of the country's veins and destroying the nation!"

At the age of twelve, Roland was forced to find work to help with the family expenses. Within a year, the work of carrying heavy coal-filled sacks had caused the naturally large and robust physique which he had inherited from his mother's side of the family, to grow enormously in strength.

One night the old man came home in a foul mood, stinking of vomit and demanding to be fed. When his mother informed him that there was no food in the larder, he flew into a rage, and as the slap to her face rang in his ears, Roland felt his own fury explode inside of him. Before realizing it, he had struck his father so hard that the old man found himself flat on his back, spitting one of his teeth out onto the floor.

His father now spent even less time at home, and the obstreperous old man began to occupy more of his day attending street rallies. There, groups of veterans and men ruined by the economy, furiously insisted that the government should resign.

They also demanded that the country stop paying reparations to France, and that Germany rearm to command the respect she deserved.

At one point his father went missing for a week, and when he finally staggered home he admitted to having been jailed for participating in a riot that had broken out at a beer hall. The crowd had been aroused by the stirring oratory of an Austrian veteran, who as a Corporal, had fought heroically, and been wounded in the trenches during the war.

For several nights the old man again failed to return home. Roland and his mother assumed he would show eventually with more of the usual rambling excuses for his absence. However, a few days later there was a knock on their door, and when they opened it a policeman loomed. He informed them that the old man's body had been found in a canal, where days earlier, probably drunk, he had fallen in.

They did not collect the body.

Roland's mother was always able to find sufficient food to ensure that he never lacked for enough to eat. To supplement her work as a chambermaid at a local hotel, she also worked at an evening job while Roland laboured delivering coal. He tried not to think about what kind of work she must have been doing, but she was still an attractive woman for her age, and there were not many occupations a woman could pursue that would provide the money she was obviously earning to help cover the family expenses. It was difficult to maintain your dignity during these times of high unemployment and diminished purchasing power.

The next three years had been very difficult ones for Roland and his mother, but despite the hardship, he managed to complete his studies. Part of that could be attributed to his naturally dogged nature, but at the time Roland might have admitted begrudgingly that it could also have been because of Maria.

Maria possessed the lithe body of a dancer, and in fact had taken regular ballet lessons until financial constraints, due to the reduced fortunes of her parent's imported fabric business, curtailed them. However, she continued to practice at home. With her pale blue eyes, fine elfin features, and long blonde curls, she was the most beautiful young lady that Roland had ever seen. She always sat near the front of the classroom, and he would rush to school in the mornings in anticipation of taking his position near the back wall. From there he would often find himself staring at her and daydreaming about situations where he would be holding her in his arms, while she gazed up at him with her face beaming in adoration.

Roland would be overcome with feelings of awkwardness whenever he got near to Maria, and as a result, his attempts to converse with her were clumsy. His voice was too loud, and his comments either too rough or mistimed in the context of any general conversation involving her and other surrounding classmates. Self-consciously he would try to cover his anxiety or embarrassment with a laugh, which always seemed to manifest itself in a way that was harsher or more sarcastic than he intended. In those moments, he caught the fleeting sideways glances of condescension from the Jewish boys and would perspire profusely as he felt the hot and conflicting emotional tides of shame and rage wash through him. Accordingly, he kept his distance from her, and them, but all the while he dreamt of vindication and revenge.

Over their last two years of classes he had noticed that her dresses, although always clean and neatly pressed, were gradually becoming less varied. Eventually, she was down to three, which then grew more worn and threadbare.

He dreamed that one day he would become wealthy and rescue her from poverty. Then, she would see the noble qualities he had always possessed, respecting and loving him for rising up from humble beginnings to save her. He would show those privileged bastards who sat in his class with their tailored clothes and soft clean hands, what a real man could do on his own without anyone's help – and she would adore him for it.

It was just before their graduation that he had finally gathered the courage to approach her. Somehow he had managed to scrape together enough money to pay for a modest meal at one of the local restaurants after the ceremony. He had made reservations. For weeks, he imagined how thrilled and grateful she would be when he sat her at the table, and told her of all the plans he had for them. He would make a great future for her if she would give him a chance.

Roland waited until the other class members were not around, and then moved closer. It still caused his pulse to race if he thought about it. She had smiled shyly when he came near her, but when he had finally stammered and blurted his awkward invitation, she had trembled slightly and tilted her head downward to avoid his gaze.

Her voice quavered. "Thank you, Roland. It is very, very kind of you, but I...I have already accepted an invitation from Jacob, who has also asked my parents to join him and his family for a dinner party at his home."

Seeing him stiffen she hesitated, and then continued. "As you know, Jacob's father owns one of the biggest furniture manufacturing concerns in Germany, and my parents are desperately hoping this will be a chance for them to revive their fabric business, which has not been doing well lately. I must accept Jacob's invitation. I...I hope you understand."

Roland felt his face flushing with the now-familiar humiliation, and then the rage beginning to rise from his stomach. He choked it down with all the self-control that he could muster, while instinctively wanting to lash out and strike her! She was rejecting the offer that he had saved and sacrificed months for! For Jacob! That fucking Jew with his family's money and business connections was destroying any chance he had with Maria! It was like the bastards had their boot on his neck and were slowly suffocating him as they crushed his dreams.

His head was spinning when he croaked. "*Ja*, I understand!"

With that, he strode out of the room without once looking back, as he dismissed her from his mind.

Later at the restaurant he ate the two servings, chewing his food slowly while he pondered his fate. Other men – lesser men – were stopping him from getting what he deserved. He now dreamt of the day when he would have power and respect. Anyone who dared to cross him then, by God, would certainly learn to regret it!

The bile collecting in his stomach was beginning to affect his digestion. He fished the coins from his pocket and shoved them onto the table. With a belch, he stood up, tore the napkin from his neck, and then threw it to the floor. Still seething with rage, he marched out of the restaurant.

A few nights later, as Roland walked home from his evening shift of delivering coal, he witnessed a huge melee taking place in front of the local synagogue. A group of men in brown uniforms and caps, wearing red armbands bearing a white circle emblazoned with a black swastika, were waving torches, shouting, and throwing paving stones at the doors and windows of the temple. An equally large number of policemen were trying to force them back. Two of them were trying to wrestle one of the brown-shirted men – apparently, their leader - toward a police van.

The man was shouting at them. "You should be helping us! Not trying to prevent us chasing these Jewish vermin from our Fatherland!"

Once again, Roland felt his anger welling up. Impulsively, he rushed over to where the policemen had taken the man and began to pound on them with his huge fists. In seconds, the two officers were lying on the ground unconscious, while their astonished prisoner clasped Roland by the arm, gasping. "Quick! Let's run for it! I know a place we'll be safe!"

Roland followed the man as they sprinted across the street. Two blocks later, the man pulled him toward a black Mercedes-Benz. The man was clearly winded, but between deep breaths he pointed to the passenger door and wheezed. "Get in."

After driving for twenty minutes, and sure that they had not been followed, the man pulled over to the curb and switched off the car's engine. Roland could see that the man was about thirty years of age, had cut his hair in the military fashion, and wore a pencil moustache which was already showing flecks of grey.

"Why did you help me?" He asked.

Roland was asking himself the same question, but finally he concluded that there was only one answer. "I don't like Jews."

"You say that like someone who has been screwed over by one of those bloodsuckers. Am I right?"

His father's words began to echo in his mind. "They fuck everybody. Not just me. They stabbed us in the back by screwing us in the bond market. That's the only reason we lost the war."

The man considered Roland's words for a moment. At the same time, his eyes appraised the young man's sweating, dishevelled appearance.

Then, he nodded his head in agreement. "You are a lot smarter than I'll bet a lot of people give you credit for. Most people hate Jews because they have personally been swindled by one of them, or someone in their family has. However, you seem to have a grasp of the big picture. Do you know why my friends and I have formed a private army to go after them?"

Roland's eyes narrowed. "The Jews are rich. They run the banks here, just like their financier relatives in London and New York. The Jewish bankers in Britain and America use their connections to pressure the German government to do nothing, while the Hebrew scum buy off our politicians along with the police and turn all our women into whores. The only real solution will be to force all of them out."

Hissing, he continued. "We must do it even if they don't want to go."

A flitting smile crossed the man's face. "My friend, I think you are just the kind of young man we could use. Eventually, one way or another, our party is going to govern this country, and we are going to need both brains and muscle to get there. I keep people I trust close to me, so if you join us you would be part of my inner circle."

Roland responded bitterly. "I would like to take you up on that, but these days I'm trying to find some way to get into the field of aeronautics. That means I'll have to do two jobs to earn enough money to get the technical training or find someone who will let me apprentice. I don't have money and I don't have connections, so I think I'm going to be very busy trying to find the means."

The man nodded again, then paused for a moment while he appeared to roll an idea around in his mind. "Let me give you a ride home. I know some people who may be able to help us out. In the meantime, I could pick you up in a few days for our group's next meeting if you are interested."

Roland grunted. "*Ja*, I definitely would be."

The man started up the car's engine again, but just before putting it into gear he seemed to remember something. Then, turning to Roland he thrust out his hand. "Forgive me for not introducing myself. My name is Heinrich Pfaltz."

He took the man's hand and gripped it firmly. "Roland Schwartz."

"Roland, I am very intimately associated with our founder Ernst Rohm, who is unfortunately now in Bolivia getting their army into shape. However, through him I have met members of Hitler's inner circle who know people in the aircraft industry. If you join us, I am sure that something can be done for you."

Over the next twelve months Roland attended several rallies, where, imposing and resplendent in his new uniform, he served as Pfaltz's bodyguard. Early in that year, as promised, he also found himself working as an assistant in the design bureau of *Bayerische Flugzeugwerke* in Augsburg.

He had a natural aptitude for drafting and copying blueprints, spending much of his time delivering them to various departments charged with turning them into real parts, and ultimately aircraft. Thus, over the months he got to know many of the important members of the production team, and they him. When returning from his deliveries, he would often also be bearing a suggestion from one of the production department heads regarding some small modification to a part design that would improve its performance, or its incorporation into the production process.

In time he became one of the most recognizable employees in the company, and often the first one people in the production department would approach with suggestions. He also became the first person the designers would query, to find out if the production engineers and mechanics had recommended any changes or enhancements.

It was on one of his trips to attend an *S.A.* rally, and visit his mother, that he saw Maria again. He had arrived on the late evening train and was just getting into a taxi when he noticed her emerging from the *Koenig's* Hotel, perhaps the most expensive accommodations in the city. She was wearing a light-green silk dress, with a grey fur shawl around her shoulders.

He felt the old rage rise once again within him, as he suddenly realized that she was with Jacob's brother Mikal - older by ten years - and one of Mikal's Jewish friends. His pulse began to race as Maria placed a cigarette between her lips, inclining her face toward the flame as the other man pulled a lighter from his pocket to light it for her. She arched her head back, while the men's eyes took in her long elegant neck and the curvature of her shapely torso. Slowly, she exhaled the smoke through her nostrils from where it rose in a lazy cloud into the amber glow of the streetlight.

He heard the two men laugh as their hands slipped up under her fur and around her breasts, while they helped Maria into the back seat of the limousine. Then, they climbed in on each side of her. After travelling a short distance, the car turned off of the main thoroughfare and disappeared down a dark side-street.

Slamming the taxi door shut behind him, Roland turned to the driver, and through clenched teeth, gave him directions home.

By 1931, Rohm was back. During *S.A.* strategy sessions which Roland often attended as Pfaltz's bodyguard, he detected the homosexual nature underpinning the relationships between all the senior leaders and some of their subordinates. Although no one approached him personally, he frequently caught glimpses of senior leaders including Pfaltz, groping their drivers and disappearing into bedrooms together during overnight conferences. After the initial shock of realization, Roland struggled to contain his disgust, but decided it was in his interest to bide his time.

The next two years became a type of hell for Roland as *Bayerische Flugzeugwerke* was forced into bankruptcy by *Lufthansa*, due to crashes of the Messerschmitt-designed M20. His major source of income aside from the temporary contracts that Pfaltz was able to find him at various aircraft plants, was the money he earned as an *S.A.* bodyguard. However, it did not sit well with him that the future of his career in aeronautics, or anything else for that matter, was entirely in the hands of these men.

In 1933, the newspapers were full of the Nazi's ascension to power. As part of their rearmament program they brought *Bayerische Flugzeugwerke* back to life, and much to his relief Roland had his old job back.

One day, to his surprise, he was summoned to a private meeting during a visit by Hermann Göring to the factory complex. The president's office had been vacated for him, and Göring was sitting alone behind the desk when he entered. He instructed Roland to close the door but did not invite him to sit down. Sweat began to trickle down his back, while Göring silently sat there and coolly fixed him in his gaze.

Göring had been a fighter pilot ace in the Great War. As a decorated hero, he had been awarded Germany's most prestigious medal, the *Pour le Merite*, also known as the *Blue Max*. Recently his career in the aeronautics industry had been superseded by his duties as a senior member of the Nazi party. His pale blue eyes took in everything and missed nothing.

After more than a full minute, he spoke. "Roland Schwartz, you are a member of the *S.A.*, and the personal body guard of Heinrich Pfaltz, are you not?"

Roland cleared his throat nervously. "Yes sir. That is correct."

Göring smiled. "Yes, that is correct."

He seemed to consider that fact a moment, then continued. "The *Führer* has entrusted me to form an agency whose sole concern is state security. Our authority overrides that of any other police or security agency in the country. We have the absolute power to investigate, detain, and arrest anyone we suspect to be a traitor. The name I have chosen for our organization is *Geheime Staatspolizei - Gestapo*. Do you understand?"

Roland shifted his weight uncomfortably to the other foot. "Yes."

Göring had placed one of his feet on the desk and was gazing at the highly polished toe of his boot. "Yes? Then tell me Schwartz, are you a loyal member of the Nazi party, and do you support the *Führer* without reservation?"

"Yes I am sir. I support Adolf Hitler absolutely!" He swore.

Göring began to tap the toe of his boot with his riding crop, then tilted his head up to look Roland squarely in the eyes. "What would you say Schwartz, if I were to tell you the *Führer* knows that the senior leadership of the *S.A.* are all homosexuals, and as such are a threat to the *Reich*?"

Roland inhaled deeply as the gravity of his situation became apparent to him. If this was some kind of loyalty test, he was trapped. In desperation he decided that his only hope was to tell Göring his true feelings, and place himself at the man's mercy. The *S.A.* had the power to destroy his career, but the man before him had the power to destroy more than that.

Shaking with fear and rage, he sobbed. "It disgusts me! I am not a homosexual and have prayed that a day would come when I could bring this very same information to someone with the power to do something about it! They are degenerates who have no right to be spoken of in the same breath as our beloved *Führer*, much less to be in the same room! Simply tell me what must be done! Please! Give me a chance and I will do anything to defend the *Führer* and the *Reich!*"

Göring held Roland's eyes a bit longer, and then removing his boot from the desk, he slowly straightened himself up in the chair. "Schwartz, I have decided to trust you – for now. I will be relying on you to be my eyes and ears during any further meetings of the *S.A.* leadership. However, before I let you go back to your duties here, I have a few documents which I would like you to sign. They simply attest to your having observed the senior leadership of the *S.A.* going to secret homosexual liaisons. Also, to overhearing them discussing plans to execute the *Führer*, other members of the government, and senior officers of the *Wehrmacht*."

Roland felt a great wave of relief pass through his body while Göring spoke. In the back of his mind there came the emerging confirmation that he had made the right decision. Betraying the *S.A.* was not a difficult choice, and in the long run he would survive and benefit.

He watched as the new chief of *Gestapo* operations opened his briefcase and withdrew a file with several official documents inside of it. Spreading them out on the table he smiled and handed Roland a fountain pen. Then he pointed. "Sign on the line there, at the bottom of each page."

Leaning over the desk, Roland did not attempt to read any of the documents, and his hand trembled only slightly as he affixed his signature to each of them.

When he had finished, he straightened up and made one last declaration. "Please be assured that you can count on me for anything, absolutely anything, in service to the *Führer* and the Fatherland!"

Göring smiled reflectively. "Very good Schwartz, but don't worry. We will of course be keeping an eye on you, but we also know how to reward loyalty. So speak to no one else about the subject of our meeting today. Return to work, and keep us apprised of what our *S.A.* friends are up to. We will be in touch with you again."

As Roland was about to exit the room, Göring called out to him. "Schwartz. Aside from serving the *Führer*, is there anything else you have ever dreamt of doing?"

Roland responded without thinking. "I've dreamt of being a pilot, sir. Like you."

Göring smiled and nodded his head. "That is interesting."

After Roland had left and closed the door behind him, Göring shook his head, and muttered to himself. "Another useful *arschlecker*."

July 7, 1934 was the day that the world changed for Roland Schwartz. Once again, the president of *Bayerische Flugzeugwerke* had vacated his office for Hermann Göring, and Roland had been summoned.

Göring was beaming. "Schwartz, the *Führer* has asked me to personally convey his appreciation for your help last week in *Bad Wiessee*. Your neutralization of all the security at the gates and entrances made things much easier for our people that morning when they captured all those *S.A.* scum in bed with their chauffeurs. Apparently they shot Heines and his boy right in the sheets. The *Führer* believes Rohm and all those bastards got what they deserved for such flagrant moral turpitude. Good work!"

Roland felt his chest expand with pride. "It was my privilege to serve the *Führer*!"

With some bemusement, Göring regarded Roland for a few moments. "As I mentioned at our first meeting Schwartz, we in the party know how to reward loyalty. We are quite impressed with Messerschmitt's latest design, the *Bf*108 *Taifun*, and he will soon be awarded a contract to develop a new advanced fighter for the *Luftwaffe*. I'll want someone on the inside to report directly to me on its progress. Your flying lessons will begin tomorrow. For the next few years, Willy Messerschmitt is going to have a new test pilot."

The year passed quickly for Roland. In ground school, he had no trouble grasping the principles of flight. With the party's financial assistance and personal interventions by Göring himself, it was made abundantly clear to his instructors that Schwartz was to be accelerated through the program, and his progress given the highest priority.

However, Roland did not need special attention while he diligently pursued his goal. He progressed from basic flying in underpowered but forgiving biplanes, to more powerful higher-performance models. Finally, he spent a relatively high number of flying hours mastering the sleek *Bf*108 *Taifun* monoplane.

Although the taciturn student was not particularly well-liked by his instructors, his skills mounted with the additional flying hours, and they could all generally agree on two things: Because of his physical strength, he tended to be heavy on the stick and rudder controls, and second, he was ready to return to the *Bayerische Flugzeugwerke*.

The austere blond secretary - a woman in her early forties - escorted Roland into the office, and then closed the doors behind him as she left.

There had been few changes to the room since he had last been here. On the shelf containing a collection of international aeronautical publications, there was a new scale model of a monoplane fighter. There was also a fresh stack of design blueprints on the drafting table. This time however, instead of Göring, Willy Messerschmitt was sitting behind the desk.

He felt the sense of apprehension experienced a year earlier, when he had first been summoned to this very room. Always, it was someone with power and authority – an authority he instinctively believed he must defer to, lest he be assigned blame for some misstep or inadvertent wrong decision. Roland tried his best to assuage these feelings by telling himself that he was a pilot and deserved the respect due to his status. These people had no right to look down on him or exercise such complete control over his life.

However, he only partially succeeded in convincing himself, and in response to the quiet confidence exuded by the great man, he clicked his heels together while drawing his considerable bulk into a rigid posture of full attention.

Messerschmitt looked up from a drawing that he had been examining, and then motioned Roland forward, but did not invite him to sit. "Welcome back Schwartz. Hermann Göring informs me that you are to be one of my test pilots. I'm fairly certain that I know the reason why he wants you here, so let me come right to the point. We are both extremely lucky to have Göring as our friend and patron. Whereas Milch would prefer to see my head on a pike, Göring wants me to build fighter planes for the *Luftwaffe*. This I am happy to do, as the alternative does not really bear contemplation. So, it is of no concern to me that you should report our progress to him as we develop the *Bf109*."

Messerschmitt held his hand up as Roland opened his mouth to protest. "I anticipate that he and the *Führer* will both be more than pleased with the performance of my new design. It is my belief that we can both benefit from this arrangement Schwartz, so I am authorizing a significant pay rise for you. I am also instructing all my senior design and engineering staff to keep you constantly apprised of any technical details or performance specifications."

He drew the fingers of both hands together to form a small pyramid and rested the apex against his lips a moment before continuing. "I already have test aviators who are much better and more experienced fliers than you. However, starting today you are to be formally known and addressed as a test pilot. I want you to spend as many hours per day as you possibly can in the air, so continue flying the *Bf108*. You are going to be part of the *Bf109* testing program and I want you up to the task. Do you have any questions?"

Roland's head was spinning over the speed and breadth of his good fortune. His initial reaction was a desire to immediately thank Messerschmitt for promoting him to his new rank and status. However, as he examined Messerschmitt sitting comfortably behind his desk in an elegantly tailored suit, with his refined features, and long slender fingers – fingers which unlike his own had never been bruised or toiled in filth - he acutely felt the social gulf between them.

At first this engendered a reflexive sense of clumsy embarrassment, replaced almost immediately by bitter resentment, and then a rising anger. He began to involuntarily perspire in his attempt to suppress this confused swirl of conflicting instincts.

Finally, having regained control, he forced himself to bow his head slightly, and then grinned obsequiously before stammering.

"N-no questions. I am at your service – and the service of the *Führer*!"

After Roland had left the room, Messerschmitt leaned back in his large leather-bound chair. His broad intelligent forehead creased as he slowly reached up to scratch his forefinger along the bottom of his chin.

He pondered the nature of this man Schwartz. Though he appeared to be oafish, the man was obviously slyer than that. Why else would Göring have picked him? Had the response regarding his service to the *Führer* been only a nervous hedge, or a not-so-veiled threat?

Messerschmitt contemplated the possibilities a moment longer, then resolved to always appear attentive to Schwartz's needs. First, there would have to be a modification to Schwartz's parachute - perhaps to reposition it from his buttocks to his chest, or somewhere else - which would allow him to lower his enormous bulk completely down into the *Bf*109's hard metal seat. Even then, it was likely that he would still fill nearly every millimetre of the relatively cramped cockpit. Somewhat amused, but not displeased at the discomfort he imagined Schwartz would experience flying the *Bf*109, he then returned to examining his drawings.

December 1939

Jack eased the lever on his jackleg drill forward, and the long pneumatic piston leg supporting the machine began to push the drill steel into the rock face while he held it steady. The ear mufflers on Jack's hardhat dulled the deafening jackhammer roar, which was amplified in volume and intensity as it reverberated off the walls and ceiling of the drift, 1,500 feet below ground.

In addition to safety glasses and steel-toed rubber boot 'muckers', Jack wore a pair of rubberized trousers and coat - 'oilers' - which protected him from the constant spray of mud that blew back onto him, as the high pressure stream of water running through the hollow centre of the drill rods forced the pulverized rock back out of the deepening hole. The battery-powered lamp on the front of his helmet pierced the stygian darkness with a narrow beam that lit the area immediately in front of him.

As he finished his last round, he switched off the drill, released the pressure from the leg, and pulled the machine back to extract the steel rod from the hole. He then dragged the entire jackleg drill with its attached high-pressure water and compressed air hoses, about a hundred feet back from the rock face. After that, he spent half an hour filling the pattern of holes he had drilled with sticks of high-explosive. Next, he primed them, and then connected all the primer charges with blasting chord, which he strung back around a corner into the cross-drift where he had placed the jackleg, before tying the chord around a blasting cap attached to a five-minute fuse. He unsnapped the top button of his jacket to retrieve a dry wooden match, struck it on a nearby rock, and lit the fuse. Finally, he turned in the direction of the main drift, cupped his hands around his mouth, and shouted. "Fire!"

Jack trudged a couple hundred feet further down the cross drift and waited. He braced himself, and a few minutes later there was a loud explosion, followed immediately by a pressure wave that travelled down the tube-shaped drift as if it were the barrel of a gun.

It was going to take at least twenty minutes for the smoke and dust to dissipate, so Jack moved a short distance further away to the small grotto where he had stashed his lunch-pail near a short section of plank placed across two blocks of stone to fashion a seat.

When the air in the blast area had cleared sufficiently, he would move the mucking machine – a small rail car with a compressed air pneumatic scoop on the front of it – up to the new pile of broken rock. He would fill it several times, and transport the gold ore to a mill hole, where he would dump it. The force of gravity would pull the rock deeper into the mine and break it against the walls of the shaft into smaller pieces on the way down to the jaw crusher, which would then pulverize it into even smaller fragments. From there, it would be carried by a skip in the main shaft to the surface, and milled. The last step would see the separated fine ore heated until it was molten, and then the gold portion poured into ingots.

As he finished off the last of his sandwiches and emptied his thermos of its last drams of coffee, Jack began to take stock of events over the past year.

It had all started and ended with Henriette. Even now he felt himself become aroused as he remembered her lithe body, lustrous long black hair, and beautiful hazel eyes. He thought they had been careful.

She hadn't told him about missing her periods, but two weeks after high school graduation and about three-and-a-half months into a pregnancy, she miscarried. It had happened at home, and there had been complications. In all likelihood, the only reason she had survived was down to her father being an experienced doctor, but there had been hell to pay – figuratively and literally.

The Lafrance family were the most devout of Roman Catholics. They had confessed dutifully to Father Albert, and he had brought the full weight of Christian guilt down upon them. He convinced them that a very terrible scandal could be avoided if secrecy were maintained, but there would have to be some genuine token of remorse and severe penitence before this vilest of sins could be forgiven, or any possible dispensation forthcoming from Rome.

There had been a substantial financial gift to the local parish, and they had all come to agree – strangely, even Henriette had agreed – that the best thing was for her to go into cloisters in Quebec, and devote her life in service to the church.

As Jack stared into the darkness, he cursed the perversity of religion. For her leaving hadn't been the end of it. He had been told as he called over several days that she was ill and couldn't come to the telephone. The last time he had rung, her mother answered, and in the background, he had heard Dr. Lafrance shout something indiscernible in French at her before she slammed down the receiver.

Within half an hour there had been loud knocking on their door, and as his mother opened it to let him in, Dr. Lafrance exploded in vituperation, cursing Jack as a 'fornicator'. As Brigit looked on in horror, he proceeded to accuse Collin of having raised an irresponsible criminal who had seduced his daughter, got her pregnant, and nearly caused her to die when she miscarried. Finally, threatening to go to Collin's employer, and declaring that as God was his witness, they would all burn in hell for this, he slammed the door and left.

His father had been livid. "How could you have been so stupid! The poor girl nearly died! If Lafrance makes a big enough stink about this, I could lose my bloody job because you couldn't keep your damned cock in your trousers!"

Jack was without an answer. He had never seen his father so angry. In desperation he looked to his mother. Shame, embarrassment, and uncertainty shifted across her face while she tried to comprehend this sudden and shocking turn of events. He was stunned, and uncontrollably he felt his own anger rising.

Before he knew it he was shouting at his father. "I didn't know! We love each other! If you can't see that, then we have nothing more to say!"

Flushed with anger, he grabbed his jacket, unable to stop the words coming out of his mouth. "I'll spare you any further embarrassment and leave now!"

His mother stammered. "Jack don't..." But he had already stomped out of the front door, slamming it violently behind him.

Months later, Jack was still mystified and disgusted by the way Henriette had convinced herself she deserved to spend the rest of her life doing penance as a nun. They had been lovers for over a year, and she had never expressed any strong religious beliefs to him, but had nonetheless always attended Sunday Mass, explaining only that it was a family tradition.

He had thought that he knew her, but clearly, he hadn't. Perhaps, because of his own lack of religious belief, she had avoided broaching the subject with him.

However, her thinking had become apparent to him when Henriette had managed to get a short letter delivered to him through a mutual friend before she left. She expressed her profound sense of guilt for having brought a life that had been conceived in sin into this world, and how the miscarriage had been God's judgment. It would take a lifetime of servitude to earn his forgiveness, and to regain any hope of finally entering the kingdom of Heaven. Jack had been an unwitting tool of Satan, and he needed to confess to a priest, thereby getting the absolution necessary to save his soul from damnation and an eternity in hell.

The indoctrination was strong, he mused. In the end she had reverted to believing the authoritarian and paternalistic tenants of her upbringing, having inculcated all the attendant religious assumptions. As a result, the passion and love of a vivacious young woman was doomed to wither under a colourless nun's habit, forever crushed by the austere supervision of some sexless Mother Superior with vinegar running through her veins.

He could see now that his love for her had been naïve. Jack vowed to himself that he would never make that mistake again. From now on, women were for pleasure, and any kind of romantic ideals could wait until conditions suited him.

At the end of his shift, Jack rode the cage to the surface where he emerged into the late afternoon darkness of early December. He made his way to the 'dry' room, and after showering and changing into his clothes, he walked over to the rudimentary office where the geologist and mine manager worked. There, he told them he was leaving to join up, and arranged to take the mail truck out to the railway crossing next morning.

Parked near the rail crossing at dawn, he and the driver shivered in the cab of the truck while its engine idled. The hot air heater blowing from under the dashboard kept them only slightly warmer in the thirty degrees below zero Fahrenheit air. As they spoke, their words, exhaled through chattering teeth, caused clouds of frozen vapour to form in the air before them.

Gus, the driver, had fought in the trenches for the Austro-Hungarian army during 1917/18, and he used his imperfect English in an attempt to dissuade Jack. "Maybe is a good idea you change your mind about going. I remember war is every time bad. This shit sometimes is bad too, but war is worse."

Jack was hunched over on his seat, vigorously rubbing his mitten-clad hands together. "I wouldn't be too quick rushing to judgment Gus. Right now almost anything seems to be a better idea than freezing our balls off in this ice box. If it gets any colder, your piss would freeze solid before it even hits the ground."

Gus could only manage a grunt in response.

A short time later, signs of a locomotive appeared in the distance, as the massive grey billows of steam and smoke shooting upward from its stack became visible above the tree line long before its dark shape hove into view. A blast from its whistle announced the train's arrival.

The huge locomotive slowly chuffing to a halt was a Hudson 4-8-4, built in Montreal, and designed for hauling long trains comprised of heavy rolling stock, or for pulling passenger sleepers at speed. It came to a stop just before the crossing, and a conductor wrapped in a full parka emerged briefly onto the steps of the first passenger car. He tossed a small canvas bag containing postage down to the mail truck driver, who in turn passed a similarly-sized sack up to him. The man then hurried back into the warmth of the passenger car.

Jack thanked Gus, then clasped the railing and swung himself up onto the stairs, which he quickly ascended before entering the Pullman.

In exchange for a few dollars, the conductor wrote him a ticket to Ottawa. Jack then made his way to a group of four unoccupied seats in the nearly empty car. He had just placed his bag in the rack above when there was a wail from the locomotive's whistle. Grabbing at a seat railing, he was nearly jolted off of his feet, as with a lurch, the slack between the resting cars was suddenly pulled taut.

A deep huffing from the belly of the locomotive exploded in dark grey blasts of smoke shooting upward from its stack as steam hissed from the drive pistons near the front of the engine. The reciprocating strokes of the long connecting arms began to turn the huge drive wheels increasingly faster, until the train grew into a thunderous black juggernaut ploughing down the tracks. It left a widening smudge in the clear blue sky behind it, and this eventually dissipated as the tiny soot particles settled silently alongside the rails to create a grey dusting on the snow-covered landscape.

For the next two hours he passed his time reading a copy of the Winnipeg Free Press. It contained stories about the destruction wreaked on Poland by the German conquest. Polish pilots and army officers had fled to England in the wake of the defeat, joining the ranks of scientists and Jews who had also decided to find sanctuary in the west, and perhaps carry on the fight from there.

France and Britain, as allies of Poland, had declared war on Germany, but thus far there had been no further attacks by the *Wehrmacht* on either country – or on any other. The pundits argued over whether it was just a matter of time, or whether Hitler had no further territorial ambitions. Some journalists had labelled this pause 'the phony war'.

Jack wondered if his brother Jason, who had acquired his pilot's license while still a student at university, would be patient enough to graduate - or would he join the Air Force in anticipation of hostilities. He resolved to call him as soon as he got to Ottawa, and sound him out. As for himself, he had decided to join the Army and see where that took him.

He switched trains in Sudbury, but there was a four hour layover, so by the time his train departed, it was nearly mid-night. When he awoke at seven the next morning, they were just pulling into the station in Ottawa.

After breakfast at a nearby restaurant, Jack used their pay phone to call his brother. The landlady informed him that Jason had gone off to the flying club airfield to get some practice time in. She gave him a number he could try, and as luck would have it, someone brought Jason to the phone moments before he was scheduled to go up.

Jack pressed the earpiece closer to dampen the sound of a column of military vehicles passing nearby. "Did I get you at a bad moment Jay?"

Jason was ecstatic to hear from his brother. "Christ no, Jack! It's good to hear from you! What the hell have you been up to these past months?"

"I've been trying my luck as a miner. The money was okay, but you don't see the sun much. I'm thinking of joining the Army."

Jason laughed. "You're joking! I thought you would be the last guy to say 'yes sir - no sir' to anyone!"

"Well, with what's going on in Europe these days, it's just a matter of time before we have to say it in German. I can fight, so maybe I'll get in early, and make my mark."

"Think seriously about that before you sign on the dotted line Jack. They're not fooling around over there."

He hesitated a moment. "By the way, there was something I needed to tell you about mom and dad."

At that moment, he was interrupted by some shouting in the background about the Jenny's engine blowing up if Jason didn't soon get it airborne.

One of the three soldiers lined up outside of the phone booth had tapped on the door and was glaring at him impatiently. "Okay Jay. You had better get into that airplane. There are also a few guys here who look like they need the phone. I'll get back to you once I know what I'm up to."

"Sorry. It looks like I have to go too Jack. Thanks for calling. Best of luck and make sure you let me know when you get settled..." Jason's voice trailed off, and then there was the clunk of the phone's earpiece as it swung against the wall.

Jack could hear him protesting, but the voices of other people in the background were angrily shouting at him. "Get the hell in that damned airplane, or we'll let someone else take it!"

Chuckling to himself, Jack put the earpiece back in its cradle. In his mind he had a picture of his brother gritting his teeth in an effort not to be frozen blue while flying in an open cockpit through the frigid December sky.

Next morning at the recruitment centre his medical examination pronounced Jack fit, and he was immediately accepted into the Canadian Army. He was then assigned to the Canadian Armoured Fighting Vehicle School that was now hastily being expanded to feed trained men into several of the tank regiments across the country. After nearly two decades of slow, often piecemeal progress, they were now in various stages of conversion from horse-mounted cavalry to the mechanized armoured regiments which would coalesce into a Canadian Armoured Division.

The first part of his basic training was to take place at nearby Camp Borden. However, nine months into the war, there was still an acute shortage of a tank regiment's most essential piece of equipment – tanks. As he settled into his barracks and took a stroll around the base, Jack was only able to recognize significant numbers of old six-ton, American-built versions of the Great War French Renault, some Vickers Mark IV B light tanks, and one ancient example of the American Mark VIII. This relic was a version of the original rhomboid-shaped tank first developed by the British to conquer barbed wire and trenches in the Great War. In addition, there seemed to be a growing supply of Universal Carriers – a light and open tracked vehicle he sometimes heard others refer to as a Bren Gun Carrier.

The initial part of basic training was centred upon learning how to march in formation, and fitness. As a boxer, Jack had for years been rising earlier than most in the mornings to go for long runs, and in the winter, he had also skated and trained on cross-country skis. Working in the mines had made his already muscular body exceptionally strong. It was soon apparent that he was fitter than most of the instructors, so he was often tasked to assist them in leading the young men through their various exercise sessions and cross-country runs.

Finally, they were taught the operation and maintenance of tanks. It was already obvious that the vehicles on the base were obsolete, but they were still able to familiarize themselves with the system of clutches and levers used to drive most tanks and the more mundane aspects of mechanical maintenance. Most importantly perhaps, they mastered the dirty and difficult job of repairing broken caterpillar treads which sometimes succumbed to the rocky terrain, or slipped off their bogeys during manoeuvres.

He did not allow his boxing skills to deteriorate and worked out on the punching bags while also sparring daily in the gymnasium. Over the weeks of pounding the bags, and his reluctant partners, he felt some of the rage over the way his disastrous relationship with Henriette had ended, begin to ebb. This was accompanied by pangs of regret over the way he had handled the confrontation with his parents.

In April, he entered an inter-regimental meet, and over the course of three days defeated five opponents, knocking all but one of them out in the Olympic style three-round bouts. Despite the sore ribs, a welt under his right eye, and his bruised and swollen lips, he was exultant to be the Canadian Army Heavyweight champion.

Jack worked hard to excel in the use of radios. Most tanks were equipped with what was known as an 'A' set which was for inter-tank voice communication. However, command tanks were also equipped with a 'B' set which utilized Morse code to communicate longer distances to headquarters. He seemed to have close to a natural ear for distinguishing the sounds of the 'dits' and 'dahs' – the dots and dashes which in various combinations, represented letters of the alphabet. Ironically, his large hands also developed a remarkably light touch on the key, and he had soon mastered the skill of tapping out transmissions which were notable for their speed and clarity at the receiving end. This did not go unnoticed by his superiors, and by May he was promoted from his rank of Trooper, to Corporal, and made an instructor in the A9 Wireless Section.

Schadenfreude

For Peter, the recent summer holiday with his cousins and their friend David, now seemed like a dream. They had made him feel completely at home, and his aunt Brigit was so like his mother, that it had been difficult to decline her suggestion that he remain in Canada rather than return to Germany.

She had continued to write to his mother, and through her he had learned that Jason was now in University and also taking flying lessons. David had taken an apprenticeship at the local iron mine, while Jack was in his final year of high school, and was apparently gaining some fame as a crushing defenseman in the local junior hockey league.

The sight of the landing strip in the distance caused him to refocus his attention to the task at hand, which was to successfully complete his solo flight by landing the tiny biplane without mishap. Earlier in the morning before taking off, he had experienced a slight twinge of apprehension, but once in the air a serene sense of confidence had taken over, so he had performed the flight plan flawlessly and almost without thinking.

Within days of returning from Canada, Peter had enrolled in the local flying school. The small aerodrome had been rapidly expanding its facilities to augment the training of new pilots, which were urgently required by the growing number of *Luftwaffe* squadrons now coming into existence. He had attacked the program with exceptional zeal, spending every minute absorbing information from both the manuals and his tutors. At the same time, he also took every possible opportunity to spend time in the air with his instructors. In less than a month they believed he was ready to solo.

It was a very routine approach, but at the last moment he experienced a gust of wind shear, which caused the airplane to suddenly drop several metres, placing him too low, and short of the runway. Reflexively, he advanced the throttle while simultaneously pulling back slightly on the control column, giving him the required increase in speed and altitude. The subsequent landing was uneventful as he did a perfect touch down, and then reduced the throttle. After losing sufficient speed, he turned the aircraft onto the access way and taxied it back to the hangar.

When Peter descended from the cockpit his instructor Sigmund Fuelbier, a grizzled veteran of the Great War, was there to shake his hand and congratulate him. He wore a black eye patch above his shrivelled left cheek, and was unable to contain the grin below his thin grey moustache. A withered, claw-like left hand rose to remove the smoldering cigarette from his lips.

He coughed twice, and gregariously clapped his other hand on Peter's shoulder. "I saw the way you corrected when that cross-wind tried to arse-fuck you! Not many would have recovered that well on their first solo."

Fuelbier regarded Peter for a moment and nodded his head approvingly. He took a long drag on the unfiltered cigarette and erupted again into a staccato series of dry coughs before spitting an errant shred of tobacco onto the tarmac.

Recovering his breath, he rasped. "Schmidt, I have a feeling you are going to be one hell of a fine pilot. Let's step into my office to celebrate with a glass of schnapps, *ja*?"

When Peter arrived home, the dinner table was already set. His parents and sister Elke all stopped to look at him expectantly.

"Well?" His father asked.

He teased them evasively. "I'm here all in one piece, aren't I?"

However, he couldn't prevent the smile from slowly spreading across his face. "I am now officially a pilot."

Elke was unable to contain her joy at the news. "I just knew you would Peter! You're going to be the best pilot in the whole world!"

Then, she whispered. "Papa has some other good news for you."

He turned to his father, puzzled. "Is there something else I should know?"

His father shrugged. "Well, I was going to wait until during our dinner so we could drink a toast, but it can't hurt to tell you now. It seems two good things have happened for you today."

"My friend Frederick, who is a design engineer at the *Bayerische Flugzeugwerke*, has called me to say that they want you to start in his department, beginning in about a month from now. There will be an official letter soon to confirm your appointment. Congratulations! You will be apprenticing to be an aeronautic engineer!"

For the next month, Peter spent as much time as possible in the air practicing various manoeuvres and gaining ever more confidence in his ability to control the aircraft. By the time he arrived at Augsburg, he was seriously wondering if he had made the right decision by choosing the field of aeronautical engineering.

With his all-consuming love of flying, perhaps he should instead be focusing on flying the world's highest-performing aircraft by becoming a fighter pilot.

Peter spent his first week just learning his way around the huge complex. The enormous *Flugzeugwerke* employed about 6,000 workers, and consisted of seven large buildings arranged in a spaced pattern around the central airfield. In the event of an aerial attack it would be difficult to destroy the entire facility, and any damage to one or more of the buildings would not necessarily disrupt production in the others.

He had barely settled into the design department before being informed that based upon his previous instructor's evaluation and recommendation, they intended to have him first concentrate on his flying skills, and eventually be able to test new designs in the air. To acquaint him with the flight characteristics of monoplanes, they had him practice with the *Bf*108 *Taifun*.

Peter easily adjusted to the higher wing loading and increased power of the sleek monoplane. He soon began to appreciate the roomy enclosed cockpit, which was more comfortable than the conditions he had experienced in the exposed slipstream of open cockpit biplanes.

In very short order his reflexes adapted to the increased speed and performance of the *Taifun*, and he felt that he was ready to take the next step in his development – to fly the *Bf*109.

His first few flights were in an earlier variant, the *Bf*109C. The seven hundred horsepower engine could speedily push the fighter along at nearly five hundred kilometres per hour. Peter found the cockpit more cramped than the *Taifun*, but purpose-built for simplicity and ease of operation.

After examining the spindly outward-retracting landing gear, he decided it would be a good idea to heed his instructor's admonition not to set it down too hard on the landings. It was not difficult to imagine how so many pilots had been lost in accidents attributed to the collapse of the slim, narrow-stance wheel struts. Nonetheless, he soon came to love the greater speed and performance of the *Bf*109, and the sense of agile omnipotence the plane engendered as his skill and confidence grew.

Within months he had graduated to the latest *Bf*109E *Emil* variant. With its larger *Daimler-Benz* 601A engine generating 1,175 horsepower, the top speed had been increased to a breathtaking 575 kilometres per hour. The fighter's incredible ability to climb, turn, and dive, was nothing short of exhilarating.

For the first half-dozen flights, Peter would land to find he was trembling from the massive jolts of adrenalin still coursing through his veins. This phenomenon eventually subsided as he became more accustomed to the plane's exceptional performance.

Shortly after he felt that he had mastered the *Emil* and could justifiably relish the thought of being a test pilot, he was informed that *Leutnant* Roland Schwartz had returned.

Peter was excited about the prospect of meeting the former head test pilot who had become a fighter ace with seven kills while flying in Spain as a part of the *Condor Legion*.

Schwartz would be acting in an official capacity as the *Luftwaffe*'s liaison and aircraft evaluation officer, but he looked forward to picking the *Leutnant's* brains for any information that would improve his flying abilities in the new fighter. Also, hearing first-hand exploits about the *Bf*109's performance as flown by Schwartz in real combat. Aerial dogfights fascinated and excited him. He felt sure that the ace would be able to provide him with hard-earned practical advice, and hopefully, the hands-on practice of flying mock engagements that would impart some of those combat skills.

Schwartz was assigned his own office, and the day after Roland's arrival, Peter was summoned. He knocked, and then entered to see the *Leutnant* sitting bare-headed in his uniform, behind the desk. He was poring over an unrolled blueprint design, which Peter immediately recognized as belonging to the *Bf*109E.

Peter nervously attempted to introduce himself. "Good morning sir. I'm Peter Schmidt. I was told to report to you."

Roland rose from behind his desk, but did not offer his hand. He had grown used to being saluted respectfully, but of course Schmidt was a civilian, unfamiliar with the formalities of rank. Nevertheless, this lack of official acknowledgement made him vaguely uncomfortable.

He regarded the young man cautiously for a moment. "Schmidt. It appears you are being trained for the test pilot position I vacated here when I was seconded by the *Condor Legion*. How well are you acquainted with the *Bf109*?"

Peter hesitated a moment as he took in Schwartz's intimidating appearance. The *Leutnant* stood at least seven or eight centimetres taller than he, and his large torso probably outweighed Peter by at least fifteen kilos. The carbuncular ravages of his teenage years had not been kind to Roland's neck or jaw line, and this combined with his dark black moustache to create a fearsome countenance.

"I've flown all the variants." Peter replied.

He hurriedly added. "However, most of my hours have been in our latest version of the *Emil*. I think you will be very pleasantly surprised by the margin of improved performance over the variants you were flying in Spain."

Roland misinterpreted Peter's attempt to ingratiate himself. *Was there a hint of arrogance in the young pilot's implication?*

A few of the *Bf109E* variants had made it to Spain before the cessation of hostilities, and he had been one of only a handful of pilots who had briefly flown them. *Perhaps he would have to teach Schmidt a lesson. By taking him down a few notches, he would firmly establish what the nature of their relationship was actually going to be.*

Roland forced himself to nod appreciatively. "That is good. From the reports I'm reading about the performance of the British Hurricanes and Spitfires, there will have to be improvements to maintain our superiority. Have a pair of *Emils* prepared for takeoff in an hour. I want to check you out, and also see for myself if what you say about the latest *Bf109E* is true."

An hour later, when Peter arrived at the hanger in his flying gear, the fitters had already started the planes' engines, and Roland was being assisted into his cockpit by one of the riggers.

As they prepared to taxi out onto the runway, Schwartz's voice came to him over the radio. "We will take off together in *rotte* formation. I want you to attempt to follow me as a wingman. Stay behind and slightly above me to my right. I will give you a warning about any manoeuvre, and I will expect you to stay with me."

After being strapped into his own cockpit by the rigger, Peter had a few moments to observe Schwartz. He was wearing a modified chest parachute, and as he lowered his bulk into the pilot's seat, one of the ground crew leant over to strap him in. Even though he sat in a position hunched slightly forward, the top of the *Leutnant's* flying helmet still brushed against the inside surface of the now-closed Plexiglas canopy.

They lined up on the runway together, and advanced their throttles, causing the two aircraft to rapidly pick up speed. In unison, they pulled back slightly on their control columns, and the two fighters leapt nimbly into the air. After retracting their landing gear, they climbed to 7,000 metres where they levelled off.

Roland, checking to confirm that Peter was correctly positioned, then barked the first of his instructions. "We will roll left, and dive!"

It took every bit of Peter's concentration to stick to his leader as the gravitational forces accumulated with the increased speed of the dive.

After several thousand metres, Schwartz levelled off and shouted. "Break right!"

Roland rolled right, and went into a tight flat turn. Their aircraft were no longer in level flight, but knifing through the air at ninety degrees. Peter was able to glance at the ground thousands of metres below him through the right side of his canopy as he maintained his position relative to the lead fighter. He was behind but slightly below as he followed Schwartz through the ever-tightening turn.

The excessive 'G' forces had just induced the first shades of darkness around the periphery of his vision, when he saw Schwartz roll level and sluggishly resume a straight course for several seconds before beginning another climb to higher altitude.

Peter was both surprised and exultant when he realized what had just happened. Not only did Schwartz seem to have a heavy hand on the *Bf*109's control column, but he had temporarily blacked out, meaning the ace had a lower tolerance for 'G' forces than Peter!

Meanwhile, at the top of their climb, Schwartz rolled over into another dive, putting Peter through several successive manoeuvres in which he was for the most part able to maintain his wingman position.

A slight edge had crept into Schwartz's voice as he finally told Peter to maintain a level course at 5,000 metres, and try to evade him after he attacked from above. In each of several attempts, Peter, thanks to his excellent eyesight and lightning-fast reflexes, was able to roll right or left as required to dive away safely and cause Roland to overshoot.

Roland grew increasingly frustrated. His voice, now raspy, was infused with adrenalin and barely-suppressed rage as it crackled over Peter's radio. "Now fly straight and level until I arrive on your tail, then try to lose me!"

The ace's experience began to tell after Roland pulled in behind Peter. Diving, twisting, and turning in every direction, Peter was never able to completely lose Schwartz, whose experience somehow seemed to have given him the ability to anticipate his every move. However, every time Schwartz moved into a position near to having him in his sights, Peter's quickness enabled him to evade being lined up for a possible kill.

Both pilots were reaching a state of near-exhaustion. Finally, Peter pulled out of a dive and rolled into a left turn that drew ever-tighter, until he could feel the impending blackout beginning to cloud his peripheral vision. Preparing to straighten out his aircraft to concede defeat, he caught sight of Schwartz in his rear-view mirror.

Roland's fighter had begun to wobble, before it levelled off and disappeared to his right. Peter, then blacked out.

Regaining consciousness seconds later, he levelled off and circled around in an attempt to locate Schwartz, until finally spotting him about two kilometres ahead and about 1,000 metres below, on a heading to the airfield.

When he pulled into his wingman position, Schwartz's voice hissed at him over the radio. "I will have a word with you after we land!"

By the time Peter stepped down from the wing of his fighter, Schwartz, bareheaded and perspiring, was already striding toward him.

He had only just removed his own leather flight helmet, when with unexpected spittle-laced fury, the purple-faced *Leutnant* launched into him. "That was an incredibly stupid move you made up there! You were flying much too tight a turn for this aircraft! It is only because you are incredibly lucky that the wings weren't ripped right off of it! If I had not decided to roll out, we would have both been killed! If you pull another stunt like that again I'll see to it that you're fired, and you will never sit in the cockpit of an aircraft again!"

Schwartz didn't wait for Peter to respond, and threw his parachute harness at one of the fitters before stalking off in the direction of the design bureau.

Peter cursed his luck, but consoled himself with the knowledge that he now knew what kind of man he was dealing with in Schwartz.

He had clearly seen him black out. Everything else was just an excuse to cover for his inability to follow him through the turn. That meant he would now have to carefully limit himself when in the air with Schwartz to avoid bruising the *Leutnant's* tender ego.

Peter glanced sheepishly at the fitters and riggers who had been standing nearby. Several of them shrugged, and a couple of them smiled, but Karl, a mechanic who had been at the *Flugzeugwerke* since before Schwartz's time, tilted his head in Roland's direction. "*Schweinhundt!*"

For most of the next six months, Peter honed his flying skills, whilst simultaneously amassing technical knowledge about the "*Emil*". He generally tried to avoid any unnecessary interaction with Schwartz, but because of the nature of their respective duties, contact was sometimes unavoidable. On those occasions, Peter usually tried to convey the requested information as quickly as possible, without volunteering any opinions other than reiterating suggestions he had made in the written submissions to Schwartz prior to their meetings.

The *Leutnant's* manner during these exchanges was brusque. Questions were brief and to the point, and his responses curt or dismissive. Peter often left these meetings believing that Schwartz lacked any respect for his opinions, whereas, unknown to him, Roland was forwarding most of this information to his superiors and taking credit for the suggestions himself.

As spring wore into summer, their meetings became less frequent as Schwartz's responsibilities on the *Luftwaffe* side of his liaison function began to consume greater amounts of time. The *Leutnant* had been gone for nearly six weeks, when in September, Peter learned from the news reports on the dormitory radio that the invasion of Poland had begun.

For the first time, the world was mesmerized by the stunning success of the German '*Blitzkreig*', or 'Lightening War' doctrine. It combined the speed, firepower, and mobility of coordinated air, *Panzer*, and mechanized infantry attack, against the more orthodox but outdated military doctrine employed by the Poles. Their overwhelming defeat by the *Wehrmacht* was total, and produced among other things, propaganda films with the contrived and ludicrous spectacle of Polish horse cavalry charging against German armoured tanks.

It was two months after the cessation of hostilities before Schwartz made his first appearance at the *Flugzeugwerke*. The gist of his report confirmed that the *Luftwaffe* was ecstatic about the *BF*109's performance, but still had concerns regarding the flimsy nature of the fighter's landing struts. Their collapse had cost the lives of three pilots in accidents during the campaign.

While understanding the delicate balance between strength and weight required to produce the exceptional performance of the *Bf*109, they were hopeful that this problem would be addressed and somehow rectified in the future. For now, they wanted every one of the aircraft that it was currently possible to produce.

The news that he had scored four more kills in the air over Poland had preceded Roland's return, and Peter offered him his congratulations at the first opportunity in the general debriefing that was held between Schwartz and the engineers.

The *Leutnant's* chest swelled involuntarily, but he prudently contained his pride, and nodded in acknowledgement to Willy Messerschmitt who was standing with his arms crossed in one corner of the room. "Nothing can compensate for the experience a fighter pilot acquires in combat, so I have to consider my time with the *Condor Legion* in Spain helped to provide me with the skills to win against the enemy. However, those victories were also possible because of the superb flying qualities of the *Bf*109, which easily outclassed everything we encountered in the air."

There was a boisterous round of applause from everyone in the room, and without acknowledging Peter's compliment, Schwartz began to make his way to the corner of the room where Messerschmitt and some of the senior engineers were standing. Relieved, Peter slid out of the room unnoticed. He then made his way down the hall and out of the building, where he climbed onto his bicycle and pedaled over to the hanger to get more flying time in the *Emil*.

Next day, Peter learned that Schwartz had returned to Berlin. Over the following several months, he reappeared periodically, but for only a day or two, and on those occasions he spent most of his time in meetings with Messerschmitt and the senior design engineers.

Unknown to Peter, Messerschmitt had proposed to begin development on a jet-engine fighter. It would be a quantum leap in terms of performance over the current crop of piston engine fighters being flown by the world's air forces.

Roland had decided that he wanted to be at the forefront of this development, but did not relish the idea that Peter would also be at the centre of the program and possibly gain more experience with the plane than he. Quietly, he pressed his contacts in the party and the *Luftwaffe* to pull a few strings.

Peter would forever remember April 15, 1940 as the day he received a telegram from *Air Reichsmarschall* Hermann Göring, personally handed to him at the *Flugzeugwerke* by Willy Messerschmitt.

The president of *Bayerische Flugzeugwerk* spoke to Peter directly. "It seems the powers that be believe you can be of much greater use to the *Luftwaffe* than you are to me. I would strenuously disagree Schmidt, but unfortunately my hands are tied. This comes directly from Göring himself, and frankly I owe him everything I have."

"He is the only person standing between me and Air Inspector General Erhard Milch, who would like nothing better than to see that I am bankrupted or worse. The man still holds me personally responsible for his friend Hans Hackman's death testing the M20 prototype."

"I'll hate to lose you because you know the *Bf*109 almost as well as anyone except perhaps me, but I have to maintain Göring's favourable consideration, so there is nothing I can do. You report to the *Luftwaffe* in Berlin on the day after tomorrow."

Once in Berlin, Peter was fitted out with a uniform, taught the basics of rank echelon, and then tested in the air to determine his flying skills. He passed easily, demonstrating skills that exceeded those possessed by some of the veteran fighter pilots at the school. A day later, the smiling *Oberst* handed him official documents assigning the rank of *Leutnant*.

The *Oberst* was convinced that Peter was a superior pilot, and nodded his head appreciatively as he conveyed the additional good news. "You're lucky Schmidt. You've been assigned to one of the best *gruppes* in the *Luftwaffe*. It already possesses one of our leading aces. By personal request, you'll be flying in the *schwarm* of *Hauptmann* Roland Schwartz!"

Peter snapped a crisp salute as he handed the papers containing his squadron assignment to *Hauptmann* Schwartz. Roland savoured the moment a few seconds longer before slowly returning the salute.

He was unable to keep the hint of sarcasm out of his voice. "Welcome to *Jagdgeschwader 26*, Schmidt. I assume you were pleased to learn that I have decided to make you my personal wingman. As such it will be your primary duty to cover me and confirm my victories in the upcoming battle."

Peter admitted to a certain degree of confusion. "Upcoming battle? What are you talking about?"

Roland smirked. "You see Schmidt, I have connections in the Party that you couldn't even dream of. I am privy to information that the world will only learn about tomorrow morning when we have successfully commenced our push through Belgium and into France."

"We are going to teach the Frenchies a good lesson this time, so gather your gear, then check out your aircraft and get yourself squared away. Be prepared to join me in the dispersal hut at 06:30 hours tomorrow morning all ready to go when we begin hostilities.

Try not to shit your pants when we start fighting aircraft that shoot real bullets."

Peter's head was spinning with the news. Tomorrow he would be in the air attacking other aircraft and being shot at in return. The suddenness with which it had all come to pass was not only startling but thrilling as well.

Before Peter could further question him, Schwartz brusquely ended the conversation. "*Leutnant* Schmidt, you are dismissed!"

At the maintenance shed Peter's eyes travelled appreciatively over the length of his *Bf109E*. Fully armed, cleaned and polished by the fitters, it was resplendent in its mottled grey camouflage pattern.

The fighter aircraft of *Jagdgeschwader 26 Schlageter* bore additional markings which distinguished them from other front-line fighting *gruppes*. On the left-side engine cowling a small white shield bore a gothic *'S'* in homage to the *gruppe's* namesake – a nationalist hero killed by the French in the 1920's for attempting to sabotage a reparations coal shipment mandated by the Treaty of Versailles. Their aircraft were further distinguished by the bright yellow colour around the nose section which served to provide easy *gruppe* recognition.

In the early morning, they attacked the enemy airfield from the east, putting the sun behind them and into the Belgians' eyes, as they screamed in at tree-top height.

Roland was commanding his own *schwarm*, and he was out in front of the entire fighter *gruppe* as they swept down upon the unsuspecting Belgians. Most of the enemy fighters were parked in a line on both sides of the landing strip, and the two *rottes* separated to better bear down on their respective rows of aircraft.

In the distance Peter could see that a large twin-engine transport plane had taken off and was in the air about half a kilometre beyond the end of the runway.

He swivelled his head to make sure that no enemy planes were diving upon him or Schwartz, as the *Hauptmann* fired his guns at the line of fighters below. The cannon shells traced two parallel lines in front of the stationary row of aircraft, and as Roland corrected his aim, they slammed into the last four machines. Topped up with fuel, they exploded in a sequence of orange blasts as he flew beyond the end of the airstrip.

Roland now had the unarmed transport lined up in his sights and moved in to point-blank range before firing. His 20mm shells tore a line of jagged holes along the left side of the fuselage and blasted the windows to pieces as they obliterated the cockpit. The lumbering aircraft slowly turned over on its back and plunged into the ground, where it exploded. The huge fireball created a mushroom cloud of thick black smoke, which Peter glimpsed again briefly as it shrunk in the rear-view mirror atop his windscreen.

As they pulled up and banked to the right, they could see that the entire airbase was aflame as successive waves of fighters strafed the remaining aircraft sitting on the tarmac. When they finally levelled off, the other *rotte* rejoined them, moving back into their 'finger four' position on Roland's right.

Schwartz's voice hissed through Peter's headphones. "You saw that did you Schmidt? I got five kills which you will confirm. That's how we destroy the enemy in combat. Do you hear me?"

Peter grit his teeth and did his best not to betray the anger he felt at Roland's attempt to belittle him before answering. "*Ja*, I heard. Five kills confirmed."

Within three weeks the British Expeditionary Force and several units of the French Army were evacuating at Dunkirk to seek safety in Britain. Peter was amazed by the breathtaking speed of the *Wehrmacht's* '*Blitzkrieg*' tactics as they laid low these formidable opponents. More astounding was how high Schwartz's score of aircraft kills had soared in this brief span of time, to over thirty. He somehow managed to know just when a group of fighter aircraft would be sitting on the tarmac or in the process of refuelling. While Peter guarded his flank as wingman, Roland would destroy the hapless aircraft as they sat motionless on the ground or fitfully attempted to take off. However, the greatest toll was taken on the unarmed French transport aircraft as they vainly attempted to resupply the ground troops who were trying to stem the relentless German tide now flowing in the direction of Paris.

Slow and not particularly manoeuvrable, they were easy victims and comprised the majority of Schwartz's kills.

Their *schwarm* was at 8,000 metres on an intercept course for one such group of transports, when suddenly they were bounced by four *Dewoitine* D.520 fighters.

This aircraft was the latest French design. With a slightly less powerful engine it was nearly twenty kilometres per hour slower than the *Bf*109, but a bit more manoeuvrable, thus making its performance almost on a par with the German fighter.

The two *rottes* immediately split, rolling in opposite directions in an attempt to dive away. Peter had no time to worry about the flight leader while he tried desperately but unsuccessfully to shake the Frenchman off of his own tail. Finally, he put the fighter into a dive which allowed him to pull away from his pursuer, who then roared past him into a cloud as Peter pulled up and climbed in the same direction he had last seen Schwartz flying.

Suddenly, he saw the D.520 that had been on the *Hauptmann's* tail. Whether Roland had shaken him or had been shot down was now a secondary consideration as he closed on the French aircraft's tail from slightly above. His stream of 20mm cannon shells grazed the leading edge of the right wing-root, and two of them penetrated the engine. It immediately began to belch smoke and a thick spray of engine oil spewed out the right side of the cowling.

Peter took his thumb off of the firing button when he saw the canopy slide back and the pilot beginning to climb out of the cockpit. In a flash, Schwartz's *Bf*109 dove in from the left. He gasped, as Roland poured a fusillade of cannon fire point-blank into the side of the D.520, causing it to explode in a massive fireball filled with debris which Peter had to bank violently right to avoid.

The other two *Bf*109s were nowhere to be seen, and as he formed up on Schwartz's left again, Peter was seething.

As hard as he tried, he couldn't keep the anger from his voice. "What the hell did you do that for? He was bailing out! A few more seconds and he would have been clear! His plane was finished!"

There was a noticeable pause before Roland answered. "I will ignore your lack of respect for a senior officer this time Schmidt, but don't ever question my methods again or you will regret it. You were allowing that pilot to escape and fight another day, when we should be killing as many of the bastards as possible. Too bad, because that would have been your first kill. Now when we land you will confirm it as another one of mine."

Brothers in Arms

For Jason, Flight School had been an exercise in impatience. They had seen war coming even during Peter's visit in 1938, so while in his first year of university, Jason had joined their flying club and got his pilot's license by practicing from a tiny grass field the group operated on a small farm west of Toronto.

Unfortunately, the club's sole aircraft was a threadbare Curtiss JN-4 'Jenny' biplane of late Great War vintage. The Canadian-built 'Canuck' version featured a stick instead of the standard control wheel, and it was often not in flyable condition. Between the frequent maintenance required for its worn-out Curtiss OX-5 V8 engine, and the depredations of student pilots upon the aircraft's landing gear, the plane was likely as not to be in the hanger for repair when he was scheduled to take it up during attempts to increase his flying hours.

Throughout the invasion of Poland, and the subsequent 'phony' war when Germany didn't seem to be doing anything, he gradually acquired more flight time, while also forcing himself to endure university classes.

However, in the late Spring, at the end of his second year, things began to change quickly when the Germans attacked France.

Jason immediately enlisted in the RCAF, and breezed through ground school at Trenton. Since he already had his pilot's license, he was allowed to familiarize himself with night-time instrument flying in the Link 'Blue Box' flight simulation trainer. He scheduled this between his normal training sessions, where they were teaching him to fly the military way in a more modern airplane. His flying skills were now rapidly improving, but between flights, he listened to the radio broadcasts describing the debacle occurring in what was now being called the Battle of France.

The announcer's grim voice – the 'voice of doom' they called him - intoned a daily litany of defeat, describing how in a completely unexpected move, the Germans had thrust through the Ardennes and the Somme to cut off the bulk of the British army in Belgium and France. With their backs to the sea, they were forced to desperately evacuate to England from Dunkirk on a flotilla of hastily assembled boats of every kind, leaving the bulk of their heavy weapons and equipment behind.

The *Wehrmacht* then subsequently outflanked the impregnable chain of fortresses known as the Maginot Line, and in less than two more weeks of being subjected to this *Blitzkrieg*, the French had lost.

Throughout this period, flights in the elegant little Gypsy Moth biplane reinforced his sense of flying in three dimensions, while his previously basic skills developed to a point where the use of various control surfaces and cockpit inputs had become instinctive.

In that very short time, he felt himself becoming an integral part of the aircraft. It was almost as if he were guiding it with his mind, as the biplane, so sensitive to any light movement of the control column, responded immediately to his will.

She was also a forgiving aircraft. The lift provided by her two large main wings gave him the opportunity to correct for most early errors, guided for an initial period by the calm advice of his instructor in the seat behind him.

Shortly after going solo, he found himself selected in one of the groups soon to be shipping out for the transatlantic crossing to Britain. He quickly arranged a short leave, and then booked a train ticket out of Toronto.

A day and a half later, he stepped onto the front porch of his parent's house in *Wawa*, where he paused a moment to let his eyes rest on the home he had grown up in. The storm windows had been taken down and replaced with screens. This spurred a childhood memory of his brother and he helping their father twist the wing latches during the twice-yearly ritual of switching the exterior frames to create a double-glazed insulation barrier for the winter, or a screen against insects during the open-window heat of summer.

Canadians who lived in northern communities like his own, contended with lengthy winters where temperatures often plummeted past -40 Fahrenheit, and summers where the heat sometimes rose to 90 or above. Such extremes of climate bred a stoic toughness in people that served them well in other realms of adversity – not least of which was the battlefield.

It was mid-afternoon, and his mother was busy in the kitchen preparing the evening meal. She had just closed the oven door on a pork roast, and had her back to him when he silently entered.

"I hope you made enough for me too," he said, in a matter of fact way.

"Jason!" She spun around, hesitating a moment to take in the first sight of him wearing his blue Air Force uniform, before rushing to embrace him.

The questions followed quickly. "Why didn't you tell us you were coming? Your father will be so happy to see you! How long are you here for?"

"Not long mom. I'm off to Halifax in three days, then shipping out to England. I'll have to leave again tomorrow afternoon."

She couldn't hide the disappointment in her voice. "But you've just arrived…"

Jason nodded. "I know. Its short notice, and I had a devil of a time just getting this leave, but I wanted to make sure I had a chance to say goodbye. There is no telling how long this war is going to go on, but it could easily last another year or two."

It seemed too long a separation to contemplate, so she changed the subject. "I've just taken some scones out of the oven. They should have cooled down by now."

She sliced one through, then spread butter and honey on both halves before handing the steaming biscuits to him. He bit into them ravenously, savouring once again the taste of his mother's baking.

Passing him a glass of cold milk, she watched contentedly as he washed down the last morsels, burping lightly before apologizing.

Jason then broached the subject that he had sensed she was avoiding. "Has anyone heard from Jack?"

She searched his eyes. "No. I was hoping that you had some news…"

"Not since he called months ago to tell me he was planning to join the army. I haven't heard a thing from him since then. He could even be in England by now if in fact he did join up."

She shuddered. "I wish he would just call or write to let us know he is okay. I'm sure your father regrets the row they had before Jack left, but he won't talk about it. He has that stubborn streak that your brother inherited, and I think neither one of them wants to admit that they were wrong."

"I'm sorry I can't tell you anything mom. I'll make some enquiries through official channels, to find out if he's in the forces at least. That might be a start."

Collin McMurchy arrived home about thirty minutes before their usual 6 p.m. dinner hour. Surprised and delighted to see Jason, he pumped his hand in greeting.

He slapped Jason proudly on the shoulder, while taking in the sight of him. "My God it's good to see you son! That's quite the uniform you're wearing. It looks good on you! The Air Force must be feeding you well because you appear to have put on some muscle since we last saw you!"

Jason grinned as a sudden wave of contentment washed over him. His father's obvious joy and the smells from his mother's kitchen had momentarily transported him back to his childhood, and the attendant sense of security he had experienced inside these walls. "I think I must have put on at least ten pounds this year dad. They work us pretty hard, and the food's not bad either, but it doesn't come anything near to mom's cooking."

His father nodded his head in agreement and patted his stomach. "No argument from me on that point. By the way, how long are you here for?"

Brigit cleared her throat. "He's leaving again tomorrow. Then he ships out to England from Halifax three days later."

His father seemed momentarily stunned, but he managed to recover, and stammered. "Well, uh, I guess a short visit is better than none at all, isn't it?"

Hesitating, he then smiled conspiratorially. "I've been saving something in the basement for a special occasion, so I think this must be it. Hang on just a moment, and then I'll join you and your mother at the table."

He disappeared down the stairs for a minute, and then re-emerged with a dusty green bottle in his hand. Moving to the kitchen sink, he took a dish rag and wiped it down before displaying the label to them. "It's a good Italian Chianti that I bought together with our Christmas wine when I was in the Sault last November. I'll get the cork out of it, and we can all have a nice glassful to celebrate your upcoming embarkation."

Later, before falling asleep, Jason laid awake in his dark upstairs bedroom listening to the familiar muffled sound of his parents conversing in the living room below. When, he wondered, would he find himself lying here again, and in what kind of world, if he came back to it? Was it possible to win against the Germans this time – and if they did, how many of his friends and classmates might not make it through the conflict?

Earlier in the evening he had called David, but his mother had answered. She told him he was working that afternoon and probably overtime on the graveyard shift too. Jason had chatted a bit and told her of his upcoming deployment. Apprehensively, she had wished him luck, before promising to have David call him in the morning.

The next morning Jason's mother served them a hearty breakfast of blueberry pancakes covered in maple syrup, with bacon and fried eggs on the side. Jason and his father had just seated themselves at the table when there was a knock on the door.

Brigit opened the door to see David, who was smiling and ravenously eyeing the food on the table. "Good morning Mrs. McMurchy. I thought I smelt blueberry pancakes!"

She laughed. "I just knew that if I cooked up a batch you would be over here in no time! For goodness sakes come on in David and have a chair. I've made plenty."

Jason rose from his chair and the two young men clasped hands.

David spoke first. "That's a pretty good grip you've got on you there, stranger. Do they actually make you do an honest day's work in the Air Force?"

Jason laughed. "You're not doing too bad yourself pardner. It looks like you've put on a little beef too since I last saw you – can't say that it's done much for your looks though."

David raised a crooked arm to flex his bicep. "A lot of overtime in the hole and two lunch-pails full of sandwiches every day tends to bring out the natural Charles Atlas in me. Now, are you going to bore us all to tears with small talk, or are you going to let me get at some of your mom's pancakes."

Collin McMurchy shook his head. "You guys will never change. Come on and dig in before this food gets cold."

The two young men caught up on each other's past year between mouths full of food, which they washed down with several cups of coffee. Collin listened to them with interest while Brigit refilled their plates and cups regularly. She looked on in admiration, then later, concern, as Jason described the pilot training program. Her worries silently increased while he described the performance of the Spitfires he eventually hoped to fly, and the German airplanes he would be fighting against.

As Jason's parents cleaned up the table and did the dishes, David said goodbye to them and thanked Mrs. McMurchy for breakfast. Jason went out onto the front porch with him to bid farewell.

David lowered his voice. "Have you heard anything from Jack?"

Jason steered him away from the screen door to keep them out of earshot from his parents. "Not since he called six months ago to say he was probably going to join the army. Christ! I wish he would just drop my mom a line. I can tell it's driving her nuts with worry."

David continued. "I'm sure he'll get himself sorted eventually, but he was one angry guy when he left last year. Listen, a cousin of mine is in the army, and he was passing through last week. He's a good runner and said that he had attended an inter-regimental sports meet, about two months ago. Apparently, there was a big blond guy from Northern Ontario who knocked out three other guys to win the heavyweight division. He didn't know the guy's name, but his description sounded an awful lot like our Jack. If it was, he could already be in England by now."

Jason paused a moment to take it all in. "Yeah, it could be him. I've already told my mother I would start making inquiries through official channels as soon as I get back to base. Meanwhile, please don't mention any of this to my parents. Until we find out for sure, it would just give them something more to worry about."

"You can count on me Jay. But there is another thing I've been thinking about. What the hell is Peter up to these days? We know from your aunt's letters that he is in the *Luftwaffe*, but I wonder if he saw any action in Poland or France – and what is going through his head if he has? He didn't seem to have any love for the Nazis, but now he's fighting for them."

Jason shrugged. "I don't know what he's thinking. The law of averages ensures there is probably only the slightest possibility we will ever meet in the air, but I've no idea what I would do if we did. With the headgear, goggles, oxygen masks, and closed canopies, we probably wouldn't recognize each other anyway. One of us could end up killing the other and not even know it."

David shook his head, and then clasped Jason's hand a last time before looking him squarely in the eye. "You watch your tail when you are over there. I mean it."

He forced a smile. "If you don't make it back, I won't have an excuse to come over and mooch another breakfast off of your mom."

"Don't worry about me. Coming back alive is going to be my highest priority if I've got anything to do with it."

David released his grip. "Well, good luck on that. I sure hope to see you again when it's all over."

Before he disappeared around the street corner, David turned to look back once more, to exchange a final wave.

After Jason went upstairs to his bedroom to put his uniform on, Collin went out onto the porch. He stood there a few moments with his hands in his pockets, lost in thought. He then moved into the living room, took a seat, and absently browsed through the previous week's edition of the Toronto Star Weekly magazine. However, he found it impossible to focus on the lines of print or the photographs, so he eventually folded the paper and put it down upon the table beside his armchair, and silently contemplated the fate of his sons.

Brigit used up the left-over pork roast with some lettuce and tomatoes to make Jason several thick sandwiches for the journey back. She gave her son one last hug before he and Collin walked out to the car. Watching them go, she was reminded once again of how their physically resemblance, even in their slightly forward-leaning gait. They climbed into the old Dodge, and as it pulled away, Jason leaned out the passenger-side window to wave goodbye. Choking back the tears, she waved in return, and though not a particularly religious woman, she whispered a quiet prayer that her son would return safely to her.

At the train station Jason's father put a hand on his shoulder. "You know your brother and I had words that we probably both regret now. At least I do. I understand he still may not want to talk to me, but damn it, if you do manage to get in touch, please tell him to write your mother. I know he can take care of himself, but she worries about him constantly, and it would ease her mind considerably if she just heard from him once in a while."

Jason nodded in agreement. "You know as well as I do that Jack was never the kind to write regularly, even at the best of times, but I'll do whatever I can to get in touch with him and see that he does."

He gave his father's hand a final shake, and then the train's whistle blew, as with a jolt, it clanked into motion. Grabbing his bag, he leapt onto the steps of the last car and waved goodbye. "We'll see you dad!"

Despite the gnawing sense of uneasiness, Collin put on a brave face. With as much bravado as he could muster, he called out to his son as the train pulled away. "Make sure you keep your eyes peeled, and don't ever let one of those German bastards get the jump on you!"

He stood alone on the platform, hands once again in his pockets, and watched as the train receded into the distance. A final time, he waved at the shrinking figure of his son, and even after the train had disappeared, he continued to stare silently.

In June, during one of his lunch breaks, Jack was told to report to his Commanding Officer.

Captain Willard Wright, a lean man in his mid-forties, was standing behind his desk with the stem of a telephone in one hand and its earpiece in the other, as Jack entered his office.

He liked the big instructor for several reasons, not least of which being that Wright was a devoted boxing fan. Corporal McMurchy was also a very good radio instructor - perhaps the most highly-skilled operator in the camp. The young man took his job seriously and was well-liked and respected by his students. They were inspired by his enthusiasm for the subject, and subsequently the Captain had officially noted Jack's leadership qualities. It also didn't hurt that his students regularly achieved the highest scores in the course.

Jack saluted. "Reporting as ordered sir."

Wright raised his two outstretched arms, holding the telephone in front of him sarcastically. "They didn't tell me when I was commissioned that part of my job would be to operate a telephone exchange. However, it seems there is a Flight Sergeant McMurchy on the line who says it is imperative that he speak with you."

Jack cleared his throat sheepishly. "That would probably be my brother, sir."

The Captain handed him both parts of the phone. "Well there you go. We can't keep the Air Force waiting now, can we? I'll head down the hall and attempt to restore my wounded pride by gloriously relieving myself whilst reading some of that inspiring doggerel scribbled over the urinals. Indeed, some much-needed enlightenment, and a few minutes of privacy for you."

"Thank you, sir." Jack replied.

After Wright had left, Jack spoke into the phone. "Jason? How the hell are you doing!"

"I'm doing fine brother, but I don't mind telling you it has been one hell of a job tracking you down. I hope you are not pissed off at me for getting dragged away so soon into our last phone call. What the hell are you doing in the Army?"

"No, no." Jack reassured him. "As a matter of fact, I tried to call you about a month ago, but your landlady said you had already upped stakes and joined the Air Force."

"Yeah, that's right." Jason replied. "In fact, I'm in Halifax right now, and will be shipping out tonight to finish my training in England. It seems they want me to be a fighter pilot, which as you well know is for me a dream come true - but c'mon little brother, what are you doing at the Tank School?"

"A little bit of everything at the beginning. I pretty well know a tank inside out, but right now they have me working as a radio instructor."

"Radios?" Jason was puzzled. "The only time I ever saw you near a radio was when you wanted to listen to some American music from across the lake, on dad's set."

"Well it turns out they think I'm some kind of wizard when it comes to Morse Code, so I've spent the last few months in a nice warm classroom teaching Morse while the other poor bastards have been freezing their arses off outside, marching up and down the parade ground, or inside of some ice-cold tank."

"You never cease to amaze. Is there much chance you will be landing up in England anytime soon? It would be great if we got the chance to tear up London together sometime, eh? You could be the fighter, and I could be the lover. The place wouldn't stand a chance!"

Jack laughed. "I think we could do some damage brother. However, they actually let things slide so badly in the Army over the last twenty years that it is probably going to be quite a while before we can send anything like an effective tank force over there. However, you can bet it will come to pass eventually. So, look out London! Oh, and speaking of fighting, you may be interested to know that I am now the heavyweight champion of the Canadian Army."

"Shit! A few days ago, I was talking to Davey in *Wawa*, and he said a friend of his in the army had seen a guy in a boxing tournament that we were sure must have been you. Congratulations brother, I always knew you had it in you!"

The mention of *Wawa* caused Jack to pause a moment. "How is old Davey doing?"

"He's put on a little beef, and is still working on his electrician's ticket at the mine, but…"

He had noticed Jack's slight change of mood and decided to change the subject. "Listen, I know you didn't leave on the best of terms with dad, but mom is worried sick about you. Why haven't you dropped her a line?"

Again, there was some hesitation. "I don't know. I guess now I just feel stupid about how I handled the whole thing – walking out on them that way, when you can be pretty sure there was going to be hell to pay for them with the local gossip mongers. Dad had plenty of reason to be angry after the way Lafrance threatened him, and I can imagine mom will be worried out of her mind about you now too - going over to fight in Europe."

He paused again. "Listen, I promise to write her soon, and I'll try to put her mind at ease. Maybe even see if dad and I can patch things up."

Jason was relieved. "I'm glad to hear you say that. Everything will surely work itself out if you just give it a try. I know for a fact that they are both hoping to hear from you."

There was an interruption, and after a moment Jason came back on the line. "They're telling me my time is almost up. Let's try to keep in touch, eh? I'll write you once I'm settled in England."

"Okay. I'll look forward to hearing from you."

He hesitated another moment. "You be careful over there. Like they say, watch out for the Hun in the sun."

"Funny, someone told me almost the same thing just the other day." Jason replied, reflecting on how his brother and father were much more alike than either of them would care to admit.

He tried to lighten the mood. "Don't worry about me brother. You just stay alert, and make sure one of those great iron monstrosities doesn't accidentally drive over your big toe, eh?"

Jason then paused as the seriousness of the moment began to reassert itself. "I guess I don't need to tell you, but when you get the chance to have a go at them, watch out for yourself too. We can drink a beer to our luck when it's all over."

Jack heard the click at the other end of the line, and as he was putting the phone back down onto the desk, Captain Wright strode into the room.

"Is everything okay?" He asked.

"Yes sir. My brother ships out for England tonight to train as a fighter pilot."

Wright considered this for a moment. "Excellent! Let's hope he shoots down lots of bloody Germans!"

That evening Jack wrote a letter to his mother, trying as best he could to apologize for his behaviour over the past year, and telling her about his present situation. Underneath his signature, he etched a line in Morse code. (.. .-.. --- ...- . -.-- --- ..-)

Jason spent a week in relative comfort sharing a cabin on one of the newer liners which were capable of a speed that made them virtually immune to potential U-boat attack. Upon arrival, he was posted to an airfield in the midlands where he began the next stage of his training.

The North American 'Harvard' was a big step up. With the snarling power of its R-1340 radial engine, and the higher loading tolerances of its single wing, mastering the monoplane felt like learning to fly all over again. When raw power became the essential ingredient to remaining airborne and maintaining manoeuvrability, a crucially new factor had been added to the equation whose sum total resulted in survival.

Although a far less-forgiving aircraft than the biplanes he had trained on earlier, the Harvard did approximate the performance and handling characteristics of a modern fighter plane. In relatively short order, with the patient tutelage of Flight Lieutenant Maltby, with his duplicate set of controls in the instructor's position behind him, Jason gained confidence in his ability to fly the aircraft. Meanwhile his reflexes adjusted to the plane's greater performance, and the forcefulness of its responses. Eventually, the Harvard too, began to feel like a second skin.

Jason liked the acerbic instructor, whose first bit of advice had been to wear a silk scarf. "It's not an affectation old boy. *Jerry* will come at you from every direction, so your head has to be on a swivel, constantly turning, searching the skies all around so that you see him before he sees you. That wool collar on your uniform will wear your neck rawer than a freshly deflowered virgin if you don't wrap it in a silk scarf first. If it excites you old boy, just think of it as an elegant condom."

Maltby, though only three years older than Jason, had cut his teeth on the Hawker Hind biplane before transitioning to the Hawker Hurricane when the RAF's first monoplane fighter became operational. Subsequently, he had also been one of the first to fly the Spitfire.

An aggressive pilot, Maltby had been posted back to Hurricanes for the Battle of France, and by mid-June 1940, had run up a score of four kills, all on bombers. On two of these occasions his victims had reciprocated by shooting him down in the process. In each case he had survived unscathed. Two days after his final kill he'd been bounced by a *Bf*109, and the injuries that resulted had ended his operational career, relegating him to his current role of flight instructor. Jason enjoyed his sardonic sense of humour, and progressed rapidly under his tutelage.

One day, after Jason had completed the navigational section of his training, Maltby approached him to declare in his matter of fact way. "I think you are about ready to solo now, old boy."

He pointed to a Harvard sitting in front of its hanger. "I've reserved that bus over there for you. Why don't you take it up for a spin?"

Though surprised, Jason agreed immediately. He gathered up his flying kit, and the two of them walked over to the hanger. Now, this first time all alone with the Harvard, he would find out for certain what kind of relationship he had forged with the aircraft.

Maltby's last cryptic bit of advice had been not to work up a set of nerves over something he had done many times before. "Remember, if you get into any kind of funk up there, rely on the procedures you learned in training. In the worst case, you can always take a break by climbing out onto the wing for a little think, and something will probably come to you."

"That would be the ground then, at about three hundred miles per hour." Jason responded.

Maltby was unperturbed. "Well, you do have a parachute you know. I've tried my own a few times, and I must say you get a cracking good view of the countryside."

"Yes, but do the people down below mind several tons of airplane coming through the ceiling and into their parlours during tea time?" Jason asked.

"Not at all old chap. We British are a resilient people – stiff upper lip and all that. Anything for the old war effort you know. Besides the War Department have loads and loads of airplanes. They won't miss one. I really wouldn't worry about it if I were you."

Jason grinned. "Well, don't worry sir. I'll make sure to miss your particular parlour if it comes to that."

"That's awfully good of you, old boy. Mrs. Maltby gets her knickers into a dreadful twist when people make a mess. It gives me all sorts of trouble getting them off of her after that."

He paused a moment, contemplating his previous statement. "If you must visit, just aim for the duck pond. It's no bother, really. Actually, come to think of it, I never much cared for ducks except for potting at them. The only thing better is shooting the Hun, which I expect you will be doing in due course if you don't prang your kite today. I'd love to be joining you shooting at *Jerry*. Its great sport, but unfortunately some of them seem to be able to fire back. Especially that blighter who got the right ear I'm missing and those two fingers on my hand."

He held up his mangled digits for Jason to examine. "Mrs. Maltby was quite fond of the big one which used to be in the middle – says she would have divorced me if the blighter had got my tongue too."

He paused, and then thrust out his chin to reveal his profile. "I used to be quite handsome you know. I still am actually, under certain paler shades of moonlight."

He then shook his head ruefully. "I can't imagine what got into him, that impertinent Hun bastard!"

Jason glanced at the wide purple scar that ran from where Maltby's right ear had once been. It continued near the edge of his right eye, and down his cheek to the corner of his mouth. "Maybe the sauerkraut he had for breakfast was a little off. I know some of the meals I've had to eat since arriving in England have made me want to kill somebody – usually the cook."

"Tut, tut, now. You Canadians really need to raise your culinary standards to a more refined level. Only then will you stop pining for your bacon and eggs, and beefsteaks. You should learn to appreciate the exquisite cuisine of Britain. My personal favourite for breakfast is a succulent combination of burnt wieners and pickled herrings. Surely you see my point."

"Yes," Jason lied. "Now if you would just 'point' me to the latrine, I think one of those herrings is getting ready to swim upstream."

"Oh dear, not a case of nerves, I hope. Don't worry, old boy. It's in a herring's nature to swim, that's all. Now, here is the map we have prepared for you. Just follow your heading over to Hendon – and be sure to let them know it's you, in case they get it into their simple minds to shoot you down. Then, do a nice little U-turn and come back to us. It should be a piece of cake."

With that final comment, he strode purposefully toward the edge of the runway, from where he would signal to Jason when it was time to taxi toward the starting point for takeoff. It took several minutes for the runway to clear, so while waiting there, between turgid imaginings of her knickers, Maltby fixed his mind upon the very limited options regarding what Mrs. Maltby might actually be preparing for his dinner.

Once he was in the air, Jason's solo flight in the Harvard was uneventful and went completely to plan. Over the next few weeks he subsequently mastered night flights and instrument flying, until he was finally handed his transfer papers to an Operational Training Unit.

There, he spent a brief time learning the cockpit instrumentation and flight controls, before he was informed by the O.I.C. that he should be prepared to solo in a Spitfire the very next morning.

Jason got a fitful night's sleep as nervous energy and dreams of flying in combat caused him to repeatedly wake, after which his imagination would race with the prospect of finally flying the airplane he had been dreaming of since arriving in England.

Occasionally, while learning to pilot the Harvard he had caught sight of a Spitfire's elegant shape cruising through the sky. He thrilled to the purr of its Merlin engine as it flew by in flight formation 'Vics' of three, either during training exercises, or on course to intercept the German bombers that had been attacking England since July.

Maltby had often rhapsodized about the power and speed generated by the Rolls-Royce Merlin engine, and the nimble handling characteristics of the aircraft. Now the day he had longed for was approaching, and at last he would take to the air in the sleek fighter.

Jason rose early, wolfed down something scrambled and burnt for breakfast, drank an extra cup of coffee, and then made his way to the dispersal hut to pick up his parachute. After giving it a thorough check, he threw it over his shoulder and made his way toward the revetment where his Spitfire would be parked. As he rounded the reinforced berm where it stood under its camouflage netting, Jason's eyes took in the full length of the aircraft. Its three-bladed variable-pitch propeller and triple exhaust manifolds revealed it to be a Mark II.

A ground crewman helped him to climb into the cockpit, where the parachute strapped to his buttocks fit nicely as a cushion into the scoop-shaped bottom of his armoured seat. The rigger finished strapping him in, while on the opposite side of the cockpit, a fitter who looked to be no more than a teenager, tested the tightness of the connectors for Jason's oxygen mask and radio microphone.

Jason began to verbally recite a checklist of the various instruments and controls in the cockpit. Finishing, he turned to the ground crewmen and joked. "Everything seems to be here – including the kitchen sink!"

The rigger was a sandy-haired man in his late forties. He had seen innumerable young pilots off for their first solo flight, some of whom had not successfully returned. "Mr. Mitchell thought of everything when he designed this little beauty sir. However, I'd not toss the sink just yet. I'm sure that it has been put there in case you experience any unpleasantness. We mustn't be landing one of His Majesty's precious Spitfires with soiled undies. It can leave a terrible stink in the cockpit, and that's very bad for the fitter's moral. If necessary, just give them a little wash before landing, and that should make everyone happier all around, sir."

Jason, who could take a ribbing as well as anyone, stared blankly into the crewman's eyes while appearing puzzled. "I don't quite follow you chief. Do you mean that I'm supposed to be wearing underpants?"

The crewman, struggling to keep a straight face, shook his head sorrowfully. "Well sir, I've always assumed that underwear would interfere with a Canadian's ability to shag polar bears. However, it is highly recommended that you keep your goolies well-insulated and inside your trousers above 10,000 feet, on account of how if you don't, they freeze up and turn all purple and green, which on good authority, the ladies don't like much."

Jason seemed to ponder this advice a moment before replying. "This turning purple and green stuff sounds absolutely dreadful. In fact, I think it would be a very good idea to resign from the air force right now and enlist in the British infantry. I hear they will actually let you run around in a plaid dress or with no clothes on at all if you just promise to kill a few Germans."

He paused. "On second thought however, I guess I should take just one little spin in this airplane before I do that, to justify all the training and such. Don't want to waste the King's shilling, eh? Now, if you could just lend me your underwear…"

The rigger pulled a face. "I'd love to sir, but it appears that I've forgot to wear mine today too. It must have something to do with hanging about with too many bloody Canadians. However, if I could offer a little advice sir, you might try saying something very toffee-nosed and noble on the way out. Tallyho, or something like that, to stir the fitters."

"Very well then Corporal, ballyhoo it shall be! Now get the fuck off of my airplane so I can get this over with. Considering all your good advice, I'm absolutely sure that I'll now cut a very dashing figure as I carve a swath through the clouds."

"I don't doubt it for a moment, sir."

Then grinning, the rigger closed the small access door on the left side of the cockpit, and leapt down from the wing. He next jogged off for a safe distance from which to observe.

After checking to make sure his microphone was firmly plugged into the radio, and confirming that there was oxygen flowing to his mask, Jason flicked the petrol flow switch on the instrument panel. He then pumped the manual primer a few times to spray fuel into the cylinders of the Merlin engine. Then, switching on the ignition, he checked to make sure his brakes were locked before signalling the other ground crewmen to stand clear of the propeller. Finally, he reached forward to push the starter button on the instrument panel.

Suddenly, there was a loud explosion and bright flash, followed by a large puff of black smoke exiting the exhaust stacks as the Coffman cartridge detonated and turned the engine over. The Merlin coughed once, and then like a startled beast, it roared into life.

Jason checked his radio and received the reassuring confirmation that they were hearing him in the tower. He throttled back and signalled the ground crew, then saw them use attached ropes to pull the chocks away from the main wheels of his undercarriage.

Because the Spitfire sat on a small tail wheel, its long engine cowling and propeller rose at a sharp angle in front of the cockpit, blocking a pilot's forward vision when on the ground. Jason released the brake lever on his control column, advanced the throttle a bit, and began to taxi the aircraft, utilizing the brakes on his rudder pedals to induce a fishtailing motion. Combined with occasionally sticking his head out of one side or the other of the still-open canopy, it allowed him to acquire some forward vision as he advanced toward the take-off area near the end of the runway.

Nosing the aircraft into the wind, Jason pulled the brake lever and did his final check, beginning with the magnetos, to confirm the ignition system was performing its function properly.

The Merlin tended to overheat quite easily if left running too long on the ground without the necessary airflow through its radiators, and Jason noted that the glycol temperature was starting to edge over the one hundred degrees mark, which was near the top of its optimum operating level. He adjusted the fuel mixture to full rich and set the propeller pitch at fine. The other gauges indicated that he had adequate fuel, the electrical system was functioning, and that the oil pressure was normal. He then confirmed that he had set his trim tabs for take-off, and that the flaps were set to full up.

Jason slowly advanced the throttle and felt the increasing rush of power from the Merlin engine. Requesting permission to take off, he received it immediately from the tower, and then released the brake lever on the control column. The Spitfire surged forward and began to accelerate faster than he had ever before experienced.

He maintained constant pressure on the rudder pedal to counter the Merlin's enormous torque, which was making the aircraft want to veer left. Part way down the runway Jason felt the tail lift, and then he eased the throttle all the way forward. Feeling the rush of increased acceleration, he pulled back on the column, and suddenly, after a twelve-hundred-foot sprint, the Spitfire leapt smoothly into the air.

As he gained height, Jason squeezed the brake lever on his control column and turned the undercarriage lever to the "up" setting. Within seconds the red light on his instrument panel indicated that his landing gear was now retracted.

He smiled to himself under the oxygen mask and reached up to slide his canopy hood shut. The radiators had been in the fully open position for takeoff, but now with the increased speed and air flow, he was able to partially close them to improve the aircraft's aerodynamics. As his altitude increased, he again went through the process of readjusting his fuel mixture, throttle, and trim tabs to improve handling and performance.

Glancing at his watch, Jason was surprised to learn he had been in the air barely more than a minute. He reached for his map to confirm he was on the right compass heading, and then began climbing to altitude.

The Spitfire was a revelation once he was airborne. The in-line Merlin was much more powerful than the Harvard's radial engine, and the aircraft had been designed from the beginning to acquire every possible bit of performance from the V-12. Its rate of climb, roll, and the tightness of its turning radius were breathtaking.

As he did his circuit, Jason took the opportunity to practice the manoeuvres he had already mastered on the Harvard. He climbed above the clouds, diving and rolling the airplane through various turns and quick changes of direction, while marvelling at how the Spitfire responded to its controls with so much power and agility.

Reluctantly, he turned the airplane back toward the aerodrome and prepared for his landing approach. Lowering his flaps, he brought the Spitfire around into the wind at about 140 miles per hour as he lined up the end of the strip. Then, keeping his nose up, he bled off speed in an attempt to get down to the recommended seventy-five miles per hour for final touch down.

He came in slightly above speed, which resulted in a single bounce before the aircraft's wheels began to run smoothly along the surface of the grass runway. Conscious of not wanting to cause the aircraft to nose over, Jason applied the brakes lightly to reduce the Spitfire's speed. Eventually, he came to a halt at the end of the landing field, and then used the same fishtailing technique to finally steer the aircraft back to its revetment. There, the maintenance crew awaited his arrival with mixed expressions of joy and relief.

After opening the small door on the left side of the cockpit and assisting Jason out onto the wing, the crew chief made an exaggerated inspection of the interior. Twitching his nostrils until obviously satisfied, he grinned. "Everything is very sweet and tidy indeed sir. I do believe we can safely remove Mr. Mitchell's basinet for the duration."

Jason had not stopped smiling since he climbed out of the aircraft. Jumping down from the wing, he turned to look up at the rigger, and then over to the other two fitters.

Exultantly he exclaimed. "Ballyhoo boys! Ballyhoo!"

Still smiling, Jason threw his parachute over his shoulder, and with a spring in his step, he strode off in the direction of the officer's hut.

The crew chief chuckled, as the bewildered fitters exchanged puzzled looks and scratched their heads.

With every training flight, Jason fell more deeply in love with the aircraft. By the time his group Captain had given him the green light to go operational for combat, the Spitfire felt as if it had become an extension of his own body whenever he took the controls.

The mid-August sun was shining unusually hot in the early morning sky, and much of the dew had already evaporated from the short-cropped grassy tarmac of the airfield as Jason climbed into the new Mk II Spitfire for his first operational sortie.

He had been briefed earlier in the morning after a quick breakfast. Intercepting the Germans relied upon a systematic process, now established, whereby after detecting the first wave of bombers, the front-line radar stations would relay the pertinent information to Fighter Command Headquarters, who would plot the enemy's track, and convey this information to Group Headquarters who alerted their individual airfields. Accordingly, Jason's flight of fifteen fighters would fly to "Angels" (altitude) 25,000 feet today to fly top-cover for the Hurricanes that would be attacking incoming bombers at 18,000 feet.

Similarly, *Bf*109s often flew top-cover for the German bombers, and could be expected to dive down upon the allied defenders once they engaged. It was the job of the Spitfires to intercept the *Bf*109s before they could disturb the Hurricanes as they went about their grim task of shooting down as many of the bombers as possible before they reached their targets.

He and Flight Sergeant Carson, a Yorkshire native with five operational sorties under his belt, would be the wingmen for

Lieutenant James Edwards, who was a veteran of the Battle of France, and an ace with six kills to his record.

While in the dispersal hut, Edwards had warned him. "Try to keep to the right and slightly above my tail. Stay generally abreast of Carson, and for God's sake never stop scanning the skies above and behind you for enemy aircraft."

Edwards grumbled incessantly about the incompetence of the old-guard senior officers who insisted they fly in the more vulnerable and less efficient three aircraft "V", or "Vic" formations. They obdurately refused to heed recommendations that they switch to the finger-four formations that he had seen the Germans use so effectively and with devastating effect against them in France.

Now, dashing to their Spitfires, he shouted one last bit of advice. "Just remember McMurchy, those four plane German formations can do a ninety degree turn faster than you can blink. So, if we see a group either coming or going on a parallel track to us, I'll be rolling into it as fast as possible before they can try the same thing on us. They will always start out with a one-man advantage, so it is vital that we get at least one of them on the first pass. If you do get bounced, remember that there are likely going to be at least two of them on your tail, so try to evade by getting them to follow you into a turn. The Spit can go tighter than a 109, so that should shake 'em."

The coastal radar arrays had detected several waves of bombers approaching from the southeast, and within minutes their course had been plotted and the fighters scrambled.

From 25,000 feet Jason saw them first appear as an indistinct dark line in the distance to his south. This soon transformed itself into waves of twin-engine *Dornier* 17s distinguished by their slim pencil-like fuselages, and the more bulbous, broad-winged *Heinkel* 111s. Filled with high-explosive bombs, they sped doggedly on toward their targets, boldly emblazoned with the *Luftwaffe*'s menacing black cross *Balkenkreuz* insignia.

Edwards' voice crackled over the radio set. "Resist the urge to dive down on them boys. I can see two squadrons of Hurricanes coming from the north. Keep your eyes peeled for 109s. They should be arriving at the party any time now."

The flight leader had barely stopped speaking when Jason saw a group of tiny dots appear about a mile off to his right. They suddenly grew into the yellow-nosed, mottled grey shapes of eight *Bf*109Es, rolling left to dive on the Hurricanes who were now busily engaging the bombers below them.

"109s at three o'clock low and diving!" He shouted into his microphone.

Edwards had seen them at almost the same instant and responded tersely. "Follow me boys."

The three aircraft rolled slightly to their right before nosing down to attack their diving German prey as Edwards' voice came once again through Jason's headphones. "Concentrate on those two at the rear. We'll hit them from the side and roll right to come back around onto their tails."

Jason's fingers gripped the ring on top of his control column tightly, and his thumb hovered over the firing button. One of the *Bf*109s loomed in his sights, but just as he was about to fire, German tracer flew past his canopy, and in his peripheral vision a few hundred feet to his left he saw Carson's aircraft explode in a massive fireball. He felt the thud of two 20mm cannon hits in his rear fuselage, and immediately rolled the Spitfire into a turning dive to the right. Edwards, whose first burst had blown the tail off of the *Bf*109 he'd lined up, did an equally quick snap-roll to the left, and threw his aircraft into a diving turn, while the *schwarm* that they had been bounced by, overflew them.

He and Edwards both came out of their diving turns with about 2,000 feet less altitude. Jason formed up on the right behind his leader's tail as with all speed they resumed their original line of descent toward the melee below.

There were at least a dozen smoke trails from the bombers that had been shot down, and he could see three others spiralling down in flames. Suddenly, half a mile ahead of them he saw another *schwarm* diving from the left onto the Hurricanes below. Edwards' high-pitched adrenalin-laced voice was in the earphones again. "Full power! We'll take the two nearest, and then try for the other two as we cross over them on the same pass!"

Approaching from the side at more than four hundred miles per hour, they lined both aircraft up in deflection shots, firing slightly above and ahead of the *Bf*109's, so that they flew into the streams of bullets. Jason saw Edwards' bullets tear into the German's engine, then the canopy flew open as the pilot leapt free of the shattered aircraft. Jason's own target passed directly into a full burst and immediately exploded as some of the bullets found the German's fuel tanks.

Instantly the second *rotte* took evasive action as Jason's next intended target, the *schwarm* leader in the index finger position, snap-rolled to the right into a dive away and under him - a vector that was impossible to follow at this speed. Meanwhile, the wingman in the forefinger position, who had been furthest away and behind, used the extra second of time this provided him to roll into a right turn toward Edwards and get off a short burst. One lucky round ripped through the spinner and into the hub, tearing the Spitfire's propeller off the front of the Merlin, and putting the aircraft into a spin. As the German dove away, Jason saw Edwards' hood slide back before the flight leader launched himself out of the cockpit. Seconds later his parachute popped open, and he began a slow drifting decent to the verdant fields of Kent, thousands of feet below.

Assured that Edwards was okay, Jason turned his attention to engaging more German aircraft, but to his dismay the sky appeared to be empty. He detected activity far to the west, and was about to turn the Spitfire in pursuit, when he was shocked to see that his fuel gauge was registering nearly empty. There was also a small ragged hole in the left side of his cowling, forward of the windscreen, through which the precious substance was streaming. Worse still, the cockpit was rapidly filling with the noxious odour of high-octane aviation fuel.

Jason cursed out loud. "So much for self-sealing gas tanks!"

In addition to the danger of an explosion, Jason was also aware of the possibility that he could be overcome by fumes, so he pulled back his canopy, tightened his mask, and left the oxygen flowing below the altitude where it was normally unnecessary. However, he was conscious of the fact that the oxygen would also make any fire in the cockpit burn much more fiercely.

As he approached the airfield he glanced once again at the gauge. It was registering empty.

He radioed the tower to advise them of his predicament, and that he would be attempting to land immediately, and they informed him they would have a fire truck standing by.

Aware that a belly-landing would result in enough heat and friction to set off a huge explosion in the aircraft, Jason mentally crossed his fingers and hoped that whatever the cause of the damage to his fuel system, it had left his landing gear unscathed.

He bled off speed, held his breath, and then raised his flaps as the wheels touched down and began to roll across the grassy strip. Just before he came to a halt at the far end of the runway the Merlin suddenly coughed and stopped cold, freezing the propeller motionless in front of him. Jason immediately released the harness with his right hand, swung the left-side cockpit door open with the other, and literally leapt out onto the wing. From there he jumped to the ground and quickly moved away from the aircraft. It was only then that he noticed the two gaping holes torn through the fuselage just aft of the Spitfire's cockpit.

Jason had barely finished reporting Carson's death and the approximate location where Edwards had bailed out, when he was ordered to scramble with a new Vic. One of its wingmen had been wounded in the leg by a bullet passing through the cockpit door and grazing the pilot's thigh before exiting through the other side. After the wounded pilot was taken to hospital, the fitters and riggers had repaired the punctured metal, rearmed the guns with fresh belts of .303 cal. ammunition, and topped up its tank with fuel.

His new flight leader, Lieutenant Stephen Morris, an English pilot with two kills to his credit, instructed him to take the left-side wingman's position. As they climbed to 25,000 feet, he informed Jason and the other wingman, Flight Sergeant Raymond Allum, that they would be intercepting a formation of bombers on their return leg from London. Because the *Bf*109s had very little loiter time over target due to their limited fuel capacity, it was unlikely that they would be disrupted by fighter cover during this attack on the Germans. However, it was probable that there would be significant numbers of the twin-engine *Bf*110 *Zerstorers* embedded in the bomber stream, which could pose a serious danger to unwary Spitfire or Hurricane pilots.

Flt. Sgt. Allum was the first to spot the leading wave of *He*111 bombers travelling in a south-easterly direction from their right, at about 20,000 feet.

Lieutenant Morris spoke calmly into his microphone as he pushed his aircraft over into a dive. "Follow me down boys."

They dove at full throttle, and even through his protective earphones Jason was nearly deafened by the roar of the Merlin as they passed through four hundred miles per hour.

Morris was leading them to a group of three *He*111s which had only just now seen them, and flashes of light began to twinkle in the rearward open ends of the cupolas located behind the bombers' cockpits. Bright streaks of German tracer passed harmlessly above his canopy, as he saw Morris's wing-mounted .303 cal. machine guns erupt...stitching a line of holes along the length of the nearest *Heinkel*'s fuselage. It had begun to roll over as they flashed by it, but before they could begin their own roll right to begin their loop around, a *Bf*110 slid in behind Morris's tail and began to fire its forward mounted 20mm cannons. Several rounds penetrated the Flight leader's engine, and Jason saw the Malcolm hood slide back before the Spitfire rolled over and Morris dropped out.

Without waiting to see if the parachute had deployed, Jason slid in behind the *Bf*110 and fired a burst that missed, except for two rounds that caught the right rudder as the Messerschmitt rolled violently left into a dive. Jason instantly performed the same manoeuvre and was once again on the German's tail. The aircraft rolled violently again in the opposite direction as it sought to shake him off. The nimble Spitfire was easily able to follow that attempt to evade him, and once again he found himself closing on the *Bf*110 as he followed it through the diving turn.

Jason could see the rear gunner attempting to overcome suddenly shifting gravitational forces to aim the gun at him, but the erratic nature of the *Bf*110's desperate manoeuvrings was causing the German's shooting to go hopelessly wide of the mark.

For a split-second he found himself directly behind the German, and he thumbed the firing button to unleash a stream of bullets that tore up the length of the Messerschmitt. The cockpit shattered, and suddenly the entire aircraft disintegrated in a massive fiery explosion, forcing him to bank left to avoid it.

As his breathing began to slow, he chirped into his microphone. "Allum, are you anywhere nearby?"

To his surprise there was an immediate response. "I'm behind you to your right. Don't ask me how, but I managed to follow you through all of that. Nice kill on that one-ten. I can definitely confirm it for you."

"Thanks Ray. Did you see whether Morris's chute opened?"

"Yes, I saw it deploy. He didn't seem to be wounded, which is nothing short of a miracle when you consider all the lead that Messerschmitt poured into his kite."

"Yeah, that damned thing seemed to come out of nowhere."

Jason was scanning the skies to the southeast. "I don't see any of those bombers now. We'd best radio in Morris's general location, and head back to base."

While Jason transmitted Morris's position, a *schwarm* of yellow-nosed *Bf*109Es was midway across the English Channel on the return leg of their earlier escort mission to London. Even with tanks fully loaded they had still carried barely enough fuel to linger over the city for a minute before they were forced to reverse course for home. This left the *He*111s and *Bf*110s to fend for themselves. As they neared the French coast, Peter gazed down at the landscape below while maintaining his position behind and to the left of *Hauptmann* Roland Schwartz.

The previous month had not added much to the *Hauptmann*'s score of victories. The enemy pilots over Britain were often skilled, and a generally tenacious lot, while the Spitfires were every bit a match for the *Bf*109s. Even the older Hurricane in the hands of an experienced pilot could be lethal. Several times Peter had come to Schwartz's rescue, as the overmatched flight leader was about to be shot down by an RAF pilot he could not shake from his tail. This had caused Peter's personal score to rise to three, whereas Schwartz had only managed to dispatch one already damaged Hurricane over the same period.

Today they had flown top-cover for the bombing mission, but Roland had failed to spot any opportunities to descend on the attacking RAF fighters. Their only engagement had been with a flight of Hurricanes that had attacked them head-on from below on the way out from their target. Neither side had got any hits as they flew past each other at a combined speed of seven hundred miles per hour, and by the time they had come around to engage them, the attackers had disappeared somewhere into the endless expanse of a cloud-filled sky.

Schwartz had grown even more difficult than usual to be around during this past month, and as they made their final approach to the grassy airstrip, Peter was trying to think of some excuse to avoid dinner in the mess this evening.

They touched down simultaneously, as smoothly and disciplined as usual, but this time the *Hauptmann*'s undercarriage suddenly collapsed. The aircraft slid along on its belly until one of the spinning prop blades caught in the tarmac and spun the *Bf109* around sideways. Peter was unable to avoid the fighter as it slewed into his path, and his right wingtip caught Schwartz's *Bf109* flush on the cowling.

Immediately, his own aircraft began to cartwheel across the runway, and Peter saw the world spin crazily through his windshield. There was a final wrench of tearing metal, as his now wingless aircraft, its fuselage grotesquely twisted and cockpit shattered, came to rest on its back - a mangled, smouldering wreck.

For three harrowing weeks Jason flew an average of two or three sorties per day. After only a week of operational duty, so many flight leaders were lost in the conflict, they had promoted him to that position. By the end of August, he had become a double ace.

Both he and Edwards, along with two Australian Flight Lieutenants, had decided to buck official protocol by forming their four "Vics" into three "finger-four" formations whenever they got airborne. The new formations immediately became more effective on the attack. They were now six pairs of leaders with one wingman each, as opposed to only four flight leaders with four pairs of wingmen, thus improving their offensive potential by fifty percent.

By the end of September, Jason could feel the effects of exhaustion settling over his weary frame. However, the daylight raids had tapered off as the Germans resorted to doing most of their bombing of London by night. Then, as the *Blitz* wore on and fighter interception by Spitfires at night proved to be less effective than in daylight, this increasingly became the duty of more specialized night-fighter groups equipped with Hurricanes.

The Squadron Commander now felt confident that he had adequate daytime assets, with enough flexibility to order Jason and a few of his fellow long-timers to step down for a week, so they could get some rest.

By the time he returned, rested and refreshed, to active duty, it had been decided that daylight operations would now focus on patrols over the English Channel to provide protection for shipping against German aerial attack. They were also to engage the enemy on the other side of the channel in an activity the Squadron Commander curiously labelled "rhubarbs".

As he lay in his hospital bed Peter reflected on how it was a lucky thing that both he and Schwartz's fuel tanks had been virtually empty when they crash-landed two weeks previously. Roland had suffered only a superficial cut that left the thin red line of a scar, beginning above his right eyebrow and running down to the left side of his nose. However, Peter had suffered a compound fracture of his right shin, which was fortunately not dislocated. Nonetheless, he would be off his feet for at least six weeks, while Schwartz had just yesterday been recalled to Berlin to discuss recent developments on some new project at the *Flugzeugwerke*.

Over the next month, he periodically received reports from his squadron mates that JG26 was continuing to enjoy a two to one kill ratio against the British fighters, which were now flying across the channel and attempting to engage them. Some of this was attributable of course to the fact that the R.A.F. fighters were flying at the limits of their range, and much like the *Luftwaffe* fighters a year before over England, they were often bounced on their return leg while low on fuel.

He took the opportunity to spend some of his spare time writing several letters to his parents and sister. At first they had been very concerned when they were notified of his accident, but he reassured them that all was well and he had got off lightly, all things considered. This most recent week had involved some physical therapy, which largely amounted to abandoning his crutch and cane to walk around freely upon his now nearly healed leg.

Within weeks, he returned to active duty, which largely consisted of attempts to intercept British fighter incursions into France that often took the form of ground attacks, or efforts to ambush German aircraft at altitude. Contact was random and usually brief because the enemy aircraft were operating at the limits of their range, so were generally restricting themselves to hit and run tactics. The opposing fighter arms played these cat and mouse games throughout the winter and early spring, but things suddenly changed in late April.

The mail delivery came in the morning, and today there were two letters addressed to Peter. The first, from his sister, he put aside for a moment, to read the telegram from Schwartz, who had once again been seconded for most of this month to a liaison function in Berlin.

Inside there were transfer orders.

Something big must be in the works, he mused. A large portion of JG26 *Gruppe* in Abbeville were being moved east to a new station inside of Germany, but very near the eastern border.

Rhubarbs, as Jason discovered, involved either low level strafing on German targets of opportunity, or seeking to engage at higher altitudes with German transport and fighter aircraft.

He disliked the low level attacks because the lack of recovery room limited the number of useful evasive manoeuvres possible in the nimble Spitfire. Critically, it also reduced the possibilities of a successful bail-out by parachute if necessary. As well, it made the aircraft vulnerable to ground fire, which normally had shorter range than the less-concentrated shelling from anti-aircraft guns he had to contend with at higher altitudes. This additional firepower greatly increased his chances of being shot down.

At higher altitudes he found himself engaging with fighters from two different German fighter groups. JG26 were referred to as "the yellow nosed bastards", or "the Abbeville boys". This was because of the yellow colour painted under their engine cowlings, and on the spinners and the rudders. Also, their main airbase was located in Abbeville, in addition to the smaller fields they had scattered through north-eastern France. The aircraft of this *gruppe* were flown by some of Germany's highest scoring aces, and they were extremely dangerous opponents – even when bounced – in any aerial engagement.

The other group, which he encountered less frequently, was JG2 *"Richtoffen Gruppe"*. They were identifiable by the red colouring of their engine under-cowlings and spinners. Since this *gruppe* was tasked to defend the western coastal region of occupied France, Jason came into contact with them only occasionally. This occurred when he was assigned to missions venturing west at the extreme range of his fuel supply, where engagements were necessarily of shorter duration.

Having crossed the English Channel, Jason glimpsed the coast of France disappearing behind him as he flew south at 15,000 feet. Inland, the May foliage had nearly completed its transformation to summer green from the buds and blossoms of spring.

In the previous nine months, his score of downed aircraft had risen by six. These included a single *He*111, a *Bf*110, and four *Bf*109s.

For the past six months, Jason had been flying the upgraded Mk Vb model with its more powerful Merlin 45 engine, which in addition to greater speed, also generated a faster climbing rate. Both of these factors had played a role in his last three victories against the *Bf*109s. In particular, his last kill had been one of the *Bf*109F *Freidrich* variants, which, with its rounded wingtips, more aerodynamic airscrew spinner, and more powerful engine, had stretched the Mk V to its limits, and would have easily outmatched the Mk II he had been flying last year.

They had been flying over the countryside for less than two minutes when the voice of his wingman, Flt. Sgt. Pearson came screaming over the radio. "*Schwarm* attacking from six o'clock high!"

With split-second precision, their four-plane formation immediately divided into pairs which dove in opposite directions into the patchy cloud bank that was drifting about 3,000 feet below them. Jason levelled off and called his wingman on the radio. There was no response. Repeated attempts to contact him brought only an ominous silence. Cautiously, he nosed the Spitfire down and out of the cloud cover, but when he emerged into visible airspace there was no sign of the other three aircraft, or the enemy.

Scanning the skies in every direction, he banked right, and began flying east-by-northeast to begin his return flight across the channel. As he crossed the edge of the cloudbank into clearer air, he saw the French coast a few miles ahead of him. He then put the Spitfire into a climb toward another patch of cloud nearer his original altitude of 15,000 feet.

Suddenly, he saw the winking of tracer fire in his rear-view mirror, and instantly realized that he had been bounced. Cursing, he rolled left into a dive, with the enemy aircraft close on his tail. As he reached the crucial speed where he could feel 'G' forces building up to their maximum tolerable level, he banked left slightly, pulled the control column into his belly to go into a turn, and then levelled off. The German was surprised by the suddenness of the move and overshot him. Using the kinetic energy and speed he had built up, Jason put the Spitfire into a climb to gain more altitude. He glanced into the rear-view mirror, expecting as usual to see the Messerschmitt levelling off to turn away, but to his horror he saw the German was closing on him, and that it was not a *Bf*109!

The aircraft on his tail was a new design that he had never seen before. Although its fuselage was thicker than the Messerschmitt, its contours were clean and streamlined. The cockpit was shaped differently, but the most distinguishing feature of the new fighter was its large air-cooled radial engine, which was pulling the German into the climb faster than he would have expected from a *Bf*109F.

In seconds the German would be in a position to destroy him, so out of desperation he rolled right and pulled his pursuer into a tight turn. Then, with his engine already at full boost, he went into a spiralling upward climb. The move fooled the enemy pilot for a fraction of a second, allowing Jason to put more distance between them. However, the German quickly recovered, and once more the enemy pilot was matching his spiralling climb, while slowly closing the distance between them. The macabre aerial ballet continued through 18,000 feet, where Jason noticed that the enemy aircraft was no longer gaining on him.

At that point Jason rolled out of the climb to level off, and pulled the enemy into a tightening turn. It soon became apparent to the other pilot that Jason in his Spitfire could go tighter and would eventually be on his tail, so the German suddenly rolled over and began to dive away. Anticipating this, Jason immediately snap-rolled the Spitfire into a dive, and within seconds had closed upon the other plane. Thumbing the firing button on his control column, he sent a stream of 20mm and .303 calibre shells into the tail and rear fuselage of the aircraft. He was rewarded by the sight of the canopy sliding back and the German pilot exiting the aircraft. However, before he could deploy his parachute, the slipstream slammed the pilot into the fighter's horizontal stabilizer, with back-breaking force. Jason saw him fall limply off to the left, before plunging earthward.

When he landed, Jason was informed that his wingman Flt. Sgt. Pearson was missing in action, as was Flt. Lt. Cartier, the other flight leader in his formation. The remaining wingman, Flt. Sgt. Gallagher had just been picked up by a Walrus sea-rescue floatplane in the channel. On board the rescue plane, the recovered pilot had radioed in that before parachuting into the frigid waters, he had been shot down by a new type of German aircraft. Jason confirmed that he had also been engaged by a similar aircraft, which below 18,000 feet, exceeded the Mk V's performance in all areas except turns, but above which, its fighting qualities tapered off dramatically.

After examining his gun camera footage, the boffins informed him that the aircraft he had shot down was the new *Focke-Wulf* 190A. They went on to explain that the fighter was a Kurt Tank design, with exceptional performance, and long rumoured to be in the works. Now, unfortunately, the 'Butcher Bird' as it would come to be called, was a deadly reality in the skies over Europe.

Jack eagerly followed the war news on regular CBC Radio broadcasts and in the newspapers. Every day he waited nervously during mail call for any letter that might come from either his mother or Jason, as the Battle of Britain wound down in intensity and shifted to the *Luftwaffe's* autumn night-bombing campaign. All the while, he maintained a fervent hope that one of the dreaded telegrams would not arrive with bad news about his brother.

Over time, as Jason's score began to rise, and any chance of an invasion of Britain began to wane, he was able to push some of the anxiety for his brother further into the back of his mind, where it lurked silently. It none the less made its presence known on those occasions when he realized a longer than normal period of time had elapsed since the last letter from Jason, describing his life in England, or containing uncensored accounts of action in the sky.

In November, he was promoted to Sergeant, and then made head-instructor of the camp's radio school. He settled into a routine over the next eight months, but was bitterly disappointed when he was ordered to stay behind as the Ontario Tank Regiment shipped out to England in July. However, he was soon relieved to learn that the 5th Canadian Armoured Division was now being formed, and that he had been assigned to one of the old permanent regiments, the 8th New Brunswick Hussars.

On the morning of October 9th, 1941, Jack stood on the aft deck of the liner Monarch of Bermuda, as the port of Halifax disappeared into the mist. Shivering in the cold dampness, he pulled the neck of his heavy wool greatcoat more tightly about his neck, and with a rising sense of elation he told himself that finally they were *en route* to England.

After their arrival in Liverpool it seemed as if the British couldn't decide where to put them. Their initial camp was established at Osbourne St. George near the head of the Bristol Channel, and it was here that they waited for their first tanks to arrive.

Tank crews spend less time on their feet than the infantry, so theoretically they wouldn't necessarily spend as much time marching on their proverbial stomachs. However, after a settling-in period of a few weeks, there were many complaints about the apparent transmogrification of what they were being fed.

Shiploads of nutritious and relatively fresh food arrived by convoy from all corners of the British Empire, but miraculously, the fruit, vegetables, and meat that most of the troops had eaten as standard fare in Canada seemed to somewhat magically appear most often on the plates in the Officer's Mess, and in particular, also in the British Officer's Mess. While in contrast, most Canadian troops sat down to an inferior diet regularly composed of such delicacies as fried wieners, or tinned meat, and mysterious things like pickled herring, preserved in vinegar. Fresh fruit and vegetables were rare, while to the soldiers' chagrin, macaroni and beans, in addition to native dishes with strange, almost incomprehensible names like 'bubble and squeak' or 'bangers and mash', abounded.

In November, an American M2A4 light tank arrived, soon followed by two M3 Stuarts. These tanks were small, lightly armoured, and possessed a relatively high speed. However, compared to pictures Jack had seen of the German *Panzer* Mark III and IV tanks being used to invade Russia, and the large tanks the Soviets were fighting back with, he judged they would not be very effective in combat.

In December however, their equipment finally began to improve when two American 'General Lee' tanks arrived, and at last Jack felt they were being equipped with vehicles possessing the armament and power to give them a fighting chance.

The General Lee was inelegant in its design, with a high profile topped by a small turret armed with a relatively light-calibre 37mm gun. However, it was a big tank weighing over thirty tons, and its air-cooled radial – actually an aircraft engine - was powerful enough to propel it at reasonably good speed. It possessed an excellent single-volute tracked suspension and was mechanically very reliable, but perhaps its most impressive feature was the powerful 75mm main gun, sponson-mounted on the front right side of the tank. This had less lateral range of movement than a turret, but it nonetheless gave the Lee enough punch to take on anything the Germans were currently fielding.

In January they were moved to the Headley-Lindford area in Hampshire, and a few short months later in April 1942, to their permanent training facility in Aldershot. Very shortly after this move the first Ram tanks began to arrive.

In most respects, the Ram was an excellent tank. It was Canadian-designed and built, but it borrowed the excellent engine, suspension, and drive train of the American M3 General Lee. However, the Canadians had completely redesigned the hull, eliminating the main gun and its side-mounted sponson. As well, they had replaced the tiny turret with a larger turret mounting a 2-pounder main gun. The final result was a very reliable vehicle with a much lower profile than the General Lee, thus making it a more difficult target to see or hit. At their tank testing range in Maryland, the Americans had been so impressed by the Ram that they had virtually copied it to produce the M4 Sherman. Except for a slight modification at the front of the hull, and a larger turret ring capable of accommodating a redesigned turret housing the more powerful 75mm main gun, the two tanks were virtually identical.

Over the next several months, the men were divided into crews and trained to perform as many of the tank's functions as they could master. They were also versed in tactics and manoeuvres, and how to coordinate their actions through the effective use of radios. Most of the men were assigned to specialized functions such as driving, radio/gun loader, and gunner. Some of the men like Jack, who displayed an aptitude to master all the operational functions as well as possessing a head for tactics, were made crew commanders. By summer he was in charge of his own tank.

As sufficient numbers of tanks arrived, the regiment was divided into four squadrons, each identified by one of the first four letters of the alphabet. Easily recognizable symbols were painted in yellow on the sides of each tank's turret to identify which squadron it belonged to. 'A' Squadron used a triangle, 'B' Squadron a square, 'C' Squadron a circle, and 'D' Squadron used an equilateral four-sided diamond. Later, individual tanks would acquire names painted on the sides of their hulls, each beginning with the designated letter of their squadron. Jack belonged to 'B' Squadron and he personally painted the name of his tank in white block letters. *BEOWULF.*

It might be summer, Jack thought, but only in the British sense. The Gulf Stream from Mexico mitigated the temperatures in winter, making them far milder than the arctic cold most of the Canadian men had grown up with. However, some troopers from the west coast of British Columbia, where winter temperatures rarely fell below freezing, joked that they felt right at home.

To most of the men, including Jack, the incessant rain and gloomy clouds of summer did not seem like much of an improvement over the winter months. During manoeuvres, the tanks often churned the fields into seas of muck, which frequently clogged the bogey wheels and stuck to his boots like glue.

After one such manoeuvre, Jack climbed back into the turret of the recently hosed off Ram tank and took his seat under the commander's hatch. His vehicle was one of the upgraded models with a larger 6-pounder, or 57mm main gun, but he shook his head ruefully as he disapprovingly cast his gaze around the circumference of the sixty-inch turret ring. Why the Canadian Tank Development Board had heeded the British advice to build a cruiser tank was beyond him. The evidence already existed from the Russian front that both sides were employing heavier tanks equipped with 75mm and 76mm guns to spearhead tank-on-tank clashes that no cruiser tank design could possibly hope to survive.

Too bad, he thought, that they hadn't listened to General Wolverton's calls for a tank capable of accommodating a gun of at least 75mm. If they had, the Ram would have been one of the best tanks currently available. As it was however, it could serve as an excellent training machine, but would be hopelessly outclassed if ever put into combat against the latest German designs.

He concluded that the British, who had conceived the original tank back in 1915, had somehow lost their perspective when it came to designing vehicles suitable for modern fighting doctrines like those employed by the Germans, with their extremely successful '*Blitzkreig*' or 'Lightening War' tactics.

Panzer General Heinz Guderian, the most successful exponent of the *Blitzkreig*, had learned these tactics by studying the work of Colonel J.F.C. Fuller of the British Tank Corps, who had fleshed out the general principles toward the end of The Great War in his "Plan 1919". Ultimately, Fuller's revolutionary ideas had been rejected by the British Army, so that by 1933 he had retired in frustration to become a writer and academic.

Recently there had been rumours flying, which were now being substantiated, about how poorly the under-gunned Churchill heavy infantry tank had performed at Dieppe, and as news continued to trickle out, the scale of the fiasco was becoming more apparent.

Slow and cumbersome, the Churchill's design very much resembled the old trench crossers of the First World War. It had proved entirely unsuitable for a seaborne invasion of the French coast, where most of them became bogged down on the shale beaches, and then were easily picked off by German anti-tank guns.

It was apparent to him that the key elements in any future tank engagements would include good mobility, large gun calibre, and effective armour. As they honed their skills on the fields of Aldershot, Jack developed a greater appreciation for the speed and reliability of the Ram during manoeuvres over most types of terrain. It was an excellent tank in many respects, but he rued its lack of a decent main gun.

Trap Line

David hiked about a mile up the railroad tracks leading from *Michipicoten* Harbour toward the sinter plant in *Wawa*. As the sun rose, it revealed a clear and windless day. The surrounding forest had originally been cleared for about one hundred feet on both sides of the rail bed, and in the early morning light the shadows of the spruce trees spread westward across the frozen snow-covered open ground, almost to the tracks. In the twenty minutes that he had been walking, the dark elongated tree-shapes had already receded several feet as the sun rose higher above the eastern horizon. In the crisp morning air, his breath rose like steam toward the pale blue sky above him. In the distance and out of sight, the cawing of a crow echoed through the trees, and was answered by the staccato chattering of a squirrel.

On his back, he had hung a pair of snowshoes. The single strap of a game bag also hung off of his right shoulder. In the thick wool-lined leather mitten of his right hand he clasped his single-shot, twenty-gauge shotgun. There was already a number six shot-shell in the chamber, and he had left the hammer depressed, effectively putting the gun on safety, but ready in an instant for cocking and firing should the opportunity arise.

He had set his trap line with several rabbit snares and small leg-hold traps for martin and foxes, but he carried the shotgun for the grouse that he occasionally encountered on his daily round. The rabbits and grouse augmented his mother's cooking pot, and the skins of martins and foxes provided a small supplement to his income from the mine.

This had been an unusually bad winter for both rabbits and grouse because there had been some unseasonably warm days in which the snowfall had been replaced by a light drizzle which had later frozen into an almost impenetrable layer of ice on the surface of the snow and on the branches of the trees during the night. This effectively prevented rabbits and grouse from accessing their normal food supply, and many had perished from starvation. As they, among other small animals, were the main source of food for foxes and martins, these predators had also diminished in numbers.

He stopped and laid the shotgun across one of the rails while he tied his boots into the snowshoe harnesses. Picking up the gun, he stepped gingerly off of the rail bed, and onto the deep snow. He felt the shoes sink about half a foot into the snow, and then hold his weight there. Methodically, he moved step by step westward into the forest where the snow was firmer because of the supporting underbrush. Soon David had hiked about a quarter of a mile in to where his trap line began. Here, the bush had thinned, as several small hillocks predominated and supported an assortment of defoliated deciduous trees. This increased his view to a perimeter of about one hundred yards, and from his current position he could see his first snare. It was empty, and the rabbit trail where he had set it was covered with a layer of the snow which had fallen yesterday. There were no fresh tracks.

As his eyes scanned the ridgelines ahead of him, he reflected upon his present situation. The construction of the sinter plant in 1939, and the ever-expanding output of sintered ore for the blast furnaces in Sault Ste Marie, had been for this area a significant contribution to the war effort. Arguably, it was at least partially his contribution too. It had also facilitated the rapid completion of his electrician's apprenticeship, and his attainment of journeyman's status. There had been almost unlimited opportunities for overtime work, and he had amassed enough in the way of savings to finance his education should he chose to go. Many universities in the country had experienced a decline in enrolment, as most of the eligible young men in the nation now opted to defer their educations by joining one of the armed services.

What about him? As an Ojibwa, where did he fit into the greater scheme of things? Once again, less than twenty-five years after the 'war to end all wars', the Europeans were destroying themselves with even greater intensity. Why should he want to help any side defeat the other in a distant conflict, half a continent and an ocean away? On the other hand, should they win, what did the Nazis, with their philosophy of racial superiority, have in store for people like him?

While fishing at High Falls last week, he had visited the Renaults. Mrs. Renault had emigrated from Norway as a young girl, and David had first met her at the McMurchys. During her periodic trips into town she often dropped in to have a cup of tea with Mrs. McMurchy, who was also an immigrant, and the two of them would chat in Norwegian.

Mrs. Renault's oldest son and her oldest daughter's husband were both in the army, and her next-oldest son had recently joined up. Mr. Renault was general manager of the local hydro-electric company, and a vociferous anti-Nazi. He was obviously proud of his family's contribution to the fight, but David could see that Mrs. Renault, who was normally a cheerful person, had developed permanent worry lines around her eyes. Though smiling, she seemed to have visibly aged since they had last met.

Pleasantly surprised, she invited him in. "I've just taken some bread loaves out of the oven, David. Will you stay for a while and have some with us?"

She spread butter and home-made raspberry jam on the still warm slices, while her husband Steve sat at the table reading a newspaper and puffing silently on his pipe. He smiled and nodded a welcome.

David chuckled. "Don't mind if I do." He took a seat at the kitchen table and hungrily bit into the first one she handed him.

After he had devoured three of the thick slices and washed them down with a large cup of coffee, she asked him. "Have you got any news about the McMurchy boys recently?"

Only three days previously he had visited the McMurchys, bringing a large whitefish that Mrs. McMurchy had cooked them for dinner.

"Well, as you know, Jason is now what they call a multiple ace, and apparently, he is still shooting down Germans in his Spitfire. As for Jack, they are a little worried because they haven't heard from him in the few weeks since he landed in Italy. But then Jack never was one for writing much, so I expect they will eventually hear from him sometime."

He paused, remembering. "Oh, yeah. Mrs. McMurchy also said they got a letter from her sister. It seems Peter was back for a visit, but they didn't know where he will be reassigned, because the rest of the letter was blacked out by the German censors. I guess he's a multiple ace too. Strange, eh?"

Mrs. Renault shuddered. "He seemed like such a nice boy during that summer he was here. Why in the world is he fighting for those dreadful Nazis?"

David shrugged. "Beats me, but I'll bet he doesn't have that much choice in the matter. The Nazis don't seem like the kind of people who take no for an answer. Also, things are not going well for the Germans these days, so I guess he has good reason to think he is protecting his family while he's defending his country."

Steve Renault grumbled. "Well, say what you will about it, I just hope he doesn't end up killing any of our Canadian boys while he is at it."

David gazed a moment at the bread in his hand. "Amen to that."

He then bit slowly into it, staring absently at the floor as he chewed and considered the possibilities, while outside, the gurgling of a nearby raven presaged the winter's early darkness.

As he made his way further along the trap line David continued to find the snares empty, and the nearby area devoid of any fresh animal tracks. He was rounding a bend in the trail to where his final snare was set, and suddenly came to a stop. In one smoothly silent motion, he slid his hand out of the mitten which was attached by a length of chord to his sleeve, and raised the shotgun to his shoulder while cocking the hammer.

Straight ahead of him, no more than thirty feet away, was a large male timber wolf. The animal was gaunt, and the snow around it was stained red as he ravenously devoured the rabbit that had been caught in David's snare.

The wolf's head jerked up at the sound of David's hammer cocking. At this range it would be an easy shot. However, if the wolf chose to attack him it could cover the distance in less than two seconds, leaving him scant time to make the decision to shoot.

David hesitated. *If he was careful not to damage the pelt, it would bring a good price.* The wolf's lips curled back from its teeth and a growl of warning rose from deep in its throat. He saw the animal's ribs beneath its fur and realized that the wolf too, had probably been starving. It hunched guardedly now over its meal, refusing to surrender the food, while its blazing amber eyes remained fixed upon David.

Surely the wolf knew that it was probably going to die, but something in the animal's defiant stance and burning gaze caused David to pause. Even faced with overwhelming odds, a fundamental nobility in the creature would not contemplate submission.

His finger relaxed from the trigger, and he slowly began to back away, while calmly speaking to the wolf. "Okay, fellah, you look like you could use that food more than me. Just finish that off, and I'll leave you to it."

He backed around a bend in the trail, and when he had got another two hundred feet, he turned around and started hiking back along the route in, guardedly keeping his shotgun at the ready, while glancing back over his shoulder to make sure he wasn't being followed.

Just before he reached the clearing near the railroad, he noticed a slight movement out of the corner of his left eye. Slowly turning his head in that direction, he caught another small movement, and then he saw them. Two ruffed grouse - almost invisible because their feathered colouring blended perfectly with the local trees - were standing on the grey length of an old fallen cedar log, no more than twenty-five feet away. Silently, he raised the shotgun to his shoulder and very slowly cocked the hammer. He waited patiently, scarcely breathing, until one of the birds moved closer to the other. Then, he gently squeezed the trigger and the shotgun roared, taking both of the grouse's heads off with one shot.

Stuffing both birds into his bag, he continued out to the railway, where he unstrapped his snowshoes. Hitching them over his back, he began to whistle a tune as he trudged home to his mother and her cooking pot.

The next day at work, he found his thoughts wandering from the job at hand. The millwrights had just installed an electric drive motor on the conveyor belt that carried powdery coke dust up the length of an enclosed belt-housing to a new furnace. There, it would mix with the crushed ore to assist burning the impurities out of it.

Before starting the job of wiring up the new motor, David traversed the several hundred feet from the bottom of an adjoining belt-housing, to examine and diagrammatically record how the connections had been made to that motor on top. He had not brought a mask and was nearly asphyxiated by the thick cloud of black dust. Although the interior of the enclosed belt housing was illuminated with ceiling lights, visibility was blocked beyond fifty feet by dust. By the time he emerged coughing, his face, hands, and clothing were coated in a layer of black grime.

As he was wiring up the new motor, he found himself imagining Jason flying in combat and Jack in his tank. Briefly, he even envisioned Peter flying low over a field in Russia firing his guns at soldiers below. In one such moment of inattention his screw driver slipped, and he jammed the knuckle of his index finger between it and the frozen housing of the motor, tearing away a layer of skin.

"Fuck!" He cursed, and looking at his watch, he realized it was already ten past noon. Cursing again, he pushed the screwdriver into his tool belt, and then trod off toward the lunch room.

When David entered, his shift boss Patrick O'Brian was already there. Wax paper hung out of his open lunch pail, and he was halfway through a sandwich. He looked up and grinned. "Davey, you look like you joined a minstrel show!"

David walked over to the sink and began scrubbing his hands. Looking in the mirror, he winced at his reflection, and started to rub soap onto his face. He had removed his hard hat, and after washing up, swept his fingers back through his hair. However, noticing the layer of black residue that had accumulated under his finger nails from just one sweep, he cursed, and washed his hands a second time.

He sat down across the table from O'Brian, and then opened his lunch pail. David took a bite out of the sandwich his mother had made for him that morning. "I think I'm going to join up."

O'Brian stopped chewing, and his eyes rose to meet David's. He was a tall, straight man in his fifties. A Dubliner, he'd fought for the British Army, and had survived the Somme. "Are you sure about that Davey? You don't have to, you know? You're my best young electrician – you can do a lot for the war effort right here, and I'm sure most of us wouldn't think any the less of you for not going."

"Thanks Pat, but I already got an earful from Bouchard as he was coming off shift in the change room this morning. He was going on in his usual way about how he and everybody in Quebec, where he is from, don't owe anything to the British Empire, or the French one for that matter. He says we are not their colonies anymore, so there is no obligation to help them. I'm afraid he is like a lot of the guys in Quebec. He's illiterate, thanks to the Catholic Church being in control of education there, and correct me if I'm wrong, but in any of the newspapers I've read since this war broke out, I haven't seen the Vatican condemn Hitler - even once."

David continued. "Most of the people in Quebec live in the countryside, where the church encourages them to have twenty kids and to not send any of them to school, except maybe for the brightest one, whom they groom for the priesthood. That's why the medieval place hasn't changed in 400 years. The church wants it that way. If Bouchard could ever read *Mien Kampf*, he would know that Hitler considers people like him '*untermensch*' or beneath humanity. I'm sure I fall into that category too, but what Bouchard is too ignorant to understand is that if Hitler wins, he'll use people like him and me, and those conscription haters in Quebec, as slaves, whether they have fought against Germany or not."

O'Brian nodded his head. "My Ma tried to raise me a good Catholic too, but it didn't really take, if you know what I mean. It didn't stop me from doing my bit in 1914 – 18, and I have to admit I can see your point about that lot in Quebec. However, war is dangerous. You could get killed, or so badly wounded you'd wish you were dead. If you have the opportunity, as you do, why not just play it safe and let others do the fighting?"

David considered this question for a moment. "My friends are already over there now, and a lot of the boys I knew from town are too. They are risking their lives for me, among other things. I just feel that this war is something that is bigger than any of us, or any local concern, and I should be a part of it."

O'Brian sighed wearily. It was a sigh of regret, and also a grudging acknowledgement. "Well Davey, that kind of decision is what every man has to make for himself, and every man will find his own reason to go or not to go. So, think carefully. Whatever you chose, I'll respect you for it."

At the end of the shift David showered and changed into his clothes. As he prepared to exit the building, O'Brian was waiting for him by the door. He looked David in the eyes. "Is your mind made up then?"

"Yeah." David replied. "I'll be heading out tomorrow."

O'Brian held his gaze a moment longer, and then put his hand out. "Well son, you just keep your head down and make sure you get back here in one piece. Can you do that?"

David clasped O'Brian's big hand firmly. "You can count on it, Pat. We'll be seeing you again someday, eh?"

With lunch-pail in hand, and a duffle bag full of his work clothes slung over his shoulder, he walked over to the rail crossing where he could hitch a ride down the tracks to the harbour.

O'Brian watched David as he trudged across the lot toward the small platform, and he then spoke softly to himself. "I hope so son. I surely hope so."

David waited until next morning at the breakfast table, after he had finished eating, to tell his mother. She said nothing, but bowed her head to stare silently at her hands. Slightly embarrassed and unsure what else he might say to allay her fears, he quickly told her. "Mom, there is a train leaving for Hawk Junction, and then on to the Sault, later this afternoon. There are a couple of things I have to do in town this morning before I go. Don't worry. I'll be back before lunch."

In town, David emptied his bank account, and except for fifty dollars, he put the rest in an account that he opened for his mother. Before heading back to the harbour, he stopped in to say goodbye to the McMurchys. Collin was at work, but Mrs. McMurchy insisted he take with him some of the cookies she had baked that morning.

As David left, she hugged him and wished him luck. "Please be careful when you are over there. I know your mother will be worried sick about you while you're gone. She'll want nothing more than for you to just return home safe and sound."

David shrugged. "Don't worry about me Mrs. McMurchy. I'll be alright. Sorry to dash off, but I'm on a tight schedule and should be on my way. Thanks for the cookies."

He smiled at her, waved goodbye, and was gone.

When he returned to his mother's house, his grandfather and the band's shaman were there too. His mother put her arms around his waist and rested her head upon his chest. Instinctively he put his arms around her shoulders and held her there a moment.

Looking up, she told him. "The war took your father away from us. Only part of him actually came back, but he managed to give me the best part of whatever was left when he gave me you. I don't want this war to take that away too."

He was trying his best to sound reassuring. "Mom, I just feel that I have to be a part of this and do my bit. Please don't worry. I'll do whatever I can to stay out of harm's way."

David grasped her by the shoulders so he could look into her eyes. "I know dad thought a *Wendigo* was coming for him, but I don't think I have to worry about that. I feel like I can make a difference out there by helping my friends fight, and also protect my family from something evil at the same time."

His grandfather placed a frail hand on one of David's shoulders. "I understand that you have made up your mind, so know that our prayers will go with you. We hope they will help to keep you safe."

He then began to chant a familiar tune in the Ojibwa language, and David felt the tension go from his body as he listened to the old man recite the ancient lines. The shaman stepped forward and brandished an eagle's feather which he used to caress David's forehead and shoulders until his grandfather stopped chanting. He then placed the quill of the feather into David's chest pocket.

The old shaman's face crinkled up as he smiled, telling him. "Keep this with you at all times. You never know, eh?"

David smiled back and nodded his head appreciatively. "You've got a deal."

His mother spent the remaining time helping him pack a change of clothes, and several extra pairs of socks and underwear. She fed him one last meal of grouse and rabbit stew before they made their way down to the siding.

He shook his grandfather's hand and gave his mother one last hug. Then, he kissed her on the cheek.

The locomotive's whistle blew, and he climbed the steps to go aboard the caboose. In the twilight, David stood at the railing and waved to them as the train pulled away. He remained there and watched as their figures began to slowly shrink in the distance.

Gradually, darkness fell, and the train's lights began to reflect eerily off the snow as it made its way east. Overhead, the aurora borealis began to form a green ring around the full moon, before expanding umbrella-like away from it, and then, eventually bleed down to every horizon.

As the train gained speed and chugged past the dark woods, David heard a sound - indistinct at first - rising eerily from the forest, which, as it carried sharply through the crisp night air, he recognised as the baleful howl of an ancient timber wolf.

Upon arriving in Sault Ste Marie, David walked from the station to a nearby restaurant where he ordered a breakfast of steak and eggs, which he washed down with two cups of strong coffee. He left twenty-five cents on the table, and as he paid his bill at the cash register, he asked the waitress for directions to the recruitment office.

It was not far away, and carrying his small suitcase he walked the four blocks down Queen Street until he saw the rusty-coloured brick building. On one side of the building there was an official sign over the entrance, and next to the door was a large poster depicting three young men standing to attention, each in a different uniform of the Army, Navy, and Air Force.

When he entered, there were already several young men inside sitting on collapsible chairs as they filled out application forms at a long table. Three other desks were arranged against the far wall, each with a sign representing one branch of the service affixed to the front. He walked over to the Air Force desk and told the middle-aged Sergeant sitting behind it that he wanted to sign up.

The man nodded, then handed him the application form and pointed to the table. "When you've finished filling this out bring it back to me."

When he returned with the completed form, the Sergeant scanned it carefully, stamped it, then clipped it to another official document, and handed both back to David. "Take this next door to Dr. Hendricks for your medical examination. When he's finished, bring it back to me."

Two hours later, David returned with the completed medical forms, and handed them back to the Sergeant. He carefully examined the information, nodded his head in approval a couple of times, and then looked up. "According to this you are above average in your level of fitness, and perhaps more importantly the doctor says you have exceptionally good eyesight. Welcome to the Air Force son."

He pointed to the other side of the room. "Go through that door on the right to get your uniform issued. You'll stay at the barracks over by the armoury tonight. You can have all the breakfast you want there but report back here by nine hundred hours tomorrow morning with all your gear. There is currently a demand for aerial gunners, and we'll have a ticket for you on the train to Manitoba. They will give you your basic training, and then have you shooting at enemy airplanes in no time."

Dieppe

The transfer to RCAF 403 Wolf Squadron out of Manston, found Jason flying the recently-issued Mk IXb Spitfire, which possessed markedly improved performance over the Mk V. Approaching Dieppe from the north-east at 20,000 feet, he could see innumerable dark columns of smoke rising from the beach in front of the city.

This was his second sortie of the day, and unlike the first one, the sun was no longer at his back. Earlier in the morning he had come out of its glare to bounce an unsuspecting red-nosed *Fw*190 as it began its strafing run on the landing craft running in to shore.

Now, approaching mid-day, the increasing carnage unfolding beneath him was plain to see.

In addition to the blasted and burning wreckage of several landing craft, there were other ships further out, either sinking or on fire from shellfire or bomb hits. Worse, he could see that none of the Churchill tanks had breached the sea wall. They now lay on the stony beach, broken or on fire where they had been abandoned, or destroyed by enfilading anti-tank gunfire.

The beach was also littered with an appalling number of soldiers scythed down by a merciless hail of machinegun fire, shrapnel, and the strafing runs of *Fw*190s down the entire length of the shoreline. Those who had survived huddled in small groups in the lea of the sea wall, while a withering torrent of bullets and exploding shells filled the air above their heads.

From where Jason could see them, their situation looked hopeless. A massive preliminary shore bombardment from several cruisers or battleships, which might have saved them, had apparently not been written into the plan. For now, he and his fellow pilots would have to do their best to intercept the *Luftwaffe*'s bombers and ground attack aircraft, to give the men below a chance to regroup.

A flight of *Do* 217s approached from the east at 12,000 feet as they prepared to make a bombing run on the group of destroyers about a mile off-shore.

He quickly relayed instructions to his wingman, Flt. Sgt. Gerrard through the radio mike. "*Dornier*s at 12,000! Follow me down and pick one for yourself!"

Jason banked right, and put the Spitfire into a dive that would take them down on the two rearmost aircraft. A bomber soon filled his sights, and he thumbed the firing button to send a stream of 20mm and .303 cal. fire into the *Dornier*. It tore into the wing along the outer edge of the starboard engine nacelle, causing it to fold upward and tear off. The bomber immediately rolled over and began spinning toward the sea below.

Machine gun fire from the *Do* 217 to his right poured into Gerrard's engine, causing it to spew oil over the windscreen while flames burst from the exhaust manifold. Through the rear of his canopy, he glimpsed the wingman's hood sliding back, and the pilot exiting his aircraft only seconds before it exploded in mid-air.

The parachute opened, and Jason circled momentarily until he saw one of the rescue launches change direction and begin to make its way toward where they estimated the pilot would touch down in the water.

Over the next few days, more news began to trickle in confirming the extent of the disaster. Much of the worst information was withheld from the press. However, those like Jason, who had experienced a panoramic view of the catastrophe unfolding as they flew over the battle site, knew how badly things had gone for the landing parties. The German press was having a field day with the film and photographs of burning tanks and surrendered soldiers. Although this was written off in the allied outlets as inflated Nazi propaganda, those in the know were beginning to suspect that if this abortive attempt to breach the Atlantic Wall of Fortress Europe was any indication, it might indeed be impregnable. While the planners attempted to figure out what had gone wrong, Jason was stood down for several days, so he took the opportunity to visit Jack.

Although they had been in touch by telephone several times in the past year and a half, they had never been able to synchronize their leave times effectively enough to actually meet. Out of concern over what he had seen on the beach below him at Dieppe, Jason had immediately called Jack and was enormously relieved to learn that his brother's regiment had not been involved in the operation. He confirmed a meeting with him in two days hence, and on the designated morning, Jason packed a light bag and proceeded to purchase a train ticket to the Midlands.

When he stepped off the train near Aldershot, Jack was there to meet him. Grinning, the two of them shook hands. They had not seen each other for close to two years, and the intervening events had wrought changes in them. Though they continued to share the robust physiques of brothers in their youthful prime, their boyish countenances had been replaced by the mature faces of young men who had taken on responsibilities and experiences which had seasoned them beyond their years.

Jason was the first to speak when his eyes fell upon the insignia - three khaki cloth stars, each with its yellow cloth background - freshly sewn on both epaulets of Jack's tunic. "Jesus, little brother, you outrank me! You're a bloody Captain now! You didn't tell me you'd been promoted!"

Jack shrugged. "It just came through last night. I had to sew the damned rank patches on myself this morning, just before heading out here. You're a sight for sore eyes yourself 'Loo-tenant'. How is life treating you these days?"

"Bad pun! I'm doing alright I guess – haven't been shot down yet - but you're right to guess I've had some close enough calls to wish I was nearer to a British toilet. So far, the old McMurchy luck is still holding. Yours too, I reckon. You can sure thank your lucky stars you guys didn't go on that Dieppe raid. Our boys took a real pasting."

"This is what I'm hearing too. It's all unofficial for now, but it sounds like a fuck-up from the very start. Apparently, the tanks didn't even get off the beach."

Jason winced. "From up above it looked like they didn't stand a chance. They will have to find some way to take out those anti-tank bunkers and machine gun nests first if they ever want to try that stunt again. I can't tell you how relieved I was when you answered the phone two days ago."

Jack heard the concern in his brother's voice and reached his big hand out to slap him on the shoulder. "Let's stop talking shop for a while Jay. I know a good place we can go this evening to chase some English skirts. I reserved a couple of rooms next to the pub, but things don't really get going there until 8 o'clock, so why don't we head over to the base and I can show you around some tanks."

Jason grinned. "Sounds like a good plan, just as long as I don't end up tonight with one of your retreads."

Jack laughed. "Don't worry Jay. There should be at least one or two that I haven't got around to yet...but they might not be as pretty as you like."

Jason suppressed a smile as he shook his head and sighed. "You haven't changed a bit."

On the training grounds, they watched a squadron of Rams manoeuvring at speed and simultaneously firing at targets. Jason turned to his brother, somewhat mystified. "Those don't look at all like the ones I saw on the beach a few days ago. They're much faster and have a more compact shape."

Jack nodded his head in agreement. "They're Ram tanks. Not as heavily armoured as the Churchill, but in every other respect, a much better machine. It's one weakness however, is that it only has a peashooter for a main gun. When they finally put us in the field against the enemy – likely in North Africa I suspect – we expect to get upgraded to Grizzlies, or the American-built version called the Sherman. It's got a bigger 75mm main gun, which will take out anything the Germans are currently fielding. Our crews here have had a lot of training and are very good, so we'll do some damage if they ever let us loose."

They continued over to the mechanic's shop, where a Ram tank was having its left front drive-sprocket replaced. On both sides of the hull about one yard behind and slightly above the toothed wheels, *BEOWULF* had been painted.

Jack pointed to the tank. "This one's mine. We bent our drive sprocket all to hell yesterday when we collided with another tank that cut in front of us at a pretty good clip. It looks like they are almost done."

Jason rapped his knuckles on the cast hull and turned to Jack. "It feels as solid as a battleship."

Then, he paused. "Say, do you mind if I borrow that can of white paint over there?"

Jack was puzzled. "Sure, be my guest."

Jason found a small brush, and after stirring the paint, dipped it in and began to draw the outline of a wolf's head based on the shape of Lake Superior under the name on both sides of the tank. Standing back to view his handiwork, he turned to Jack. "There you go brother. Your tank and my Spitfire now have the same artwork on their noses."

Jack clapped him on the back. "I like it, but to be honest, you probably shouldn't ever consider pursuing a career as an artist!"

Jason was not phased. "Don't worry, it'll grow on you. You'll be surprised at how much better it looks after you've bought me a few rounds of beer."

Jack laughed. "You'll look better too – after we've bought a few rounds for some of those English girls!"

August 1943. Poltava, Eastern Front

Hauptmann Roland Schwartz shrieked in terror as he clawed at the canopy release mechanism. The acrid stench of burning oil stung his nostrils as he recoiled from the flames which were now licking hungrily into the cockpit below the instrument panel. Superheated by oxygen escaping from his torn supply hose, they set both of his gloves ablaze, causing the flesh on the back of his right hand to curl and blister as he desperately gripped the control column. Fighting for breath, he cursed in agony, as with a final push, the canopy suddenly flipped open. Arms flailing, he continued to struggle unsuccessfully in a frantic attempt to extricate his bulky torso from the tightly-confined cockpit of the blazing *Bf*109G. His trouser cuffs were on fire as he fought to get his legs free from the tangle of the seat harness. The aircraft rolled over on its back, and he was violently buffeted in the slipstream, but finally kicked himself away to see the tail-fin pass within half a metre of his head. Tumbling, tumbling, the whole world was spinning as he yanked the rip cord, and there was a sudden snap! With a sharp jerk, the parachute canopy blossomed above him, knocking the wind from his lungs.

Schwartz gasped for air as his mind raced. *Where the hell were Schmidt and the two wing men?* As he drifted down beneath his parachute he scanned the skies around him, seeing the smoke trails of his and another aircraft, and then the burning wreckage of a third fighter a kilometre away on the ground.

They had been pounced upon so suddenly by the two Russian fighters that he had not had any time to react before his *Bf*109 burst into flames. When he had seen the two *Lavochkins* shoot past, the red dice on the cowling of the leader had unmistakably told him it was Lucky Ivan, one of the leading Russian aces, followed by his wingman.

Turning his head to the right, he saw a *Bf*109 from his *schwarm* cautiously begin to circle around in his direction. As it got closer, he recognized it as *Oberleutnant* Peter Schmidt's. The left horizontal stabilizer and wing were thoroughly riddled with bullet holes, and the plane looked barely flyable. Schmidt was on his radio, and waved briefly at him. He then pointed his finger in the direction of their base as he turned the fighter and flew off in that direction.

Within minutes of settling to the ground and rolling up his parachute, Roland saw the German half-track approaching. There were several armed soldiers kneeling in the back with their weapons at the ready.

The driver motioned Schwartz into the cab, and noticing his burns, pointed under the dashboard. "If you want to take care of that hand, there is a first aid kit below. There should be some burn ointment and bandages inside."

Roland reached for the first aid kit but his hand began to shake uncontrollably before he could open it, and he suddenly turned to the driver. "Let's get this piece of shit going! We're out in the open here, and there are goddamned Russian planes everywhere!"

After landing his shot-up *Bf*109G, Peter took a quick walk around the aircraft. The *"Gustav"*, with its distinctive collection of bulges on the engine cowling and nose, had held together - but barely. Fortunately, none of the hits had been on the tire in the wheel well, or on the landing strut. If the damage had been only a few centimetres closer to the fuselage he'd have lost that wing. What remained was beyond repair, and the whole thing would have to be replaced.

This was by far the worst day he'd had on the Eastern front in the nearly two years since he had arrived at the launch of

Operation Barbarossa. During those good early days, Schwartz had more than tripled his already high score of kills, while Peter in his subordinate role of wingman had achieved less than half that tally.

They were now reduced to fighting a rearguard action. After the German disaster at Stalingrad, the Russians had again prevailed at Kursk, and now were overwhelmingly on the offensive. They seemed to have vastly larger supplies of everything, including ground attack and fighter aircraft. There was also no longer any shortage of highly-skilled Russian pilots. Pilots like Lucky Ivan, who had shot down Schwartz today, and whose wingman had nearly killed Peter.

Never an enthusiastic Nazi or ardent proponent of expansionist warfare, Peter was beginning to experience a lingering sense of dread whenever he thought about where the eventual outcome of this conflict would bring him. A certain resignation and fatalism had fallen over those pilots who were not fanatical Nazis, as it became ever more apparent that the Russians were now prevailing. Ultimately, it would depend on how much of a penalty they could make them pay for every kilometre of their advance toward Germany, if they were ever going to halt them.

As he thought about his parents or his younger sister, and how they might fare after a Russian victory, it steeled his resolve to stop the enemy offensive with every possible means at his disposal – ideology or politics be damned!

It was obvious that Schwartz didn't like him. It had been that way even back in their days at the *Bayerische Flugzeugwerke*. Any recognition of Peter's role in protecting him as his wingman had been sparing. Begrudgingly forced to acknowledge Peter's relatively high number of victories over enemy aircraft, and his flying ability, Roland had chosen to keep him close out of self-interest and had only recently promoted him to leader of the second *rotte* in his *schwarm*. This still curtailed Peter's ability to take the initiative, while having to follow Schwartz's lead.

Peter did not have much confidence in Roland's leadership. He observed that Schwartz still seemed most interested in running up his score, but not necessarily by aggressively challenging the Russian fighters. Most often he would choose stragglers and transport aircraft. In recent months, the kills had come more slowly as Roland avoided attacking the heavily armoured *Ilyushin* (*Il-2*) '*Sturmoviks*' which were in ever-increasing numbers diving down to strafe and bomb German ground formations. They were hard to kill, and had a lethal sting in their rearward firing machine gun. Getting down low with them also made you vulnerable to ground fire.

However, Peter doubted that any different kind of leadership would have prevented what had happened to them today, unless they had intentionally gone very high up, looking to engage enemy fighters. They had been attacked in a perfect manoeuvre out of the sun, and it was all over before they knew what had hit them. It was quite apparent that Lucky Ivan had more than just luck on his side. He was a skilled and lethal foe in the air.

After dressing Schwartz's hand, the doctor advised him it would be at least three weeks before he would be fit to fly a fighter again. With this news, Roland decided to catch one of the *Ju*52 tri-motor flights that regularly ferried badly wounded evacuees back to Berlin, where he would visit his mother, and check with his contacts to see if he could get any more information about the *Me*262 program.

There was no replacement aircraft available for Peter, so he resigned himself to spending an idle week at the base until his wing had been replaced with a new one. First however, he had the reluctant task of writing a condolence letter to the mother of his wingman. There would be plenty of time over the next few days to write to his own mother in Germany too.

The week passed slowly, but after seven days no new wing had arrived, so Peter pressed his mechanic to see if there was one they could cannibalize from another aircraft. For several days there was nothing to be found, until the right landing strut on a *Bf*109G collapsed during a routine landing, killing the pilot and destroying the right side of the aircraft, but leaving the left wing, horizontal stabilizer, and landing strut intact. Because of a shortage of fitters and mechanics, it took more than ten days to dismantle the wing and install it on Peter's aircraft. He had only taken it up for a first test flight, when Schwartz returned from Berlin with news.

He beamed triumphantly as he announced his good fortune. "Well, Schmidt, they have placed Galland in charge of putting together the *Me*262 Squadrons, and because of my experience during the development phase of the program, they want me to join them. I'll be shipping out in a week, but before I go, I want to kill a few more Russkies, so starting tomorrow we'll be going out on more patrols. Have you found some wing men for us?"

More than a bit jealous, Peter tried to be magnanimous. "Yes, I have - and congratulations Roland. You flew with Galland for a while in the *Condor Legion* before Molders took over, didn't you? It sounds like a great opportunity. I envy you."

Schwartz was going to savour the moment. "I'll bet you do. When I am flying jets and you are still flying these propeller machines, there is no way that you will be able to match my score. Jets will turn the tide of the air war."

Peter bit his tongue. "You're probably right Roland. Let's just hope Willy Messerschmitt can build enough of them to make a difference."

Schwartz spat. "*Gott in Himmel!* You're always the pessimist. That is why people like me are the leaders, and people like you aren't. German technology is destined to triumph over everything and everyone. Nothing can stop us!"

Peter shrugged. "The Russians seem to have done a good job of that recently. I hope you are right, and that these jets are the answer."

Roland shook his head contemptuously. "You just make sure you do your job as *rotte* leader when we are on patrol. I still can't understand how you let that bastard get the jump on us last time out."

Next day, Schwartz, as squadron leader, was out in front of the flight when Merkel, his wingman, spotted the group of Russian transport planes about 1,500 metres below them.

"Enemy aircraft ten o'clock low!" he shouted into his radio.

Peter was further back, to Schwartz's right, and his wingman Frantzen was behind him - to the right and slightly above - as they flew in the classic finger-four *schwarm* formation.

Schwartz's *Bf*109 rolled left, and with his wingman closely in tow, he dove down on the slow-moving transports, sure of the opportunity to easily run up his tally of kills. Peter took a quick glimpse above and behind him for covering fighters, and saw nothing, so he led his wingman down in pursuit. The transports had scattered as Roland's first burst caused one of the aircraft in the centre of the flight to explode in a huge blast of flame. As he dove through the remaining aircraft, Schwartz fired another burst, which tore a second hapless transport's right wing off at the root, causing it to roll over and plunge uncontrollably toward the ground, trailing flame and smoke behind it.

As Peter lined up behind another one of the lumbering transports, he suddenly saw Schwartz's wingman explode in a ball of flame, and the camouflaged silhouette of a Russian fighter plane flash by. Simultaneously, Peter saw tracer pass over his right wingtip. Instinctively, he rolled left and rammed the throttle forward. As he threw the *Gustav* into a diving turn, he caught a glimpse of the *La 5* in his rear-view mirror just before it overshot him. Circling round, he saw the smoke trail from Frantzen's plane as it plunged earthward.

He desperately searched the skies above and in front of him for the Russian aircraft. His keen eyes soon detected a tiny distant speck that quickly resolved into the shape of an aircraft flying alone about two kilometres ahead and 1,000 metres above him. With it's stubby *Shvetsov* radial engine, as opposed to the sleeker *Mikulin* or *Klimov* V-12s powering the *MiG* 3 and *Yak* 3, it was unmistakable as a *La 5*. Checking behind him every few seconds to see if there was a Russian wingman in the area, he began to climb to a position directly behind and slightly below the *Lavochkin*.

It had initially been difficult to see from a distance, with its camouflaged underside painted blue/grey, but now it loomed in his windscreen. The red stars on the side of its brown and green patterned fuselage, and on the undersides of its wings, stood out clearly. It was with a brief rush of surprise that he recognized the pair of red dice on the aircraft's cowling. Lucky Ivan! The Russian was known to have more than sixty kills and was an exceptionally skilled pilot.

As he closed the distance, Peter had noticed periodic eruptions of black smoke from the aircraft's exhaust ports. Clearly, Ivan was preoccupied with the failing *Shvetsov* and hadn't seen him. He lined-up the *La 5* in his sights and deliberately fired a short burst into the area below the cockpit and engine. There was a flash inside the cowling, and instantly smoke and flame began to stream out of it as the aircraft went into a shallow dive. Checking behind him, he cautiously began to follow it down, and immediately saw the canopy slide back. The pilot was trying to climb out of the cockpit which was now also filled with flames. However, part of the flyer's harness was tangled in the controls.

The slipstream suddenly tore off the pilot's flight helmet and goggles, and at first sight of the long auburn hair Peter was shocked to realize that the enemy pilot was a woman. Flames were pouring out of the cockpit now, and as the pilot flailed about in desperate agony, they first set her flight suit and hair afire, then began to burn her blistering exposed flesh black. Horrified, he pressed the firing button, and heard his own desperate scream above the roar of his guns as he fired a stream of shells into the writhing figure. It disintegrated instantly in the hail of bullets, as the *Lavochkin* then rolled over onto its back and plunged toward the ground.

There was still no sign of the other *La* 5.

Peter searched frantically for any sign of Schwartz. He soon spotted the flame and smoke pouring from another transport about 1,000 feet below him to the right, while Roland continued to fire rounds into it from behind, seemingly oblivious to the recent dogfight above him. As Peter pulled up alongside him, Schwartz shouted into his radio transmitter. "You saw that didn't you? You will confirm that was number three today!"

"*Ja*, I can confirm it Roland, but Merkel and Frantzen have bought it. *La* 5s got them. However, I managed to nail one of the Russians. It was Lucky Ivan."

"You got Lucky Ivan?" There was a hint of suspicion in his voice.

"Yes, except it was Lucky Ivana – Ivan was a woman. I saw her failed attempt to bail out before she burned up. I'd heard the Russians had women pilots, but I didn't believe it until now!"

Roland was skeptical. "I guess I'll have to take your word for it, Schmidt, but you know I didn't see any of it, so I can't confirm your kill. Maybe your gun cameras will. Those are the rules. Now form up with me. We are returning to base."

Schwartz's departure coincided with two promotions for Peter. In addition to an increase in rank to *Hauptmann*, he was now also by default, the *schwarm* leader.

He immediately switched tactics and began to take his *schwarm* to higher altitudes where there was a greater likelihood of being able to bounce Russian fighters. As a result, his score of downed aircraft rose by thirty over the ensuing year as he was forced to stretch his superb flying skills to the limit engaging increasing numbers of *Yak* 3 and *La* 5 high-performance Russian fighters. By the time his transfer orders to the Western front came through, the number of downed aircraft insignia painted on his aircraft's rudder had risen to fifty.

When Roland arrived at the *Me262* program headquarters in the *Flugzeugwerke*, he was informed that they had only recently solved a major problem experienced during the jet's takeoff phase. The *Me262* had initially been designed with a tail wheel. During takeoff, the only way to get the tail to rise, and thus provide the steering control required while accelerating down the runway, was to tap lightly on the brakes at precisely the correct speed. This would cause the tail to jump up, and then the lift generated by the horizontal stabilizers kept it there until the jet was airborne.

Miscalculating when to perform this manoeuvre could result in the tail dropping again, and rather than becoming airborne, the aircraft might instead run off the end of the tarmac at high speed. Even if brakes were applied at the correct moment, too much pressure could result in the jet nosing over into the runway with an equally catastrophic outcome. Ultimately, the problem was solved by moving the *Me262*'s centre of gravity forward, and equipping it with a tricycle landing gear. This lowered the nose onto a steerable wheel, and also had the added benefit of improving the pilot's forward visibility during takeoff.

Roland diligently acquired enough flying hours at the controls of the *Me262* to master it. Then, when enough of the jets had rolled off the assembly line to equip a Wing, he was personally informed by Göring that he had been promoted to *Major* and made a *schwarm* leader in *Jagdverband 44,* out of deference to his more than one hundred aerial victories.

Göring took this opportunity to pin Oak Leaf clusters to the Knight's Cross he had awarded Roland a year before. He nodded his head approvingly. "You see Schwartz, the *Führer* and the Fatherland can show gratitude to those who serve the *Reich* so heroically. Congratulations! If you continue to serve the party well, the swords and diamonds cannot be far behind."

As Göring stepped back, Roland's chest swelled with pride and he thrust his right arm into the air to give the Nazi salute. "*Heil Hitler!*"

North Africa

Jack threw his pack down onto the floor of his tent and reached for the jerry-can beside his bunk. Tilting it carefully, he poured the water into his tin cup, and then thirstily gulped it all down.

It was only eight-thirty in the morning but already the Algerian sun was radiating its baking heat through the canvas walls, turning his temporary domicile into an oven. Jack's shirt and shorts were soaked through with sweat from the morning's five mile hike through the Atlas Mountains. This exercise was staged daily to keep the members of his advance party in shape while they waited for the main body of the regiment to join them from England in preparation for their invasion of Italy.

Several crews, including his own, had been sent ahead, but for the time being they were without tanks, and once the initial set-up at Blinda had been accomplished, time began to pass with interminable slowness.

On the way to the showers, he ran into his gunner, Mike Robertson. Robertson was from New Brunswick and had grown up on a farm only twenty miles from the regimental headquarters at Gagetown. He had been visiting his cousin in Northern Ontario in 1941 as he turned 19, and the two of them had joined up at the same time. Ironically, he had gone through basic training at Camp

Borden, becoming part of Jack's crew there before they had been transferred back to his home town.

Meanwhile, his cousin had been slotted into the navy and was now serving on a destroyer in the Pacific.

Jack liked the sinewy young gunner. Though tough as nails, Mike had a great sense of humour, and an infectious grin. He was a born scrounger and explorer – always venturing into nearby towns or villages if he could get a pass while off duty.

Although his crew was a tightly-knit, well-oiled machine inside of their tank, Jack encouraged a fair degree of informality among them. Mike saluted casually as he approached. "Hey Jack, I took a drive into Algiers with our supply boys from the mess yesterday to look around, and I spied this place called Madame Fifi's. One of the locals spoke some French and told me it was a house of ill repute. It was closed at the time, but apparently they open at seven in the evening, so a few of us are planning to take a jeep into town tonight to check out the talent. Are you interested in joining us?"

Algiers was about 20 miles from the base-camp in Blinda, and it took them about an hour to drive the jeep along the dusty unpaved road. The early December sun was just setting as they arrived.

The lights were on at Madame Fifi's, and the voice of a chanteuse accompanied by accordion music wafted from a gramophone within. They were greeted at the door by an elderly North African man in a white suit. He was tall and thin, with a pencil moustache and oiled hair which was combed straight back. Both had been dyed black. He spoke in heavily-accented French as he directed them to a room where several young women were lounging on chairs, some smoking, while others sipped either tea or water.

Several of the women were obviously of local Arabic or North African origin, but two were black Sub-Saharans, and a few more appeared to be Europeans. Jack was eying one of the slender African women when Madame Fifi entered the room and announced in English that the bar was open. She also suggested that the gentlemen should find a lady who was to their liking, and then they could negotiate with them individually.

Madame Fifi was a Frenchwoman in her early forties. Even without the high heels she was taller than average, and the burgundy-coloured sleeveless dress, with its twin slits that ran from mid-calf to her knees, accentuated her slim figure. She was fine-featured, and her long light-brown hair was styled with a soft curl that fell to just below her shoulders. In her right hand, she balanced a long cigarette-holder with a smouldering *Gitane* lodged in its end. Her eyes possessed a calculating hardness, but they suddenly grew large and interested when she saw Jack. They travelled admiringly up and down his tall, powerfully muscled physique, and with a slightly exaggerated swaying of the hips, she crossed the room to approach him.

She touched his forearm lightly. *"Vous et un Canadien. Parlez-vous francais?"*

Jack smiled. *"Je parle une peu madame, mais Anglais c'est mon preference."*

She returned his smile and transitioned effortlessly into English that was only slightly accented with French, as her hand softly traced a path up his firmly muscled arm to rest on his broad shoulder. "Very well then. English, it shall be. My name is Fifi, and you are…?"

"I'm Jack – *Jacques.*" He laughed, and then took the hand she had just removed from his right shoulder and kissed it. He let his lips linger a second there as he inhaled the perfume on her wrist. "I'm very pleased to meet you Fifi. You have a nice place here."

Her mouth parted as her tongue ran slowly along a top row of perfect white teeth. She lowered her eyelids and her fingers once again gently massaged the large muscles of his upper arm. "Mmmmm. I think I will give you my personal attention tonight Jack. Let's retire to my quarters and I will have champagne delivered. You must be very thirsty after such a long day in the desert."

For the next two weeks, Jack was able to obtain daily transportation into Algiers, where he and Fifi lustfully pleasured each other into the early hours of the morning. She had made it plain from the beginning that this would not be a business transaction, but rather a mutually beneficial situation where no money would change hands. He found her experienced and talented ways literally intoxicating as she aroused every bit of his physical stamina and power to sate all of her hungers and desires.

They acknowledged that this was at best a temporary arrangement because Jack would eventually be moving on with very short notice once the planners had fixed a date and destination for their departure. For now, they would enjoy what time they had remaining, while exploring the intense physical attraction they felt for each other.

One night after hours of love making, as they sprawled atop the sheets, catching their breath, his curiosity got the better of him. "Fifi, what was it that brought you from France to live in Algiers?"

She hesitated, prepared to invent a story before deciding to tell him the truth. "Well darling, my name is actually Catherine. Catherine Bruneau. I was born and grew up in Lyon where my parents had a modest shop which sold stationery and office supplies. At eighteen I moved to Paris where I worked for several years as a secretary for an importer. The owner's nephew and I entered into an affair, and like a foolish girl I followed him here when the firm decided to open an export office."

Fifi's voice was edged with bitterness as she continued. "After a few years, his family found out about our relationship and they were not pleased. They began to squeeze his budget, and in truth he was not a very good businessman, so we started to have money problems. In the end, he decided to abandon me and returned to the security of his family in Paris where I understand he is now doing quite well. I sold what insubstantial assets remained from the business and opened a very small cabaret. However, I soon learned that there was less money in selling watered-down drinks than the favours of young ladies."

Jack was weighing this information. "Have you ever considered going back to France?"

"My elderly parents are aware of the rumours and won't hear of me returning to Lyon where I would bring scandal down upon them. These days, with the Nazi occupation, the idea of going back to Paris – where my former boyfriend's family is happily and profitably collaborating with the *Boche* – does not appeal to me. No. I will make do here for now, at least until this war is over, and then perhaps, I will move – or perhaps not. For now, I have a comfortable life, don't you think?"

She languidly raised her arm and expansively made an arc with the back of her hand to mutely display the sumptuous quality of her boudoir. She dropped it lightly upon his chest and moaned as she moved it in a slow downward caress to below his firm stomach.

Well, there it was, Jack thought. *Fifi was a survivor, and like him, she was not investing too much into a nebulous future but taking what pleasures from life as came along.*

However, they both knew it would at some point come to an end, and on the night of December 18th they spent their last hours together before he was dispatched with the advance party to Matera, Italy. As a crescent moon shone dimly upon them through the gossamer curtains, they made desperate love until two o'clock in the morning, neither of them wanting to be the first to climb out of their bed.

Finally, when they did part, Catherine stood alone in the darkness by the upstairs window, wrapped in her white satin sheet, suffused with the last traces of his scent, while her loins ached from the passion of their lovemaking. Over the past decade, she had intentionally erased every man from her mind the minute he had left that room. Now, for the first time in almost as long as she could remember, she began to wonder beyond this moment, and about the fate of her young Canadian. *Would he even survive the war?* Strangely, an unfamiliar moisture welled in her eyes as she watched him shift the jeep into gear, reluctantly wave to her one last time…and then drive away. She continued to watch after the headlights eventually disappeared, as she too was swallowed by the vastness of the desert night.

————————————————————

May 1944. Reconnaissance

A tiny frozen crystal of ice had formed on the inside of Flight Lieutenant Jason McMurchy's Perspex canopy. It hung diamond-like, to the right of the central bulletproof section of the windscreen. A ray of sunlight refracted through it, stabbing a flickering beam into the corner of his eye. Besides disrupting the expanse of sky before him, it poked at his retina, shattering the fatigue that had begun to creep over his body after six hours at the controls of his FR Mk XIV Photo Reconnaissance Spitfire.

While most of 403 Wolf Squadron were now flying rhubarbs and escort missions out of Kenley, Jason had been transferred to 430 'City of Sudbury' Squadron's PR unit. In the early morning darkness, he had taken off from their aerodrome near Ashford.

The Robin-egg blue Mk XIV PR variant was nearly invisible at its operational high altitude, and additionally, it was fitted with an extra belly-tank to increase its range. To compensate for the weight of its high-resolution cameras, most of its armament and ammunition had been removed. That brought an increase in speed and a higher ceiling, but in a concession to its pilots, this had been compromised slightly to allow the retention of a single 20mm cannon in each wing with minimal rounds loaded.

Instinctively turning his head left to avoid the annoying

glimmer, he reached up to brush away the frozen crystal. It was then that he saw the pair of tiny specks more than a mile in the distance, which quickly resolved into two aircraft beginning to dive on a target below. Focusing more closely, he saw them assume the shape of German *Fw*190A fighters.

Jason knew from experience that the *Fw*190 had inferior high-altitude performance to his Mk XIV, but at lower levels, it was the equal of most allied fighters in the skies over Europe.

Glancing below, he saw the dark shape of a four-engine Halifax bomber. Its inside starboard propeller was feathered, and the outboard port engine trailed black smoke, as the aircraft skimmed along barely five hundred feet above the English Channel. The tail-gun position had been blasted away by German flak, and the mid-upper gunner had rotated his turret to the rear position to take aim at the diving fighter. He'd obviously alerted the pilot too, as the heavy bomber began to jerk from side to side in a desperate attempt to evade the German firing down upon them from astern.

A line of watery explosions marched across the sea's surface in front of the bomber, as the German pilot, now approaching at a speed in excess of five hundred miles per hour, tried to line up the erratic bomber in his sights. The mid-upper gunner in the Halifax began to fire, and Jason saw the tracer begin to snake upward toward the approaching fighter. Whether the bullets found their mark, or whether the German pilot had misjudged his speed, the lead fighter failed to pull up out of its dive and shot past the bomber, crashing with a huge explosion into the sea directly below.

However, the German's wingman had judged his descent perfectly, and was now streaking in at full speed behind the bomber to make his pass. Two of his 20mm shells tore into the top of the Halifax's fuselage. About a half dozen more of his rounds from the same burst missed their target, sailing past the leading edge of the port wing. However, the last of these shells cleaved the cowling just forward of the port inboard nacelle, taking a piston-head from the Bristol radial with it on its path to the sea below. Immediately, a stream of dark black smoke began to trail out behind the damaged engine, while bright orange flames licked around the saxophone exhaust manifold.

The pilot activated extinguishers on the engine and feathered its prop. He quickly adjusted his main flaps to prevent the port wing from dropping, which would have induced an uncontrollable spiral into the waves below. The stricken Halifax partially regained its trim, while the *Fw*190 pulled up and climbed past the bomber. Banking to its left, the fighter circled around in an attempt to get behind the bomber for another pass.

Jason had rammed the throttle forward into full boost. The Rolls-Royce Griffon roared with all the power of its 2,500 horses as he kicked the left rudder pedal and snapped the Spitfire into a power-dive, straining the aircraft's wing tolerances to the limit. He nearly blacked out from the G-load induced by this sudden change of direction, but within seconds he was down behind the *Fw*190.

The German had lined the bomber up once again and his first few rounds were kicking up huge geysers of spray in the sea ahead of the Halifax when Jason opened fire. The enemy flyer never saw him coming and died instantly as the short burst of 20mm cannon shells marched up the spine of the *Fw*190 and into the cockpit, disintegrating the Plexiglas while tearing the pilot to shreds. One of the rounds, entering the onboard gas tank, caused the entire aircraft to explode in a massive ball of flame, smoke, and debris. Parts of the destroyed aircraft sailed past him, but to his shock and dismay Jason saw a fist-sized glutinous red object adhere itself to his windscreen, and then leave a wide crimson smear when the tremendous velocity of the airflow over his canopy tore it away.

He circled around to pull up alongside the bomber pilot's window as he throttled down the throbbing Griffon. The flyer flashed a quick 'thumbs up' at him, but was unsuccessful in his attempt to force a smile. The strain of flying the wounded bomber was demanding every ounce of his strength and concentration. His facial muscles were drawn taut as he struggled with the wheel and fought the massive forces pressing against the bomber's damaged control surfaces. As Jason's eyes slid back along the fuselage of the Halifax, he saw a hole where one of the German's 20mm rounds had exited through the side of the mid-upper turret. What was left of the gunner's lifeless torso lay slumped over his weapons.

The same flak burst that had destroyed the rear turret had also shredded the ailerons along the trailing edge of the bomber's horizontal stabilizer. As a result, the aircraft's nose was subject to pitching which the pilot was attempting to counter with the engines and main wing flaps. At the same time he had to contend with the bomber's tendency to yaw left because of the loss of power from the port engines. Exhausted, he was in imminent danger of losing the struggle. Jason could also see the flight engineer, hunched beside the pilot, frantically working the throttles of the two remaining engines while juggling fuel sources from what little remained in the undamaged tanks.

Jason pointed to himself, then up, and circled his finger over his head to indicate his intention to climb to a higher altitude where he would guard the crippled bomber against further attack. The other pilot acknowledged with a quick nod of his head, and then returned his attention to struggling with the bomber's flight controls.

Jason switched frequencies to advise coastal rescue units of the bomber's position and direction of flight. He then put the Spitfire into a climb which took him to 12,000 feet, where he could keep an eye on the bomber as it skimmed over the sea below, while also frequently checking behind him through the canopy and his rear-view mirror to ensure that no one was diving upon him from above.

From there, he saw the pilot gradually lose his battle to stay aloft. The aircraft's shadow inexorably crept back from ahead of the bomber until it was directly underneath and darkening the sea below. He succeeded in one last heroic effort to get the nose up just before the Halifax pan-caked onto the water.

A great sheet of spray shot forward as the bomber skipped once across the surface before burying its nose in a wave. This sudden slowing of momentum caused the aircraft's tail to pitch upward, but before the plane could summersault, its fuselage snapped just behind the main wing, bringing the nose back up while the entire rear section fell back into the sea and quickly disappeared beneath the waves.

The bomber had gone into the water less than two miles from the Yorkshire coast, but Jason knew it would be impossible for anyone to survive a swim to shore before succumbing to hypothermia in the Channel's frigid waters. He circled lower to see if he could spot survivors, and miraculously he saw the pilot, flight engineer, navigator, and bombardier all scramble out onto the port wing.

The front part of the bomber was settling into the water and sinking slowly as the weight of its engines began to drag the leading edge of the wings under the waves. It stayed afloat long enough however, to allow the men to retrieve the inflatable raft from its storage locker close to the port wing-root near its trailing edge. The men managed to clamber into the life raft and began paddling furiously toward shore, as with a final rush of air bubbles, the aircraft sank from sight beneath the sea's churning surface.

Jason circled the raft briefly until he noticed the small coastal patrol motor-launch chugging its way toward the downed airmen. He'd memorized the bomber's squadron markings, and with a final waggle of his wings, he flew over the raft once more, opened the throttle, and pointed the Spitfire inland.

The fighter's big five-bladed Rotal propeller bit hungrily into the air, leaving the Channel far behind, as the Mk XIV sped past the English coastline toward Ashford Airfield.

Jason was about to bank left in a southward turn, when a powerful explosion just beneath the aircraft slammed him against his seat, and flipped the Spitfire over on its back. Shrapnel from the flak burst had pierced the engine compartment, and Jason cursed as oil and glycol filled the windscreen, making it virtually impossible to see past the front of the cockpit.

He immediately dropped the unresponsive stick from his fingers, tore the oxygen mask from his face, and began to claw at the canopy release mechanism. It opened, and with a violent jerk he pulled the canopy back along its runners. However, instead of where the sky should have been, he saw the whirling English countryside rushing down toward him.

Upside down in a flat spin, his ears were deafened by the loud whine of the stricken engine and shrieking air rushing past his windscreen. For a fraction of a second he was temporarily disoriented. Realizing that he was still locked into the plunging Spitfire by his seat harness, he tugged desperately at the release, and finally felt it unhook, while the force of gravity pulled him down and out of the open canopy.

The air screaming past the plummeting aircraft slammed into him like a gigantic fist. Tumbling in the slipstream, he narrowly missed the Spitfire's rudder while groping frantically for the ripcord. Catching it in his hand, he gave it a hard yank, and was rewarded with the loud snap of the parachute bursting open - nearly dislocating his shoulder blades with the sudden change in velocity and direction.

Jason turned in his harness just in time to see the Spitfire slam into a fallow wheat field, sending huge gouts of flame and earth shooting skyward. As the clumps of soil and aircraft fragments fell back to earth, the smoke from the explosion drifted away from the point of impact to reveal a gaping crater from which only a few twisted scraps of metal protruded like a bizarre set of smouldering broken teeth.

He descended the final few hundred feet to earth, then remembering his rudimentary parachute training, bent his knees and rolled along the ground to dissipate the force of impact.

Back on his feet, he began to gather in the parachute, finally rolling it up into a manageable ball which he intended to sit upon while thanking his lucky stars and awaiting eventual pick-up. Before he could accomplish this, a khaki-coloured army truck came speeding down the road which ran parallel to the field he had just landed in.

An officer driving the flat-nosed, fifteen hundred-weight Chevrolet, was waving frantically at him out of the right-side window. As the truck pulled alongside, the driver slammed its brakes, and it squealed to a halt, raising a huge cloud of dust. Through the settling particles, Jason noticed another man sitting motionless in the passenger seat with his eyes rather strangely downcast.

The driver was an artillery Captain. He leapt out of the truck, and with a curious limping gait, bounded over to Jason.

"Thank God you're alright!" He exclaimed, while excitedly brushing bits of soil from the epaulets of Jason's flight jacket. "For a moment there, you gave us one hell of a fright!"

"Gave you a fright!" Jason retorted. "Was that your anti-aircraft burst that knocked me out of the sky?"

The Captain was pensive. "Yes, I'm very sorry to say. One of our new NCOs with a very bad case of buck fever I'm afraid. He mistook you for a *Jerry*."

"My Spit doesn't look anything like a fucking *Jerry*!" Jason exploded.

The Captain's brow furrowed, and appearing somewhat

chastened, the dawning of an idea spread across his face.

Trying his best to sound sympathetic, he replied. "Yes, I quite agree and I'll see to it that the lad is disciplined. However, for now perhaps you could find it in your heart to join me at my mess to help you celebrate your lucky escape with one of the bottles of fine cognac I liberated from Dunkirk during that bit of unpleasantness back in 1940?"

It was then that Jason remembered the Captain had a noticeable limp, so he nodded at the man's leg. "Did you pick that up in France? It looks like it should have been a ticket out of the war."

The Captain shook his head in disagreement. "Not a chance old chap. I wouldn't miss this show for anything. I was prepared to get down on my hands and knees to service His Royal bleeding Majesty himself to stay in."

He grinned. "I suppose the twits took my threat seriously enough to let me have my way, just this once."

Jason was starting to like the insouciance of the man and decided that he actually wouldn't mind a few ounces of alcohol in his system to iron out the tensions of a long day before heading back to the airfield for his debriefing. "I think I'll take you up on that offer Captain. By the way, my name is Flight Lieutenant Jason McMurchy. And yours is...?"

"Artillery Captain Reginald Brown, at your service. I'm very pleased to make your acquaintance, although I wish it had been under slightly happier circumstances!"

He thrust out his hand, and Jason returned the captain's solid grip. "Can't quite say it's been a pleasure for me yet Captain, but from what you've told me of your war booty, things should improve shortly I expect."

"I certainly expect they shall," he said, still grinning.

Pausing, he glanced at the country designation on Jason's shoulder sashes. "What part of Canada are you from? Montreal?"

"No, I'm actually from a small place in Ontario called Sault Ste Marie. You've likely never heard of it." Jason replied.

Captain Brown knit his brow for a moment. "I seem to remember the name from an old geography lesson. It's on the junction of two Great Lakes if memory recalls. Is it Superior and Huron?"

Jason was unable to conceal his astonishment. "Bang On! Not

too many people over here would have known that."

"Geography is a bit of a hobby of mine," Captain Brown admitted.

"Actually, to tell the truth, I was an upper-form geography teacher at one of those schools where the 'toffs' send their little chinless wonders. That was before this show began. But I digress! Let us hurry back to barracks where we can drink a few toasts to your hometown."

"Amen to that," Jason agreed, as he rolled up the last of his parachute and walked toward the truck.

As Jason trod past the tailgate toward the passenger door, Captain Brown pointed at the young man who had climbed out of the Chevrolet's cab. He looked no more than eighteen and was doing his best not to make eye contact. "Flight Leftenant McMurchy, this is Corporal Alexander, one of my gun crew leaders. A dead shot he is. He once knocked down an aircraft with one round of flak from his piece."

Cpl. Alexander stiffened to attention and snapped a crisp salute. "Sir!"

Jason was curious. "What did you bag Corporal? Was it a one – eleven or a two - seventeen maybe?"

The Corporal's eyes shifted nervously over to the Captain, who replied. "Well actually...he, ah, bagged himself a Mk XIV Spitfire. Today, as a matter of fact."

Jason swallowed hard first but couldn't prevent the irritation from creeping into his voice. "Is there any particular reason why you decided to shoot down fifty thousand quid worth of Spitfire today Corporal?"

The young man winced and began to shift his weight from one foot to the other. "Well sir, we were quite busy today. Several doodlebugs and Messies went over, along with a lot of badly damaged Lancasters and Halifaxes. A Lanc had just gone over trailing smoke from three engines when you popped up over the ridge from the same direction the Messies had been coming from. We were prepared for the next one, and the sun was in our eyes, and..."

His voice trailed off, and then he earnestly began to apologize. "I'm awfully sorry sir. It was a reflex action. I don't think the shell was hardly out of the barrel before I realized we'd made a mistake.

We were horrified when we saw your ship go in. I'm just so relieved to see you made it out alright."

Jason raised an eyebrow before responding. "Understandable I guess Corporal, but it doesn't make losing my favourite fourteen feel any better. She was a delight in the air and had got me though quite a few tight spots before today. Let's hope you're just as good a shot when the next real *Jerry* comes over."

He glanced at the still smouldering crater. "The boys at Recon HQ aren't going to like not receiving their film footage from Bremen today, but I guess I can live with that, and so I guess, shall they."

Captain Brown's truck was equipped with a wireless set, and Jason called in to his group to apprise them of the situation.

Putting the microphone down, Jason turned to Captain Brown. "Air-Sea rescue has apparently got things well in hand. The surviving crew is on its way in and the poor sodden bastards have even confirmed the *Fw*190 that I downed. Group isn't exactly thrilled about the lost camera footage, but they seem almost happy that I'm alive. They've also given me permission to accompany you back to your HQ to finish up any paper-work you might have before returning to base."

"Excellent plan old chap," the Captain replied.

"I'm sure there must be mountains of paperwork to do on this one. No harm in sampling a bottle of cognac during the process. Don't want to miss dotting those 'I's, or crossing the 'T's by rushing, do we?"

Jason hesitated. "Captain, you don't suppose the hospital where they'll take that Halifax crew is nearby, do you? I wouldn't mind looking in on them if it's possible."

"Actually, we'll drive right past it on the way back," the Captain offered. "However, I don't know how keen they'll be on letting you see them this soon."

The morose Corporal brightened suddenly and interjected. "My sister's a nurse there sir. She's on duty right now. I'm sure she could get us in!"

Brown caught Jason's eye and shrugged. "It can't hurt to give it a try. Let's go."

The Corporal walked round behind the fifteen hundred-weight and climbed into the covered bed, where he took a seat. Jason eased into the passenger's side of the Chevrolet's cab, and soon Captain Brown had double-clutched the truck through its full range of gears, speeding them along the coastal route back to the battery and toward the hospital. Less than fifteen minutes later, they were pulling into the hospital parking area, and Brown carefully selected a spot to leave the vehicle where they wouldn't block any ambulance access to the entrance.

The young soldier standing guard duty snapped a crisp salute as they passed through the front doors and into the reception area. Approaching the front desk, Captain Brown asked the receptionist where they might find the four airmen recently brought in by the rescue service.

The greying receptionist stared down a thin nose through her glasses at him and attempted to be firm. "They've only just arrived and were looking a bit hypothermic. I don't know if they'll be ready to see anyone just yet until they've been fully examined."

Brown pointed to Jason. "This is the pilot who shot down the plane that attacked them and provided cover until they went in. He'd like to see how they are doing, and I'm sure they would be more than glad to meet him."

The receptionist hesitated a second, pursing her lips. "Very well, but you will have to be escorted into the examining area by a nurse."

"Is Olivia Alexander in? She's my sister." The Corporal interjected.

For a few seconds, the receptionist peered at the young man through her spectacles. The lips relaxed a bit. "Ah yes, I see the resemblance. One moment please."

She reached for the large black telephone and flipped one of the switches on her console. "Send nurse Alexander to reception please."

The matron then turned to them. "Excepting young Alexander, you two must now spell your family names before I can officially enter them into the visitor ledger."

Within a minute, Jason detected the sound of approaching footsteps. Then, out of the adjoining hallway stepped one of the most beautiful women he had ever seen. Her blond hair was swept up beneath her nurse's cap, and her radiant blue eyes lingered on him for just a moment, before shifting to the young Corporal beside him.

Her mouth spread into a wide smile, and Jason noted it was filled with perfect white teeth, as she gasped. "Bobby!"

She rushed over to give him a brief hug. Then, she drew back. "Whatever are you doing here? I haven't heard from you in weeks!"

Momentarily avoiding her question, he motioned toward the Captain. "This is my commanding officer, Captain Brown."

Then pointing to Jason he told her, "This is Flight Leftenant McMurchy."

"Jason." He said, extending his hand. "It's a pleasure to meet you, Miss Alexander."

She clasped the hand while her eyes took in his tall frame, not disliking what she saw. "I'm Olivia."

Smiling, she arched an eyebrow. "The patch on your shoulder and your accent tells me you're a Canadian. I think I've heard that you fellows can be quite old fashioned, still singing songs from the last war and such."

Jason failed to suppress a slight grin. "All I can say in response to that is I'm only old fashioned from the neck down, ma'am. In fact, after a few lessons I've even recently learned how to use what the *avant-garde* British quaintly refer to as a water closet. Although, I must say that compared to the way we do it back home, it is a damned uncomfortable way to take a bath."

She held his steady hand a brief time longer than necessary, interested, as her eyes lingered on the bright spark of intelligence she saw in his. This was a man who flew airplanes at over four hundred miles per hour in deadly combat, 25,000 feet in the air. It was a serious business not normally lending itself to humour, but this fellow seemed to have his wits about him in every sense of the word. Most of the men his age became tongue tied around her, but this Canadian seemed to exude a strength and confidence which was uncommon in her experience.

Her smile warmed as she told him, "Flight Lieutenant McMurchy, I really can't imagine you needing lessons in anything – except perhaps in how to keep your uniform neat and clean."

Jason brushed one of his epaulets lightly. "Well, Miss Alexander, uh, Olivia, I must confess to the need for some tutelage. Apparently, they are not making parachute rides as genteel as they might once have been."

She turned to her brother. "Parachute rides? Bobby, just what are you doing here?"

The Corporal's eyes were again cast downward as he mumbled. "It's a rather complicated story. Something I'll tell you about later, when we have more time. Suffice it to say that Flight Leftenant McMurchy prevented the *Jerries* from shooting down those four chaps you've got here from that bomber which landed in the drink."

"Could you take him to see how they are?" He pleaded.

She gave her brother a suspicious look, and then turned to Jason. "I suppose it can't do any harm to show you to them. From what my little brother says, they'll probably want to thank you, but somehow I get the impression he's not telling me everything."

She was looking at her brother again, eyes slightly narrowed.

Jason glanced at the corporal then back to Olivia. "Well, I wouldn't sell him short just yet Miss Alexander. One thing I can tell you is that your brother is a dead shot with that anti-aircraft gun of his. You should ask him about it some time."

The corporal continued to stare at something invisible on the linoleum.

Olivia took another look at Jason's scruffy uniform and resolved that she would definitely get to the bottom of things later.

She then turned to Captain Brown. "If you and my brother don't mind waiting here Captain, I'll take the Flight Lieutenant to the bomber crew. Follow me, Lieutenant."

Jason walked half a pace behind her to better take in the lithe shape of her body. The knee-length skirt revealed the athletic tone of her legs, and as his eyes took in the long arabesque of her slender neck, he felt his pulse begin to race as an intoxicating scent from the perfume in her soft hair rose into his nostrils.

"Miss Alexander, uh, Olivia, how long have you been working here? As a nurse, I mean."

"About three and a half years now."

She hesitated. "When my older brother Matthew was killed in France, I just knew that I had to do my bit. I wanted to do something to help our chaps, and of course they wouldn't let me fight, so this is it."

She stopped to ask a seemingly unrelated question. "Why is it the Army people call you Leftenant, but your people say Lieutenant?"

Jason could tell mentioning her brother's name had conjured up a memory that she had not yet come completely to terms with, and that she wanted to change the subject, so he tried to lighten the mood. "It's definitely a strange Army preoccupation. Maybe you've got to have a severe overbite before they'll take you. However, come to think of it, your brother's teeth are almost as perfect as yours. Also, my brother who is in a bloody big Sherman tank tearing hell out of the Germans in Italy has a flashing good set of teeth, and he says Leftenant too. I've learned that about the only thing you can do to save yourself is to try to be upwind when they salute you."

Olivia felt herself warming to him and couldn't suppress a smile as they continued their way down the corridor. "There seems to be a fair number of you Canadians about these days. Do you expect you'll be able to defeat Mr. Hitler with lassoes and hockey sticks?"

Jason gave her a look of mock disdain. "We did it to the Germans in 1914 -18, didn't we? No reason we shouldn't be able to do it again. We're always happy to help out our cousins-Jack!"

"Oh no! You're not one of those fellows who is full of himself are you?"

Jason replied. "Actually, the only thing I long to be full of this time of day is cold beer, and I'd like to buy one for you too if you are free sometime."

"Oh." She replied. "You're very fast!"

"You can get used to going five hundred miles per hour. Sometimes it distorts your timing a bit, on the ground – but never your eyesight." He looked at her approvingly.

She smiled and looked into his eyes. "Let me think about it a while, will you? I don't normally have my beer cold. However, I think I might have a few days off at the end of next week. You can always call me here."

Jason's heart began to race when he realized she hadn't completely said no. "Sure. I'll get the number when I've finished my visit."

She led him into a large examining room filled with cots and medical apparatus. "We're here."

The four fliers were sitting on individual hospital cots, and their uniforms had been replaced with thick sleeping gowns. They each had a heavy woollen blanket wrapped around their shoulders.

Jason approached the pilot and thrust out his hand. "Glad to see you guys are doing all right after that landing in the channel. I'm Flight Lieutenant Jason McMurchy, the Spitfire pilot."

The bomber pilot was about Jason's height but much slimmer with a shock of curly blond hair on the top of his head.

He took his hand and pumped it firmly, glancing briefly at the country patch on Jason's shoulder. "Good to meet you. I'm Sergeant Keith Green, lately of Christchurch, New Zealand. I'd say that those of us who made it owe our skins to you Lieutenant."

"I think the way you kept that shattered piece of junk aloft as long as you did probably had more to do with it. You were doing some serious flying there mister."

The Sergeant shrugged as his face grew downcast. "A case of necessity being the mother of invention, I guess. Unfortunately, we still lost half my crew."

Jason put a reassuring hand on the man's shoulder. "From what I could see, your tail-gunner was gone already, and your mid-upper guy bought it during the first pass from that second *Fw*190. I'm going to confirm that he nailed that first *FW* in my report."

He continued. "There are not many pilots who would have been able to put what was left of your Halifax into the drink as well as you did. There really wasn't much more you could have done."

"Thanks, but it's sure not going to make writing those letters much easier."

Olivia had been taking the conversation in with a growing sense of both interest and awe, when the doctor arrived. "I'm afraid I'll have to move you along Lieutenant. I must run a few tests on these chaps. Will you see him out nurse?"

Olivia waited at the door as Jason wished the men good luck.

As he turned to exit the room, the New Zealander called to him. "By the way Lieutenant, I just transferred over from Lancasters in 419 Squadron two weeks ago. There is a tail-gunner in another kite there who has a wolf's head exactly like the one on your Spit, painted onto the base of his turret. Anyone you know?"

Jason scratched his head. "There is only one person I can think of, but he's training air gunners in Manitoba. I'm definitely going to look into it though. Thanks Sergeant."

He stepped into the hall, and once again into the intoxicating presence of Nurse Alexander.

As they neared the lobby, Jason threw caution to the winds. "Olivia, I see two gigantic Canadian beef steaks and a bottle or two of Claret in our future if you'll come out with me this Saturday evening. I can actually be quite civilized when I'm well-fed and watered. In addition to lisping a Shakespearian soliloquy or two, I might also regale you with tales of thrilling wilderness adventure amidst the fearsome and exotic creatures of the north woods – of which I am one".

She had slowed, and he was looking directly at her now. "How about it? You've got nothing to lose but that incredible waist-line of yours."

To her surprise, Olivia realized she was experiencing an involuntary physical response to the handsome Canadian pilot, and her face began to colour. There was something about the confident sound of his voice, and the slight hint of irony in his smile. As she looked up into his strong intelligent face, a warm flush passed through her.

Stopping, she placed her hand lightly upon his upper arm and coquettishly arched one of her eyebrows. "Lieutenant, if you'll bring those steaks and the Claret to my home this Saturday evening, you are cordially invited to join me, my sister, and her American pilot boyfriend, for dinner. He is apparently bringing steaks from America, and Burgundy, I think."

Jason looked into her large blue eyes and felt his heart pounding. Regardless, he smiled calmly. "Nurse Alexander, I do believe we have a date."

Bomber Base

Captain Brown had been a generous host. Nearly a full bottle of cognac had been consumed before Jason made his belated way back to the aerodrome at Duxford.

The Base Commander, Major Peabody, was a small, officious and moustachioed old-school officer who had shot down two observer planes as a pilot in the Great War. He was a stickler for protocol and had been impressed neither by Jason's obviously hung-over appearance, nor the loss of a highly specialized Mk XIV PR Spitfire.

He proceeded to expound vociferously. "Flight Lieutenant McMurchy, it is my belief that you intentionally deviated from your mission so that you could go swanning about in an egotistical attempt to run up your score of German aircraft kills. I am probably wasting my breath with you, but I cannot emphasize too strongly that Photo Reconnaissance, as the name implies, exists for a purpose, and that purpose does not include facilitating the personal ambitions of one Flight Lieutenant McMurchy!"

Jason's head was throbbing, and he was not in a mood to be diplomatic. After four years of defending Britain, he had had a belly-full of condescension from career officers. Before the commander could continue, he interjected. "I encountered two *Fw*190s attacking a damaged Halifax. I merely did my duty."

Barely attempting to conceal his irritation, he continued. "I'm sure you would have done the same thing if you had been in my position."

The Major drew himself up to his full height, leaning forward, but he still had to crick his neck uncomfortably to stare Jason full in the face. "Lieutenant, what I would do or not do in any situation is absolutely none of your concern. People with your lack of self-discipline are obviously more suited to less-important duties, and to that purpose I am transferring you back to 403 Squadron at Kenley. There, your lack of professionalism will undoubtedly be less noticeable while you reacquaint yourself with the Mk IXb Spitfire."

"That squadron is slated to be upgraded with new Mk XIVs and assigned to buzz-bomb interceptions, but until then you will be flying over the channel to mix it up with ground targets or anything you can find in the sky for daily rhubarbs. Surely, this will be an occupation where you might possibly be able to perform your duties without destroying any more of his majesty's aircraft – and if you do manage to do so, there is happily the very high probability that it will be in the process of blowing yourself up at the same time. Now, Flight Lieutenant McMurchy, you are dismissed!"

Jason responded with a deliberately sloppy salute, and locking eyes with the Major, whose face was now flushed with anger, very slowly drawled. "Yes sir."

He then intentionally performed a poorly executed about-face, and sauntered casually out of the Major's office.

The transfer paperwork was going to take over a week to process, so Jason took the opportunity to ride the train north to Middleton St. George, where 419 Moose Squadron was located. He was immediately impressed by the sight of the massive four-engine Lancaster bombers doing their warm up and testing runs before being 'bombed up' for that evening's run into Germany.

After inquiring at the base commander's hut, he made his way over to one of the giant aircraft, where he immediately recognized the wolf-head design painted on its rear-turret base. Also, with his back to him, was the familiar broad-shouldered form of an airman, checking the machine-gun breeches.

Jason cupped his hands to his mouth and raised his voice to a raspy falsetto. "Hey buddy, have you seen my canoe around here anywhere?"

The airman's head snapped around at the jibe, as a broad smile of recognition flashed across his face.

"Jason! You crazy bastard!" David shouted, as the two men stepped toward each other.

Stooping low, he clasped Jason around the waist with both arms and lifted him bodily off of the tarmac.

Jason gasped. "Whoa there, pardner! I ain't ready to lay in the *teepee* with you just yet, but I've got to say you sure are a sight for sore eyes! I thought you were in Manitoba teaching them how to shoot straight. How long have you been in 'Old Blighty'?"

David lowered Jason to the ground, stepped back, and pretended to throw a punch to his mid-section. "I've been here for about a month, but hey, more importantly, tonight's op has been cancelled, so let's head over to the mess where you can use some of that officer's pay to buy me a beer while we catch up."

Later, in the Sergeant's mess, Jason sat down across from David at a table situated near one of the quieter corners, where it was more suitable for conversation. With practiced bemusement, he handed him one of the steaming cups of brew he had poured at the urn. "I know the limeys like their beer warm, but this stuff is way too hot, and it smells an awful lot like coffee."

David shrugged. "Being an officer and all, you can probably get a beer in your mess, but for those of us in the less-exalted ranks, assigned to more humble accommodations, it is strictly *verboten*."

"Welcome to the military buddy, where the lower ranking scum are forced to learn humility, to make up for the lack of it in higher ranking scum. Maybe it's time for us to practice a little subversion." Jason suggested.

He leaned closer to his friend. "What are you up to this evening? I'm cooling my heels all this week waiting for my transfer to come through, and since your op has been scratched, why don't we hit a pub and down our fill of the local ale?"

"Due to an unfortunate incident last week, we are not allowed off-base, and that's effective for an indefinite period of time, until the Commanding Officer's sphincter relaxes enough to let us resume our recreational activities."

Jason glanced down at the barked knuckles of David's right hand and chuckled. "Would the aforementioned incident be referring to a donnybrook, and would the 'unfortunate' part be the condition of the other guy's jaw?"

David sighed. "It couldn't be helped. A rather large Scots Guardsman took exception to my ethnicity."

Jason conspiratorially raised a finger and slowly tapped the side of his own forehead. "I'm wondering if it's possible that he may have referenced a term used in the more rarefied levels of anthropological study for people of your highly regarded ilk, and called you a fuckin' Indian?"

David feigned an exaggerated wince, accompanied by a sharp intake of breath. "The man was clearly a confused individual. I informed him that no person in my exalted lineage has ever been near the subcontinent, much less fornicating in the vicinity. Furthermore, I patiently explained my surprise at how he had been mistaken, considering how obvious it was that a woman in his ancestry had apparently lain with one of those dusky-skinned buggers in Malabar. I then professed an interest in learning the Hindi language and suggested I would be willing to pay him to teach me a few expressions."

"Did the fellow take you up on your offer?" A convulsing Jason asked, while he unsuccessfully attempted to keep a straight face.

David shook his head. "The ingrate screamed some unintelligible Scottish words and began to swing his fists at my face. Before I knew it, I had forcefully raised the toe of my boot deep within the recesses of his kilt, and then we were rolling around on the floor."

"Hoot mon! I hope you didn't do too much damage to his bagpipe. Otherwise he may *nae ha'* any progeny to pass down this new-found wisdom to!" Jason chortled.

"I'm sure his instrument will still be capable of making its wretched music, albeit at a slightly higher pitch, but as you know, some people are slow learners. Considering the conviction of his obviously uninformed opinions, it's possible that when he regained consciousness he might have imagined that it was all a dream, and my efforts to inform him will have been wasted."

"Ah yes. There are always some who cannot, or will not, learn, but I'm sure that the nobility of your gesture will have registered with many of the onlookers. I would wager that recently there have been fewer people expressing confusion about your bloodline."

David shrugged unconvincingly. "Imagine that, huh?"

Jason chuckled. "So, fill me in. When did you get here, and how did you get out of Manitoba?"

"Well, as you know, when I finished my electrician's apprenticeship, I joined the Commonwealth Air Training Program, but they're usually only making pilots out of university students or guys like you who already have a license. I must have inherited the old man's eyesight, because when I did the aerial gunnery course, I got one of the highest scores ever recorded."

"They decided to make me an instructor, which I didn't mind doing for a while, but after a year of flying around in the back of an Anson teaching other guys how to operate the turret and shoot down Germans, I really felt I should be over here firing at real airplanes."

"In retrospect, I must have been nuts. I told my C.O. that if they didn't transfer me over here, I was going to develop a serious long-term case of insubordination and spend the rest of the war in the stockade. He finally relented, and I got here about a month ago."

He pursed his lips a moment before continuing. "It turns out that at this end, the odds are stacked pretty high against you. The average lifespan of aircrew here is only ten missions, but you are required to complete thirty ops to finish your tour. I'm just trying to survive each trip these days. It probably would have been better to have just kept my mouth shut and stayed in Manitoba."

"Yeah, but think of all the interesting people you would *nae ha'* met if you hadn't come?"

Jason was making light of the situation, but only to disguise the anxiety he was experiencing as realized just how long the odds were that his friend was going to survive this war.

"You're right." David admitted. "Bestowing enlightenment on boneheaded types actually makes it all seem worth-while doesn't it?"

The slight edge of sarcasm that had crept into his voice suddenly disappeared. "Bye the way, my mom writes to me once in a while. In the last letter, she said your mother told her that you're a multiple ace now. Have you run the score up any higher in the last couple of months?"

"Not really. I've been doing photo reconnaissance until recently. I bagged an *Fw*190 last week, but right after that I got shot down by one of our coastal defence antiaircraft batteries. This seemed to put a burr in my C.O.'s britches, so I've been transferred. Next week, I'll be back to doing rhubarbs across the channel, so you never know. Judging from the decline in quality displayed by some of the German pilots, it's possible I could bag a few more before this show is over. On the other hand, they have still got some guys with ten times my score, and I sure as hell don't want one of them getting on my tail."

David nodded his head in agreement. "I guess from what your mom said, she still gets the odd letter from her sister in Germany. Apparently, Peter went on a real tear over on the Eastern front. Over fifty kills. I know he probably doesn't fly at night, but all the same, I hope I never run into that guy in the air."

"Me too. I'm pretty confident in my flying skills, but I'm fairly sure that neither one of us would realize we were attacking each other until one of us had been shot down, and I frankly don't know how I would react if I was mixing it up with him. I know he's flying for the *Luftwaffe* and may have shot some of our boys down, but he is my cousin and we know he was no Nazi."

"I know what you mean, but people change, and even though I can imagine him thinking he is just defending his home when he gets a kill, he is also defending Hitler. Sometimes I wonder how he deals with that fact."

David paused a moment, then asked. "Have you heard anything recently about Jack?"

"Not much – mostly second-hand through my mother. I got a letter from him about two months ago, full of photos. Some were of him and the crew of a Sherman tank he's commanding in Italy. They're a really tough-looking bunch. The rest were of battle damage to his tank, and some were of burnt-out German tanks they had destroyed in combat. It looks like they have been having one hell of a fight."

David grimaced. "From what I'm reading in the newspapers, it's not going to get easier any time soon. You'd think with Mussolini gone and the Italian surrender, the Germans would have given Italy up as a lost cause. Apparently however, they have decided to use crack troops and a heavily fortified set of defensive lines across the north of the country to prevent us breaking out into the Po Valley, and through what old Churchill calls 'the soft underbelly of Europe'".

Jason was pensive for a moment. "Well you can't really blame them for wanting to cover their arses though, eh? The Russians are giving them all they can handle on the eastern front, so the prospect of guys like Jack and a tank army tearing through from the south must be giving them nightmares."

"Good point." David chuckled. "Especially if Jack ever gets to Germany and takes his shirt off. The whole female half of the master race would surrender *en masse*. How many of those Italian beauties do you suppose he has seduced by now?"

Jason grinned back at David. "I'm betting that you and I would probably run out of fingers and toes if we counted them. When it comes to women, there never seemed to be enough of Jack to go around."

David shook his head. "No, no. I think it's just the opposite of that. Jack's got more than most to go around, and good news travels fast among the fairer sex."

Jason was still grinning. "There's nothing fair about sex when one guy seems to get so much more of it than the rest of us!"

They both laughed, and then Jason had an idea. "Listen. Why don't I head into town and buy some beer? I could smuggle it into your barracks and then we can spend the evening doing some serious catching up. I'm not expected back at my base tonight, and I'm sure your room-mate wouldn't complain if we shared a few with him. The way things go, this might be the last time we get together for a long time."

David nodded in agreement. "That is the best idea that I've heard in a good while. I've got some spare coin of the realm in my pocket here, so take it and pick up some bread and cheese while you are at it. By the time you get back, I'll have had the butler lay out our finest china and silverware. Will you be requiring a dessert fork?"

"No. I'm mostly a bare fingers man myself. About the only thing I'll require, is a bottle opener."

Jason borrowed a bicycle and David's rucksack before pedaling the short distance into town. He had never liked his beer warm as the British preferred to drink it, so he had to struggle mightily not to laugh when the clerk apologized because the last dozen-and-a-half bottles he possessed had been stored in the cellar and might be a tad cold for immediate consumption.

The grocer he met next was a more taciturn fellow, but he warmed up to Jason when he saw the pilot's wings on the chest of his tunic. He eventually allowed that his youngest son, a navigator, had gone missing two months earlier when his Short Stirling bomber had been lost over Germany. Still obviously grieving, the mourning father seemed to cheer up a bit when Jason replied to his query as to how many of the 'German bastards' he had shot down, and he noticed that the man didn't charge him extra for the wedge of cheese, which was significantly larger than the 250 grams he had requested.

When Jason got back to David's room, he was introduced to a pimply-faced nineteen year old tail-gunner from Saskatoon.

The young man stretched out a long gangly arm with an enormous hand on the end of it. "Earl Cooper. I'm glad to make your acquaintance. I just got here from Manitoba last week, and you can imagine how shocked I was to find myself bunking with my old instructor. It's damned lucky though, because he's been bringing me up to speed before I go on my first op."

Jason pried the tops off of three bottles and handed one to each of the others before taking a long draught from his own. "Well, I reckon you'll get all the speed you want once your *Lanc* is airborne, but more importantly, did this guy teach you how to shoot?"

Earl nodded. "He sure did. The Sergeant here is the deadliest shot I've ever seen, and I've always been pretty good with a gun myself."

Jason saw David nod his own head in agreement. "The kid has got an eye. Some crew is going to be really glad they have Earl watching out for their rear ends."

Their bottles clinked as they knocked them together, and David offered up a toast. "Here's to rear ends. Speaking of which, my Spitfire flying friend, have you had any of those English skirts in your sights recently?"

Jason then described his encounter with the *Fw*190s attacking a damaged Halifax over the channel, and subsequently being shot down by a British anti-aircraft gunner who had mistaken him for a *Bf*109.

They laughed when he told them that the young man's older sister was a nurse, who he was now over the moon for. When he described her appearance, the two tail-gunners nodded their heads and smiled knowingly at each other. With enthusiasm, they approved of his plan to pay her a visit when she was off-duty in a couple of days.

Mood Music

Jason eased himself into the back seat of the cab and gave his driver the Alexander address in Chatham. He removed his cap and passed a hand back through his tangled hair, expelling a sigh of relief while the hectic events of the past week raced through his mind.

He'd bagged a *Fw*190, got shot down, transferred to a new squadron, and reunited with his best friend David.

Yet, despite all this, his thoughts were constantly being drawn back to Olivia. She intruded so persistently into his consciousness that he found himself in an almost constant state of arousal.

His daydreams were interrupted when the taxi pulled to a halt by the curb. The driver turned around and caught his eye. "This is it guv."

He pointed to a large two-story Georgian style house finished in the local stone. At each end of the slate-covered roof, chimneys poked their soot-stained tops into the late afternoon sky. Two large broadleaf trees, taller yet than the chimneys, stood sentry in the front yard, where their wide-spread limbs concealed most of the second floor from view.

The building was one of many similar houses along this tree-lined street. It conveyed a sense of the familiar – that pre-war aura of security and upper-middle-class comfort - which on this day at least, continued to permeate the neighbourhood. There was no evidence of any bomb having fallen here. In actuality, however, this was due largely to luck, as the town lay on a route often used by the *Luftwaffe* during their regular bombing runs, which were now almost always at night.

Jason had intimate knowledge of the skies directly above, for they had been filled with contrails - some undoubtedly his own - in the summer and fall of 1940, as British aircraft duelled daily with German fighters and bombers overhead.

Like homes all over Britain, since the declaration of war, there had been blackout curtains in every window, and no bulbs in any of the outdoor lighting fixtures. So far, this had been a lucky street, but everyone here would know that by accident or design, on any given night, their number could be up.

Jason reached into his pocket. "How much do I owe you?"

"Half a quid should do it guv." The driver was a small man with evidence of old burns on his left hand and the same side of his neck. In his early fifties, he was of an age that made it quite possible that this had happened in the Great War.

His white collar was soiled and in obvious need of an ironing and starch. Years of vitamin deficiency had left a sallow pallor on the man's face. The recent defeat of Germany's submarine wolf-packs in the North Atlantic had led to a gradual increase in the accessibility to fresh fruit as more and larger convoys began to arrive in British ports, but very little of it seemed to have got to him yet.

Feeling a touch guilty about the two bottles of claret and the beefsteaks in the satchel beside him, Jason passed the driver a one-pound note. "Keep the change, and fuck the *Führer*, eh."

"Thanks guv."

He tipped his hat and caught Jason's eye. "And next time you see one of them Messies up there, you put some lead into him for me, will you guv? Tell him Ypers 'Enry wishes him a fond *auf wiedersehen*."

Jason grabbed his bag and stepped out of the cab. Then, before closing the door, he poked his head back inside. "I'll certainly do my best to express your kind farewells next time I'm on *Fritzy's* arse Henry."

"Appreciate it guv. Best of luck to you."

The cabbie was grinning as he depressed the clutch, shifted the old taxi into gear, and gunned the engine to pull away.

He ascended the steps and pressed the front door-bell. It vibrated lightly beneath his finger, and presently he heard footsteps approach from within.

The door opened and Jason felt his heart race, as he caught sight of Olivia in her high-heeled pumps and a shimmering powder-blue silk dress. It was slightly padded at the shoulders and gathered above the hips to accentuate her slim waist. Her hair was no longer pinned up, and it now fell to below her shoulders where it curled under, Vera Lynn style.

Olivia gasped. "My goodness, there is a Canadian at my door, and he appears to be carrying a rucksack full of swag. Should I call the police?"

Jason feigned confusion. "Swag you say? I have so much trouble trying to understand British mispronunciation of the English language. Surely you mean swig? The plural form actually. A lot of them - and not looted mind you, but purchased from the vintners of Bordeaux and cowboys of Alberta with hard-earned cash money."

His hand moved instinctively toward her hip to draw her nearer, but she stepped back, a teasing pout on her lips. "I daresay you don't think me the type of woman whose favours can be purchased so cheaply?"

He attempted his best impression of an upper-class English accent. "I daresay, there is nothing in this bag that came cheaply, and I double daresay that I shall attempt to seek your favours, whatever the cost."

She crooked a finger to her lip and cooed. "Then you must surely enter to ply your gifts...and also regale us with exciting tales of aerial adventure my dear Flight Lieutenant."

Olivia took him by the arm, and Jason felt the heat rising in him with the brush of her body against his elbow.

She pointed through a double doorway. "Let us retire to the parlour, were I can introduce you to my sister and a smitten young American who shares some of your peculiar interests."

He smiled. "Do I strike you as someone who is interested in something peculiar?"

"Well, I don't know." She replied. "I suppose we would first have to define our meaning of peculiar. I for one would think it peculiar to fly four hundred miles per hour, high in the air, firing bullets into other airplanes that are trying to do the same thing to me."

Jason shrugged. "Why, I've never considered that peculiar. I thought everybody did it. Besides, if you can keep a secret, there is something else, or perhaps I should say, *someone* else that I am even more interested in."

She smiled at him again as they entered the parlour. "Yes, my suspicions were right all along, because you really do seem to have a lot in common with this particular gentleman, Major Charles Dentine of the United States Army Air Force, who seems quite similarly interested in my sister Mildred."

Major Charles Dentine was about an inch shorter than Jason, with light brown hair, green eyes, and a Clark Gable style, pencil moustache. Like many fighter pilots, he was of a wiry build, and was at least twenty pounds lighter than Jason.

He was wearing his brown pilot's uniform and winked at Jason as he thrust out his hand. "Y'all kin call me Charlie. 353rd Fighter Squadron out of Boxted Airdrome. I'm sho' nuff glad to make your acquaintance Loo-tenant."

Jason gripped his hand firmly and was about to reply when he was interrupted by Mildred, who had just walked into the room. "Oh Charlie! Anyone would think you were one of those absolutely dreadful hillbillies, the way you speak sometimes."

She turned to Jason. "Don't be fooled for a moment by this scoundrel Lieutenant McMurchy. Major Dentine is a university graduate and I'm certain he only speaks that way because he knows it annoys me. I'm Mildred, and I'm very pleased to meet you."

Mildred was every bit the beauty that her sister was. She shared the same elegant figure but her hair was a deep shade of red, and she possessed a pair of startling pale blue eyes.

Jason smiled at Charlie. "Well it's a pleasure to meet you too pardner. Feel free to call me Jay or anything you like for that matter. Just don't call me late to the chuck-wagon. These days between meals, I'm flying out of Kenley."

He released Charlie's hand, and took Mildred's out-thrust fingers. "I reckon it's a real pleasure to be meetin' you too ma'am."

Mildred wrinkled her nose and turned to Olivia. "My God, where ever did you find this cowboy? Are you sure he didn't ride in here on a horse? You'd better not imagine for a moment Lieutenant McMurchy that we will tolerate you riding your mighty steed around in our home."

Then she giggled. "It would be unseemly."

Before Jason could respond, Charlie interrupted. "Speakin' of beasts, I brought a couple of U.S. number one t-bones with me, so why don't we start marinating them a while before cookin' 'em up? Meanwhile, I'll pull the cork out of one of these bottles."

Jason reached into his rucksack and pulled out his package. "I'm right with you there, pardner. I just happened to bring a couple of Canadian grade 'A' beefsteaks myself. I tried to get moose meat, but for some strange reason they were all out."

At this point Mildred was gnawing her lower lip while smiling adoringly at Charlie. Olivia took the package from Jason. "Mildred and I will prepare this along with Charlie's offering and some vegetables in the kitchen, while you two gentlemen get to know each other. There are wine glasses on the table in the dining room."

Jason removed the two bottles from his bag and placed them on the table while Charlie screwed the cork from one of his own. "I know you are supposed to let his stuff breathe for a while, but how about you and I have a sample anyway just to get started?"

"I'm with you pardner." Jason replied. "Start pouring."

Charlie half-filled two glasses, passed one to Jason, and then he raised his own in a toast. "God bless the French. They may not be very good at fighting Germans, but they sure know what to do with a bunch of grapes."

"Amen." Jason smiled, and they both took a long draught from their glasses.

He then added. "Speaking of the French, I thought it was '*de rigueur*' to sip this stuff instead of gulp it."

"Maybe for them, but after a few sorties, I like to get a buzz started early. I'll go slow and stick the little finger out after the ladies return to the room." Charlie jibed.

167

Jason stuck his little finger out and raised his empty glass. "Just for practice mind you, but I'm about ready for a refill *mon ami*."

Charlie grinned and refilled both of their glasses. They took a seat next to each other in a pair of comfortable armchairs, and stretched their legs out. The American took a casual glance around the room. "Nice digs, huh?"

Jason's eyes also did a circuit of their surroundings. The room was tastefully decorated with patterned wallpaper, landscape paintings, some delicate china, crystal figurines, and several flower-filled bowls or vases. Much of the trim and furniture consisted of polished walnut. "A little classier than I'm used to. Mr. Alexander must do okay in whatever line of work he's in. I gather this isn't your first visit, so have you ever met the parents?"

"Yeah, this is about my fourth time here, but I only met their parents on the first visit. The mother is a beauty just like the girls. The old man seemed a bit aloof. He's some kind of lawyer. I can never get this Barrister – Solicitor thing straight. He doesn't say much about the war. Still seems a bit sensitive about losing his son in France."

"Olivia seems a bit that way too. I think for now I'll just avoid the subject and let her bring it up if she wants to." Jason observed.

Charlie nodded in agreement. "That would probably be a good idea. The first time I asked Mildred about it, the poor kid bawled her eyes out for the next hour. He must have been a hell of a guy, because they sure miss him."

He paused. "So, what are you flying?"

"Mostly Spits." Jason replied. "I was flying a Mark IX before they transferred me to photo-recon. There, I was flying the Mark XIV. That's a real improvement in speed. I'm cycling back to a combat squadron the day after tomorrow, so I'll be back in a Mark IX, which is one hell of a fighter. How about yourself?"

"I started out a year and a half ago in P-47s. They are a big powerful brute of an airplane. *Krauts* can put a ton of lead into one and they still keep going. I'm flying a P-51D Mustang now. We call it a Cadillac of the sky, and man that is an airplane I love."

He continued. "Your Spit just might be a little prettier, but I think we're both running the same Merlin up front - except mine's a Packard instead of a Rolls Royce like yours. You can't believe the range on that airplane. The thing can fly all the way to Berlin and back. I really love that bubble canopy too. My first P-51 was a 'C' variant with the faired-back fuselage. P-47 was the same – a Razorback. Once I got into a 'D' with the bubble I could see a whole lot more of the world around me."

Charlie's voice had lost its drawl.

The girls rejoined them and were sitting at each end of an adjoining sofa nearest to their particular guest, holding their empty stemware. Charlie filled Mildred's glass, and then handed the bottle over to Jason who did likewise for Olivia.

She then raised her glass and rhymed a toast. "To our two noble knights of the air…and the gifts they bear!"

Jason responded. "To our two lovely hostesses and may the cattle herds of North America not have sacrificed their finest in vain."

They tapped each-others glasses together and drank to their toast. Jason, noticing the first bottle was empty, reached for one that he had brought, and twisted the corkscrew into it. Once he had extracted the cork, he refilled Charlie's empty glass, and then his own. In a few minutes, he did the same for each of the Alexander sisters.

Mildred had looped her hand under Charlie's arm. "Lieutenant McMurchy, did you know that Charlie is an ace?"

She shifted her gaze up to Charlie's beaming face. "How many of those nasty Germans have you shot down now darling?"

The wine and Mildred's affections were starting to get to him, and Charlie's face was flushed as he smiled down at her adoringly. "Well sweetheart, I've finished off nine of them, confirmed. One more and I'll be what they call a double ace."

Charlie turned to Jason, who had been following the conversation while taking in Olivia's profile, and imagining what it would be like to kiss that beautiful mouth. "How about you Jay? Have you managed to bag any *krauts*?"

Jason tore his gaze reluctantly from Olivia and answered casually. "Sure".

Charlie was looking at him expectantly. "Well, how many?"

All eyes were upon him now, and Jay responded slyly. "I've bagged a few."

Graciously, Charlie tried to coax a number out of him. "Don't worry, we won't think any lesser of you if you haven't made ace yet. C'mon. How many exactly?"

Jason looked down, trying to prolong the suspense, and then looked up teasingly at Olivia. "Well, actually there have been a few that I claimed that were not confirmed, so I can't really count them."

Olivia continued to press him. "Come on now, don't be shy. Tell us."

Jason cleared his throat. "Well, uh, I'm credited with twenty-two."

A temporary silence fell over the room, and then Charlie whistled. "Jeezuz Christ man. Twenty-two! Damn! You've been holding out on us boy! Twenty-two! Pass your glass over here Jay."

Addressing the ladies, he enthusiastically proclaimed. "I'm going to buy this man another drink!"

Charlie filled his and Jason's glass, after which, they both took another long sip. "I had to bail out of a P-47 once. Have you ever been bounced?"

Jason was smiling at Olivia now. "I was nearly shot down a couple of times back in 1940 when I was still learning the ropes, but then I just barely managed to land the crates both times. However, it did actually occur once, quite recently - on the same day I met Olivia. Right after I'd bagged a *Fw*190D."

Charlie was leaning forward now. "What happened? Did his wingman get you?"

"Well, no he didn't. I actually happened to get shot down by Olivia and Mildred's little brother."

The sisters were both staring at him with their mouths open.

Olivia spoke first. "What are you saying? I thought something was up with the way Bobby was behaving that day. Tell us, what was going on?"

"Just a bit of a mix up really. I was coming out of the sun from the same direction that a Messerschmitt had recently flown. He mistook me for another one and let me have it with his anti-aircraft gun. It was an easy mistake to make given the circumstances."

Charlie was laughing. "What? Bobby shot you down? Hah! That's what I call unlucky!"

"Well, truth be told, it was just the opposite. I met an Artillery Sergeant with an incredible supply of excellent cognac, and of course I had the good fortune to meet one of the two most beautiful women in England afterward." Jason was eyeing Olivia wolfishly.

Now, Mildred cooed. "He's very smooth, isn't he?"

Charlie was still grinning. "Jay. Are you sure you didn't fly your airplane into that shell deliberately?"

"I'll leave you all to speculate on that one." He replied archly, while managing to catch Olivia's eyes again.

Olivia's eyes narrowed coolly. "At the speed anti-aircraft shells travel, I suspect that kind of feat might be beyond even our Flight Lieutenant McMurchy's apparently considerable flying skills. Tell me Lieutenant, are you what we might refer to as a masher?"

Jason shrugged while still maintaining eye contact. "Of the worst sort, I'm afraid."

Then he changed the subject deftly. "Is that your stomach rumbling Charlie, or do the Alexander sisters have a bull terrier tied up behind your chair?"

Charlie drained the last drops from his glass. "Guilty. I tell you, I'm so hungry I could just about eat a Clydesdale. Are you hungry yet Jay?"

Jason nodded. "That bacon and eggs I had for breakfast have faded into history. I'm not quite ready for a trip to the glue factory with you Major, but I swear I can hear one of those steaks in the kitchen calling my name. How about it, ladies? Should I work my magic on the stove, or shall I pull the cork out of another bottle?"

Olivia formed her full red lips into a sultry pout that was driving Jay crazy. "Don't worry Lieutenant. The Alexander sisters are capable of taking a hint – even those as subtle as yours. So why don't you and the Major just relax for a few minutes while we prepare your tribute. Come Mildred. Let us arrange a feast suitable for these two brave warriors and leave them a while to regale each other with their heroic exploits."

Mildred tore her adoring eyes off of Charlie. "Why yes. They must be absolutely famished after a hard day of slaying the beastly Hun."

With their meal finished, Jason and Charlie retired once more to the parlour, while the Alexander sisters cleaned up. When the ladies rejoined them, they finished the last half bottle of wine, and shortly afterwards Jason was surprised to discover that Charlie and Mildred had discretely disappeared into another room, somewhere beyond the darkened hallway.

On the sofa, Olivia snuggled up to Jason and he felt her soft blond hair caress his neck as he spoke. "Miss Alexander, I think I'm now going to do something I have wanted to do from the first moment I saw you."

He felt her lips part as he pressed his upon them. A soft moan escaped her throat as he slid his tongue between her teeth, and deeper into her mouth. His other hand rose instinctively to clasp her breast as they drew each other closer, and in the heat of their passion she tightened her embrace. Her trembling hand slid slowly up the inside of his thigh and stopped there briefly. Then wordlessly, she rose to grasp him by the tie, and gently tugged him to his feet. She drew him closer to kiss him fully on the lips, then, still holding his tie, began to pull him toward the dark hallway.

They passed silently through the corridor and into her bedroom, where in the darkness she kissed him again, and began to undue the buttons of his tunic. Simultaneously, Jason reached behind her to release the clasp of her brassier, and next pulled at the shoulders of her gown until it slipped softly to her waist. She pulled on the sleeves to help remove his shirt, and as their lips came hungrily together once more, he pulled Olivia close to feel her full breasts pressing hard against his chest.

Stepping out of the remaining clothing now gathered about their feet, Jason reached down behind her thighs and effortlessly lifted her above his waist. Thrilling to the strength in his hard muscles, Olivia clasped her arms behind Jason's neck and moaned, while thrusting her tongue deeply into his mouth as he took her.

Easily bearing her weight, Jason turned and lowered her gently upon the bed. Their panting bodies thrust and moiled upon the sheets as they exchanged the energies of their turgid passions – giving physical expression to an urgent need to satiate emotions engendered by the heightened anxieties of a precarious existence. Biological in origin, the intensely human will to survive - to continue - had brought them together in a shared desire that all young adults must necessarily feel in wartime.

Later, as they lay beside each other, satiated, Jason pulled her closer to feel her heat, and kissed her once again.

As he drew back to take in the full vision of her flushed beauty, she smiled and sighed. "Lieutenant McMurchy, I do feel as if I have just been... I think the medical term for it is... ravaged."

Jason couldn't prevent a grin of satisfaction from spreading across his face. "I assure you Miss Alexander that I'm just a simple country boy who was overcome by alcohol and lust. You will not have your way so easily with me again."

She smiled, but there was a nervous moment of hesitation in her voice. "Jason, honestly, I want to make love to you forever, but please don't break my heart. I've experienced that once already when my brother died at Dieppe. If I fall in love with you, I think it's possible that I might be able to get over your leaving, but if you get killed, I'm certain it would finish me."

Jason recalled the day of constant sorties he'd flown over the beaches of Dieppe on that disastrous day, including the sight of flaming tanks and scores of dead bodies lying on the shale in horrific testimony to the carnage unfolding below.

He realized then that this was not the time to tell her of his involvement in the battle, as it would undoubtedly generate questions or resurrect additional painful memories, perhaps ending these moments of intimacy they were now sharing.

Instead, he assured her. "You don't have to worry about me leaving. I don't think that I've ever met a woman more interesting than you. Truthfully, I can also say that I'm a damned good flyer, and as far as I'm concerned there isn't any German pilot out there who can stop me from coming back to you."

Olivia looked into his eyes and saw the certainty there. Then sensing his passion rising once more, she drew him closer and whispered huskily into his ear. "I'll hold you to that Lieutenant. Now make love to me."

Italy

As part of Operation Timber Wolf in November 1943, the 5th Canadian Armoured Division replaced the British 7th Armoured Division, and took possession of the Sherman tanks that they had used to help defeat the German *Afrika* Corps.

The tanks had arrived in Italy full of dust and sand. Before cleaning out the one that had been assigned to him and his crew, Jack did a thorough inspection of the vehicle. It was an M4A4 model, so was quite distinct from most of the Sherman tanks that had been manufactured in Canada and the United States. In 1942, there had been a shortage of the air-cooled radial engines used to power the tank, and a stopgap solution had been developed with the creation of the Chrysler multibank engine. This involved installing five of their six-cylinder, in-line, liquid-cooled engines around a common crankcase. Since this resulted in a power-plant that was longer than the radial engine, the chassis and hull of the tank had been extended by 11 inches, with a corresponding larger spacing between the bogey-wheel assemblies in the suspension, which also required the provision of a longer track.

After a six-month production run of the modified version at the Detroit Tank Arsenal, radial engines again became available in sufficient numbers, and the U.S. Army made a calculated decision. With the differing track lengths, and regular gasoline being used

174

by the multibank instead of the aviation fuel used by the radial, it was believed that the M4A4 would disrupt the uniformity of their supply and logistic efforts, so they opted to sell the entire run to the British Army.

The two identity patches on both the front and rear of Jack's tank had already been painted the solid dark red of the Canadian 5th Armoured Division, with the standard white maple leaf superimposed on the right-side square, and the numeral 52 on the left. When the tank had been cleaned out, the first thing he did was find some white paint to print *Beowulf* on the extra armour plates welded to both sides of the hull above and aft of the drive wheels. After that, he drew a version of the Lake Superior wolf-head emblem under the names. Next, he used some tape to trace the four inner and outer edges of a square on both sides of the turret and painted the lines yellow. The square outline symbolized 'B' Squadron. This, along with the other bold symbols for 'A', 'C', and 'D' squadrons, made visual identification of the various elements easier in combat.

The next few months passed quickly. At the end of January they were peripherally involved in the battle for Ortona, and five weeks later, a few miles north of Ortona, they participated in an indirect shoot at the village of Tollo. This was excellent practice with their new 75mm main gun and its lethal high-explosive round. It proved very effective in dislodging the enemy infantry that had dug in to cover a broader retreat to where the bulk of German forces intended to set up more effective defensive fortifications further north.

At the end of April they massed on the Cassino Front overlooking the Rapido River in preparation for the coming assault up the Liri Valley, and eventually, it was hoped, to Rome.

As they punched through the Gustav Line, and then the Hitler Line, the muddy terrain often forced them onto higher ground, where their silhouettes became easier prey for the deadly 88mm mobile anti-tank guns, augmented by strategically dug-in Panther tank-turret bunkers armed with their deadly long-barrelled, high velocity 75mm guns.

During this campaign, Jack lost two of the tanks in his troop - destroyed with all ten crew-members killed. The first had been obliterated on the Gustav line when an 88mm anti-tank gun hidden in a wood to their left, fired a round that tore through the turret of the rearmost tank, partially dislodging it. The ammunition stored inside had exploded, simultaneously killing not only the three men in the blasted turret, but also the driver and co-driver in the hull below. Fortunately, a pair of Typhoons circling above them had sighted the 88's muzzle flash, and immediately dove down to destroy it with a rocket attack before it could take out any of the remaining tanks in his troop.

Three weeks later, a hidden bunker with a Panther turret affixed to it put a 75mm armour-piercing round through the front of the tank on Jack's right. The driver and co-driver were both killed by ricocheting shards of metal as the shell travelled through the tank and into the engine compartment where it ignited the gasoline, immediately engulfing the tank in flames. Before the rest of the crew in the turret could escape, the ammunition began to cook off, and they were incinerated as the tank "brewed up". Jack had been talking to the crew commander, Sgt. Walsh, on the inter-tank radio when it had been hit. The other tank's radio continued to broadcast, and it took several hellish seconds before he was able to turn his own receiver off - *to silence the horrific screams of the men being burned alive in the other turret.*

In desperation, the three remaining tanks split their troop apart to attack the German bunker. Its turret had been installed in a concrete base at ground level and was also strategically stationed on a hillock at the edge of a small open valley. It presented an almost impossible target to kill from the front where the armour was thickest. Fortunately the Sherman's speed over undulating terrain made it a difficult target to hit. The German gunner missed twice while at least three 75mm armour-piercing rounds bounced off the Panther turret without any observable effect, as the tanks continued to flank it on both sides.

The long-barrelled 75mm had trained directly on Jack's tank as Mike's last armour-piercing round deflected harmlessly off of its frontal turret armour. Fortunately, his troop-mate who had flanked the German from the left, fired a round from close range a fraction of a second later through a narrow gap at its base. When it penetrated, shells stored inside exploded, and the violent eruption threw the turret fifty feet into the air before it fell back, landing upside down while billowing smoke. Meanwhile, flames roared from the top of the concrete bunker beside it, devouring the men inside while cooking off its large store of ammunition. As he thanked his lucky stars, it occurred to Jack that he was not feeling even a twinge of sympathy for the German soldiers being incinerated inside.

In late May, they punched through the Gustav Line, then breached the Adolph Hitler Line, subsequently crossing both the Melfa and Liri Rivers. In those vicious battles, they lost a grievous number of tanks and men as they fought their way through well-designed and stubbornly held German positions. Despite this great cost, the superbly trained Canadian tank and infantry regiments tenaciously continued to assail this intractable enemy's lethally effective defences until they had finally smashed them into submission.

By June they had advanced to within twenty-five miles of Rome and could anticipate liberating the city within a day or two, before they were suddenly ordered to halt. To their chagrin, this was done to allow the Anglophobic U.S. General Mark Clark to pull his troops out of the area where they were more usefully deployed opposite the German positions in the Gothic Line, to liberate the city himself.

Jack's thoroughly blooded regiment retired to the Voltura River area North of Naples to spend June and July refitting, and getting some rest. It was while they were there, licking their wounds, that they learned of the inter-forces boxing tournament being organized among the American, British, Canadian, and New Zealand regiments.

The tournament was held over a weekend, and the respective weight classes fought three-round bouts under Olympic rules.

Jack won his two preliminary bouts by knockout, and on late Sunday afternoon, he stepped into the ring to fight in the final bout for the heavyweight championship. His opponent was a black American who stood about two inches taller than Jack, with a correspondingly longer reach. He was fit and well-muscled, although Jack outweighed him by at least ten pounds.

The first round was mostly a feeling-out process. Surprisingly light on his feet for a heavyweight, the American possessed a sharp jab which he used effectively to prevent Jack from moving close inside. He could also slip punches well. Several times he merely tilted his head sideways to evade one of Jack's own well-timed jabs. Jack spent the round pursuing him and puzzling out his opponent's style, but he was unable to get him cornered.

Later in the round, he changed tactics and began throwing hard punches at the other man's arms whenever he got him close to the ropes. This successfully slowed the rate of the jabs his opponent threw, but he was only able to get inside once, where he used the opportunity to land two crunching right hooks to the ribs.

The second round followed the same general pattern, but Jack got inside three times to throw vicious hooks with both hands to his opponent's ribs and abdomen. By the end of the round, Jack could feel that when the American's jab landed to his face or head, it lacked a lot of the sting it had possessed earlier in the fight.

Round three began like the previous two, but early into it, Jack got the American in a corner, where he landed several hooks to the body. The fighter's arms dropped and Jack just missed with an uppercut to the head, which his opponent slipped before desperately tying him up in a clinch.

The referee moved them further into the centre of the ring before signalling them to begin again.

The American surprised him by stepping forward to land three quick jabs in stinging succession to Jack's face, and a vicious right hook that just grazed his chin. This caused him to stagger backward as a sudden swelling rose beneath his left eye.

However, as a result of Jack's bruising body attack earlier in the round, the American had slowed, and he failed to pursue Jack in time to prevent him from squaring up.

Jack dropped his left shoulder to fake throwing a right, and when he saw the expected right cross coming from the American, he shot his left arm underneath to block it. Then, rotating through the waist he put his entire upper body behind a powerful straight right hand which hit his opponent with devastating force square on the chin.

The American's eyes rolled up and his knees buckled as he crumpled to the canvas with a thud heard throughout the arena – knocked-out cold by the blow.

A huge cheer rose from the Canadian section, and after the count, the American's handlers helped their fighter up and got him to his stool in the corner. After Jack got his gloves off, he rose from his own stool and went over to wish the man well. By this time, his opponent was standing again and his head appeared to be slowly clearing.

Jack clapped him on the shoulder. "That was a good fight – you led me a merry chase for most of it. You really are hard guy to hit."

The American grinned, and then explained awkwardly. "Well, I got to say you sure hit me good that last one. I used to spar with Joe Louis a bit before the war, up until I turned pro, and I'd say you hit just as hard as he does, but you might have to work on your finishing game if you ever plan to go up against him. Except for when he was just extending the session, he used to put me away in under two rounds."

Jack laughed. "I think I'll leave mixing it up with the Brown Bomber to you my friend. A cousin used to call me Max Schmeling when I was a teenager, and we both know how Joe finally tuned him up!"

The banquet that evening was well-attended by the various contingents who were seated at tables in their own sections throughout the hall. Earlier, there had been some negotiating with several of the local farmers, and the fare was several cuts above the standard military issue that most of the men had become accustomed to. There was also a liberal amount of beer provided, and as the event proceeded many of the participants began to feel the effects.

Midway through the evening, the winners of each weight division were presented with their medal by a local Count and *Countessa*. He was a frail man in his seventies, but his wife, on the other hand, was a vivacious and petite young woman in her early thirties. Her soft black hair held a natural curl and fell in a thick tangle down her back to a point just above her shoulder blades. She possessed flawless olive skin, wide pronounced cheekbones, and the tip of her slim nose curved delicately upward above slightly flared nostrils – all atop full, sensuous lips.

While the count placed the ribbon around Jack's neck, her large brown eyes caught his seductively, while her fingers caressed the inside of his forearm, sliding lightly down to his hand, where unseen, she slipped a folded piece of paper into his palm.

For the remainder of the evening after the local dignitaries had departed, Jack nursed a single beer, and as the last inebriated celebrants exited the hall, he made his way to the service doors at the rear of the building, following the instructions in his note.

When he stepped out into the narrow unlit street, Jack saw the dark rounded silhouette of a *Bugatti* coupe facing him from the opposite side of the lane, and parked in the shadows. The driver's window rolled down, and a slender arm clad in mink emerged to motion him forward.

Jack opened the passenger door and slid into the soft leather seat beside her. The *Countessa* purred seductively in English adorned with a lilting Italian accent. "I thought you would never get here."

She leaned all the way over, placing one hand on his right shoulder, and passionately kissed him. A soft moan arose from deep in her throat, while with her other hand she frantically undid Jack's trousers. She gasped, as he placed both hands around her waist, lifted her effortlessly, and then forced her hips down upon him. Panting heavily, she groaned into his ear. "*Bastardo!*"

They climaxed, and she collapsed in exhaustion against his chest, catching her breath as he drank deeply from the fragrance of her hair, while even more intoxicating scents had arisen from a combination of perfume and the exertions of her perspiring body. She kissed him languorously again before sinuously sliding herself back into the driver's seat.

Smiling as her eyes travelled appreciatively over him once more, her voice grew low and husky. "Come, I want to take you to a place I think you will like. Don't worry. I will have you back to your base by morning."

Jack had hitched up his trousers but was not ready to call an end to the evening with this woman. *Not by a long shot,* he assured himself. "Lead the way *Countessa*. I'll go anywhere you like."

She depressed the clutch, smoothly shifted the car into gear, and then drove them carefully down the narrow lane, then finally exited onto a larger thoroughfare. This eventually took them out of the town, and soon they were traveling down a winding country road. It was overhung with the boughs of ancient trees and illuminated only by the long cone of their headlights. At last, they emerged into a small clearing on a bluff overlooking the sea.

A nearly full moon had risen in the clear sky, covering the mild swell below them in a glistening blanket of silver.

She switched off the lights and stopped the car's engine. "This is where I come to be alone. My husband has no time for me now. This war has consumed him, and I think he is very near his end - but I am not near mine."

She smiled. *"Capisce?"*

Slowly, she began to undo the buttons of his shirt, while he reached over to remove her coat and released the clasps on her blouse. Naked now, they made love twice more through the night, before a thin strip of light on the eastern horizon signalled that it was time for her to go home, and for Jack to return to base.

Over the ensuing two months they met at every available opportunity. He learned her name was Francesca, and that she possessed a lively and ironic sense of humour. She was at first surprised to learn that he understood and appreciated her ideas. In her social universe, it was incomprehensible that someone from Jack's relatively humble origins would possess that capacity.

Raised in a privileged and somewhat socially insulated environment, she had assumed at first that his robust physical attributes, and what she regarded as colonial origins, would necessarily include the predilection for an undeveloped intellectual curiosity. Being nine years older than he and having had the advantage of an excellent private education, it was natural to expect that she would be better read, and more broadly conscious than he. However, while this was generally true, she was also delighted to discover that he was in fact at least aware of the references and studied allegory that she often introduced to their conversations.

Francesca gradually began to open herself to him with confidences and ideas she had never imagined sharing when first sighting him as he stood like a gladiator in the boxing ring. Much of it was esoteric – art or philosophy – but she seemed most concerned with the causes of this war and how it would play out, and where people of her status would find themselves at the end of it all. She also seemed obsessed with the idea that communists would take everything away from her, and that the illiterate peasantry would destroy all the vestiges of civilization that families like hers had contributed to society for centuries.

For his part, Jack found that he couldn't help developing a genuine affection for her vivacious wit and personality. Things had grown to a point where he eagerly anticipated spending time with her – even beyond those hours of passionate love making.

In August, just before his regiment moved north to prepare for their upcoming assault on the Germans, they spent their last weekend together in one of her private villas. For the last time, they were lying naked upon her bed in the darkness, as a warm summer breeze wafted through the partially open window, gently ruffling the diaphanous white curtains. Ghostlike, they occasionally parted, to reveal the moonlit branches of leafy trees, towering like guardians beyond the protective stone wall which surrounded the villa's traditionally cobbled courtyard.

It was then that she had told him of her husband's prognosis. "His doctor says the cancer will take him before Christmas. He probably will not live to see the end of this war."

She then turned to regard his profile a moment. A note of concern had crept into her voice. "How about you Jack? Do you think you will be alive when this war is over?"

Tank crews often deflected their thoughts of a grizzly death by employing pithy and fatalistic witticisms. Alternatively, they feigned a lack of concern - to avoid pondering the uncomfortable issue. However, this was the first time he had ever been seriously asked the question by a woman, and in this secluded moment of intimacy it caused him to reflect a moment. "I don't ever get drunk before a battle the way some guys do because I always want to be sharp in combat, but when you get down to it, I must believe I'm going to make it, or else I'd be trying a lot harder to become oblivious to my fate."

He laughed at the analytical nature of his own response, and tried to lighten the subject with humour. "Besides, I know a soon-to-be rich widow who may need a husband and consort to squire her about the post-war social circuit, so I have no choice except to survive."

He was disconcerted, but not to the degree he may well have been in a younger, less experienced incarnation, when she laughed sharply. Not realizing that he had been half-joking, she spoke what was from her perspective, a harsh and fatalistic truth. "Hah! You really do not understand the ways of the world! It is ridiculous that you can even imagine moving in my social circles. They would consider you coarse and unrefined, and refer to you as my *'torre'* – my 'bull'. I would be ridiculed for my lack of taste, and low, base instincts. It would be far too humiliating for someone in my position to bear!"

At the last moment, when she caught his eyes, she realized something that had been in them only a few short seconds earlier, was now gone. She briefly experienced a stab of regret, but was unable to fathom it. Whereas a minute ago, to her pleasure, he had seemed to be looking into her soul, there had now occurred some new and undefinable withdrawal. As well, something intangible had also risen as a barrier to her again looking into his. In their moments of intimacy, away from her friends and family, she had loved what she saw there, and how it made her feel, but it was as if a curtain had now been drawn. Uncomprehending, she saw him shrug, while the hint of a knowing smile spread across his lips as he reassured her. "Francesca, I'm quite certain you don't have to worry about ever finding yourself in that position."

Next day, sitting in the turret of *Beowulf,* Jack reflected upon how Francesca's remarks might have cut him to the quick before the promise he had made to himself in the subterranean darkness of that mineshaft, years earlier. Women were for pleasure, not falling in love with, and accordingly, he should invest nothing more than his lust in them.

Yet grudgingly, he had to admit that with the *Countessa* he had made the mistake of allowing himself to entertain a fantasy in which these seductive meetings would continue indefinitely. When in fact, on the conscious level he had always known that she was from a world that he could never be a part of, nor when he thought seriously about it, did he want to be.

Instinctively, he understood there was no truth in her belief that she was somehow inherently superior, or deserving of her privileged status. With equal certainty, on a rational level, Jack also knew that he was not in that sense inferior, or otherwise deserving of his lower social ranking. It was an accident of birth that had put them in separate realms, which in her mind at least, could never be reconciled, because of arbitrary but strongly-perceived social barriers like money and status.

When he considered it, he believed these barriers were probably irrelevant in terms of how human beings should actually relate to each other, but in reality, they consigned most people to subordinate roles that justified the egos, power, and excessively self-serving behaviour of their masters. Near the top of society, self-interest was self-evident to those who consciously cherished their privilege, and there was no limit to the lengths that some people would go to either justify or maintain it.

Their physical attraction to each other had overwhelmed them both, but in the end, even though she had come to know Jack was more than the equal of most men from her own class, self-interest and pride had ultimately asserted itself.

Chagrined, bemused, and with his convictions now firmly reinforced, Jack shook his head and cursed at himself. "Smarten up, you stupid bastard!"

That week they moved up the east coast toward Tuscany, where they were tasked to spearhead the attack on *Feldmarchall* Albert Kesselring's crack *SS Panzer* Corps and *Fallschirmjäger* parachute regiments. There, the tenacious Germans had dug-in, with the resolute intention to hold their last major defensive barrier in Italy – the Gothic Line.

Fair Trade

With part of a week off duty, Jason had confirmed with Charlie that he too wouldn't be flying for a few days and arranged to take him up on the offer to check out his P-51. In turn he had agreed to reciprocate by letting Charlie take his Mk IX Spitfire for a spin. Their luck held when he contacted Olivia to find that she and Mildred too, were free for a few days.

South of Colchester, the American G.I. standing guard near the gate at Boxted Aerodrome eyed Jason suspiciously, and was just about to challenge his credentials when Charlie arrived.

"It's all right sergeant." Charlie said, as he reached his hand out and slapped Jason on the shoulder. "The Lieutenant is here for a little test drive. I'll keep an eye on him to make sure he doesn't steal any of the silverware."

As they exited the guard shack, he pointed to a Quonset hut at the edge of the runway. "Let's go over and meet some of the boys. I see you brought your helmet and goggles, so all we'll have to do is fix you up with a parachute and 'Mae West'. There should be some hot coffee brewing too."

The morning was cool and damp, with just a hint of mist rising off of the surrounding fields. Jason rubbed his hands together and grunted. "Amen to that Major. Is that your machine over there?"

He was pointing at a covered revetment where the sleek silver form of a Mustang with its canopy open, was crouching inside.

"Yes sir, that's my hoss Jay. I think you'll find she's a pretty hot ride. A bit temperamental on occasion, but I'll give you all the information you need pre-flight so you can put her through her paces."

They entered the dispersal hut and Jason was impressed by the relatively lavish appearance of the place. There were several sofas, shelves full of magazines, and a large refrigerator in one corner. On the other side of the room, there was also a large wood-burning stove with about eight or nine airmen standing around it. Several were smoking cigarettes, while some took turns pouring coffee into their metal cups from a large percolator on top of the stove.

All wore the standard American Army Air Force issue of crumpled brown officer caps and similarly coloured tunics, with tan shirts and trousers. This was in distinct contrast to Jason who was entirely in blue, except for his white shirt. A few of the Americans began to eye him curiously.

One of them noticed the Canada patch on his shoulders and came across the room, thrusting out his hand. "Lieutenant, I'm Joe Haadland, from Duluth, Minnesota. My cousin joined the Royal Canadian Air Force in 1940. He flew Wellingtons until he was lost over Denmark in forty-one."

Jason took his hand and pumped it. "Sorry to hear that, Captain. It took a lot of guts to fly a bomber anywhere over the continent back then."

"Yeah, well he never lacked for that, but I think my aunt and uncle would have preferred a live coward. All the same, I'm one of the guys who know how many Canucks were getting killed over here while Uncle Sam took nearly three years deciding he wanted to be a part of it. Can I get you a cup of coffee?"

"Thanks. I thought you would never ask. Why don't you join Charlie and I? He's going to give me some last-minute advice about flying a P-51."

For the next fifteen minutes Jason listened to the two Americans describe the prop, throttle, and manifold settings for takeoff, and the speeds for various stages of the landing approach.

One of the pilots by the stove had picked up snatches of the conversation, and in a deep southern drawl hollered sarcastically across the room. "Hey Charlie, after you teach him how to fly a Mustang do you think you can show your Canadian pal there how to shoot down some Germans?"

Charlie stopped in mid-sentence, and the room went suddenly quiet before he spoke. "I'll tell you something Hank. You might want to be taking some lessons from my friend here. Last time I looked you had six kills. Lieutenant McMurchy here has already bagged twenty-five."

The other pilots were now staring at Jason with renewed interest. A few of them crossed the room, and they began to pepper him with rapid-fire questions. What kind of fighter was he flying? What did he think was the best thing to do when a *Bf*109 dove away? How good was the *Fw*190D?

Jason attempted to answer as many of the young pilots' questions as he could, but after a few minutes he just grinned and explained. "Truth is, you keep your eyes peeled, and just do your best to make sure you bounce his tail before he bounces yours. Now if you guys will excuse me, the Major here has a bronc he wants me to bust."

Captain Hank Smith of Lubock, Texas, scratched his head, and with a puzzled expression, turned to one of the other pilots. "I thought them Canadians were supposed to have French accents."

The other pilot, from Seattle, Washington, just shook his own head. "Hank, you ain't really been around, have you?"

"Nope, but with twenty-five kills, I reckon that feller has."

Joe had gone into another room, and soon re-emerged holding a parachute and an inflatable yellow life vest. He handed Jason the parachute, and then accompanied him and Charlie out to where the P-51 was parked. Several of the other pilots stepped just outside the door to watch.

As they approached the fighter, Jason slipped the Mae West over his uniform and Charlie helped him into his parachute. They did a circuit around the plane to familiarize Jason with the airframe, and to point out any peculiarities.

Jason stopped a moment to gaze at the radiator air-intake located below the fuselage under the main wing.

Charlie saw him examining the large mouth-shaped opening. "Yeah, I know it's a strange place to have the thing, but it seems to work pretty well down there".

Jason next walked over to the wingtip and looked down its length toward the cockpit. "So, this is the laminar flow wing that everyone refers to when they talk about the P-51. What is the big deal?"

Charlie pointed to the bulged top portion of the wing. "You'll notice that the thickest part of the wing is further back than on a normal wing. I don't think it alters the chord length or aspect ratio, but it apparently reduces drag and moves turbulence to a point further back along the airfoil. Since all the Mustangs I've ever flown have had the laminar flow wing I can't really confirm that it increases speed, but I think you'll find it improves the roll rate."

He pointed to the engine. "As you know, the Packard Merlin V-1650-7 is a virtual replica of the Rolls Royce Merlin 60 series you have in your Mk IX Spitfire, so you've got lots of power. Just be sure to ease the throttle back a bit on this one right after you start it up though, because if you don't they will sometimes do a ground loop, and you know how much aircraft mechanics hate changing propeller blades."

Jason had cocked an eyebrow. "I can't say I've actually ever had one of those in my Spit. Is that the voice of experience speaking?"

Charlie cleared his throat. "Uh, maybe, but the only thing I can say is that if it happens, you'll be wishing you'd brought a second pair of underpants."

Jason winked. "Never wear 'em myself. Just get in the way when I'm in a hurry."

"Well, you just make sure to bring my girl home safe and sound with her virtue intact. She can bite awful bad if you don't treat her right."

"Don't worry Charlie. I'll treat her like the lady she undoubtedly is."

"Yeah? I was afraid of that."

The two Americans helped Jason onto the wing, where he marvelled at the relatively spacious confines of the cockpit. They assisted him again as he pushed the parachute hanging beneath his buttocks into the scoop formed by the metal bucket-seat, then adjusted his shoulder harness.

Charlie and Joe stood on both sides of the cockpit while pointing out the various instruments and controls as Jason slid his feet into a comfortable position on the rudder pedals. They next talked him through the start-up procedures, and as the engine roared to life, reminded him once more to actuate the rudder when the tail first lifts, to counter the torque which normally pulls the nose to the left. After that, to completely open the throttle and maintain full rudder until lifting off at about 150 miles per hour.

Jason found that the P-51, like his Mk IX, also featured a long snout containing its Merlin engine. It protruded upward in front of the cockpit, causing the Mustang to share his Spitfire's poor forward visibility while on the ground. This also produced the same general handling requirements, causing him to utilize a weaving technique similar to the one he normally used to steer his own aircraft before takeoff. However, this plane's wider landing gear gave it a much greater feeling of stability.

The takeoff went smoothly. As he began his climb, he backed off the manifold pressure and adjusted his prop pitch, while gradually continuing to increase throttle through his ascent until it was at last fully open. When he passed through 18,000 feet, he turned on the second-stage booster and felt the surge in power as he continued to climb to 40,000 feet, which was only slightly below the aircraft's maximum ceiling. There, he increased his manifold pressure another 30 percent, raised his prop pitch, and at 3,000 rpm 'military power', with the engine screaming, he kicked his right rudder and rolled the Mustang over into a dive.

For the next ten minutes Jason put the Mustang through all the manoeuvres he had honed as a skilled fighter pilot. The P-51 was exceptionally responsive in every sense, and he delighted at the clear rear-view afforded by the bubble canopy, and at how easy it was to move around and handle the controls inside of the roomy cockpit. Satisfied that he had explored every aspect of the airplane's performance, he climbed to 20,000 feet and lined up the top end of the runway. He then put the Mustang into a near vertical dive. Travelling at over five hundred miles per hour, he levelled off about one hundred feet above the tarmac and did a complete 360 degrees roll, kicking up a huge dust cloud as he screamed past the astounded pilots. Pulling up, he bled off some of his speed, reduced the manifold pressure and prop pitch, and then made his way around to the approach end of the aerodrome.

He began to lower his speed as the end of the airstrip came back into view off to his right. Since he would be landing from downwind he waited until he was below 250 miles per hour before starting his sweeping turn into a short approach. Partially applying the flaps, he lost more speed, and at 175 miles per hour lowered the landing gear. As Jason passed below 165 miles per hour, he applied full flaps, lined up the centre of the runway, and continued to bleed off more speed. At 120 miles per hour the Mustang's wheels set smoothly down upon the tarmac. Heeding Charlie's advice, he went easy on the brakes while simultaneously raising his flaps to ensure his tail wheel stayed firmly on the runway, and thus avoiding any possibility of nosing over.

As Jason climbed out of the cockpit Charlie was already on the ground beside the aircraft waiting for him. Grinning, he put his hand out to steady Jason as he jumped down from the wing root. "That was a nice smooth landing, but what the hell did you do with my girl up there? Just look at her! She's bleedin' from the ears!"

Jason nodded in the direction of the Perspex canopy. "I love that rear visibility you get in the bubble, and all that space in the cockpit. I swear pardner, there's enough room in there for all your illegitimate kids."

The half dozen pilots who had gathered around hooted and laughed.

Charlie sighed. "Afraid you'd need a B-17 for that my poor frozen and infrequently laid friend. Meanwhile, the only advice I can offer your sorry Canadian ass in that department is to make damn sure your igloo has a back door, just in case papa *Nanook* comes 'round with the shotgun."

"You have nothing to worry about Major. I always keep my sled dogs ready to roll. They're almost as allergic to buckshot as I am!"

Charlie ran his hand adoringly along the polished side of the rear fuselage. "She's a beauty all right. How do you think she handles compared to your Spit?"

Jason shrugged and then grinned. "Pretty close on all accounts. As you well know, once you get their knickers off, there are lots of similarities – and that seems to be the case here."

He then winked lewdly. "It feels like she has a faster roll rate, but maybe not quite as tight during the turn."

Charlie, who was not immune to a double-*entendre*, shook his head ruefully to a chorus of whistles and catcalls from his squadron mates. "Now, that's no way to be talking about a lady."

Then, more seriously, Jason suggested. "We still have half the morning left. What say we grab a taxi over to my base and you can take a Mark IX up to see for yourself."

Charlie nodded in agreement. "Great idea, but hang on to your dough for a second. The sergeant in charge of the motor pool owes me a favour. Give me a minute to see if I can round us up some free transportation."

They looked at Joe, and Charlie asked. "You want to come along?"

Joe shrugged. "Maybe next time, but right now I've got a bit of paper work I've been putting off, and it won't wait any longer. See you later."

As Joe walked back to the dispersal hut, Jason turned to Charlie. "What's up with him? The paper work can usually wait."

Charlie was watching Joe's back vanish through the door of the Quonset hut. "Not this time, I guess. He's got the worst kind of paper work – lost two men this week, and he's been putting off writing to their families. One of the guys was married, and as you know, there isn't any way you can sugar-coat that kind of pill."

"You can say that again pardner."

Charlie disappeared behind the hill separating the Quonset hut from the main runway, and Jason took another walk around the P-51 to once again examine its contours and admire its sleek lines. He was standing below the port side of the engine cowling, peering at the huge air intake hanging from the belly of the aircraft when the humped shape of an olive-coloured Dodge sedan screeched to a halt behind him.

As the dust settled, Charlie stuck his head out of the driver's side window. "We're flush Jay. Hop in. I'll pick up my flying gear and we'll be on our way."

Jason slammed the door of the big sedan as he slid into the passenger seat. He grabbed the armrest on the door to steady himself as Charlie pumped the clutch and rammed the shifting lever on the steering column into first gear. With a roar, the car accelerated down the access road toward the dispersal hut.

Within an hour, they were at the Canadian aerodrome in Kenley, and Jason was helping Charlie squeeze into the cockpit of his Spitfire. On the walk around the airplane Charlie had remarked upon the relatively narrow track of the landing gear and wondered if that would present any problems with landing. Jason assured him that although it was not as robust as the wider-tracked gear of the Mustang, it was adequate for the slower landing speed of the Spitfire.

After Charlie had familiarized himself with the instruments and controls, Jason gave him a bit of last-minute advice. "The propeller tractors right, so just like you do in your P-51, you'll have to apply some rudder to counter the engine torque which causes yawing to the left on takeoff. The cockpit is a fair bit tighter than your Mustang, and rear visibility is somewhat less than in your bubble canopy. However, the mirror on top of the windscreen helps, and the Malcolm hood is bulged, so when you look back over your shoulder you can actually get a pretty good view of what is behind you. Don't forget that since your landing gear is a lot narrower you won't want to make any sudden turns on the ground, or you might end up looking at the grass sliding across the top of your canopy."

After giving him a final rundown on the controls, Jason put his hand on Charlie's shoulder and winked. "Now don't forget that this is not your old man's Ford, so I don't want to see any used condoms behind the seat when you get back."

Charlie shook his head. "Honest son, you don't have to sweat it. If your lady here surrenders her charms to me, I'll be sure to clean up."

Jason chortled. "Now I really am worried!"

Jason watched Charlie line up at the end of the runway and point the Spitfire into the wind. The Merlin roared as he opened the throttle, and the airplane accelerated down the strip. Unused to the superior lift generated by the Spitfire's thin elliptical wings, Charlie let the aircraft travel about three hundred feet further along the ground than necessary, before pulling back on the control column to rotate the aircraft into the air. Almost immediately he raised the landing gear, and Jason grunted with satisfaction as he watched the Spitfire do a smooth half roll to the left. Charlie now looped south of the airfield, and then began to climb into the distance. Within minutes he was out of sight.

Half an hour later, Jason observed a small dot appearing on the southern horizon. He watched it quickly grow into the silhouette of his Spitfire as Charlie slowly looped around to the downwind end of the runway. Levelling off, he lowered his landing gear, and despite the fact that his approach speed was higher than proscribed, Charlie put the plane down without a bounce.

In minutes, Charlie was bringing the airplane to a stop in its revetment and sliding back the hood of his canopy. Jason leapt onto the wing and pulled the left-side cockpit door down to help Charlie ease himself out. The American was grinning as they hopped from the wing root onto the ground.

"Well pardner, what did you think of my girl?"

Charlie was ebullient. "Damn! That was sweet. I felt like I was wearing that airplane."

"What did you think about the handling?"

Charlie thought for a second. "I agree with you. It's a tad slower on the roll and a bit tighter in the turn. Damn near even-steven. If they could figure out a way for it to carry enough gas to get to Berlin it would be a great bomber escort."

"I agree." Jason grunted. "The photo reconnaissance version I flew had a belly tank built into it, and I took her to Berlin several times, but unfortunately they had to compensate for the extra weight by removing almost all the armament and ammo to pull that one off."

On their way back to Jason's dispersal hut, they encountered a pilot who had just left the ready-room, who passed on the news. "Met office still says they are going to be socked-in over the continent for at least the next three days. Nobody is going up until the weather clears."

Jason turned to Charlie. "Hey, I've got a great idea. Since we already have our three-day passes, why don't we head over to my friend David's base where you can get a look at a Lancaster? Later, we can collect our food and booze, and then the three of us could head over to the Alexander's for the evening? I'll get us a lift on the Anson that heads up there every afternoon with the dispatches. Later in the day, we and David could catch it again on its return leg to get back here."

Charlie smirked. "Every once in a while, you actually make sense. Now show me where the telephone is, so I can call my base and arrange to keep the buggy for a couple more days."

"Okay, and while you are doing that, I'll call David, and then the Alexander sisters to let them know we are all coming."

An hour later, strapped into their fold-down seats, they were landing at Middleton St. George, home to RCAF 419 Moose Squadron, where David was waiting for them with a battered khaki-green jeep.

Jason introduced his two friends to each other and climbed into the back seat, while Charlie sat in the front next to David. It took two attempts to force the unwilling transmission into gear, but soon they were driving down one of the maintenance roads along the side of the airstrip.

As they passed in front of the looming row of four-engine bombers squatting in their revetments, Charlie joked. "They must have had a sale on black paint down at the local hardware store. They look like a flock of giant crows!"

David agreed. "Yeah, unlike the U.S. 8th Air Force who have guys like you to mind their tails, we mostly fly without escort at night, so as they say, 'out of sight, out of mind'"

David pointed to a Lancaster standing in the revetment ahead of them with its bomb bay doors open. "That's mine. I'll turn in just on the other side of it so we don't get in the way of the maintenance guys."

After he parked the jeep, the three of them got out and walked over to the huge bomber.

David gestured toward the front of the bomber. "Except for the mid-upper gunner and I, everyone else in the crew works up there. Let's take a look."

As they walked under the plane toward the nose, Charlie looked up into the cavernous bomb bay and whistled. "Jeezus Christ! You could park a Buick in there!"

Nodding his head, David agreed. "Yeah, she'll easily carry twice the load of a B-17 or a B-24 most places, and if you are lucky, get you all the way back home too."

He then pointed to the *H2S* bubble just to the rear of the bomb bay. "They originally designed this plane with a ventral turret where that radar dome is, but in the trade-off between armament and armour versus bomb load, the top brass in their wisdom have opted for tonnage on the target as their highest priority. Needless to say, none of them are usually ever in one of these things over those locations. No white-hot shards of flak coming through the seats to interfere with the clarity of their thinking. Of course, those processes naturally function at maximum capacity behind the security of a large desk, where they can be unimpeded in their efforts to come up with those, uh…big ideas."

Jason and Charlie had heard the edge of sarcasm creeping into David's voice, and they caught each other's eyes apprehensively, for they both knew how massively the odds were stacked against him and his crewmates every time they went aloft over Europe.

They took another moment to stare up into the bomb aimer's blister at the very front of the bomber, and then they moved under the port wing to look up at the inboard engine, which was now being worked on by two mechanics.

Jason turned to Charlie who was gazing intently upward at the exposed engine. "They're Packard Merlins, just like the one on the front end of your ship, except these are from the 'twenty' series, and this crate has four of them."

Charlie nodded appreciatively.

One of the mechanics recognized David and waved before resuming his installation of a new manifold cover. The tail gunner nodded back in silent acknowledgement.

Turning to his two companions, he pointed to the rear section of the Lancaster. "C'mon, let's have a look at my office."

After they had walked behind the tail assembly, their eyes were drawn to the Perspex turret with its four .303 calibre machine guns mounted in their rearward-pointing position. "This is my humble abode in the skies. As you can see, I've removed the clear panel in front of the sights. It makes things a little draughty, but greatly improves the visibility."

Charlie was scratching his head with disbelief as he stared into the cramped quarters of the turret. "It must be some kind of cold up there being jammed into that thing."

"That would be putting it mildly. There is cold, and then there is damned cold. At 20,000 feet, as the British would say, it's bloody damned cold!" David replied.

Charlie shook his head again as he leaned over to look into the turret. "Boy, you've got to be sporting a massive set of *cajunies* to be hanging your ass out of this here spot. Those German fighter pilots must look at you like a hungry bass eye-balling a big old bug swimming across the surface of a pond."

Jason, somewhat surprised by the directness of Charlie's observation, saw David's face crinkle into a pained grin as he replied. "Well, if you are going to insist on indulging in folksy metaphors, let me put it this way: I'll heartily confirm your anatomical evaluation, and also state that I am one deadly fucking shot, so for me it's actually more like shooting fish in a barrel."

"Whooee!" Charlie hooted, while Jason grinned.

"I'm damned well going to have to buy you a drink for that one! You Canadian bastards are like to clean me out. Any more of those and you'll have me writing home for my walking around money!"

Just then he noticed the symbol painted on the bottom part of the turret.. "Hey, ain't that the same nose art Jay has on his Spitfire, there, along the bottom of your turret mount?"

"That's right." David replied. "It's the Lake Superior wolf-head. If you ever see a German plane with one on it, watch out. That would be Jay's cousin Peter, and from what I hear, he must be one shit-hot pilot. Apparently, he has more than twice as many kills as even Jay has."

Charlie whistled. "Kee-ryste! I'll be sure to keep my eyes peeled for that feller. Say, those are two *balkencreuzes* down there beside the wolf's head. Are you telling me you've plugged two krauts son?"

"Yup, that's me, the author of their misery – in the frozen flesh."

"Well damn my nearly flat-busted ass. You boys have no end of surprises up your sleeves, don't you?"

The two friends glanced at each other and grinned as Jason declared. "Among the fairer sex, many a tale is told of how Canadians are a legendary surprise."

Charlie was looking sceptical. "Maybe you fellers ought to keep those stories for someone who will believe them – and that sure as hell ain't me! Right now I'm working up a powerful thirst, and I do hanker for the lovely ladies if you get my drift."

Laughing, Jason and David each put a hand on one of Charlie's shoulders, and began to chant an oft' heard refrain, sung since the Americans had begun to arrive in England. "He's over sexed, over paid, and over here!"

Charlie shrugged his shoulders in mock resignation and following a round of spirited guffaws they agreed it was indeed about time to pursue their plans for the evening.

Jason was first to declare. "I do believe the Alexander sisters are expecting us and have been preparing a culinary surprise. I've managed to acquire a couple bottles of the Languedoc region's finest fermented grape juice. Do we have anything else we can bring to the table?"

A sly expression crept over David's features. "A guy who disappeared on his first op brought an extra pair of brand-new shoes with him from Canada, which I managed to retrieve from below his bunk before they packed the personal stuff off. A grocer in town exchanged two excellent bottles of a Tuscan vintage for them."

Charlie slowly smiled. "Well it may interest you two cheap skates to know that I've got four, yes count 'em, four bottles of Bordeaux, which I flat-out stole from a Texan squadron mate of mine who has way too much money for his own good. The bastard has the stuff shipped in by the crate."

Charlie was basking in the glow of their astonished approval. "So, what are we waiting for boys? Let's catch that Anson back to Jay's airfield so we can climb into my chariot and head on over there. I've started to develop an appetite!"

Mr. and Mrs. Alexander were away for the weekend, so it was Mildred who answered the door. She gave Charlie a passionate hug before inviting them all into the parlour. Just as she was telling David how pleased she was to finally meet him, Olivia and her brother Bobby emerged from the kitchen.

Olivia threw her arms around Jason's neck and gave him a peck on the lips before turning to introduce herself. "You must be David. Jay has told me so much about you. I am very glad to finally meet you in person. I'm Olivia."

He lightly shook her outstretched hand, and immediately decided he liked her smile and the way she frankly held his gaze. Jay had not exaggerated when describing her. She was unquestionably a beauty.

She interrupted his thoughts to introduce her brother. "David, this is my brother Bobby. He's an anti-aircraft artilleryman."

The young man took his hand, returning the firm grip while staring in nervous amazement at David. "Incredible, I mean, very nice to meet you."

David grinned. "So, you're the guy who managed to shoot down the infamous Jason McMurchy. Congratulations! You are one of a very elite few."

The young man flushed with embarrassment and protested. "Not intentionally of course! It was an accident…really! He was coming out of the sun! It could have happened to anyone!"

David, still grinning, tried to reassure him. "I don't think he holds it against you. After all, you were instrumental in him meeting your sister. Believe me, I've known him a long time and I've never seen him that head over heels for any girl."

This seemed to put Bobby more at ease, and he relaxed a bit as he began to regard his new friend. Although they were about the same height, the young man was still a teenager and had not yet filled out to David's more robust proportions. There were a dozen things he would have liked to ask him, but he wasn't sure whether it would be polite.

Finally, his excitement and curiosity got the better of him, and he blurted. "Is it true? Are you really a proper Red Indian?"

David wore a look of consternation while pretending to examine the back of his hands. "Where did you ever come up with an expression like that? I'm not even pink, much less red."

Blushing, Bobby rushed to correct any offense he may have inadvertently created. "No. No. I mean like they say in the western novels. I've read dozens of them. Really, it sounds like it would be terrifically exciting to ride horses bareback and kill huge wild beasts like bison and bears!"

Although struck by the absurd naivety of the young man's questions, David was also warmed by the obviously earnest desire on Bobby's part to know more about him, so he tried to answer him seriously. "My people never really rode horses. Sometimes we used them as pack animals though. Also, there aren't actually any bison in my neck of the woods - which is Northern Ontario - although the moose can grow quite large. As for bears, they will usually be long-gone before you ever knew they were around."

Bobby was hanging on every word as David continued. "The horses and buffalo stuff all happened out west on the Great Plains, and a lot of what you see about that in the movies is Hollywood bullshit. Certainly no one has even tried to live like that for over fifty or sixty years."

David's tone became ironic. "Meanwhile, the government seems to think they can civilize us by making us more like white people, but not everyone completely agrees with that idea."

"I guess that pretty well lets the air out of my balloon. It is not at all as I imagined." Bobby sighed.

David gave him a friendly clap on the shoulder. "Yeah, except for ceremonial occasions, I think you can safely forget about that 'wild-west, noble savage' stuff. Like everyone else, we're more interested in cars and radios these days."

Jason had wandered over to place a glass of wine in David's hand and couldn't resist the chance to employ some banter at his friend's expense. "Don't let this guy's self-depreciating façade fool you for a second Bobby. I've known him all our lives and he's as noble as they come. As a matter of fact, back home, he is addressed as 'Sir Crosscheck'. And there has probably never been anyone more savage when it comes to chasing a puck into the corner during a hockey game. Except, possibly...me."

They clinked their glasses together, as David shook his head. "Phhht! Compared to me, you're a bloody amateur. Don't you remember that last game we played, when I took four of Cryzinowski's teeth out with my elbow?"

Bobby had been listening incredulously as they spoke, and Jason had begun humming 'Scotland Forever', when Mildred announced that dinner was served. The Alexander sisters had somehow managed to acquire a substantial amount of mutton, along with an assortment of relatively fresh vegetables which they had made into a salad, except for the potatoes which were baked whole.

After dinner, when the dishes had been cleaned up, they tuned the radio to a station playing American big-band jazz music. Over the next few hours, they diminished their supply of wine while speculating about the future course of the war, and what was to come afterward.

At one point, Bobby informed them that the science fiction movie 'Days to Come' was playing at the matinee next day, and they all agreed it would be fun to go and see it.

As the evening wore on, they began to slowly disappear to their respective bedrooms - first Bobby to his, and then Jason and Olivia to hers. David had fallen asleep on one of the sofas. However, before Charlie and Mildred retired, she stepped into the hallway and emerged a minute later with a pillow and blanket. She propped the pillow under David's head and carefully covered him with the blanket before she and Charlie turned out the lights, and then silently made their way to her bedroom.

Next day, they all slept late, and once again the Alexander sisters miraculously produced a substantial enough supply of bacon, eggs, and coffee to satiate everyone's appetite, and fortify them for the movie.

Fully restored by their meal and the recuperative vigour of youth, they all crammed into the Dodge, and under Bobby's directions Charlie drove them the five miles across town to the Paradise Cinema. It was a massive art-deco style building with seating upholstered in plush red corduroy. Having arrived early, they had their choice of seats, sitting front and centre, in the rear balcony. Eventually the theatre filled, and the thick red velvet curtains parted.

Everyone stood for the national anthem and stock footage of the king, and then they settled again into their seats to watch the Pathe News. It featured numerous scenes of the allies battling in Normandy, and more American amphibious landings in the Pacific, along with footage of the campaign in Italy. Jason and David searched vainly among the images on the screen to see if they could recognize Jack among them, but although there were a few shots of Sherman tanks, they were not distinguished by the narrator as being from a particular nation. They were also taken from a distance that greatly reduced the size of the crew faces, which together with their goggles and helmets, rendered them unrecognizable in any event.

On the way home in the car, Bobby wanted to discuss how prescient the scenes about aerial bombing of civilian centres had been, considering the movie had been made in 1936. "Really, this movie was made before the Germans bombed Guernica in Spain, or the Japanese bombed Chunking in China – and since then we've also had the *Blitz* on London, and now we're giving it back to them even worse in the Ruhr!"

He caught his breath and continued. "What did you think about that rocket taking some of the survivors to another planet to start the human race over again? When this war is over, do you think we will develop that kind of technology and leave the Earth?"

"It's probably just a matter of time," Charlie mused. "You can't stop progress."

Jason agreed. "Yeah, something like that might happen eventually. The only thing that worries me right now is that the Germans seem to be leading everyone in its development. I did a photo reconnaissance trip one time to Peenemunde because some resistance people told us the Nazis were testing one that could carry a ton of explosive at over 2,000 miles per hour. If we don't finish them pretty soon, there's no telling where all this rocket stuff could lead to."

To their horror, they were to have Jason's words ringing in their ears, as ten minutes later, within a quarter mile of the Alexander home, they rounded a turn to see three houses ablaze. Several fire trucks had just arrived, and the air was filled with a steady ringing of their bell-sirens as the men jumped off and ran their hoses to the nearest hydrants. Charlie pumped the brakes, and the car screeched to a halt.

He rolled down the window as a fire warden approached and shouted into the car above the clanging of the bells. "Buzz-bomb! We've got two collapsed houses and suspect there may be at least two families beneath the rubble. We need every able-bodied man to help dig them out!"

The four men leapt out of the car and quickly followed a fireman to the nearest collapsed building. Olivia, followed closely by Mildred, approached the Chief Warden. They quickly explained that she was a nurse and they would help with injured victims until the ambulances arrived.

As the men approached the nearest building they could see that one corner of the brick exterior was still partially standing. It rose up to the third floor but was angled precariously inward. Meanwhile, muffled cries could be heard rising from beneath the rubble in the basement below them. When enough of the broken wood and masonry had been cleared, they saw that a portion of the ground floor near the centre of the house had been cracked and forced down into the cellar, leaving a gap where it had separated from the concrete wall of the basement. Freeing a length of timber, they wedged it under one of the broken floor joists, and used the top of the basement wall as a fulcrum to raise the section of flooring higher. Bobby was the smallest of them, and he climbed under it, using the torch he had borrowed from a warden to look inside.

The light revealed several people huddled there, covered in dust and bleeding from many small cuts and abrasions. One man lying under a heavy wooden beam was clearly dead, but more urgently, flames were beginning to lick at the edges of the basement, and more debris would have to be cleared to free the people trapped inside.

Keeping their eyes fixed upon the wall fragment leaning over them, Jason and Charlie moved further toward the end of the lever. David released his grip, and moved quickly to stack pieces of broken masonry onto the top of the basement wall to brace the edge of the flooring. While he was doing this, Bobby slid further into the gap, and as David moved over to assist him, he passed up the limp body of a girl who appeared to be about twelve years old. She was wearing pajamas which were soiled with dust and mud. Aside from a large red welt on the right side of her forehead, she appeared to be unconscious, but unhurt.

Taking the child gently in his arms, he carried her for a short distance across the street to place her carefully down upon a blanket that Mildred had spread on a patch of lawn nearby. He watched as Olivia felt for a pulse and checked her breathing. However, when she lifted a large lock of the girl's hair from the side of her head, it revealed a deep indentation.

Olivia shook her head slowly as she looked up to David. "She's gone, poor thing. I'm afraid there is nothing we can do to help her now."

David helped Mildred cover the child's body with a blanket, and then made his way back to the damaged house. His friends were helping the remaining victims climb out of the wrecked basement, while the firemen hosed down the last of the flames. A rope had been tied around the timber lying atop the dead body, and as the men tugged at it, there was a sudden roar. The entire corner of the house which had been looming menacingly above them collapsed inward, raising a huge cloud of dust and burying the basement in a mass of bricks, lathe, and plaster.

The Chief Warden approached them. "We'll dig that body out later. There weren't any survivors in the other buildings, and the firemen seem to have things in hand now. Many thanks, boys. You helped us save some people tonight. I think we can handle things from here on, so you may as well head off home."

In the car, the mood was sombre as they drove the final part of their route to the Alexander residence.

David reflected upon his role in the scheme of things. *How many German houses, and how many little girls like the one he had carried in his arms this evening, had fallen prey to bombs dropped from his own aircraft. Could the children of every German be held accountable for the actions of Hitler and the Nazis?*

High above their targets, the bomber crews told themselves it was just a job – retribution for something the Germans had started. It was easy to be impersonal from a height of 20,000 feet, but tonight he had seen on an intimate level what a buzz-bomb, which was really not that much different in effect from some of the weapons he had helped to drop, could do to real people.

As he sat silently in the back seat of the sedan, it was difficult to reconcile conflicting thoughts about his duty, with its concomitant loyalty to his fellow crew members, versus the civilian lives they were indiscriminately destroying in the target zone.

In light of what he had just experienced, there didn't really seem to be any satisfactory resolution to this type of moral dilemma. He was compelled to save people like those they had just attempted to rescue, from the depredations of the Nazis…and to do this by waging war against the Germans. However, by so doing,

William Myers

they would inevitably inflict casualties of the same nature on innocent people.

From the rubble looking up, one couldn't avoid considering the element of human compassion, and how it contrasted with the usual consequences of his actions on real people each time he successfully completed a mission. The only thing that did seem clear to him at this moment was that the conviction he once held about his role in all of this would never be as firm or resolute as it had been before.

September 1944. Doodlebugs

Flying again with 403 Squadron RCAF, Jason glanced over his right shoulder to reassure himself that his wingman's sleek Mk XIV Spitfire was locked to his 4 o'clock position. He and Flt. Sgt. Dan Shaugnessy, now based in Illier L'Eveque, France, were flying a sweep today along the Belgian coast at 10,000 feet - assigned to pounce on any of the *V-1* missiles frequently being launched from there toward targets across the channel in England.

With the allied capture of the Pas de Calais region in late August, the *V-1* launch sites had been shifted to sites further east in still-occupied parts of Belgium and Holland.

The unguided missile resembled a small aircraft, and it was aimed simply by launching it up a long ramp toward London. When the pulse-jet engine located atop the rudder engaged, it was propelled along the rising slope, and then through the air at about four hundred miles per hour until the small spinner on its nose had measured a predetermined distance. This triggered a spring mechanism pulling down the elevators located on the trailing edge of the *V-1*'s horizontal stabilizers, thus putting it into a dive. The 'doodlebug' then plunged randomly from its cruising altitude of

3,000 feet, carrying a one-ton explosive warhead into the city below.

In addition to its destructive capacity, the weapon's random and indiscriminate nature proved extremely effective when it came to generating fear. As people heard the ominous sound of one flying above them, they often froze in their tracks, helpless, and could only pray in guilty hope that the sound would continue until it had passed well beyond and dropped on someone else.

When its thrumming engine did suddenly go silent, the people below held their breaths for seemingly endless moments of sheer terror, until the blast. Afterwards, their hearts eventually stopped racing, and they would begin to breathe again, thankful to still be alive. Often enough, they died instead, and when the dust settled, the better part of an entire city block had sometimes been obliterated.

Jason and his wingman were flying genuine thoroughbreds today. Having been recently upgraded from the Spitfire Mk IXb, their new 'F' series Mk XIV E had the more powerful V-12 Rolls-Royce Griffon engine. Augmented with a five-bladed propeller, it had the extra horsepower and speed necessary to catch a *V-1* in level flight.

The longer nose needed to accommodate a larger engine and its conical spinner, gave the aircraft a hungry shark-like appearance. The sleek design sported a standard grey and green camouflage pattern, while a 20mm cannon and two 50 cal. machine guns in each wing gave it a lethal bite.

This variant of the 'fourteen' had a lower-profile rear fuselage with an experimental bubble-top canopy over the cockpit, and Jason appreciated the improved visibility that he now enjoyed. It compared favourably to the reconnaissance variant of the Mk XIV Spitfire he had flown previously, with its Malcolm hood-style canopy and the standard-design faired-back fuselage.

He was also grateful for the extra firepower and ammunition. Behind the white circle with its red maple leaf on the aft sides of his engine cowling, the 28 tiny black crosses painted along the fuselage below his cockpit attested to the lethality of this combination in Jason's skilled hands.

He looked up through the Perspex canopy, and saw that they were gaining on a flight of American P-51 Mustangs climbing about 5,000 feet above them.

He dialed in their frequency, and recognizing the flight leader's voice, he called nonchalantly. "Charlie, is that you up there? I'm gaining on you fast at 10,000 feet. Going to be right below you pretty soon, so don't any of you guys crap your drawers when you spot *Jerry*. Over."

Major Charlie Dentine drawled back into his mic. "What are you boys doin' down there? Didn't fergit yore toilet paper agin', did you? An' how the hell are you goin' so fast? Is that really a Spit you flyin'?"

Jason radioed his confirmation. "It sure is pardner, but I've traded in my Mark Nine for a Fourteen. I'm chasing buzz-bombs today."

Charlie chortled. "Whooee boy! Fourteen's almost higher'n I can count – and I didn't know Spits had bubble-tops. You ain't lyin' to me, are you?"

"You know I would never lie to an over-paid Major. One of the egg heads in the air ministry liked that bubble on the P-47 so much he decided to try one on a Spit. They work pretty well on Typhoons and Tempests too, apparently. I sure do like the rear-view in this baby."

"Far as I can tell, you're always viewin' rears – and what's underneath 'em too. You should try watchin' where you're goin' some time. How the hell you movin' so fast? I thought Spits and Mustangs was just about even-steven."

"Well pardner, she's got the Merlin's big brother Griffon up front generating about twenty-five hundred horse. She'll do nearly 450 miles per hour level if I get her liquored-up on 150 octane gas. Maybe more if I sweet talk her."

"Kee-ryste boy! Twenty-five hundred horse? The Merlin in this here Mustang of mine only puts out around seventeen hundred and fifty, which is about all the haul-ass I've ever needed."

"Well, like I've always told you pardner, mine's bigger than yours..."

"Hah!" Charlie exclaimed. "Sounds to me like your imagination got lost in your underpants, boy!"

Jason tried hard to sound insulted. "Underpants? Only a Yankee boy like you would need to wear underpants. Real men – that's Canadians for the uninformed – don't wear underpants. Not even in January."

"You be careful who you're calling a Yankee, son. An' you'll be callin' me your daddy if you don't buy the first drink tonight down to the usual waterin' hole."

"I'm looking forward to it pardner. Shall we invite the Alexander sisters?"

"I'm always two steps ahead of you, son. I invited them already. An' like I said, you better be ready to buy a whole lot of rounds tonight 'cause I'll be poppin' the question to Mildred."

"Well then, congratulations pardner. The celebration tonight will definitely be on me!"

Jason suddenly noticed movement below. "I'd like to chat all day with you slowpokes Charlie, but I just spotted some trade launching over the channel. Say hello for me to your buddies in the B-17s."

"Trade? You're starting to talk like those British queer fellers. You just drill that *kraut* boy, and never mind tryin' to swap him a Ford or a Frigidaire!"

"Danny, follow me down but stay well back!" Jason warned his wingman.

He then snap-rolled his Spitfire to the left and threw the aircraft into a dive that would get him onto the missile's tail. His wingman duplicated the manoeuvre and followed him down.

The *V-1* was skimming above the sea at 3,000 feet. Except for the pale orange flame shooting out the end of its rear-mounted engine, the missile was nearly invisible because of the dappled grey-green camouflage on its stubby wings and slender fuselage, which blended well against the dull grey waters of the channel below. It was traveling at full speed, but with his throttle to the firewall, the raw power of the 12-cylinder Griffon was pulling Jason through a dive speed in excess of five hundred miles per hour, and he was perceptibly gaining on the target ahead of him.

Jason knew from experience that the powerful force of a *V-1* exploding in mid-air had the ability to destroy an attacking aircraft traveling too close behind it, so he warned his wingman again to hang further back. Prepared at any second to snap-roll away from exploding debris, he closed to within 250 yards of the missile, aimed along the left side of its fuselage, and fired a short burst of 20mm cannon shells which converged on the target's wing root.

The shattered airfoil disintegrated, and the *V-1* rolled over into a plunging spin toward the sea.

Jason and his wingman both pulled back hard on their control columns to point the noses of their aircraft upward in an effort to use the kinetic energy accumulated in their dive to regain altitude while simultaneously bleeding off any excess speed. They banked slightly right to witness the buzz-bomb's death spiral into the frigid channel waters. On impact the warhead detonated and the massive explosion thrust a huge fountain of water hundreds of feet into the air.

"Scratch another doodlebug Danny," he chirped to his wingman as the 'G' forces and resultant rush of adrenaline drew his vocal chords taut. Jason then pointed the aircraft's nose at a rising tower of cloud. "Let's get around the top of this cumulus. That should put us back on station."

"Roger that. I want to take a squirt at the next one though." His wingman replied.

"Next one's all yours, pardner."

The two Spitfires began a smooth, turning climb, while continuing to maintain their relatively tight formation. Impelled by the powerful Griffon engines, their huge props dug into the air and pulled them effortlessly to higher altitude. They passed through a lower layer of thin cloud and emerged once again into the momentarily blinding glare of sunlight. Banking to the right, they finally swept around the nimbus pillar to a scene that was both startling and awesome.

The sky above the white cloud layer was swarming with aircraft.

Dentine's flight of sixteen Mustangs had been bounced by a mixed German formation of at least that many *Bf*109s and *Fw*190s. The P-51s had jettisoned their long-range drop-tanks, and were now swirling about with their German counterparts, diving, rolling, turning and spinning across the sky in over a dozen individual duels. Already, the smoke trails created by two stricken aircraft had disappeared into the cloud layer below. More German planes were arriving on the scene, and without pausing to consider the odds, Jason rammed his throttle forward.

With the Rolls-Royce power-plant roaring in his ears, he literally shouted into his mic. "Let's go Danny!"

They dove at full speed into the melee. Jason spotted Charlie Dentine's P-51 with its distinctive set of dentures and pencil moustache painted on the engine cowling. It was behind a *FW*190D which suddenly disintegrated in a hail of Dentine's .50 cal. bullets.

Flashes suddenly appeared in the rear-view mirror attached to the top of his windscreen, and Jason realized to his horror, that a *Me*262 swept-wing jet fighter, with its hundred mile per hour speed advantage over the propeller-driven Spitfire, was diving down upon him and his wingman.

"Break right Danny!" He shrieked into his microphone while reflexively rolling left in the opposite direction.

The jet's tracer shells streaked off to his right, and out of the corner of his eye he had time to see the *Me*262, with a black boar's head painted prominently on its nose, moving in behind his wingman and beginning to fire.

Shaugnessy responded to Jason's warning a fraction of a second too slowly, and one of the *Me*262's 30mm cannon shells tore through the back of the wingman's armoured seat ripping his torso in half as it continued through the instrument panel and into the fuel tank located directly behind the Spitfire's engine. The aircraft completely disintegrated as it exploded in a huge ball of flame.

A cascade of charred body parts, along with a few smoking pieces of airframe and the blackened engine with its attached propeller, now succumbed to gravity as they tumbled earthward.

Jason pulled the stick into his belly and felt the 'G' forces push him back into his seat as he brought the Spitfire around in a climbing turn, searching for the jet. To his amazement, the sky was almost empty.

One of the remaining aircraft was a P-51 with its engine spewing a long trail of smoke. The windscreen was covered in oil and the pilot had just leapt from the cockpit. As the doomed Mustang fell past him, he recognized the grinning teeth of Charlie Dentine's nose art. Craning his neck to see below the trailing edge of his port wing, he was relieved to see the white bloom of the American's parachute successfully opening.

Off to his left, a *Fw*190D circled alone from behind a cloud and hadn't noticed Jason approaching from the right. His thumb hovered for a fraction of a second above the firing button near the top of his control column, preparing for the deflection shot, but instead of firing he froze, as suddenly, in the periphery of his vision, the black boar emblazoned *Me262* reappeared, roaring out of a cloudbank to the left above him. With a sickening realization, he saw that it was bearing down on the figure of Charlie Dentine dangling helplessly below his parachute. A streak of flame shot from the jet's 30mm cannons, and to his horror, Jason saw Charlie's body explode into a mist of bloody fragments as several of the shells passed through him.

At the same time, the German pilot in the *Fw*190 turned his head, and as their eyes met, he registered a look of shock and recognition before snap-rolling into a dive and disappearing into the clouds below.

A scream of helpless rage burst from his throat as Jason snap-rolled the Spitfire into a turning dive in an attempt to get on the jet's tail. Then suddenly, ahead of him, three American P-51s were also diving on the *Messerschmitt* as it rolled over into a reverse loop and with incredible acceleration dove away, escaping to the east.

As Jason levelled-off he saw that the sky was once again empty. His breathing began to slow, and memories of the *Fw*190 flooded back into his mind. Its rudder had been decorated with over sixty victory bars, but this was not why he had hesitated long enough for the German to escape. No, there had been a distinctive wolf-head design painted on the engine cowl of the enemy fighter. It was exactly the same as the one on the nose of his Spitfire, and the pilot in his sights had been Peter.

Because of the *Me262*'s superior speed, Schwartz arrived at the airfield ahead of the slower piston engine fighters. He immediately sighted the two *Fw*190Ds with their easily identifiable red and white striped undersides circling above to cover him as he throttled back on his approach. Unmolested by opportunistic allied fighters, he nonetheless put the jet down roughly in what should have been a routine three-point landing because of the adrenalin induced stiffness in his arms. He taxied over to the revetment, and there he pulled off his flight helmet and clambered out of the jet's cockpit. Matted hair stuck to his forehead, and his flight suit was drenched in sweat.

Walking across the tarmac toward the officer's mess, Roland saw Schmidt's *Fw*190D land and taxi its way over to one of the revetments near the maintenance huts. There, the maintenance crew would conceal the fighter with camouflage netting to hide it from strafing attacks. These were becoming ever more frequent as allied aircraft now based in France, and seemingly in endless supply, roamed continuously further east.

As he saw Schmidt descending from his cockpit, the rage rose in him once more and he increased his pace, nearly breaking into a trot, and shouting as he approached from behind. "Coward!"

Before Peter could turn around, he shoved him hard against the side of the *Fw*190. Schwartz had a height advantage of nearly 10 cm and outweighed him by 15kg, but in his rage, he had underestimated Schmidt, who at 182 cm was a very fit 90 kg. Peter spun around and launched a powerful right hook into Schwartz's jaw, staggering him.

Schwartz stepped back. There was the taste of blood in his mouth, and he had nearly blacked out with the shock of the blow.

Stunned, but still enraged, he shouted over the heads of the maintenance chief and young fitter who had stepped in between them. "You bastard! You cut and ran from that Spitfire, and let him get on my tail! I saw the insignia on the side of his engine! It was your fucking cousin, wasn't it? You were willing to let an enemy pilot shoot down a German because you were too gutless to defend the Fatherland instead of attacking that Canadian bastard!"

Peter's fists were still clenched. "He is the one who had me in his sights and let me go, you arsehole! The only reason he was able to get on your tail is because you were too busy scoring another of your glorious victories by shooting down a defenceless man hanging beneath his parachute. Now they will be more than happy to return the favour to us, so think about that the next time you have to bail out, you piece of shit!"

"You're a traitor. You're afraid to fight, or kill them!" Schwartz spat the words in a spray of spittle and blood.

"My sixty-four victories say different."

"I have twice as many kills as you, and your fucking Canadian cousin will be my next one if I ever see him again!" Schwartz sneered.

"I got more of my victories here you *schwein* - against these western pilots who are excellent fliers - not like the poorly trained novices and transport pilots you ran your score up against on the eastern front. I noticed my cousin had nearly thirty '*balkankreuzes*' below his canopy. You might find you've bitten off more than you can chew if you find yourself in a dogfight against him. Those Spitfires move a lot faster than transports - or parachutes!"

Roland felt the rage boiling up in him again. *How dare this arrogant bastard question his methods? The enemy was the enemy!* It was every German's duty to defend the Fatherland against these invaders who now threatened to destroy the *Reich*.

"We are going to liquidate these vermin by whatever means necessary, and if people like you don't have the stomach for it, get out of the way of people who bloody well do!"

He stabbed his finger at Peter. "I'm going to see to it that you never fly in combat again Schmidt!"

"Hah!" Peter laughed. "You don't outrank me here Schwartz, so you can go piss yourself as far as I'm concerned."

Roland was not used to being spoken to in this way. His normal inclination would have been to use his huge fists to club the man into submission, but as he rubbed his swollen jaw, he noted that Peter's casual stance belied the fact that he was still on the balls of his feet, and his fists were still clenched.

His eyes narrowed, and he hissed. "You have no idea who I know Schmidt, and believe me, you'll be drinking buckets of my piss by the time I'm through with you."

He left abruptly, and Peter's hands slowly unclenched while he pondered the threat and watched Roland marching purposefully toward the officer's quarters. Alarmed, the fitter was staring expectantly at the maintenance chief, but nonplussed, the old mechanic merely shrugged. "That was a very good punch. A right hook, *ja?*"

Bad News

With the approach of autumn, the evenings had grown appreciably cooler, and as she prepared to exit the hospital, Olivia slid a navy-blue woolen sweater over her shoulders to protect against the damp chill.

She had spent an exhausting day applying dressings to innumerable wounds while also assisting the doctors in their unsuccessful attempt to keep two of the young men from expiring. As the fighting grew more intensive in Normandy, the numbers of wounded soldiers arriving from the front had been increasing – gradually stretching the limits of space available at the hospital. In addition, there had also been a growing trickle of wounded from the big push on the Gothic Line in Italy.

As she passed through the outer lobby, her mind was preoccupied with thoughts of the evening she and Mildred had planned with their two fighter pilots. She had told Olivia that Charlie seemed unusually anxious on the phone yesterday as he settled on the venue, and also the time that the two men would arrive at their home to pick them up. At this point however, she was thinking that a warm bath and a well-deserved night's sleep would be preferable.

Unexpectedly, she saw Jason standing at the entrance to the lobby. He was in his blue air force uniform, but there was something different about his appearance. In addition to looking a bit dishevelled, his body language was unnaturally tense.

She saw the grim look on his face, and her heart sank. "Oh, no, not…"

Before she could finish, he stepped forward…grasping her shoulders as he choked out the words. "Charlie's dead. Shot down this afternoon over France. I saw him buy it."

There was a sudden hollow sensation in the pit of her stomach, and she threw her arms around his neck as her legs grew unsteady. Olivia felt Jason's shoulders stiffen as his arms encircled her waist to take the weight.

She regained her balance, and lifted her face from his collar, searching his eyes for any hope. "We'll have to be the ones to tell Mildred. It's going to be so awful for her. Thank God my parents are back!"

Desperately she pleaded. "Is there no chance he somehow survived?"

He responded hoarsely. "None."

They sat silently in the back seat of the taxi during the ride to the Alexander home. There, Olivia sensed the distant nature of Jason's thoughts. He appeared angry, rather than sad about his friend Charlie's death. What had he seen?

Worried for him, she took his hand. "It's unbelievable that Charlie's gone. He was a close friend. Are you sure that you're alright darling?"

He squeezed her hand gently and looked at her profile. *She was so beautiful,* and he was certain that he loved her. However, the war had already brought more than enough tragedy to the Alexander family. If they continued their relationship, there was a good chance she would have to endure even more if he was fated to die before the fighting was finally over.

His voice was a flat monotone when he told her. "He was going to ask Mildred to marry him today. He had the ring in his pocket."

As they came through the door, they saw Olivia's father, who had just pulled a dusty leather-bound volume of statute law from a collection on the upper shelf of his bookcase. Turning, he called over his shoulder. "Oh, hello dear! Hello Jason!"

Mrs. Alexander had her back to the door as she adjusted some fresh flowers in a vase on the mantle over the fireplace. She called into the hallway toward the bedrooms. "Mildred! Your sister and her Canadian have arrived! Come out and let us all have a look at that dress you've been fussing with!"

Mildred emerged, radiant in a figure-hugging indigo satin dress. She was carrying a large emerald broach in her hand.

As she stepped into the parlour she asked. "Isn't it perfect mamma? What do you...?"

Her voice trailed off as she saw the tears that had begun to flow down Olivia's cheeks. Jason was standing there holding her hand as she leaned against him for support. His jaw was working, and it was with immense difficulty that he began to speak. "Mildred, I'm afraid..."

Mr. and Mrs. Alexander had both stopped what they were doing, and were staring at him with growing alarm as they recognized the gravity in his voice.

Jason cleared his throat. "I'm...I'm afraid I've got some bad news. It's about Charlie."

The broach dropped out of Mildred's hand and softly she began to moan. "No, no..."

Her parents looked on in shock and disbelief as Jason's features appeared to strangely alternate between sadness and anger as he struggled to continue. "Charlie was shot down...killed, this afternoon. I'm sorry...so sorry..."

Mildred groaned. "No. Charlie..." And then, she swooned and slumped to the floor.

Mrs. Alexander and Olivia both rushed to where she lay. Embracing her, they helped Mildred slowly struggle to her feet, as she continued to sob uncontrollably.

Gently, they steered her toward a bedroom while Mrs. Alexander spoke soothingly. "There, there dear. You've had a terrible blow. You must lie down now. You'll need to rest..."

Mr. Alexander put his hand on Jason's shoulder and searched his face for a moment. "It's bloody awful news you've brought us son, but if you don't mind me saying, you don't look so well yourself. Do you feel like talking about it?"

Jason words were clipped, his voice taut with anger. "I saw it happen. Charlie was okay – he got out. His parachute was deployed. Then this German bastard in a jet deliberately went at him. Shot him to pieces when he was just hanging there, helpless. I swear, if I ever see that son-of-a-bitch again…"

Olivia's father took a breath, and slowly shaking his head, he guided Jason to one of the large easy-chairs. "Have a seat son. You've had a long day, and I think you might need a stiff drink."

He took a decanter out of the liquor cabinet and poured two large glasses of whiskey, and then handed one to Jason, sighing. "Some of Scotland's finest. I save it for special occasions, but sadly I daresay, it will do both of us well to have some now…to drown our sorrow a bit."

He tapped his glass against Jason's. "Well now my boy, its bottoms up for our Charlie Dentine. He was another fine young man who has left us far too soon."

Mr. Alexander nodded toward the liquor cabinet. "There is plenty more where this came from, and we both know it's going to be one bloody long night."

It was after midnight when the bedroom door quietly opened and Olivia tip-toed into the parlour, where she found her father snoring in one of the easy-chairs. There was no sign of Jason, so she woke the old man.

He blinked his eyes a few times and shook his head. "We drank most of a decanter before I passed out. I don't know what the boy got up to after that."

His eyes then fell upon the liquor cabinet, and he snorted. "Well, where ever he has got to, he's taken a full bottle of my best Scotch with him!"

The American Military Policeman regarding Jason was exasperated. Half an hour earlier, this very annoying Canadian airman had shown up at the gate, demanding to be let in. The guard had finally lost patience and called an M.P. to deal with the situation.

Observing the disheveled state of the flyer's uniform, the M.P. also noted his tie had been loosened, and he obviously hadn't shaved for at least a day or more.

"What's in the bag?" The M.P. demanded.

"I already told the guard. It's none of your damned business. Now get me Major Haadland!"

The M.P. squared up and puffed out his chest. Squinting at Jason, he roared. "Lieutenant, you're drunk!"

Jason belched. "Wrong! I was drunk eight hours ago, but I'm not now, so if Major Haadland finds out I've been here and you failed to notify him, you'll have hell to pay."

The M.P. eyeballed Jason sceptically and made a disdainful sucking noise through his teeth. He reached for the guard's telephone, and asked the base operator to connect him to the officer's quarters.

In less than five minutes, a jeep pulled up, and Major Joe Haadland leapt out of the driver's seat. The M.P. saluted and began to explain, but the Major cut him off. "It's okay Sergeant, the Lieutenant is with me. I'll take over from here."

As the two officers sped away in the jeep, the M.P. was left standing in a cloud of dust. Placing a hand on his hip, he turned to stare at the guard, and with a look of disgust he emphatically spat on the ground.

Haadland reached over to shake Jason's hand. "Glad you came. A bunch of the boys are having breakfast over at the mess right now. Let's head over there to get some coffee and eggs into you."

Several of the pilots shook Jason's hand before he sat down at the table, while a few of the newer fliers looked on in curiosity at the Canadian.

He quickly drank two cups of coffee, and after he had wolfed down four eggs, he began to talk. "Some of you might not know it, but I was in that mix-up too when Charlie bought it yesterday. He wasn't hurt when he jumped out of his aircraft, and his parachute worked perfectly. Some Nazi son-of-a-bitch in an *Me262* shot him to pieces when he was hanging defenceless under his canopy."

Several of the pilots cursed, while some of them began to nod and knowingly catch each other's eyes.

Jason noticed their reactions and turned to Haadland. "What's up Joe? Did you know this already?

The Major swallowed. "No, we didn't Jay, but if that's what happened, it means that bastard has finished off at least four members of our squadron in the last month. He waits for stragglers – guys with engine trouble, or damaged aircraft – then he jumps them and accelerates out of there before we can catch him. Those *Me*262s have got so much speed on us, there's no way that you can overtake them. What kind of insignia did the guy who nailed Charlie have?"

Jason's head had completely cleared. He looked at Joe. "A black boar's head."

Several pilots began to mutter to each other.

Joe was nodding his head. "Yeah, that's our boy. It looks like we're going to have our hands full with this guy. Just when you think we might have these Nazis licked they seem to come up with something to throw a monkey-wrench into the gears."

Jason jabbed the table with his forefinger. "The good thing is they don't seem to have very many *Me*262s, and if you get some diving speed on your side you can stay up with them long enough to get a few good shots off – and maybe kill one of the fuckers. They also seem to have some problem getting back up to speed in a hurry when on their final landing approach. However, you have to be careful going in low for them because they usually have a few of those *Fw*190Ds circling overhead to keep them out of trouble."

Jason slowly pulled the bottle of Scotch out of his bag. "Fuck it! Gentlemen, will you join me in saluting a fighter pilot?"

He stood up, pulled the top off, and poured some whiskey into his cup, before emptying the rest of the bottle into the dozen or so extended cups. "Here's to a one hell of a good guy – Charlie Dentine – and other absent friends!"

Major Haadland responded. "Hear, hear! To Charlie Dentine. One hell of a fighter pilot!"

The pilots all echoed the Major's toast, then raised their cups and drained them dry.

As they prepared to leave, one of the newer pilots sitting across the table from him, learning of Jason's previous visit, grew curious, and then asked him. "Lieutenant McMurchy. Have you added to your score of bogeys recently?"

Joe smiled knowingly and there were nods of approval from several of the other pilots when Jason replied. "A few. I think I've got about thirty now, but I don't give a damn if I ever get another, as long as I get the chance to nail that bastard who murdered Charlie yesterday."

The other pilots cursed and muttered in agreement.

As they exited the mess, Joe turned to Jason. "Thanks for coming over today Jay. I know some of the boys appreciated that. Why don't you let me lend you a razor, and while you're cleaning up I'll arrange for some transportation to get you back to base."

Jason ran his fingers over the stubble growing on his chin and nodded. "Thanks Joe. I would really appreciate that."

"Not at all Jay – it's my pleasure."

Jason said little to the pimple-faced nineteen-year-old driver during the trip back to his base. His mind was preoccupied with the *Me*262.

After depositing him at the gate, the young driver spun the tires as he pulled away, throwing up a small spray of gravel as he moved rapidly through the gears. In less than a minute the humped shape of the sedan disappeared as it sped down the road into the distance.

Jason gave the guard an absent-minded salute as he passed through the gate, then made his way toward the dispersal hut. He still had a day left on his leave pass, and he knew that he should give Olivia a phone call to see how she was doing, but he had something more pressing that he wanted to try beforehand.

It took him over an hour to compose the short letter to Sgt. Shaugnessy's parents. Because he had been a new pilot and a recent addition to the squadron, Jason had known him for only two weeks. Dan had been a good flier and was learning quickly in his role as wingman. More than four years into it now, he could no longer abide the loss of good young men who had been leading normal, peaceful lives until the Germans had started this damned war. The frustration rose in him as he struggled against telling them that if their son's reflexes had been only a fraction of a second faster, he might be alive today. In the end he didn't, and instead he focused on the young pilot's virtues of reliability, steadiness, and dedication to duty – all the ubiquitous platitudes that one used in these letters about someone you barely knew – to help assuage the loss of a son who had died too young.

A few of the pilots were sitting around chatting when he entered the officer's mess, and although a couple of them looked up and waved, he didn't join them. Jason quickly gulped down one more cup of coffee, then went over to the stores area behind the dispersal hut to gather up his flying gear. After that, he hiked over to where the aircraft maintenance crew chief was, to explain his intentions.

The 20mm and .50 cal. ammunition for the guns in the wings of his Mk XIV Spitfire had already been reloaded. He watched while the last few drops of bright green 150 octane fuel dripped out of the nozzle as one of the men removed it from his forward tank. Another one of the crew leaned over the cowling and screwed tight the gas cap located just in front of the aircraft's windscreen. The rigger then helped strap him into the cockpit. Soon after, he was rewarded with a snarl of raw power as he started his engine and the Griffon roared to life.

Using the now familiar fishtail motion that allowed him some minimal forward vision past the Spitfire's long nose, he made his way to the end of the runway, and after a brief take off run he was retracting his landing gear while climbing into the sky from the other end of the airfield. Wasting little time he ascended to 30,000 feet, and then he rammed the throttle all the way forward while rolling the fighter over into a near vertical dive.

Even with the speaker pads in his flight helmet protecting his ears, the roar from the V-12 engine at maximum revolutions was deafening. The 'G' forces from the acceleration pushed him hard against the back of his armoured seat, forcing air out of his lungs and making it nearly impossible to inhale. He watched the needle on his airspeed indicator pass the five hundred miles per hour mark and continue well beyond the final markings on the dial.

Jason gripped the control column in his hand, and although he feared the wings might rip off of his plunging airplane, he resisted the urge to pull back on it. The Spitfire continued to hold together as the wind shrieked past his canopy, and he could barely draw a breath as the 'G' forces pressed stronger against his chest.

When the altimeter indicated that he had passed through 10,000 feet he somehow found the strength to pull back on the column. To his horror, he realized it was not moving, and that the aircraft was not responding! With both hands he now put everything he had into pulling on the column, and to his relief it gradually began to move slowly back toward his stomach. The nose of the Spitfire had pitched up slightly, but the altimeter revealed they were already passing through the 5,000 feet level. It took everything he had to keep the column moving toward him, but slowly the nose was beginning to lift, and finally at 1,000 feet the aircraft had levelled off.

Before he throttled back, he estimated that the aircraft must have been travelling at least 550 miles per hour!

It took a minute or so for Jason's breathing to return to a normal rate while he checked both wings, which appeared to have been unaffected by the stresses of the dive. Then, he opened the throttle and put the Spitfire back into a climb to altitude. At 30,000 feet, he rolled the airplane over, and once again put it into a power dive.

For the next hour he repeated the manoeuvre, until getting low on fuel, he brought the Spitfire in for a landing.

As he climbed down from the wing, he told his crew chief to give the aircraft a good going over to determine if there had been any structural damage.

The crew chief's reply was bucolic. "If there was any structural damage in this bird sir, the way you were flying it, I reckon you would be strawberry jam at the bottom of a hole in that wheat field over yonder. That's if you don't mind me saying sir?"

Jason considered the remark a moment then answered seriously. "No chief. If she's held up as well as you think she has, I don't mind. I don't mind at all."

As Jason walked away, the chief glanced at the other ground crew. "He's bloody daft!"

His aerobatics had not gone unnoticed by the other pilots on the ground. While he was walking back to the dispersal shed, a few caught each other's eyes and shook their heads knowingly, as if to indicate that they too thought he had gone off his rocker.

Jason was suddenly feeling very tired. He eventually made his way back to his room, and without removing his uniform, threw himself down upon the bed where he immediately fell asleep.

The next morning when he awoke, Jason mulled over his plan, and then ate a hearty breakfast in the officer's mess. After his third cup of coffee, he made his way to a phone and called Olivia. When she answered, he felt his heart quicken at the sleepy huskiness in her voice.

"Sorry I've been *incognito* the past day or so. There were a few things I needed to do right away. How is Mildred holding up?"

"Not so well. It has been an awful shock for her. I'm taking some days off from the hospital to help mamma get her through it."

"You sound tired. How are you doing?" Jason asked.

"I've been getting some sleep, but Mildred was having nightmares which were waking her up, so mamma and I would have to sit with her a while until she went back to sleep. I gave her a sedative last night, and that seemed to help."

She paused a moment. "What about you Jay? I've missed you."

"I've missed you too darling."

He hesitated. "I had to visit Charlie's base to have a word with his squadron mates, and later I spent some time checking out my Spitfire. This afternoon I'll be going up to look for some more buzz-bombs."

He paused again. "Listen Olivia, everyone was so upset about Charlie that I didn't tell you I lost Dan Shaugnessy, my wingman, in the same action. He was the new guy I mentioned once to you, but the same German who got Charlie got him too."

"I haven't told you the whole story about how Charlie bought it because it was bad, and Mildred didn't need to hear it. Maybe someday I'll feel like I can give you the details. Right now, I'm thinking that I just want to get some payback, so it may be a while before I take some leave again."

Olivia shuddered. "Jason, you can't win the war all by yourself. I love you, and I don't want you to take any unnecessary chances that could cost you your life. Do you understand what I'm saying?"

"Thank you darling, but you don't have to worry about me. It is that German bastard who should worry if I ever see him again."

He was realizing that she too needed some relief from the stress of the past few days, so he tried to lighten the conversation. "You can tell your father that I put that bottle of scotch I borrowed to very good use, and that I promise to replace it with some even better Canadian whiskey as soon as I can."

He could almost see her beginning to smile over the phone when she replied. "Father is very fond of his scotch, so this Canadian brand had better be as good as you say it is."

Jason responded slyly. "Just tell him it was Al Capone's favourite, and his most profitable brand. That should get him interested."

Olivia whispered. "Were you a gangster before the war? Are you going to kidnap me some day and hold me for ransom?"

She had managed to get him out of his funk. The beginning of a smile was spreading across his face as he told her. "Yes, I have actually considered that option. Let's say the next time we are alone I tie you to a four-poster so you can get used to the idea."

"I'll be there in a minute!" Olivia said, before he realized she was speaking to her mother and not him. "Sorry Jason, I have to help mum clean up. Will you call me again soon?"

"You can bet on it darling. Give my regards to your mom and dad. I'll call you later."

William Myers

September 1944. The Gothic Line

The battle for Coriano Ridge started out very badly. The British had cleared the southern slope, and the plan was for the Hussars to follow through next morning, supporting the Westminster motorized infantry regiment while advancing up the ridge to take the fortified medieval town on its summit. Through a gap in communications, and unbeknownst to the Canadians, the British had withdrawn in the evening and the Germans had returned to their positions with anti-tank guns that covered the entire valley below.

As the Hussars advanced across the valley, they were caught in a withering barrage of well-sighted anti-tank fire, and then swarmed by German troops attacking them with *Panzerfaust*s. They suffered several losses before the tanks were able to retreat to more sheltered positions, and over the next nine days, using any available cover, Jack's 'B' Squadron slowly advanced as the infantry cleared out potential ambush positions ahead of them. Simultaneously, 'C' Squadron tanks supported by infantry, outflanked the ridge, where bitter fighting ensued.

Progress was slow against the crack German *Fallschirmjäger* regiment defending the slopes and the deadly 88mm anti-tank guns, but eventually they cleared the ridge and destroyed several German tanks in the process of capturing the town on top of it.

Jack rested his buttocks against the front of *Beowulf's* transmission housing as he took swigs from a recently liberated bottle of *vino rosso*. Off to his left, the sun was setting behind Coriano Ridge, while three hundred feet to his right a German *Stug III* tank destroyer smouldered, with its 75mm gun depressed and blackened. One charred skeletal hand rose out of the open hatch over the driver's compartment, and Jack knew from experience that by tomorrow the stench emanating from the wreck would be unbearable.

Further behind the *Stug III*, in a low-lying, well-concealed area, the turret of a Panther tank lay on its side next to the ground-level concrete pillbox it had previously been built into. A Sherman's armour-piercing shell had penetrated through the turret ring and then ricocheted inside with devastating effect. In addition to shredding the crew, it had set off the 75mm shells stored there, and the resulting blast had blown it completely out of its mountings.

Captain Bob McLeod, crew commander of *Byng*, another nearby 'B' Squadron tank, sauntered over to settle beside him against the prow of *Beowulf*. Like Jack, he was exhausted after the day's brutal but victorious fighting. He gratefully took a long draught from the bottle when it was passed to him.

Jack liked the lanky Captain whose troop usually went into battle on one of his own troop's flanks. He appreciated how McLeod - an energetic and inspirational leader - was capable of instantly adapting to any situation by adjusting his tactics in the field, which more often than not put him up front in the thick of the action.

McLeod pointed directly ahead to a location more than a mile beyond the burnt-out wreck of a German *PzKpFw IV* tank. There, sheltered from sight by low, rolling hills, the distant battered remnants of Kesselring's *SS Panzer* division and elite *Fallschirmjäger* units were in retreat after the comprehensive defeat they had suffered against the Canadian tank army and infantry units. Further north they would reinforce previously-established defensive positions and prepare to be hammered by the Canadians again.

There was no mistaking the tone of bitterness in his voice. "There they go Jack. The whole Po Valley could have been wide open for us now if we'd had the resources to exploit this breakthrough. We might have have driven all the way into France or the other way into Austria and finished the bastards off once and for all before Christmas."

Jack grunted his agreement. "Yeah. No thanks to that American arsehole, General Clark. He stops us only twenty-five miles south of Rome – which we were sure to take - so he could get all the glory of liberating the eternal city. His guys should have been in their end of the line instead of the Limeys in the middle having to move a lot of their guys west to fill the vacuum. Now General Leese apparently doesn't think he can spare any of his British troops to send here and follow through on the shit-kicking we just gave the Germans. I can almost guarantee that bastard Clark will end up with a chest full of medals, but you can bet a lot more of our guys are going to get killed now because this war will last longer than it had to."

Jack's eyes searched the skies above him before wandering over the surrounding hills. Most bore the scars of war, but in many places they were still covered in vines heavy with ripening grapes. Unfortunately, within a few months the weather would be changing dramatically.

The 5th Canadian Armoured Division was not the first army to pass through the Tuscan countryside. Etruscans, Hannibal, and the Visigoths had all sought to possess this fertile soil and have their place in the sun. However, they, much like the Canadians, had seen the Mediterranean climate, with its cold rainy winter, swell the rivers and produce soggy impassable fields, which effectively precluded serious campaigning during that part of the year.

Frustrated, he growled. "It's too bad we can't chase the Germans down now and make hay while the sun shines. In two months, we'll be over the axels in mud and going nowhere fast."

McLeod also scanned the surrounding area and remembered the carnage of the day as he absently kicked at a spent rifle cartridge on the ground in front of him. "Well one thing's for sure, we are going to need a bit of time to replace and repair some of these tanks, and I can't say I won't enjoy the break."

Jack expelled a tired breath and nodded toward the bottle in McLeod's hand. "No argument with you there, Bob. You know, Robertson scrounged a whole crate of this stuff, so later this evening when you're all squared away, why don't you ask Myers and Crosby and the rest of your crew to join us, so we can do a little celebrating?"

McLeod passed the bottle back to Jack. "Sounds like just the tonic. I'm pretty sure the boys will agree."

Jack clapped his hand onto the shoulder of McLeod's rumpled, sweat-stained shirt. "You deserve it Bob. Your tank looks like you had more than a few close calls today. Why does the barrel-end on your seventy-five appear dented?"

"Christ Jack, you wouldn't believe it. An 88mm anti-tank gun fires one straight at us, and damned if it doesn't deflect off the end of our barrel. Instead of punching a hole all the way through us, it carved that groove along the side of the turret, right next to where Myers was sitting inside. The sound was like having your head inside of a huge cathedral bell. I swear it knocked every single mote of dust in the tank loose. The end of the barrel was completely bent in, so Myers slams an armour-piercing round into the breach while Crosby, cool as a cucumber, lines up on the 88 and fires. The AP round popped the barrel back into shape on its way through, then penetrated the shield of the anti-tank gun, tearing off one of its recoil cylinders in the process. For good measure, Crosby fired an HE round into it, and after that there was nothing left but the gun tube – and bloody pieces of dead Germans everywhere!"

Jack shook his head. "It sounds to me like your number just wasn't up today Bob."

They continued to gaze at the fresh groove along the turret, and other deflected shot scars on the exterior of *Byng,* as McLeod laughed. "Well, the way I see it Jack, I was probably born to be hanged, not killed by a German shell!"

The *'Op'*

Despite having made it through sixteen 'operations' by the end of summer, it had not been a good autumn for David. In September, he contracted a persistent case of yellow jaundice which hospitalized him for over a month. It was during this convalescent period that he was visited by Jason bearing the rare gift of fresh oranges. After they had peeled two of them, Jason told David of his strange encounter with Peter in the skies over Belgium – and the shocking death of Charlie Dentine.

He confessed that judging from the location of the various aircraft in the melee it might well have been Peter who had damaged Charlie's P-51, but it was the merciless bastard in an *Me*262 who had deliberately shot him out of his parachute.

"Christ!" David cursed. "Charlie was a good guy. Except for some of the boys who came up to Manitoba to train with us before the U.S. got into the war, he was the only American I ever met who wasn't some bigwig hunting moose just for the antlers. What kind of miserable bastard would shoot a guy hanging from a parachute?"

"I don't know." Jason replied tersely. "But I memorized his insignia, and if I ever see that son of a bitch again in the air or on the ground, I'm going to put every bullet I've got into him."

"Jeez, I imagine Mildred is taking it hard."

"She's taking it very hard. Olivia and her parents are staying close to her, but I don't think she's going to be in any kind of shape for quite a while."

"Are you getting any flak for not pulling the trigger on Peter?"

"No, but that is probably because I've only told you and Olivia about it. I don't want to give any of the stuffed shirts an excuse to accuse me of having a lack of moral fibre, or any such nonsense. If Peter and I both make it out of this war alive, he can buy me a beer to show his appreciation."

He paused and grinned. "But don't worry. I'll insist that he buy you one too!"

David chuckled. "There's a fat chance of that. The way this jaundice yellowed me up has caused a few of those crazy Limeys to give me some very strange looks. I'm sure they've mistaken me for a *Jap*. I wouldn't be surprised if they were thinking of some way to slip a cyanide pill into my soup."

Jason shook his head and pointed to the old man asleep in the bed next to David's. "Well pardner, the only advice I can give you on that one is to switch bowls with that duffer there every time they serve you."

David frowned. "I've always suspected you fighter boys were cruel, unsympathetic types. I can't for the life of me understand what it is that the women see in you insensitive ruthless bastards."

Jason laughed. "You should try flying in the front of the bomber some time pardner, because flying backwards in the tail has obviously skewed your perception. Otherwise it would be immediately apparent to you – as it is with most women – that I possess a very deep and sensitive nature."

David stroked his chin thoughtfully. "You're right of course. I really don't know how I could have missed it. No doubt I was too busy enjoying those sunsets on the way out to fuck the *Führer*. But just remember that you're on officer's pay, and I'm not, so that means reaching into your deep and sensitive pockets to buy the first three or four rounds."

"It will be worth it if you're not wearing that jaundiced mug of yours by then. I feel like I've just spent the last hour solving a mystery with Charlie Chan!"

David glowered. "Hah! Admit it! You have always been jealous of my profoundly handsome visage."

He nodded toward the elderly sleeping patient. "Although I have to admit I'm starting to feel like 'Number One Son' over there. As 'The Duke' says. He 'don't get around much anymore'."

Jason winced. "Confucius say, 'man who play with himself only expand very small circle of friends.' Therefore, I propose we remedy that when they finally parole you out of this place - maybe by going somewhere you can meet a few girls and get very insensitively and ruthlessly plastered."

David was grinning. "I forgive you."

By mid-October, David had completely recovered and was posted back to his squadron, but bad weather precluded any *'ops'* for the next two weeks. Although the skies eventually cleared up, there was less need now for raids on population centres, and over the next month they flew only six more missions – mostly against specific infrastructure targets like railheads, canals, and port facilities.

He experienced a very painful swelling in his throat during the second week of December which was subsequently diagnosed as tonsillitis. After two weeks back in hospital, during which he failed to respond to treatment, they were removed. This required a further two weeks of convalescence, so it was mid-January when he was once again posted back to his squadron.

There, the news that his old crew had failed to return from their run over the Ruhr three days earlier struck like a body blow. He was still reeling from the loss of his crewmates as the Flight Commander informed David he was to be assigned to a new aircraft.

On his new crew's previous *'op'*, the tail-gunner had lost his nerve when the bomber became temporarily trapped in a cone of searchlights. Screaming wildly as the flak exploded around them, the man had crawled out of his turret, and in a blind panic, exited the aircraft through the rear door without attaching his parachute harness...only seconds before the pilot succeeded in escaping the beams.

As it was, they had another *'op'* scheduled in three days, so after introducing himself to his new crew, David decided to join them at a party that was being held in one of the hangars later that evening. There was to be a live band, and a large number of the local English girls were expected.

David stretched out on his bunk to relax after dinner, but unintentionally fell asleep. He awoke two hours later, and after washing up a bit, he headed over to the hangar.

The party was well under way. Inside, the air was heavy with a thick haze of cigarette smoke, and the band was playing popular swing numbers while more than a hundred couples moved over the dance floor. David saw his aircraft's mid-upper gunner, Neil, dancing with a petite brunette, and gave him a wave, but in the crowded hangar he could not recognize any other members of his crew. He got himself a bottle of beer, and stepped outside to escape the cloud of tobacco fumes. Shortly after that, he was joined by Chris, his flight engineer, and Freddie the radio operator, who were also non-smokers. In periodic exchanges for a beer, the guard allowed them to share the warmth from a heater in his relatively spacious shack.

They took turns over the next three hours retrieving beers for themselves, while generally speculating on how much longer the war would drag on and what they might do once they got back home. Amazingly, over this same period of time they saw Neil, first with the brunette, next with a blonde, after that a red head, then in turn two different blondes, emerge from the hangar, then escort the woman into a dark area near one of the maintenance sheds. They would emerge fifteen or twenty minutes later, and invariably Neil would be adjusting his belt buckle while the young lady hitched up and straightened her skirt.

Under conditions of total war, it was quite natural that young people who might not live to see tomorrow would feel a stronger and more urgent need to satisfy their desires. However, next morning at breakfast, somewhat incredulous and more than a bit hung over, the three crewmen confirmed among themselves that they had indeed seen Neil apparently 'shag' five different women in one evening!

The January sun had nearly set by late afternoon, and the few remaining poplar trees at the southwest end of Middleton St. George airfield cast long shadows over the runway of Number 6 Canadian Group's 419 'Moose' Squadron. A brisk northerly breeze gusted sporadically, raising miniature whirlwinds of dried leaves that clattered noisily across the concrete before coming to rest in the small patches of snow along the perimeter fence.

Glancing up at the broken grey overcast, David pulled the collar of his flight jacket more tightly around his neck and climbed into the back of the flat-nosed Chevrolet van assigned to take him and the rest of the crew out to the waiting Lancaster. As he took his seat he nodded to their pilot, the Squadron Leader, Captain Robert James.

At about six-foot-two in height and athletically built, the twenty-five-year-old captain's square-jawed clean-cut face bore a strong resemblance to the idealized young warriors staring purposefully out of the recruiting posters on nearly every street in Canada. The steady and watchful look in his deep-set green eyes bespoke a kind of cool confidence that was an inspiration to the other members of his crew.

In fact, it took a lot of confidence to climb into one of the huge bombers, and then endure the freezing cold of high altitude, with the sure knowledge that the odds for your long-term survival were stacked heavily against you. Flak was always deadly, but despite the fact that growing numbers of American P-51 fighters which accompanied the 8th Air Force B-17s and B-24s had swept a high percentage of the daytime fighter interceptors from the skies over Europe, the German night-fighter force remained effective.

There was also '*Schräge Musik*'. A dual cannon system that fired obliquely upward from mid-fuselage in twin-engine night-fighters into the bomb-laden bellies of aircraft, it was almost impossible to defend against. In addition, there had been the appearance of the *Heinkel* 219, a very high-performance twin-engine aircraft, which had been specifically designed for the night-fighter's role.

The enemy night-fighters carried '*Naxos Z*', a device that homed in on a bomber's *H2S* target radar. Some of these aircraft were no longer confining themselves to the ground-radar-controlled box patterns. Like hungry sharks swimming through a school of fish, they slipped almost invisibly into the bomber stream. Following along undetected, they sometimes shot down several aircraft before exhausting their ammunition and fuel.

The results for Bomber Command had been disastrous, especially on the long raids to Berlin and beyond. While thirty operations or '*ops*' were considered a complete tour of duty, most aircrews were not making it much past their tenth.

With twenty-four missions under his belt, and at age twenty-five, Captain Robert James was one of the 'old men' of the squadron in more ways than one. You matured quickly in this game, and with his age, experience, and the attrition rate of his fellow pilots, he had inevitably risen to the rank of Flight Leader. He was aware of the respect with which his crew regarded him, and it strengthened his resolve to get his aircraft successfully to the target, and then take his men safely back home.

As the last man into the truck, David was seated closest to the open back end, and as they swung past the control tower, he could see the dark figure of Major Bruce McKellar, the Chief of Operations for 419 'Moose' Squadron surveying the dispersal area through his field glasses. Originally from Ottawa, but in England on scholarship, McKellar had traded in his Oxford tie for Royal Air Force blue upon the outbreak of war. He had graduated to the controls of a twin-engine Wellington bomber.

In September 1940, he had participated in the first air raid on Berlin. He was one of an elite group of men who could claim to have personally, on that night, forced *Air Reichsmarschall* Hermann Göring to choke on his anti-Semitic boast to the *Führer* and the German people that "if any bomb should fall on Berlin, you can change my name to *Meyer.*"

Bomber Command soon became aware of the need to preserve veteran bomber crews for the benefit of their experience. Strategic bombing was still in its infancy and although valuable lessons were being learned, the extraordinary casualty rates were creating a genuine danger of losing continuity in the command and training functions. As this perception grew, there was eventually a general acceptance of the philosophy that aircrew should have a limited tour of duty.

Earlier, after his twenty-third mission, McKellar had been promoted to Flight Leader and assigned to fly a twin-engine Manchester out of Waddington with 207 Squadron. A direct precursor to the Lancaster – which inherited many of its design features – the Manchester had experienced a great many teething problems, particularly with the Rolls-Royce Vulture engines, and had been a disappointment during its brief operational career.

While returning from his third Manchester sortie, an oil leak in the hydraulic system of his landing gear fouled the micro switches in the aircraft's undercarriage, causing it to fail during touchdown. In the resulting crash, the bomb aimer and flight engineer had been killed. McKellar had suffered compound fractures in both legs and his left arm. Recovery had been slow, and over a year later he was assigned to 419 Squadron to fly one of the new Lancaster bombers.

Whether by design, or simply through bureaucratic oversight, he had flown with 419 Squadron for another seventeen operational sorties. He rose quickly again to the position of Flight Leader and then Formation Leader. At this point the higher-ups at Bomber Command had recognized his extraordinary ability and promoted him to his present rank. By the time he stood down from operations, he had completed forty-three missions, very justifiably earning the admiration and respect of his fliers.

As David watched him standing in the control tower window he wondered if any part of McKellar still longed to be going with them into the air tonight. Flying in the mighty bomber as it carried its lethal cargo deep into German territory, some crew members experienced a kind of taut exhilaration knowing that death could come suddenly from any angle. Most however, would have truthfully described the experience as terrifying.

The truck arrived at their dispersal site, and as the crew clambered out, David peered at the brooding form of the Lancaster. The bulges at the base of both tires on the forward landing gear testified to the eight thousand pounds of high-explosive ordinance hanging in the bomb bay, and the nearly ten tons of fuel loaded into the wing tanks of the huge aircraft.

The Lancaster had been designed to carry the heaviest tonnages of bombs in the European theatre, and to operate at a similar altitude, speed, and range as its best American counterparts, the B-17 and B-24. However, the four-engine bomber had impressed even the most critical pilots with its exceptional flight characteristics. Some claimed that its manoeuvrability was more akin to a fighter plane than a heavy bomber, supposing of course that a pilot had the upper arm and shoulder muscles necessary to handle the control column.

This aircraft was an older variant of the Canadian-built Mark X model, which had originally seen duty with 405 Pathfinder Squadron. Upon being transferred to 419 'Moose' Squadron it had undergone some upgrading. The shallow bomb aimer's blister had been replaced with the deeper, more rounded version. Narrower, originally issued 'needle blade' propellers had been upgraded to the wider 'paddle blade' variety, and the unused ventral turret mount just behind the bulged-style bomb bay doors, had been replaced by the Perspex *H2S* radar blister. The mid-upper turret still conformed to the original Mk I / III design, and had not been moved forward nearer to the trailing main wing edge, or replaced with the Martin turret, with its more powerful twin .50 calibre guns, which were now being mounted in the newer versions of the Mk X.

Small white bomb silhouettes arranged in rows of ten were painted on the port side of the bomber's nose just behind the front turret. They indicated that the Lancaster had flown forty-five missions – twenty-one as a Pathfinder, then twenty-four bombing *'ops'* in 419 Moose Squadron where Robert had taken over the flight controls. A bit further forward, just behind the bomb aimer's blister, the original crew had painted the picture of a nearly naked blonde clinging lustfully to the front end of a falling bomb. Alongside the picture in bright yellow letters, had been printed the bomber's name: *'Penetrator!'*

Robert had winced at the picture's lack of subtlety the first time he saw it, but his crew had responded enthusiastically, so it had remained unchanged. A personal adherent to the 'out of sight, out of mind' theory when it came to evading enemy fighters, Robert would have preferred to eschew the more flamboyant decorative efforts that distinguished some of the other aircraft in the squadron. However, he had to admit that some of the flourishes, for example the shark's teeth and eyes that some of the crews had painted on the engine nacelles of their bombers, did improve morale – and that was at a premium in this business.

Robert did a final circuit of the Lancaster, pausing occasionally to peer up at some part of the aircraft until he had completed his inspection and satisfied himself that everything was as it should be. After they had all done their ritualistic urination on the aircraft's tail wheel, Robert climbed into the bomber and made his way forward, squeezing through the space between the ceiling of the inner fuselage, and the main wing spar, then up into the cockpit where he strapped himself into the armoured pilot's seat.

David watched the men climb into the bomber through the large entrance hatch in the rear starboard side of the Lancaster's fuselage, while he casually reflected upon the nature of the crew. With the exception of himself and Sgt. Chris Wilson, the taciturn flight engineer – both twenty-four – and Captain James who was twenty-five, the other four members of the crew shared a common age of nineteen. The crew also generally reflected the geographical and social diversity of the broad Dominion of Canada.

Robert, from Montreal, and Chris, from Vancouver, had both attended university where they played hockey for their respective varsity teams – though they had never had occasion to play against each other. Chris had been a speedy centre, while Robert with his naturally robust frame had been a bruising defenseman. He had been good enough that several professional scouts were disappointed to learn of his enlistment.

Neil Everett, the mid-upper gunner, possessed of blue-eyed eagle-like vision and trip-hammer reflexes, hailed from small town southern Alberta. After graduating from high school, he had briefly tried his hand at being a cowboy before turning nineteen and joining up. His ruggedly handsome face was already slightly weathered, and the perpetual far-away squint in his eyes combined with the single wing on the upper left breast of his uniform to make him almost irresistible to women. His prowess with the English ladies was legendary, and as could be expected, Neil was constantly subjected to a litany of good-natured jokes alluding to his earlier experiences as a bare-back rodeo rider.

Jocular Freddy Campbell, the radio operator, was from a family of lobster fishermen on Prince Edward Island. With two older brothers on Corvette escorts doing anti-submarine patrols in the North Atlantic, the stocky fisherman had chosen the air force, to avoid, as he put it: "Freezing my arse off on convoy duty."

Recently, Freddy had been talking about the potential of getting into the business of shipping lobsters by air freight after the war. He had been picking Robert's brains for ideas, completely oblivious to the fact that the Captain considered the young man an incredible optimist to be thinking so far into the future.

Marc Beliveau, the diminutive bombardier, was muttering to himself as he squirmed into his cramped position in the nose of the aircraft. The son of a geologist, he had grown up in several of the small mining towns dotting northern Quebec. He could play the fiddle with a furious passion but had gone into a serious funk the previous September when his older brother, an infantryman, had been killed near Ortona in Italy. On subsequent missions, he could be heard cursing softly to himself in French when releasing bombs over the target.

The navigator, Frank Romaniuk, was from Winnipeg, and had always excelled at mathematics. He had given up a scholarship at the University of Manitoba when the air force accepted him. Generally contemplative and not easily ruffled, he was the squadron's chess champion.

David climbed into the aircraft and squeezed through the sliding doors on the back of the rear turret. After closing them, he settled into his seat. The front of this turret was only partially enclosed in Perspex, a panel having been removed for improved visibility. The entire unit perched precariously in the tail of the bomber and was invariably buffeted by a 250 miles per hour slipstream.

Even with his electrically heated flight suit, David had the coldest seat in the aircraft. This was mitigated only slightly by the fact that he had eschewed the standard chest-mounted parachute - which was normally stored next to the rear door and only clipped on before actually bailing out of a stricken bomber - for a pilot's version. That type hung just below his buttocks, and even though the turret was already cramped, he was willing to endure some slightly reduced headroom for the extra padding and insulation it provided to his seat.

Fortunately, he was by temperament a loner, which was befitting his rather isolated aircrew position as 'tail-end Charlie'. David only occasionally attended the squadron parties, and generally tended to socialize quietly by sometimes playing cards with the guys in one of the squadron's ground crews.

Robert called back to Freddy to confirm that the *H2S* was functioning normally and received a humourless response. "Everything is good, but I would still rather have Harris's balls hanging where that ventral turret used to be before he ordered them all removed."

"You won't get any argument on that from me." Robert grunted.

Chris looked up from the main engineering panel where he had been scrutinizing the gauges, to signal all was well.

Robert nodded. "Let's start them up then."

He leaned forward to depress the starter switch for the number three, right inboard engine. With a high-pitched whine, the propeller began to slowly turn over. The engine coughed twice, and then the blades quickly became a blur as the big V-12 belched a cloud of exhaust and roared to life.

Robert nudged the throttle forward to the idling position, glancing briefly at the gauge and checking that the correct number of *rpms* had been attained. He then closed the bomb bay doors. This confirmed that the plane's hydraulic system, powered by a pump on engine number three, was functioning normally. He repeated the starting procedure for engine number four, right outboard, then engine number two, port inboard, and finally, engine number one, port outboard. At last, all four of the Merlins were thrumming in ear-splitting harmony, while the heavy bomber squatted on its dispersal pad, awaiting the summons skyward.

Presently, from the direction of the control tower, a green Aldis lamp began to flash against the dusky sky.

Robert motioned for the ground crew to remove the chocks from the main wheels, and then inched the throttles forward until the Lancaster began to creep off of its pad and onto the access strip leading to the end of the runway. Using a combination of brakes and outboard engine throttle to steer the aircraft, Robert taxied down the access strip where he was able to see several of the heavily-laden lead-bombers taking off. Soon he found himself approaching the access ramp. Once onto the runway he turned the bomber's nose a bit right of the airstrip centre-line and prepared his aircraft for takeoff.

More to calm his own nervousness than anything else, he cautioned his crew through the headset. "Make sure you are strapped in securely everyone. We are about to weigh anchor."

There were several grunts in response. In the tail, David stopped chewing his gum long enough to utter a mild sarcasm. "Aye, aye, Captain!"

Robert confirmed that the wing flaps were down, and as the Lancaster ahead of them rose into the air, he and Chris began to ease the cluster of four throttles forward. They kept the port outboard engine's throttle a little advanced of the others to compensate for the bomber's tendency to torque strongly to the left. Simultaneously, he adjusted his right aileron up to counter the crosswind coming from that direction.

When the aircraft had attained sufficient speed, Robert nudged the control column and Chris rammed the throttles forward. This, combined with the increase in speed, caused the tail to lift into the air, where the rudders could come into play to steer a straight course down the runway.

With the roar of the four Merlins filling his ears, he felt the massive aircraft surge forward. The speed indicator moved further around the dial as the big bomber accelerated down the concrete strip. Robert was dimly aware of the dark shapes of stationary aircraft still on their dispersal pads, whizzing past in the periphery of his vision. All this time, his own thundering aircraft continued to gain speed, while the end of the runway rushed ever nearer.

Robert felt like a part of the aircraft now. It was as if his own skeleton had fused with the Lancaster's airframe, and each nuance of its motion was travelling up the column and deep into his bones. With every nerve in his body suffused and tingling with adrenalin, he sensed a subtle shift in the weight of the bomber from its wheels into its wings, as the force of the onrushing air began to do its work.

Waiting until the last possible moment, Robert pulled back on the column, raising the nose of the Lancaster just as the end of the runway flashed by beneath him, while with a mighty roar, the huge bomber leapt into the skies. Amid this din, the powerful wash from its four churning propellers flattened small shrubs beyond the airstrip as the massive aircraft tore through the air just a few yards above.

Chris removed the lock bolt from the undercarriage selector and flipped the lever to raise the Lancaster's landing gear. Now began the tedious but demanding job of climbing to altitude, circling slowly, collecting, and funneling the bombers into a general 'stream' formation. Gradually, like flocks of geese, they were joined by flights from other airfields in the south of England, as by the hundreds, elements of other squadrons arrived and formed up over the eastern counties. Eventually, they coalesced into one giant elongated procession of nearly a thousand aircraft.

For those observing from below as the formation headed out over the channel, the stream of bombers seemed endless. The droning throb of the engines filled the air and strangely resonated through the ground which vibrated beneath their feet. As dusk slowly changed to night, their low humming grew fainter, while the myriad black silhouettes disappeared eastward into the gathering darkness.

High over the channel, Robert called for his gunners to do a weapons check. He was immediately rewarded by short staccato bursts from each of the three turrets, and the brief sight of orange tracer shells arcing into the blackness below.

Even with a full bomb load and wing tanks topped up with fuel, Robert could feel the Lancaster's agile response to the control column which he now gripped firmly in both of his hands. On the southern edge of the stream, he had the luxury of enough space to sideslip a bit as a brief pocket of air turbulence buffeted the aircraft. He was glad not to be in the centre of the formation where the pilots not only had to contend with the normal problems of maintaining course, speed, and altitude, but also the danger of collision with the more densely arrayed and nearly invisible elements of their squadrons.

Craning his neck to look back over his shoulder through the Perspex blister on the side of his canopy, Robert tried without success to discern bombers in the stream that stretched out behind him. The exhaust shields on the engines and the camouflage paint on all of their metal surfaces made the bombers almost impossible to see on this moonless night. However, he knew they were out there, in front of him, and trailing back from his position for a distance of nearly fifty miles.

Turning to look behind the starboard wing, he could just barely see the Lancaster of a new man, Sergeant Pilot Jenkins. It grew in size and came more clearly into focus as it began to drift in too closely. Robert calmly made the adjustments to cautiously move his own aircraft further off to the left.

Jenkins, on his first operational mission, had never met the man or the crew that he and his men were replacing.

That man, Flying Officer Rouseau, was lost on his seventeenth sortie, and had been due for promotion to lead a flight of his own. Known as an excellent pilot, he had been respected for his flying skills and cool head when under fire.

On only his second '*op*', he had very calmly landed his aircraft despite the fact that the entire starboard rudder and half of the stabilizer had been shot off by an *Bf*110. Exploding debris had wounded the rear gunner and destroyed the tail wheel, yet his navigator had sworn Rouseau was actually humming some classic tune to himself when he put the bomber down with hardly more than a gentle bump on the runway.

Robert couldn't even guess which tune Rouseau had been humming six nights ago over Hamburg when he was caught in the triangulating beams of two searchlights at 18,000 feet. Pinned like a moth in the rapier-like shafts of light, the unfortunate aircraft had been caught at the very beginning of its bombing run with the bay doors wide open. Within seconds, the first radar-guided 88mm round had exploded just beneath the fully loaded Lancaster. The resulting blast had illuminated every aircraft in the sky for more than a cubic mile and seared its horrific image on the minds of those who had witnessed it and lived to remember.

The fireball seemed to hang in the sky for an infinitely long time, when in fact it must have only been seconds. However, in those first few fractions of a second, seven very young men had been vaporized. They had been someone's father, son, brother, cousin, husband, or lover, and suddenly they no longer existed – remembered now as the physical and emotional vacuum they represented in someone else's life.

Robert recalled how his first reaction had been resentment that the light from the explosion was exposing his aircraft and increasing his vulnerability to the night-fighters prowling in the darkness. It later dawned on him that he needn't have worried, for the bright flash had temporarily blinded friend and foe alike. In the seconds that it took for pupils to dilate back to night-vision circumference, he had been safely swallowed again by the black night.

Tonight's target was Magdeburg, and as the coast of Holland passed below, Robert noticed the first traces of St. Elmo's fire forming across the top of the nose turret. Slowly it grew into an electric blue outline over the entire profile of the gun station and then began to dance weirdly back along the front of the bomber toward the cockpit. It was a familiar phenomenon, and it would eventually spread along the entire length of the wings and fuselage until the whole aircraft was enveloped in its eerie pulsating glow.

In the rear turret, David observed the blue iridescence forming first along the leading edges of the rudders and horizontal stabilizers on both sides and just ahead of his turret. Eventually it would spread over the surface of his turret and radiate along the length of his gun barrels.

Though disconcerting, he knew from experience that it would soon dissipate as the four hungry engines of the bomber consumed more of the aircraft's fuel, thus lightening its all-up weight and enabling it to claw its way higher – toward the Lancaster's ceiling of 22,000 feet. There, ionization tended to draw the strange effect off into the surrounding atmosphere.

For now though, the aircraft in his flight, with their huge wide wings, resembled nothing so much as the ghostly forms of Banshees howling through the night sky with their swollen bellies heavy and full to bursting with death and annihilation.

Three more hours to target David thought, *and if he was lucky, another four hours back to base.* He tried not to do the mental calculation that would tell him how many of his squadron, based upon past percentages, weren't going to make it home tonight.

Long ago he had stopped trying to calculate his own chances. Less than ten percent of aircrew survived to complete their allotted thirty missions, and now on his twenty-third he was living on borrowed time. This had been the case for months since he had put down safely after his tenth *'op'*.

He guessed that he'd been lucky so far. In this line of work there was an overriding element of randomness to death that seemed to transcend prudence or skill, and it could pluck life away at the most unlikely of moments. For example, one casualty associated with his previous aircraft had been Flannery. The mechanic had fallen off the wing when stung by a wasp while doing engine maintenance and had subsequently died from a broken neck.

David was glad now for the second cup of coffee that he had gulped down only seconds before climbing aboard the small transport that whisked him across the tarmac to where the fully loaded Lancaster had been waiting for him. He reached down and was reassured when the fingers of his glove came in contact with the dented cylinder of his old thermos – still mostly full – in its usual position beside the seat.

The last traces of St. Elmo's fire had dissipated and David's attention was drawn to the accumulation of cloud that had begun to appear below him. Although only patchy, it could be a mixed blessing. While clouds provided some cover from the flak gunners below, they could at the same time make the contrasting dark shapes of the bombers more visible to any night-fighters circling at higher altitude above them.

Schräge Musik

Oberleutnant Eugen Mueller cast a wary eye across the darkening skies as one by one, stars began to appear in the patches between a partial overcast. They had already received news of a large enemy force forming up over eastern England and the channel. Bomber command would be visiting them tonight, but it would still be a while before the intended target became clear to his ground controllers. With fuel rations being what they were, it would be only at the last possible minute that they got orders to take off and hopefully intercept the enemy, preferably on his way in, but also perhaps on the way out from the target.

At approximately 183 cm and 90 kilos, the blond, blue-eyed Mueller was the physical embodiment of what most people would have described as a typical German, but in fact he had grown up in Vilnius, Poland, where his father, the descendant of German immigrants, had taught science in the local *Gymnasium*.

After Hitler and Stalin had signed the non-aggression pact agreeing to carve up Poland and the Baltic states, the Russians had moved in. As part of a Soviet program which involved seizing private lands to convert them into gigantic collective farms, Mueller's three uncles had been put up against the walls of their respective barns, and shot. Eugen's own family had managed to escape westward, and had settled in Hamburg, where he had finished his last year of schooling.

Mueller was a natural athlete who excelled at track and field sports, particularly throwing. In his last year at school he had set a city record for the javelin. With his excellent eyesight and an admiring recommendation from his *Gaulieter*, he had joined the *Luftwaffe*, and then easily made the selection for pilot training.

As he moved up to more advanced aircraft, it was determined that his reflexes were not quite fast enough to qualify for the fighter program, and he had been assigned to bombers. There, he displayed a higher than average aptitude, and developed a reputation for steadiness and reliability in circumstances that might have tried the nerve of less committed pilots.

After surviving the debacle of Operation Sea Lion, which the enemy was now referring to as the 'Battle of Britain', he had risen to the position of group leader. A mere ten months later had found him in the vanguard of Operation Barbarossa, bombing railheads and airfields as the *Wehrmacht 'blitzkreiged'* its way through the Ukraine and Russia.

In the early stages of the assault while temporarily flying from bases in Lithuania, he had taken a day while his aircraft was being repaired to visit his home town. There, standing on the sidelines, he had watched with grim satisfaction as the '*Einsatzgruppen*' lined up hundreds of collaborators – mostly Communists and Jews – on the edge of long pits, and shot them in the back of their heads.

With pitiless efficiency, the bulldozers had buried them like stacks of cordwood under the fertile soils that his murdered relatives had tilled for generations. Silently, he applauded this collective justice for collective thieves.

They had been good days initially, but as the Russian aircraft and pilots improved, and after the setbacks at Stalingrad and Kursk, operations had taken on a more defensive nature. It was during this period that he learned his family had perished in the Hamburg firestorm.

Eventually, he had been pulled back to the Fatherland, where he was reassigned to night interceptor operations. This was essential to defend against the growing numbers of aircraft from Bomber Command raining destruction from the dark skies upon German cities and industry.

He relished this new role, which had changed from dropping bombs on impersonal targets, to shooting down the very men who had been the agency of his own personal loss. Only yesterday, with grim pride, he had painted yet another roundel on the rudder of the *Ju*88, indicating his eleventh kill. Not bad, he thought, for a guy who supposedly didn't have the reflexes to be a fighter pilot.

Mueller watched as his radar operator *Oberfeldwebel* Bernt Esche, and observer *Feldwebel* Jurgen Raul, finished the last drams of their coffee before he raised his hand to signal them across the crowded ready room. Seeing their pilot had already slung the parachute harness over his shoulder, the two crewmates reached for their own, then followed him out of the building onto the tarmac.

The portly *OFw.* Esche, was at age 26, prematurely bald. God only knew how he had passed the stringent physical examinations for aircrew but his undoubted skills with the radar set were in short supply, and had probably overridden any fitness deficiencies in the minds of their superiors. He was affable enough on the ground, but Mueller had noted with some consternation that his radar man would begin to sweat profusely whenever they entered the aircraft to prepare for their takeoff run. He was inordinately proud of his mother's baking skills and tended to prattle on about her strudels and cakes, which the other airmen, including Eugen, found quite exasperating in this time of restricted rations.

Their observer, *Fwl.* Raul, was Esche's physical opposite. A small wiry man in his late twenties, Raul's oiled black hair descended in an exaggerated widow's peak near the centre of his forehead. In addition to his large ears, he possessed a thin pendulous nose which hung off the front of his narrow face above a small receding chin. He was a chain smoker, and exhibited a pronounced over-bite, which gave him a rodent-like appearance. This invariably resulted in other members of the group referring to him as "*Maus*", a nickname he detested.

As they approached the aircraft Raul spat a piece of tobacco from between his teeth, then tossed his cigarette to the ground and extinguished it with the toe of his boot. Coughing, he spat again and cursed. "This '*ersatz*' dog shit they call tobacco is even worse than the boiled sawdust they serve us for coffee. Somewhere a fat businessman is doing his duty for the Fatherland and getting rich by producing these arse hairs for us to smoke. I'll bet you Göring doesn't use this crud."

Esche, following behind Mueller, looked over his shoulder as Raul caught up. "Göring probably has his own plantation in Virginia, and maybe the 8th Air Force delivers them by air mail once a week for all we know, but those arse hairs might explain why your breath usually smells like a dead pig fart."

"That is still an improvement over the stench of your mother's piss-hole coming out of your mouth, you fat piece of shit!" Raul spat back.

Esche clucked. "Now we mustn't let your jealousy of my mother's baking - and the fact that your own mother only fed you little bits of mouldy cheese - distract you from our mission, *Maus*. So why don't you stop dreaming of *Gouda* and just concentrate on being a good little *fleidermaus*."

Mueller was well aware of how the endless weeks of spending their nights in the dark skies stalking bombers had frayed everyone's nerves, but as pilot and crew commander it was his job to prevent personality clashes detracting from the effectiveness of their task intercepting bombers.

There was menace in his voice. "You two shut up and get focused on our job, or when we get to 5,000 metres, I'll throw you both out of the airplane!"

The two crewmen nodded obediently, and grudgingly proceeded from there on, silently.

It was completely dark now, and the hulking silhouette of the *Junkers* 88G-6 sat at an angle on the dispersal pad as they walked under its large glassed-in nose section. With the fuel tanks full and ammunition loaded, they were ready for tonight's hunt. All of the crew positions were in the front of the aircraft, and they took turns handing their parachutes through the hatch above them before pulling themselves up inside. They then climbed into their stations under the bulbous Plexiglas canopy.

After strapping himself into the pilot's seat, Eugen went through his usual check of the switches, gauges, and controls, before initiating the engine start. After much rough coughing and one stoppage, the first engine roared to life, soon followed by the second. Confirming that the electric and hydraulic systems were performing as expected, he nodded to Esche, who switched on the *Lichtenstein SN-2* radar set and went through the necessary checks to confirm that it too, was operating normally.

Eugen let both of the *Jumo* 213A engines run a few minutes longer to bring their temperatures up. The German engines ran on relatively normal octane-level fuel compared to the higher-grade aviation mixture used by British and American aircraft. However, standards had declined quite noticeably since the disasters of early 1943, which had denied German refiners much of their oil supply from the Caucuses, and as the allied bomber campaign began to take its toll on refining capabilities. Synthetic fuels may have taken up some of the slack, but there was no denying the lessening of fuel quality and the corresponding loss of performance when some of the lower-grade stuff made its way into his wing-tanks.

These days it was taking all of his skills as a veteran pilot to coax the maximum possible performance out of his aircraft's power plants. As the temperatures began to creep up on the two gauges, Eugen synchronized the *rpms*, and noted with satisfaction that the engines were running much smoother now.

Checking to see that Esche and Raul had both properly strapped themselves into their seats, he signalled the ground crew to remove the wheel-chocks, then released the brakes and eased the throttles ahead until he felt the aircraft begin to roll forward.

Turning onto the end of the runway, Eugen pointed the *Junkers'* nose into the wind. He then opened both throttles, and with a roar, the big night-fighter began to accelerate down the runway. As the aircraft reached critical speed he felt the wings gain lift, and then the *Junkers* rose into the air as the runway began to slip away beneath him. Confirming his heading, he continued to keep the aircraft's nose up as they climbed into the ever-darkening sky.

On the horizon, Robert could see the glow emanating from Magdeburg. The Pathfinder boys from Calgary 627 Squadron in their twin-engine Mosquitos, travelling ahead of the main force of bombers at nearly four hundred miles per hour, had dropped their target flares, so most of the aircraft at the front of the stream were already releasing their incendiary and explosive payloads onto the hapless city. As they drew nearer, he checked with his bombardier to confirm all was in readiness for their own bomb run.

"Are you all set Marc?"

"*Chalice de tabernac!*" Marc hissed. "I'm always ready to drop our eggs on those *boche* bastards...uh, sir. Bomb bay doors open!"

Robert corrected for increased drag created by the open doors. "Just make sure we are over the designated target before letting them go. I'm detecting quite a bit of creep-back down there tonight."

'Creep-back' was a phenomenon created by the natural fear that overcame bomber crew as they approached the target zone, where they could see leading aircraft passing through the explosions and searchlights of the flak boxes ahead of them. As they witnessed some of their squadron mates being caught in the beams and shot down, the instinctive response was to try to get through the target zone as quickly as possible, and after dropping their bombs, do the turn-around for home. A number of crews, through either inexperience or loss of nerve, would drop their loads prematurely as they neared the outer edge of the raging inferno, with the result that the bombs would fall short. The resulting fires gradually crept back further in the direction of the bombers' approach as successive crews also dropped their bombs prematurely on the new leading edge, and then turned thankfully back for their bases. Bomber command was aware of this, and constantly hectored its pilots about the wasted tonnage.

About a mile ahead of them Robert saw another Lancaster suddenly pinned in the triangulating cone of three searchlights. Within seconds, bursts of flak began to explode all around the aircraft. Its pilot threw it into a gut-wrenching corkscrew dive to the left, which seemed to lose two of the beams. However, the last light held him doggedly until the pilot had lost most of his altitude. Then, in a manoeuvre that must have strained every rivet in the aircraft, he somehow pulled the bomber out of its dive, to level off in the reverse of his original direction.

At that point the remaining searchlight beam seemed to disappear, possibly a victim of the hundreds of tons of high-explosive being dropped from above. Just before the bomber was enveloped in darkness, Robert saw the right stabilizer and rudder tear off of its rear fuselage.

David gazed out from the rear turret of the Lancaster at the scene below him with a sense of wonder undiminished by the fact that he had been on over twenty *'ops'* and had seen similar sights on many of those occasions.

The city was a sea of fire. A faint cross-hatching of streets could just barely be detected in the glowing orange inferno. In the centre of the conflagration a taller pillar of bright yellow flame rose skyward on the updraft of hot air created by the blaze, which was itself fed more oxygen by the screaming winds that roared in from the edges of the dying metropolis.

This was the classic firestorm. Hot enough at its heart to melt steel and vaporize flesh, it became a perpetual cyclone as the air at its centre raced upward, creating a vacuum that sucked everything from the periphery into the furnace at its core. Building materials, along with any other loose objects - including helpless human beings - were carried inward by the howling winds to where they were utterly consumed by this ravenous engine of destruction. Even those cowering far below the surface in their bomb shelters were baked alive or suffocated as the air was literally pulled from their lungs.

Over the flaming tableaux beneath him, David occasionally saw the silhouette of another Lancaster or Halifax as it dropped even more bombs into the cauldron below, then slowly slid off to the left as it made its turn for home.

Sometimes, as earlier, he would see one of the aircraft trapped in the cone formed by two or three searchlights, and then the explosions of flak would begin to appear. Typically, the desperate bomber would perform a series of extreme manoeuvres as it attempted to escape the targeting lights. More often however, it was unable to elude the illumination as flashes and puffs of black smoke crept ever closer, until a direct hit caused the aircraft to explode.

Other times, a wing would disintegrate when hit by the white-hot shrapnel from an exploding 88mm anti-aircraft shell. More than once, David had gazed on in horror as a stricken bomber would then commence its tumbling spiral downward, and occasionally an airman would exit the blazing craft.

A few parachute canopies might sometimes bloom as a bomber disappeared into the boiling cauldron of smoke and flames beneath. The canopies would hover over the conflagration, held aloft by the upward rush of superheated air, until after less than a minute in their stationary position, they too would burst into flame, and the blackened bodies of the airmen, already roasted alive, would plunge downward to be rendered in the hellish furnace below them.

There, they would be completely consumed in the unimaginable temperatures, where even the metal buttons on their uniforms and flying suits would be reduced to tiny molten rivulets. These eventually solidified into the unidentifiable liquid shapes visible on the ground days later, after it had finally cooled sufficiently for walking upon. The only remains of what had once been young men.

David reached into the right-side pocket of his fleece-lined leather bomber jacket. The sheepskin was only partial proof against the -30 C cold at 20,000 feet, and he was grateful for the extra warmth provided by the electric heating system in his flight suit, which was now plugged into its socket at the back of the turret.

From one pocket, he pulled a handkerchief and stuffed it inside his oxygen mask to cover his mouth and nose. Before takeoff he had placed a large dollop of 'Vicks' between the folded layers of soft cotton. Despite the jibes from fellow crew members and other tail-gunners that it was impossible for odours to rise the nearly four miles up, David believed his oxygen mask did not completely protect him from the noxious smell of burning human flesh. To him, it seemed to waft up interminably on the thermal currents, and he had discovered that the pungent camphor smell of the ointment somehow filtered out or overrode the sickly-sweet scent ascending from the crematorium beneath him.

Neil had told him it was just a figment of his imagination, and that he had never smelt anything of the sort in his mid-upper turret. However, whether it was the product of an over-active imagination, or of the heightened nature of his senses during long hours of nearly total darkness - with the knowledge that death was all around him - the question for David was moot. The 'Vicks' successfully suppressed his strong reactive urge to vomit, which had been his unhappy experience the first time out. He remembered now how the stuff had frozen quickly at that altitude, somewhat reducing the disgusting reek in his turret on the trip home.

The maintenance guys had taken special pains to let him know that they had not enjoyed the task of hosing out the thawing vomit in his turret before they re-armed and oiled the quadruple-mounted guns. He'd felt chastened at the time, but in retrospect, as his experience grew, he began to regard the guys' behaviour as some weird transposition of values, or priorities. Maybe it was just their way of coping with things that earlier in life they could scarcely have imagined. They had, after all, used those same hoses many times to wash out the blood, guts, and sometimes charred remains of his fellow gunners.

David felt the Lancaster lurch upward as its four-ton bomb load dropped away, and lighter now, the huge bomber began a gentle turn to the left. Exiting the flak box, they began to gain speed in a shallow dive toward a cloudbank to the west as they put more distance between themselves and the flaming city. Their aircraft became more invisible to those below as the black painted under-surfaces of the wings and fuselage reflected less of the distant fire's light and began to blend more completely into the darkness that enveloped them.

In the rear turret of the Lancaster, the glow from the burning city receded as the bomber, assisted by a tail wind, approached its maximum cruising speed of three hundred miles per hour. His night-vision, temporarily reduced by the light of the fires, had started to return, and he scanned the skies around him for any sign of the enemy. In the mid-upper turret and in the nose turret, he knew Neil and Marc would be performing a similar vigil. The night-fighters would all be up now looking for stragglers, crippled aircraft, and most of all, revenge.

Their headsets only partially muffled the roar of the four mighty engines. Regardless of this, the crew was thankful for the omnipresent drone of smooth power, because it signalled that with luck, the Merlins would propel them with all possible haste back across the channel to safety. After their harrowing night in the skies above Germany, the reassuring thump of the main landing wheels on tarmac could come none too soon.

Reaching into his oxygen mask, David removed the sweat-saturated handkerchief, and as his natural sense of smell returned he was relieved to find that not the slightest hint of the repulsive charred scent still lingered in the turret.

As the last flicker of the dying city disappeared over the eastern horizon, he could feel some of the tension slowly start to drain from his body. However, this was not a time when he could afford to be careless. He nervously attempted to maintain the blood circulation in his fingers by flexing his gloved hands around the cold gun handles. His night-vision now completely restored, he peered intently into the dark void in search of the deadly enemy predators that he knew must be circling out there somewhere, looking for a kill.

Oberleutnant Eugen Mueller turned the wheel on the steering column of his *Junkers* 88G-6 night-fighter slightly more to the left and adjusted his rudder trim to maintain the smooth counter-clockwise pattern that his aircraft described at about 6,000 metres, as he circled inside the RAF bomber stream.

For defensive purposes the entire area of Northwest Europe had been divided into a grid-like pattern of "boxes" behind a line of '*Freya*' radar sets stretching the length of the coast from France to the Baltic. At night, behind the eponymous *Kammhuber* line, each box contained a night-fighter referred to as *Zahme Sau* 'Tame Boar' sent aloft upon the first radar warning of an inbound bomber stream. There, it circled continuously, equipped with a forward-scanning radar set, and always in search of the nearly invisible four-engine Lancaster or Halifax heavy bombers seeking either to penetrate or exit Germany.

The introduction of 'Window' – tens of thousands of thin foil strips dropped from each individual bomber – had eventually reduced even the longer-range *Wurzburg* radar's ability to locate individual aircraft or guide the night-fighters toward them. In an effort to counter this, individual single engine night-fighters had been given leeway to roam around the night sky as *Wilde Sau* 'Wild Boar', entering the bomber stream at will to use their airborne '*Naxos*' radars to locate the nearly invisible enemy droning through the night sky.

This effectively augmented Mueller and his fellow *Zahme Sau* who were now equipped with the newer *Lichtenstein SN-2* radar, which could home in on the signals emanating from the *H2S* ground-tracking radar attached to the bottom rear fuselage of most RAF Bomber Command aircraft. These *Zahme Sau* were most often twin-engine types like the *Bf*110 or *Ju*88, equipped with upward firing cannon.

As he glanced behind him Mueller could see the ghostly features of his flight engineer, Bernt Esche, illuminated by the faint greenish light from the screen of his radar set. Hunched over the device, he was intently examining the signals that where being picked up by the spindly array of antennae projecting from the nose of the aircraft. Seated just forward of Esche, and holding a pair of binoculars to his face, the observer, Raul, was peering intently into the night skies ahead of them.

Further in the distant Northeast, they could just see the glowing pyre of Magdeburg reflecting pinkish-orange on the bottom of the far-off cloud cover.

"Keep a sharp eye on that screen Bernt," Mueller growled. "They'll be heading home by now and we'll want to play a little *schräge musik* for the bastards. Then we'll see if they like dancing to our tune for a change."

The *Ju*88's two engines droned steadily and he stole a brief look at each, confirming that there was no trace of exhaust flame to warn prospective prey of their approach. The ports on each of the two power plants had been covered - much the same as those on the enemy bombers - to conceal any flash emitted by the engine's exhaust manifolds.

As the engines were located nearly abreast of the *Junker's* cockpit, the shields provided the additional effect of preserving Eugen Mueller's night-vision, which otherwise would have been considerably diminished by the peripheral flashing of a standard exhaust port. He was scanning the dark skies ahead of him when Esche's voice broke in over the headset.

"I'm locked onto one of the *schwein* at ten o'clock high, about five hundred metres above us."

Eugen responded by bringing the aircraft about 30 degrees left as he pulled the yoke slowly toward his chest to put the *Junkers* into a slow climb. After about a minute, he was able to detect a slightly darker patch of sky directly above him as he drifted in from the right.

At almost the same moment Raul called out. "I've got him! It's either a Lancaster or a Halifax. Wait, I can see the rudders – rounded. It's a Lanc!"

Eugen flattened out at two hundred metres below the bomber's altitude and adjusted the throttles until he was directly underneath the dark shape above him. Slowly, he began to climb, matching the larger aircraft's speed so as not to pull out in front of it and thus alert its forward-located bombardier/nose-gunner or the pilot, to his presence.

The huge black shape above him ploughed on steadily. Its lack of evasive manoeuvres convinced him that it was completely unaware of his existence. As he eased the *Junkers* upward and closer to the dark shape, it slowly took on the familiar outline of a Lancaster. The four slim liquid-cooled Merlins distinguished it from the otherwise similarly-shaped Halifax, which was powered by the rounder air-cooled Bristol Hercules radial engines.

When he was about fifty metres below the Lancaster, Eugen hissed. "Esche! Cue the orchestra!"

There was an audible click, as the safeties disengaged from the pair of 30mm cannons, now projecting upward at an oblique forward angle, just aft of the cockpit. Eugen eased back slightly on the throttle, which allowed his aircraft to drift back to a position just below the tail section of the Lancaster.

He steadied the *Junkers*, and in a strained, adrenalin-pitched voice, shrieked the command. "Esche! Overture!"

Eugen was temporarily blinded by the muzzle flash of the cannon as they erupted behind him. The crescendo was deafening, and after less than a dozen rounds had been fired, he threw the *Junkers* into a steep twisting dive to the right, praying the bomber would not explode or shower his aircraft with jagged debris before he had put enough distance between them. After plunging 1,000 metres, with his night-vision partially restored, he pulled the yoke into his belly, and with great effort levelled the aircraft off.

Frantically searching the sky, he called out to Raul. "Do you see it?"

"*Ja*. It's at seven o'clock, a bit above us – there!" The observer pointed.

He was gesturing at the stricken Lancaster through the rear of the *Junker's* Plexiglas canopy. The bomber was losing altitude in a steady, shallow dive. Its left inboard engine was trailing a blazing streak through the night sky, and the entire rear fuselage was aflame. Just before it disappeared into a cloud, he thought he saw a solitary figure, on fire, leap from the doomed airplane.

The night suddenly exploded around him, and David's headset was filled with the sound of Neil screaming in the mid-upper turret amid the shattering din of cannon shells tearing through the fuselage of the bomber. Just as suddenly the firing stopped, but Neil continued to shriek. David thought he saw a darker form slide off into the night, far to his left and below them. He was unable to hold it in his sights as his night-vision left him, and his irises damped down to compensate for the streak of flame trailing from the inboard port engine. It was just outside the Perspex wall of his turret, seemingly close enough to touch.

In the cockpit of the bomber Robert was struggling, as he tried with all his strength to hold the control column steady. Most of the nose section of the Lancaster, as well as the crew positions directly behind him had been destroyed by the 30mm cannon shells as they passed through the front part of the bomber. Something jagged and hot had penetrated his ribs, and he clenched his teeth to prevent himself screaming in pain every time he flexed the muscles in his left shoulder and arm, as he desperately attempted to control the aircraft.

The freezing wind howling into his face through the gaping holes in the front of the aircraft's fuselage was deafening. On his port wing, the twisted, stationary propeller was locked, un-feathered, to the flaming engine, inducing massive drag as the stricken bomber yawed left while it rapidly lost altitude. It took every ounce of Robert's strength to counter with his feet on the rudder pedals and pull the control column closer into his chest.

The screaming had stopped, and David heard Robert's voice coming high and tight through the headset as he struggled with the bomber's damaged controls. "Davey! Davey! Are you alright back there?"

"Yeah, I think so!" David shouted. "How are we holding together!"

"I think everyone but us has bought it." Robert rasped. "I'm hit in the ribs. It feels bad, but I think I can hold the ship steady for a minute. Neil's still moaning into his microphone. See if you can help him but make it quick if you want to get out yourself!"

David grunted and tore off his oxygen mask. Unplugging his electric suit-warmer, he twisted around, opened the turret doors, and crawled into the shattered fuselage.

The interior was rapidly becoming engulfed in flames. Through the fire and smoke, he could see Neil hanging in the mid-upper turret, his eyes wide and staring, as red foam bubbled from his lips. There was only his upper torso left. Everything else had been obliterated by the cannon rounds. His organs and glistening shreds of viscera hung beneath him, while fluids dripped from his open abdominal cavity.

He turned instinctively from the gruesome sight just as a sudden explosion of flame blew him back through the open doors into his turret.

The aluminum skin of the Lancaster's tail section had begun to glow red, and the parachute strapped to the seat of David's flight suit was aflame as he struggled to his knees and slammed the doors shut behind him. Meanwhile, the blackened panels of Perspex on his turret were beginning to blister with the incredible heat. He stomped frantically on the turret rotation pedal, and miraculously the system still functioned. It spun through ninety degrees as he desperately slid open the rear doors, which were now so hot that they scorched his gloves. Gasping in terror as the flames licked all around him, David launched himself through the open doors into the night sky above Germany.

The pain across his buttocks was excruciating as the flames from his parachute pack began to burn through the leather flying suit. David writhed in agony, and contorted his body in repeated efforts to release the tangled straps which held it to him. Flailing desperately in the plunging slipstream, he felt the last clasp finally release, and the screams choked in his throat as the blazing wad of canvas and string sailed away into the night.

Almost immediately the pain stopped, and a quiescent numbness embraced him as even the sound of the frigid air racing past his ears faded into silence. Knowing he would die in only a few moments, he rolled over onto his back, where he felt the wind rushing past his arms and legs.

Gazing at the soundless cold stars above him, he heard his grandfather's voice, chanting. It was a song that they had sung together often around the winter fire when he was a boy. The refrain enveloped him, warm and reassuring. He joined the chant and knew that nature was about to accept him again into some part of its great cycle. No longer struggling, he closed his eyes as a glowing vision of his father's distraught face at *Agawa* drifted strangely across his mind. Numbly, he felt the wings of a great eagle that had come to bear him away, brushing against his back. Then suddenly, everything went black.

Reunion

Peter was on his second cup of coffee as he sat in the officer's mess staring out of the heavily-taped window while the first glow of dawn began to illuminate the airfield. The snow was especially deep this year, and although the tarmac had been cleared over the past two days, it remained completely surrounded by huge white banks where the ploughs had pushed it up. Through these massive walls more than a dozen wide openings had been carved to clear the various access roads necessary to give the aircraft, fuel trucks, maintenance carts, and emergency vehicles, some way on and off of the frozen strip.

Surrounding the strip was a natural palisade of tall, snow-covered conifers, which grew in a large swath through central Germany known as the *Teutoburg* Forest. This was the location of an historic victory by Germanic tribesmen in 9 C.E. over the Roman General, Publius Quintilius Varus. This was not lost on Peter, who now pondered the irony of his current location in this last-ditch defence of the Fatherland against an airborne Legion of aircraft constantly threatening to attack, both day and night, from the skies above him.

The growing light revealed a thermal inversion, manifesting as a low heavy overcast. However, the air at ground-level was freezing, and smoke from the assorted chimneys on the airbase rose straight up before flattening itself into a thin horizontal pattern just below the cloud layer. Not that finer weather would have increased the odds of him going aloft today in any case.

His *Fw*190D had been sitting in the maintenance hut for five days waiting for a new fuel-injector set. With the invaluable assistance of his brilliant engine mechanic Reiner Grundt, he'd kept the *Jumo* 213 purring despite the injectors having gone at least fifty percent beyond the amount of usage which normally warranted them simply being thrown away. Inevitably however, the combination of continually declining fuel quality and freezing winter temperatures had finally done them in. There had come a day when even Reiner's most powerful and profane incantations could only rouse six of the twelve cylinders to fire, and he had moved on to engines where his misplaced alchemy had greater prospects of success.

Three days ago he'd received a supposedly new set of injectors from the factory, but it was in even shoddier condition than the one he was replacing. Peter had been so frustrated, that before discretion prevailed, he had considered telegraphing the armaments minister, Albert Speer, to tell him that anyone thinking it was a good idea to staff an industry producing highly sophisticated and technologically advanced war machines with half-starved slave labourers, needed to have their head examined.

Nothing ever arrived on time anymore. Everywhere, the *Luftwaffe* was in the same lamentable condition. There was a shortage of aircraft, shortage of fuel, shortage of parts, and crucially, a shortage of well-trained pilots. Most of the boys they sent up these days were merely cannon fodder for the veteran allied pilots, who, on the western front at least, suffered from none of the *Luftwaffe*'s shortages of anything.

In fact, their numbers seemed to increase daily. Not just fighters, but bombers too. It was the American 8th Air Force 'aluminum overcast' by day and Bomber Command's thousand bomber raids by night. As a result, even the skies over the Fatherland were becoming an extremely dangerous place for German pilots. This included skilled veterans like himself.

Twenty-four hours per day, the hunters were becoming the hunted. The P-51s, with their extraordinary range, not only escorted American bombers all the way to their targets in Germany, but also swarmed in separate groups, seeking to engage German aircraft in the air, or strafe them on the ground.

Things did not improve at night either. The British and Canadian Mosquitoes were as fast as any fighter and painted an inky black for night operations, which made them nearly invisible. They often joined the bomber stream and had the range to accompany the four-engine heavies all the way to target. While preoccupied with their stealthy approach on a Lancaster or Halifax, many a German night-fighter had been brought down by these heavily armed high-speed 'wooden wonders'.

He took another gulp of coffee, and the caffeine began to energize him. By a great stroke of luck, he had ample supplies of the real stuff. It was not the *ersatz* sludge, but actual coffee, courtesy of an old friend in the *Panzer* Corps who had liberated huge quantities of the ground beans from an American supply dump during the recent and very temporary victory in the Ardennes salient.

At least one small kind of a victory he thought, while gulping another enervating mouthful.

A few droplets escaped near the corner of his mouth, and as he reached instinctively inside his tunic for a handkerchief, his fingers came in contact with an envelope. He'd received the telegram more than a month ago, but for some reason he couldn't bring himself to throw it away. *Why? Was he saving it as some kind of macabre souvenir, or did it serve the more sinister purpose of filling an aching vacuum by fuelling a lust for revenge – as a final poignant memento of that night his parents had ceased to exist?*

Their house on *Waldestrasse* was to the west of the city, nestled in a small valley where the local farmers still tended the orchards which they had somehow managed to save during the decades of surrounding development. His childhood there had been idyllic, filled with days of hiking, first with his parents, and then with his young sister through the fields and nearby hills. Thank goodness Elke had been away at her boarding school outside of Berlin. As bad as it had felt for him to convey to her the awful news, its effect had been much harder to bear for his sister.

The notice had been written in the impersonal bureaucratic style normally employed in official government communications. "… regret to inform you that your parents, *Herr* Arnold Schmidt and *Frau* Ingrid Schmidt perished when their house was destroyed by bombs during the air raid of…etc., etc." There followed the usual uninspired harangue about the criminals of Bomber Command, eventual victory over the subhuman enemy, and how the beloved *Führer* shared his grief.

He had immediately flown to an airfield near his parent's small town, and commandeered a taxi which took him to the location of the solid brick house he had grown up in. Nothing remained, except a large crater surrounded by still-smouldering rubble. It lay amid several similar craters, which now represented all that remained of what had once been a quiet, tree-lined street.

Even now, the mere thought of his parent's final moments caused the gorge to rise in his throat. Why had some idiot bombardier released his bombs over what was a site of absolutely no military significance? There was no evidence in the region of a crashed aircraft that might have made a desperate last-minute effort to lighten itself and remain airborne. The target that night had been fifty kilometres away, and to the east.

More likely someone had got nervous, or simply decided he didn't want to risk his skin in the flak over the target and had released the bomb load prematurely so they could begin the trip home. That particular bomber crew had probably gone back to a warm breakfast and clean sheets, but as Peter had stared into the gaping black hole, he felt the cold chill of death. His home, along with his mother and father, were gone forever. 'Perished', the telegram had said. 'Obliterated', was closer to the truth.

He could still picture his mother's face as it had been during his last visit, a look of concern and pride upon her face as she gazed at him in his pilot's uniform. Her blond hair had become streaked with grey, and she wondered aloud if he was being fed well enough as she served up a second helping of his favourite pork roast. She and his father had gone for two months without their meat ration to be able to serve the meal but had assured him they were fine.

His father, always a quiet man, had looked thinner than before. The stress of working his regular shift as a metallurgical engineer, and then doing the hours of nightly drills with the *Volksturm* was taking its toll. However, he seemed more concerned about Peter's long-term prospects for survival in the air. He was silently proud of the fact that his son was a highly-respected pilot and a multiple ace, but he did not think the course of the war for Germany could end in anything but disaster.

A near-pacifist and apolitical, Peter's father had regardless joined the other old men and young boys to train with his *Panzerfaust* and ancient rifle, as some symbolic recognition of his duty to protect his family or neighbourhood. Not that there was much chance they could prevail against the Russian *T-34s* and *Stormoviks* advancing relentlessly from the east. He'd put on a brave face for his son, but ironically, when they had parted, Peter realized his father was actually thinking that it was probably his son's days that were numbered. His embrace had lasted just that bit longer, as though imagining he might never hold him again.

Now, as the Eastern Front was collapsing before the onslaught of overwhelming Russian military strength, his thoughts turned with increasing dread upon his sister. Yesterday he had sent another unanswered telegram urging her in all haste to join him here. His thoughts grew even more troubled, but he dared not contemplate what might happen if she were ever captured by Soviet troops.

Peter swallowed hard and tried with difficulty to push the thoughts from his mind. Noticing the activity outside, he tapped on the frost-covered window, motioning at one of the young fitters who had been shuffling by to come in. With the collar of his wool great coat turned up and wrapped in a scarf, Hans Wend, barely seventeen, shook the snow off the bottom of his boots and apprehensively entered the room.

"Did my fuel injectors arrive yet?" He asked the boy.

"No. Nothing at all has arrived." Hans answered warily.

Peter could see the other boys huddled together and waiting impatiently outside as they stamped their feet to maintain circulation in the cold morning air.

"What are you fellows in such a hurry about then?"

The fitter was surprised. "Oh, I guess you haven't heard. A British heavy went down last night no more than a few kilometres from here. Mueller from *Nachtjagdgeschwader 1*, says he got it. You can still see a bit of smoke. We were going to take a look."

Peter thought for a moment. He had nothing but time on his hands today, so he reached for the keys to the *Kübelwagen*. "Wait. I'll drive us over there."

They came across the wreck just over two kilometres from the airbase and about a hundred metres off of a secondary access road. The bomber had come in over the road at a relatively shallow angle, clipping dozens of the lofty fir trees. The snapped trunks and branches bore mute testimony to the dying aircraft's direction of approach. The fresh gashes of yellow wood beneath the greyish bark of the splintered trees stood out in contrast to the predominantly white snow and green shades of the surrounding forest.

The path of broken foliage ended in a smoking crater. The dark steaming earth on the periphery had been exposed by the force of impact, and the fierce heat of the fiery explosion had melted the deep snow for several metres around it.

Very little that was recognizable remained of the bomber. Peter saw part of the tail section sticking up out of the crater, and as he approached the smoking edge, he recognized three of the aircraft's Merlin engines - solid and heavy - buried deep in the exposed soil.

Near the far lip of the crater where the nose and cockpit had impacted, Peter recognized several assorted clusters of scorched and blackened bones with charred shreds of flesh still attached to them. He counted the parts of at least four skulls which he thought he could identify as such because of their teeth. *There would be no survivors here*, he thought.

For a moment, he tried to imagine what it must have been like to be one of the crewmen in the final moments of the bomber's plunge. Those who had not escaped by this last stage of the descent would know that death was certain. If they were trapped and burning, they would probably welcome it. He shuddered and thrust the thought from his mind. The odds were high that his own particular end would be something quite similar.

He made his way back around the part of the crater nearest the road. The young fitters and riggers were pointing, wide-eyed, at parts of the wreckage. One, who had brought a *Leica*, was snapping photos of the other fitters who were standing in front of the twisted tail section that loomed up out of the hole.

Peter noticed that due to the force of impact, the rear turret had detached from its base in the tail section and was nowhere to be seen. Out of curiosity he calculated the bomber's angle of descent through the broken trees, imagined the impact, and then tried to estimate how far forward the turret would have been thrown. He scanned through the trees about fifty metres past the crater and thought he saw something dark there, poking up through the snow.

Past the melted area on the far side of the crater the snow was at least two metres deep, and it was only with the greatest exertion Peter was able to slowly make his way toward the object.

His efforts were rewarded however, when he reached the spot and immediately recognized the outline of a Frazier-Nash FN20 rear turret, with its quadruple mounted .303 calibre guns. The few remaining bits of shattered Perspex were thoroughly scorched, and the metal back of the turret, with its doors gaping open, was completely burnt to a rusty brown colour.

Hans had now made his way up beside him. He was also staring at the broken turret when Peter, thinking out loud, absently mused, "I wonder if the poor bugger made it out?"

"Mueller claims he saw one jump, but on fire!' Hans piped excitedly.

"Phew!" A great cloud formed in front of him as Peter expelled his breath into the frozen air. The enemy airman's fate did not bear thinking about, and he consciously chose not to dwell on the subject.

He'd successfully pushed the thought from his mind and was about to turn away, when Hans, bending down to brush some snow from the turret's base, exclaimed. "What the hell? It's the same as yours!"

Hans moved his hand from in front of the image. There, on the semi-gloss black paint remaining near the bottom of the turret was an image that caused Peter's breath to catch in his throat. He bent closer, at first not believing his own eyes, but finally there was no escaping it. On the turret, its former occupant had painted a wolf's head that was identical to the one on his own aircraft. Next to the wolf-head were two German *balkenkreuzes*.

Hans whistled. "This gunner was a dead shot. Two kills."

Peter wondered ruefully for a moment if either of the two kills had been pilots that he had known, then turned and looked back past the crater, and further through the tunnel of broken trees created by the bomber during the last seconds before impact.

He made a few brief calculations in his head and then turned to the fitter. "Hans, let's return to the *Kübelwagen*. As soon as we get back to the airfield, I want you to run up the *Storch*. I'm going to see if we can find our tail-gunner."

Hans looked puzzled. "Why?"

Peter was already forcing his way through the deep snow along the trail leading back to the road. He called back over his shoulder to the fitter. "If there is any possibility that man is alive, we must find him. I think I know him!"

Thirty minutes later, the little high-winged monoplane was sitting on an access ramp with its uniquely air-cooled Argus As10c

V8 engine producing a smooth, muffled thrum, while its hot exhaust gasses clouded the frigid air behind.

Peter snugged the collar of his fur-lined leather flight suit up under his chin and climbed through the left-side door of the *Fi*156 *'Storch'*, where he wedged himself into its spartan cockpit.

Hans leaned in and cupped his hand over Peter's ear to be heard over the engine noise. "Everything appears to be running smoothly sir. You've got two hours-worth of fuel."

"Very good, Hans. I hope to be back sooner than that. This bloody crate is freezing!"

Hans nodded his acknowledgement, shouting. "Good luck sir!" Then, stepping back, he slammed the tiny aircraft's door shut.

Peter radioed the tower and received permission to take off. Holding the control column in his right hand, he advanced the throttle and eased the *Storch* onto the access ramp. After lining the aircraft up with the strip, he pushed the throttle all the way forward, and slowly the little plane began to gain speed as it moved down the runway. Barely a third of the distance down the strip, the wheels on its fixed undercarriage rose off of the tarmac and the aircraft began to climb nimbly into the sky.

The *Storch*'s relatively small engine lacked the massive power and torque of the fighter planes Peter usually flew, and as a result the control column felt very light to his touch. He banked the little monoplane into a gentle left-hand turn, while below, the growling of the *Storch*'s engine echoed off the hanger walls. There, Hans watched him fly off to the east, holding steady at not much more than one hundred and fifty metres above tree-top height.

He arrived over the crash site in less than a minute, and after circling around the still smouldering crater, he lined the aircraft up along the stretch of broken trees and headed off in the direction from which the bomber had descended.

Below him lay a sea of tall conifers, their branches covered and bent with an enormous burden of white snow. Because of the low ceiling, his visibility was limited to only five kilometres, but he maintained his line of flight on a steady compass heading, constantly scanning to the left and right of the forest passing below him.

At about three kilometres out, he was traveling roughly parallel to a fire-break on his left. Just before reaching the intersection of two small local supply roads, he noticed the dark green patch of foliage below him. Slowly circling around, he came down lower for a better look, skimming barely fifty metres above the tallest branches.

The trees were growing close together, and it was impossible to see the forest floor beneath them. However, something had caused the snow to drop off of an area of the boughs on three trees growing so close together that their branches partially overlapped.

The lowering ceiling had caused the temperature to rise since dawn, but Peter doubted that the air had warmed enough yet to cause the weight of snow to slip from the branches by melting. To corroborate these thoughts, there was no evidence of this on any of the surrounding trees. No, he thought, the branches must have been cleared by something falling through them from above. There was no parachute to be seen, but except for the possibility of a falling piece of debris from the bomber, there was a very good probability that this was where the rear gunner had come to earth.

Peter reached for the radio and called in the general coordinates, requesting that a search party be dispatched immediately. Then, he circled once more and turned the aircraft onto a heading that would take him back to the airfield.

As he taxied up to the hanger, Peter saw Hans standing there beside the *Kübelwagen,* and he had the vehicle's motor already running. By the time he had shut down the *Storch*'s engine, the grinning fitter had materialized at the door to assist him out of the cockpit.

"The search party has left already, and they took three dogs with them. With their halftrack breaking a trail along the fire road, you should be able to follow them in the *Kübelwagen!*"

Peter noticed the fitter's expectant expression. "You look like you'd like to come along. Have I got your interest up?"

Hans replied tentatively. "Well, sir, you seem pretty intent on finding this guy, and I've never actually seen an enemy flyer, dead or alive. Would you mind terribly if I came along?"

Peter had already slid behind the wheel of the *Kübelwagen*. The young fitter was standing beside the passenger door with a look of boyish enthusiasm spread across his wide freckled face.

"Well, what are you waiting for?" Peter demanded. "Hop in!"

Peter slammed the stick-shift into gear, and with a sudden lurch, the little utility vehicle sped off down the frozen ruts in bumpy pursuit of the search party.

David slowly opened his eyes, and was seized by an overwhelming sense of shock. He was still alive! Everything was black, but something wet and cold covered his face. Instinctively, he moved his hand up to wipe it off, and instantly felt a stab of pain in his shoulder and in the bruised tri-cep of his upper arm. Sweeping his gloved hand across his forehead, he realized the freezing substance was snow, melting from the heat of his skin. As his eyes became accustomed to the gloom, he discovered that he was lying on his back, spread-eagled upon a deep blanket of snow, with the dark indistinct forms of trees looming above him.

Slowly, the memory of falling from the doomed Lancaster, and the struggle to get out of his burning parachute harness – followed by the fatalistic moment when he had accepted his impending death – all began to seep back into his consciousness.

The increasing light of dawn revealed the snowless boughs directly above him. With a sense of grateful astonishment he realized that the large flexible branches of the fir trees had slowed his decent enough to allow the several metres of soft snow to absorb the force of his impact. The aching muscles on the back of his legs, arms, and upper body, together with the throbbing pain in his right temple, were a bruised testimony to the nature of his downward passage through the snow-laden canopy.

He lay there trying to take it all in and wondering at the absurd odds against his having survived. His head continued to throb as his mind drifted, and he eventually sank again into unconsciousness.

He was jolted awake by the howling of wolves.

The overcast daylight of mid-morning revealed the snow-covered floor of a mature coniferous forest that was relatively clear of underbrush. Looking up, David could see that he was entirely surrounded by the towering fir trees. The trunks were at least two or three times the thickness of a man's torso, and they seemed to create an impenetrable barrier to his vision in nearly all directions, except to the north, however, where it was slightly less-densely treed. It was from that direction he'd heard the lupine cries.

The wound on his temple had opened again, and wiping the blood from his eye, he tried unsuccessfully to stem the flow as he attempted to focus on the forms moving in the distance.

He had risen to his knees and could see the bobbing tips of their ears and tails in the distance as the pack closed on him. Their hot breath formed clouds of vapour above them as the three animals leapt and clawed their way through the deep snow, struggling to get nearer. Growling and snarling with the excitement of the hunt, they were now close enough for him to see the three sets of burning eyes, and their quivering wrinkled lips drawn back tightly over gleaming fangs.

Some primordial instinct rose up from inside of him, while everything seemed to slow, as he stood up, took a deep breath, and felt a new strength possess him. His senses took on a new acuity, while events seemed to reduce in speed even further, and the sound of his grandfather's chanting began once again to echo through his mind. Strangely, he seemed to be detached and drifting above his body, but at the same time, a part of it. He heard the slow, exaggerated sound of his own breathing, and felt the muscles in his neck swelling. Reflexively, the powerful howl of a Timber Wolf, which he had learned to imitate as a child, rose chillingly out of his throat.

The two rearmost animals stopped in their tracks, transfixed with fear, but the leader of the pack had already launched itself through the air – jaws wide in slavering anticipation of a kill.

David rotated smoothly through his hips to throw a vicious right hook, and the full force of his gloved fist smashed its way through the animal's teeth, continuing deeply into its throat. The Alsatian's gag reflex sent a spasm into its throat, and the bleeding jaws opened even wider now as it attempted to regurgitate David's arm. Imbued with a desperate strength, he rammed his fist deeper, and twisting the dog around on its back, he grasped the hindquarters, fell to one knee, and with enormous force drove the thrashing creature down upon his other. There was a terrific crack as its spine snapped, and the animal went suddenly limp, before a last breath slowly gurgled up out of its throat.

As the adrenaline slowly drained from his muscles, David felt his heartbeat and breathing regain their normal rate, while the world around him also resumed its usual pace. He rose to his feet and dropped the body of the black Alsatian to the ground. Meanwhile, the other two dogs were on their haunches a few metres off, whimpering in fearful contemplation of the sight before them.

There was a sudden guttural shout of surprise as the dog-master and half a dozen fellow members of the search party emerged into the small clearing from the north and pointed their rifles at him.

In resignation, David slowly raised his hands into the air to surrender. "*Kammerad!*"

However, there was no appeasing the dog-master. As the *Feldwebel* in charge, his face went purple with rage when he spied the body of his lead-dog lying at David's feet. He was a huge man, puffing from the exertion of wading through the thigh-deep snow. Incensed and bearing a look of fury, he advanced on David, shrieking German invective.

David tensed as he saw him reach down, undo a snap on the holster of his *Luger*, and then pull the pistol out. He raised it and took aim at David's chest, but the huge dog-master suddenly froze when a commanding voice from behind him barked an order to desist.

"*Halt!*"

At first the big German seemed confused as he partially lowered his weapon, hesitated, and then slowly raised it again to David's chest. The dog-master's jaw muscles clenched, and his chest heaved as his eyes darted from the carcass of his beloved lead-dog to David's bloody glove. Then, they narrowed as he took aim down the barrel of his gun…

Peter and Hans were gaining on the search party as they struggled up the forest trail broken by the soldiers and their dogs. Suddenly about a hundred metres ahead they heard the blood-curdling howl of a wolf, followed by the strangled sounds of a choking dog. Drawing nearer, they heard angry shouting from the search party, and as they burst into the clearing Peter saw the dog-master raising his *Luger* to fire at something that was blocked from his view by the *Feldwebel*'s hulking figure.

"Hold your fire!" he commanded.

He saw the dog-master begin to lower his weapon, then tense his shoulders, and raise the *Luger* again with an obvious intent to shoot.

Peter drew his own pistol and pulled back on the action so the man could hear the round chambering. "*Feldwebel*! I am giving you an order. Lower your weapon. Do not shoot that man!"

The dog-master glanced over his shoulder at Peter, his eyes blazing. "He's killed my best dog! The *schwein* deserves to die!"

Peter's tone was firm. "Don't worry. I will deal with this myself. Put your weapon away."

The *Feldwebel* reluctantly holstered his pistol. Peter kept his *Luger* raised and stepped out from behind the dog-master to regard his captive more closely. He saw the tattered enemy flight suit, and his finger instinctively tightened on the trigger. The airman's gaze shifted from the *Feldwebel*'s holster to Peter, as his eyes went wide with recognition.

"Peter Schmidt!" The words leapt out of David's mouth.

It was then, puffing with exertion, that the fitter emerged into the clearing, carrying the burnt scraps of a parachute. He stopped in his tracks, staring in surprise at David.

Peter continued to point his pistol at David's chest. His gaze shifted between the airman and the fuming dog-master.

The dog-master was insistent. "He is one of the murderers who kill our families. Shoot him!"

David could see that Peter was struggling in his mind, blinking once as a troubled look flitted momentarily across his face...which was now a torment of indecision.

Music of the Spheres

Dawn found them paddling east under a cloudless sky, and by midmorning David signalled that they should go ashore. It was very rocky here with no natural landing, so he pointed at a location to the left of a steep cliff face.

A short distance before their destination they came upon a cleft in the rock. Open to the lake, and perhaps five or six yards wide, it penetrated the shoreline for about fifty yards into the rocky cliff. Basaltic lava had filled this folded dike between adjoining igneous layers a billion years before, and had long-since eroded, leaving this wide water-filled crack. Deeper in, it narrowed to a steep rocky slope before disappearing into the forest growing on top of the bluff. The two walls of this corridor rose straight up, with some variation, for approximately fifteen to twenty yards. Part of the way in, a huge block of granite, probably deposited as part of some ancient glacial moraine, had jammed about a quarter of the distance down into the crevasse. It hung there menacingly, high above the waterway beneath it.

It was only after some difficulty that they were able to clamber out of the canoes and tie them to the gnarled protruding root of a cedar tree, which was itself clinging precariously to a jumble of gigantic square granite boulders.

David led the others. They gingerly stepped around mossy indentations still full of rainwater, and large boulders which in some places nearly blocked their passage.

The pictographs were located on a flat part of the northern wall, facing outward in the direction of the lake. A rounded ledge of rock projected out from the base of the cliff for about six feet and about the same distance down to the surface of the water. They would have to make their way along this sloping ledge to view the images.

There was a slight breeze, and insects buzzed lazily in the air as David approached the spot where he knew the images would be. However, he hesitated for half a step as the memory of his father flooded back into his mind. Again, he saw him reach out to press his hand against the strange pictures as if to draw some mysterious strength from them, but seeming instead to have his own drained away. Sadly, he recalled his father's shoulders sagging from the failure to commune with spirits he had hoped would give him the power to wrestle his demons, or to help him reconnect with the world he had known as a younger man.

When David first caught sight of the ancient images, they appeared to be subtly shifting position as dapples of iridescent light reflecting from the lake behind him danced rhythmically over the rock-face. Heat radiated from them, which he ascribed to a combination of direct sunlight and that also mirrored off of the lapping surface of the water onto the hard granite.

The pulsating light and blazing heat made him slightly dizzy. As he turned his head away from the glare, he saw a small flock of seagulls had suddenly appeared above the water nearby, shrieking voraciously as they dove upon a school of tiny fish. Literally plunging though the surface of the lake, the birds relentlessly continued to target the hapless minnows as they made their perilous journey down-shore.

As the spectacle receded, David resumed his inspection of the pictographs.

Jack was the first to approach. "This stuff is spooky. Those snake images give me the creeps."

"I don't think they are supposed to represent something evil Jack." David tried to reassure him.

"Perhaps not, but I got goose bumps all the same. When I first looked at them, they seemed to be on fire. Maybe it was just the light reflecting off the water..."

Before David could venture a response, Jason and Peter arrived.

Jason scanned the pictographs in amazement. "Look at that reddish colour. How do you figure they were able to make paint that would hold up for so long?"

David pointed to a grouping of rusty streaks on a nearby slab of fallen rock. "There is a lot of iron in the local geology, and as you know there is almost every other kind of mineral too in the pre-Cambrian rock of the Canadian shield, so I imagine that over time a normal process of trial and error would result in the discovery of how to combine them with bear fat, berry juice, or something like that to get the pigments."

Peter was intently examining one of the paintings of a creature with horns and a serrated ridge on its back. He had moved from image to image with Jason next to him. Both were fascinated by the shapes and colours, trying to puzzle out the different symbols for some significance or meaning.

"How old do you reckon these things are?" Jason asked.

"Don't really know." David replied. "The shaman says they were here long before the arrival of Europeans. One of the images looks like a horse with a cross. If that's what they are supposed to be, then they can't be pre-Columbian. However, it might not be a Christian cross the artist was trying to represent, and a female moose looks a lot like a horse."

He continued. "Of course, there is no written record of their origin, but there is an oral tradition that mentions them in stories. I can't say how much you can believe. Every story teller is bound to embellish things a bit. Do you know what I mean? Parting the Red Sea? Endless supplies of loaves and fishes – that sort of stuff."

Jack laughed. "Hah! You better not let Reverend Wilson hear you talking like that. He'll want to baptize your heathen arse for that one."

David grunted. "Don't worry about me. The reverend knows better than to come anywhere near me with that voodoo bullshit!"

Jack cackled again. "Now Davey, that's no way to talk about a man so filled with the spirit of the Lord!"

David chuckled. "The way that moonshine lush puts it away, I'd say more often than not he's filled with the spirit of the gourd!"

By now all semblance of seriousness had disappeared as the boys, gasping for breath between bursts of laughter, in turn tried to outdo each other with various kinds of word associations or puns disparaging religious authority.

Peter shook his head gravely and strove to prevent a grin from spreading across his face. "I'm afraid you boys won't be able to go to heaven after all that smutty talk. Fortunately for me however, I'll be inheriting the fortune of my uncle Otto, inventor of the synthetic ribbed condom, which means I'll be able to bribe my way in."

The other three shook their heads in obvious disbelief, and deliberately groaned.

Peter then furrowed his brow pensively. "Actually, I laid awake for most of last night worrying about the *Führer*. You must have heard the rumour about him having only one ball. I suspect that he may not have even one, and that what has been mistaken as the single ball is actually a descended haemorrhoid. In which case we will have to address him much differently."

"What do you mean?" Jason asked.

Peter suddenly shot his hand into the air in a Hitler salute and shouted. "*Sieg* Pile!"

Momentarily stunned, his two cousins shrieked with laughter as they returned the salute. "*Sieg* Pile!"

David was shaking his head. "I knew it was a mistake to bring you cretins here. I was prepared to give you an anthropology lecture, and instead you've reverted to your basest preoccupations."

Looking down his nose at them he continued. "As for me, I'm focusing my attentions on more highly evolved types than the ones that exist in your fevered imaginations."

Then, turning to Peter he asked. "Where was it you saw that mermaid?"

Jack groaned. "I knew it! He's been fantasizing about fish!"

David winced. "Not just any fish, you amateur! I'll have you know that only mermaids raised on the finest of trout are up to my standards."

The implications of this caused the boys to collapse into another round of breathless laughter. Upon recovery, David led them to a blueberry patch nearby, and they spent the next twenty minutes stuffing their mouths with the ripe fruit.

By late afternoon they were back in their canoes, and paddling west along the shoreline. They trolled a length of fishing line with a lure attached behind both craft, and after about an hour of this, David felt a tug. After a strenuous ten minutes of wrestling with the line, he pulled in a lake trout which they guessed weighed about twenty pounds, or about eight or nine kilos as Peter described it.

A few hours later, the sun began to dip toward the western horizon, and as it sunk lower, it took on an orange hue. Eventually, as it touched he skyline, the surface of the lake was transformed into a shimmering sea of gold.

They pulled the brims of their hats further down over their faces to shield their eyes from the reflected glare as they paddled their canoes into a small inlet that had a clearing with adequate space for their tents.

Later, having cleaned and roasted the trout over their fire, it took the ravenous boys only a few minutes to reduce it to a pile of bones, which having been flensed of every last morsel, were tossed carelessly into the glowing coals.

The moon had not yet risen and the dark sky was speckled with the illumination of countless stars. After the obligatory belches, they reclined on blankets to gaze at the heavens, while trying to recognize the various constellations. In time, the Big Dipper rose above the horizon, and as the night grew darker the Milky Way became more apparent as a pale band traversing the cosmos above them.

Jason allowed his gaze to trace a path along the outer edge of the Dipper, starting from its bottom, and eventually he was able to locate *Polaris*, the North Star. It appeared to hover motionless there, and he knew from experience that over the next few hours the other stars and clusters would seem to rotate slowly around it.

At this time every summer, Earth was transiting through a band of debris left by the tail of the Swift-Tuttle comet which passes by the planet once every 133 years. When some of the generally tiny pieces tore through the planet's atmosphere, friction caused them to glow white-hot while streaking across the night sky as meteors. This was known as the *Perseid* shower, and for a brief second or two they would become visible as 'shooting stars' before disappearing when they had been completely consumed.

Occasionally, if large enough, one would partially survive its passage through the air, and impact the Earth's surface as a meteorite. Although meteors from other sources had sometimes been huge and catastrophic, the vast majority of the *Perseids* were tiny and never seen again. However, once in a while, a meteorite was found, and those were treasured by museums and collectors.

Staking out different quadrants of the sky, they had each pointed out a handful of brief flashes to the others, when suddenly Jack shouted. "Shit! Look out!"

What had started as a tiny orange dot in the dark sky had expanded in a fraction of a second into a brilliant white light directly above them. As it streaked past them, there was a deafening explosion, loud as a shotgun blast, as it broke the sound barrier. A fraction of a second later, it tore through the surface of the lake with a ripping sound, not more than a hundred yards from the shoreline.

"Christ!" David cursed. "Did you see the way that thing went in?"

The others were also staring, open-mouthed, into the darkness toward the place where a sequence of circular ripples radiated outward from the point of impact.

"I wonder how deep it is out there?" Jason asked himself out loud.

"No more than about thirty feet if I recall – and the bottom is sandy – so it should be easy to spot." David had already anticipated the next question.

They were all looking at Peter now. He grinned. "Yeah, I should to be able to retrieve it, as long as David's love-besotted mermaid doesn't get to it first."

For another hour, they speculated about what it might look like, longing for daybreak and the light they needed to begin their search. Eventually, they all fell into a restless sleep.

The morning fog rising off of the lake's surface diffused the dawning sun's rays, imparting a shimmering golden hue upon the water's edge and along the topmost branches of the trees ridging a small peninsula lying half a mile east of the boy's campsite. The ghost-like mist drifted further into the forested hills, sometimes settling into the small valleys, where it lay until dissipated by the growing heat of the day, or was eventually carried skyward by a strengthening wind.

Jack had already risen by the time the other three boys emerged from their tents, still wrapped in blankets against the early morning chill.

The smell of freshly percolating coffee wafted through the air as Jack reached for two tins of beans and the frying pan, and muttered. "What will it be my adventurers *extraordinaire*? Beans, or, uh, beans?"

"Beans please!" Jason sang out joyfully.

"Me too please!" Chimed David.

"Oh yes!" Peter responded enthusiastically. "I think beans are my favourite food in the whole world!"

"Yeah, I'll bet they are." Jack growled. "Just remember that I insist on sitting in the front of the canoe today."

"But we had beans yesterday, and you didn't seem to mind steering afterwards." Peter replied innocently.

"The wind was at our backs yesterday, but it's come around into our faces today." Jack answered. "As much as I enjoy the unending charms of your arse music, I have no intention of being ass-phxiated!"

Peter appeared to be confused. "But I was intending to do Beethoven's 9th today. I thought it was your favourite?"

"Oh, it is." Jack retorted. "However, I prefer it as background music, even though I'm sure your magnificent rendition wouldn't fail to assist our propulsion. In which case play on, but from the back of the canoe, my melodious, malodourous, cousin!"

Peter groaned. "You are my worst critic Jack. The boys in my glider club are far more appreciative."

Jack responded sarcastically. "I can understand why, given the unending inventiveness of the German mind. They are undoubtedly aware of how hot air rises and exceedingly grateful for any increase in lift, even if they have to hold their noses to get it."

David and Jason had been following the exchange with some enjoyment, but now the smell from the beans warming over the fire began to stimulate their appetites.

"Tell you what." David offered. "I'll pass you both a cup of this coffee if you'll load up our plates with some of those beans."

Jason agreed. "Yes, I haven't had any beans for at least twenty-four hours. I'm dying for another plateful."

Exchanging a quick glance with Peter, Jack agreed. "Pass the coffee. I always knew you guys would eventually succumb to my culinary skills."

"Done!" Jason and David responded in unison, as they passed the steaming cups in exchange for the bean-laden plates, and then hungrily reached for their spoons. Minutes later a resoundingly familiar chorus of belches signalled the demise of breakfast, and the boy's attention shifted to the spot where the meteorite had plunged into the lake.

After climbing into their canoes, they paddled to the approximate point of entry. Three of them held the gunwales tightly together, as Peter stripped to his shorts and leaned over the side to scan the sandy lake bottom below.

"It appears to be about ten metres to the bottom." He estimated, while continuing to peer into the water.

"I can just see several large objects, but I can't make out what they are. Hold steady while I slip over the side."

Peter slid into the water, took a deep breath, and then with a kick of his feet he disappeared below the surface. He reappeared about twenty seconds later and gasped. "There appears to be an old deadhead down there. It's mostly roots. There is nothing else nearby. I'll go all the way down and take a closer look."

With that, he took several deep breaths, and dove once more toward the bottom.

On his way down, Peter felt the surface of his body going numb from the freezing water temperature, but he could clearly see a black object approximately the size of an orange, lying directly beneath the tangled roots of a large waterlogged tree trunk. He wriggled his way in between two of these and grasped the heavy piece of rock in his left hand while pushing himself backwards out of the twisted limbs with his right.

He had barely reversed direction before something suddenly settled over both of his legs. Turning his head to look behind him, he realized with horror that he had become trapped in an old gill net which was itself snared in the roots of the submerged tree. The harder he struggled to free himself, the more firmly enmeshed he became. In panic, he twisted violently, vainly attempting to escape while simultaneously clenching his teeth and resisting the urge to expel air from his aching lungs. With growing despair, he realized he couldn't hold his breath any longer, and as he exhaled, the water rushed in. Darkness crept in from the periphery of his vision while slowly the world went black, and he slipped into unconsciousness.

On the surface, David was peering down into the water as Jason and Jack heard him shout. "Something's wrong! He's been under that deadhead too long!"

The two brothers steadied the canoes as David tore off his shirt and plunged into the lake. Even half-way to the bottom, the water felt cold as ice. It nearly shocked the air out of his lungs, and his head ached, but he forced himself to continue.

As David neared the old tree, he immediately saw Peter's feet in the old fishing net. He pulled his hunting knife from its sheath on his belt and began slashing at the mesh. The netting parted in large swathes as the sharp blade sliced through the threads and ropes. Shoving the knife back into its case and bracing his feet against one of the roots, he clasped Peter's feet in both hands and began to tug. No longer impeded by the net, he was able to drag him out from under the deadhead. With his lungs near to bursting, he wrapped his arms around Peter's limp torso and began desperately kicking for the surface.

He broke the surface, and the two brothers quickly dragged Peter's still form into one of the canoes where Jason immediately began to alternately pump his chest and exhale air into his mouth.

David was still in the water, from where he watched in grim apprehension as Peter's cousins continued to work over his limp body.

Having just forced another breath down Peter's throat, Jason was in the process of leaning back to do another chest compression when his cousin coughed up a mouthful of water and inhaled. He coughed a few more times, before slowly opening his eyes.

Noticing the other three boys gazing at him in solemn concern, Peter allowed a smile to slowly spread across his features before speaking. "You fellows are looking awfully glum. What's up? Did we lose our last can of beans?"

The brothers cursed in relief as they dragged David into the other canoe.

Jack was looking down at Peter's still prone form when he suddenly asked. "Hey. What's that in your hand?"

Peter raised his arm slightly to show them the dull black piece of cosmic debris, then grinned as he replied. "It's a gift from the Gods."

He then turned to David, as his face grew more serious. "You saved my life down there. I will never forget that."

Feeling slightly embarrassed, David couched his reply. "That wasn't really my initial intention. You were spending so much time under the water that I thought you might be trying to screw my girlfriend."

Peter spoke slowly, and his voice betrayed no discernable emotion as he slowly lowered the pistol. "Welcome to Germany, David."

Then, he pointed to the burnt remnants of the parachute, and a note of irony crept into his voice. "My fitter Hans and I seem to have found something that I think belongs to you."

Deep in contemplation, he stared for a few more moments at the shreds of parachute and vigorously shook his head in disbelief. He then holstered the *Luger* and staggered through the snow to David.

He quickly confirmed that the gash on his temple was only superficial, before clapping his hands upon David's shoulders. "My God man, you can't believe how incredible it is to see you here - and alive! How in hell did you ever survive that fall?"

David shrugged, and immediately regretted it as a stab of pain shot through the back of his shoulders. The adrenalin was starting to wear off, and his assortment of bruises were starting to reassert themselves. "To tell you the truth, I'll be damned if I know."

Leaning closer, Peter first examined David's forearm, and then glanced at the dead Alsatian lying near his feet. "I don't think the dog-master is very impressed with your Lon Chaney Jr. imitation. So, you'll have to bear with me occasionally as I sooth the concerns of some of my harder-nosed '*kammerads*'. But don't worry. I'll see to it that you are not harmed."

Peter looked up at the broken boughs in the overhead canopy of pine branches and shook his head again. "Let's get you back to my base. I've got real coffee there, and while I prepare all the necessary documents, we should have some time for catching up."

Turning to the stunned search party, he addressed them in German. "Believe it or not, this man is my friend whom I met years ago when visiting my relatives in Canada. If you look carefully you will see that he is a Native Indian – and I am not joking when I tell you he may possess some special kind of magic. Even though he is our prisoner, you will treat him with respect until he is processed through to one of the *Luft Stalag*s."

Holding up the charred remains of David's parachute, he continued. "I found my friend's parachute nearly a kilometre from here – useless."

Pointing to the snowless and fractured branches above, he added a tinge more irony to his voice. "There are only our footprints here, and a few of his. If you look up through those trees you can see that my friend has traveled at least five kilometres straight down, unassisted, to pay us a visit, so don't be afraid to show him a little hospitality."

It was beginning to dawn on the search party that they were witnessing something quite out of the ordinary, and they began to exchange glances of wonderment while voicing disbelief. Even the dog-master had holstered his weapon, and was now dourly regarding David with growing curiosity, which did not however, mitigate his continued feelings of contempt.

Peter turned back to David. "That's a nasty looking whack you've got on your head. How do you feel? Do you think you can manage the walk back to the vehicle?"

David was still trying to get to grips with the sudden appearance of his friend. "My head is still swimming with everything that's happened in the past several hours. It probably would be, even without the headache. Right now, I feel pretty sore just about everywhere, but I think I can make it."

Peter remained incredulous. "I still can't believe you survived that fall. You certainly are one incredibly lucky bastard. C'mon, let's get you back to my base where we can get some food and hot coffee into you."

On the way back, Hans was ebullient. The young fitter knew some English and often tried to interrupt David and Peter's conversation with eager but sometimes incoherent questions about their captive. They generally ignored him however, as they described to each other their experiences of the past five years. Still, Hans could hardly believe their good fortune. This was better than any of the western adventure novels he read voraciously every night before lights out.

When they arrived back at the airfield, Peter parked the *Kübelwagen* behind the dispersal hut before pocketing the keys.

Then, he turned to David. "Hans will take you over to my office. People will be watching, so try to behave like a POW until you get inside. Make yourself at home and I'll join you shortly, but first I want to gather a few things."

By now, Hans was beginning to regain some of the English ability he had acquired in school, and once inside, he headed to the stove.

"Would you like some coffee David?" he asked.

Then slightly embarrassed, he apologized. "I'm sorry, would you prefer I call you Sgt. Hunter?"

David couldn't suppress a smile at the young fitter's awkwardness. "David is fine."

"It's real coffee," the fitter volunteered. "It was liberated from a captured American supply dump last month."

He shuddered in disgust. "Without it we would be drinking the *ersatz*, which has caffeine, but it tastes like burnt sawdust."

"Thanks." David replied. "I could use something right now to clear my head up a bit."

Hans passed him a fresh cupful. "Would you like some sugar or milk to go with it?"

"No thanks. Black is good." He sipped at the brew, cautious not to scald his lips.

Hans was eying David with much wonderment. Finally, he blurted. "Are you really a Red Indian?"

David laughed. "You must have been reading some of those British dime novels. The only other time I've been asked that question was when I was stationed in England. Several people there asked me exactly the same thing."

"Well, are you?" The fitter asked eagerly, his eyes searching David's features intently.

"Technically I'm not." David answered. "The first European explorers to encounter Native Americans thought they had found India, and it's speculated that these American natives may have had a portion or all of their bodies painted red – hence the name Red Indian. Actually, we are all kind of light brown like me, and we don't call ourselves Indians. We usually refer to ourselves by our particular tribal name."

Hans could hardly contain himself. He longed to mine this captured airman for more Indian lore, and a slight tinge of awe had crept into his voice. "Can you ride a horse, and do you hunt with a bow and arrow?"

The earnest expression on the young fitter's face caused David to choke back his first impulse to laugh, and instead he chuckled.

"I can ride a horse and use a bow, but I don't own either. Only the tribes on the open prairies rode horses. I'm Ojibwa, and traditionally we used canoes and snowshoes to get around, depending on the season. My grandfather owns an old Ford truck which he taught me to drive when I was sixteen, and he showed me how to hunt with a rifle when I was ten."

"Have you ever shot a Polar Bear?"

"No. The bears in my part of the country are black, and quite a bit smaller – only up to 400 pounds, or I guess 200 kilos as you would probably say. I've only shot one of those because it was trying to get into our house, but I've shot a lot of moose. They're actually quite delicious."

"Incredible." The fitter sighed. "My friends will never believe me when I tell them this. The most exotic person they have ever met was probably an Italian!"

An idea continued to puzzle the young German. "Why do you fight for the Canadians? Didn't they steal your land?"

David thought before answering. This was a question he had asked himself before joining up. "I guess you could look at it that way, but actually, the country is pretty big. Maybe a dozen times the size of Europe, and still now with less than ten percent of the population. My people didn't really think in terms of private property, and there weren't really that many of us. Certainly not enough to repel far larger numbers of people with superior technology. Sure, we lost something, but maybe not so much in terms of land as in terms of our place...where and who we are in that new environment their technology created."

"But doesn't that make you angry at them?" Hans interjected.

David shrugged. "Sometimes, maybe. But try to imagine what it was like to be constantly fending off clouds of mosquitos and flies all summer, or the misery of breathing woodsmoke inside a teepee in January, when the temperature was forty below zero...half-starved and chewing on frozen jerky, sometimes with a broken or infected molar. Living without metal tools...only sharpened stones, which made every simple task more difficult than using a steel axe or knife."

As he took a look around the relatively warm office, David saw the squad of soldiers marching past snowbanks outside the window, and shivering in the cold. "The modern world isn't so bad when you compare it to some aspects of more primitive times."

"Regardless of time or place however, it's the behavior of certain people that can make things difficult. I guess at some point, everyone has to decide what they are for or against, and what they are willing to tolerate. It's maybe only if we are forced to, but we do make choices, and then carry on from there. My choice was based upon a sense of duty to protect my family and friends – even my 'country' – from an external threat. Simple as that."

Hans' eyes clouded, as in a hushed tone he confided. "I'm sorry you have to be a prisoner of war. Eventually, they will take you away to one of the *Luft Stalag*s – camps for allied airmen. They say it's not too bad there."

Conspiratorially, he asked. "Do you think you'll try to escape?"

David shook his head. "I probably won't. Likely as not, I'll just take it easy at first. The war should be over soon. Germany can't last much longer."

Hans was genuinely surprised. "What makes you think that? Dr. Goebbels has been telling us on the radio that with our new wonder weapons victory is assured, and the western allies will finally realize their best hope is to join us in crushing the Russians."

"I don't think so." David replied. "You see those bombers that come over in their thousands, day and night? The wonder weapons aren't stopping them, and the Russians are getting closer to Berlin every day. The allies can smell victory now, so they aren't going to cut any deals with the Nazis. It probably won't be long. Four or five months, tops."

"*Ja*, I guess you are right." Hans admitted hesitantly. "Every raid seems bigger than the last one. Germany will probably be completely *kaput* by the time it is all over. Nothing left but rubble, and Russkies."

He brightened. "Do you think they would let me come to Canada after all that's happened?"

"You never know. Believe it or not, Peter's cousins and I tried to talk him into staying in Canada with us back in '38. He obviously liked it there, and anyone who was paying attention could see that war was coming."

"Really, and still he came back to Germany?"

"Sure. You could see it was a hard choice for him, but he was worried about his family. Then, he spent the last couple of weeks astounding the shit out of us by diving off of incredibly high and dangerous places into any lake or river that he could. The things he could do in the air before plunging into the water were unbelievable. It's probably the same ability that makes him such an excellent pilot."

"He's a multiple Ace!" Hans volunteered.

"Yeah, I know. So is his cousin Jason. He's a Spitfire pilot. I see him sometimes. He told me several months ago that back in September he and Peter had come within a whisker of shooting each other out of the sky over Belgium, just before they recognized each other."

Hans was amazed. "He never said anything about that!"

"Well, it's probably not a good idea to tell your German squadron mates that your cousin is a Spitfire Ace. Not really the best thing for morale, you know? Anyway, Jason said he recognized the wolf's head on Peter's cowling."

"*Ja*, I was very surprised to see the same one on the turret of your Lancaster."

"Well, there's one on the nose of Jason's plane too, and I guess when they recognized each other they broke off, and I'd bet that neither one of them reported the incident to their commanding officers."

"*Ja*. That would be the smart thing. Otherwise, it would probably bring shit for both of them – and already there is enough shit in this war, without more."

The young fitter began to sob as something had opened up in him. "I hate this fucking war! In school they told us it was a great adventure. *Ja! Leibensraum!* A glorious future! Fuck! Now all my school chums are dead! Every one of them! Rotting away in some shit-hole of a grave in Russia or France! And for what? Nothing! Except we can get even more shit!"

"The whole business stinks." David interjected calmly, hoping to settle the boy down. "I just hope people finally wise-up for good after it's all over."

"*Ja*. I think that would be a good time to get wise. Some of our guys got wise too early and tried to kill Hitler last summer. They didn't succeed, and I hear that the consequences for them were terrible."

"That's too bad. If they'd succeeded, things would probably have been over with by now."

The fitter's eyes darted about to see if anyone was within listening range, then he quickly nodded his head. "*Ja.*"

It was then that Peter came through the door with two large rucksacks. "I've packed some warm clothes and blankets, along with enough canned food to keep you going for a couple weeks. There is an old line-shack near a fire break in the forest about seven kilometres from here. It is only used in the summer and fall, so you will not be discovered there. I've included as many candles as I could find to provide heat if it gets too cold at night, but make sure you cover the windows if you use them, just in case."

The fitter's eyes had grown round. "You're hiding him?"

Peter put a reassuring hand on the fitter's shoulder. "Hans, there are three hundred Russian divisions approaching Berlin from the south and the east. The *Wehrmacht* will give them a good fight, but the outcome is inevitable. Once those *SS* fanatics finally admit that it's over for them, they will be trying to eliminate any incriminating evidence. There is a very good chance they will start shooting P.O.W.s. We know they have done that before. After the surrender, we and David can head west where he can turn us over for processing. I think we will both do much better there than in the hands of the Russians."

Hans stammered. "What about the documentation for the *Gestapo*? Surely they will want to collect him."

Peter smiled. "I'm an excellent forger, and they won't want to collect David, because I haven't reported his capture to them. I will tell the search party and anyone else who asks, that you took him to the nearest *Gestapo* office for processing to a *Luft Stalag.*"

He reached into one of the packs to remove a pair of handcuffs. "Now put these on him and take a look at this map. You can drive down the fire break to here, and then you will have to walk about fifty metres in to the shack. It is almost dark so no one should see you going in, but just to be safe, go past the first break and circle around from the other direction. Try to cover your tracks as best you can on the way back out to the *Kübelwagen.*"

Finally, he turned to David. "There is a small first aid kit in one of the packs along with the food. I'll try to send Hans in with more every ten days or so, until we are ready to move. Do you think you will be alright?"

Somewhat shocked by this sudden turn of events, David took a second to respond. "Peter, you are taking an enormous chance here. Are you sure you really want to go through with it?"

Peter's grin was sardonic. "Ask me again if we three find ourselves standing in front of a firing squad, but for now my friend, you and Hans had better get going."

Darkness

Flight Lieutenant Martin Bradshaw, of Meaford, Ontario, was flying his black Mk XXX Mosquito fifty feet above the waves of the English Channel at three hundred miles per hour. The two Rolls-Royce V-12 Merlin engines generating over 1,700 hp each, could propel the plane at least another one hundred miles per hour faster, but he had throttled back to conserve fuel on the way in.

Bradshaw and his navigator/radar operator Sgt. Tommy Logan of Halifax, Nova Scotia, were members of RCAF 410 'Cougar' Squadron, part of the 2nd Tactical Air Force assigned to Intruder missions. These were operations flown after dark to shoot down enemy night-fighters – most often as they came in for landings at their bases deep in Germany.

To reach these targets, the Intruders flew for up to three hours at altitudes of fifty to one hundred feet, thus avoiding detection by German radar. In addition to extraordinary piloting skills, the job required trip-hammer reflexes and nerves of steel.

Bradshaw lacked for none of these, and he couldn't help but smile as he grunted at his navigator. "Looks like a perfect night for a little '*Noctivaga*', wouldn't you say Tommy?"

'*Noctivaga*' was a Latin expression meaning 'Wandering at Night', and it was the squadron's motto. The word was emblazoned along the bottom of the squadron's badge, which featured the face of a snarling cougar superimposed over a crescent moon.

The Lieutenant's eyes were locked on the view through the front windscreen as Sgt. Logan turned to him. "Indeed, it is Marty. However, if I had my way I'd rather be wandering around that bar near Manston where all those pretty little English girls come to meet the likes of us – or I guess I should say me, considering how homely you are."

"*Et tu*, Tommy?" Martin clucked. "Just remember that one woman's homely is another woman's ruggedly handsome. I've been getting a lot of those ruggedly handsome compliments from the ladies lately. Must be something to it, don't you think?"

"I'm struggling. More likely it has something to do with the fact that every lady I've ever seen you with was wearing glasses thicker than that bullet-proof windscreen you're looking through."

"It makes them look more intelligent my friend. I'm actually quite fond of the intelligent look."

Tommy snorted. "Really? I can't see it myself. What is it about them that gets you going? Do they recite the periodic table to you while you're pulling their brassieres off?"

"If you must know, *triganome - 'trysts'* are the best. I once dated a Welsh beauty - a brunette with a great head for that sort of thing - if you know what I mean? When she put it to work, she was always able to find some way of getting my slide rule to the right angle."

Tommy was introspective. "Funny. My math teacher, Mrs. King, was never that accommodating in high school. In retrospect, I guess I should have emulated you, and tried to get her brassiere off. Possibly then I'd have made more, shall we say, 'headway' with my studies. Oh, by the way, we need to change our heading fifteen degrees north in about one minute."

Martin pulled back slightly on the control column to gain another fifty feet of altitude, then lightly applied left rudder, gently banking as he kept one eye on the compass until the aircraft had come around to the new heading. He then levelled-off and slowly eased the Mosquito down to their former altitude of fifty feet. There, they skimmed over the wave tops toward a dark line growing more distinct in the distance, and which finally emerged as the coast of Holland.

After twelve missions, Earl Cooper had seen about as much as he had ever wanted to from the rear turret of his Lancaster bomber.

Returning from his very first *"op"*, he had witnessed one of the squadron's aircraft arriving late with a 2,000 pound bomb partially hung-up in the racks. It had been badly shot up in the rudders, left outer wing, and nose. The mid-upper gunner and the navigator had safely parachuted before the bomber's final approach. The rest of the crew, except for the pilot and flight engineer, had been too badly wounded to make the jump. One engine had failed and smoke was trailing ominously from another.

Every eye in the aerodrome had been riveted on the Lancaster as the pilot performed a heroic job touching down, light as a feather – but not light enough. The bomb had been jarred loose, and then upon impact with the tarmac it detonated, causing the entire aircraft to disappear in an enormous explosive fireball that killed everyone on board.

On other occasions, he had also seen squadron aircraft get pinned in the searchlights over the target and blown to pieces by flak. Worst of all, however, was when David had been lost last week.

Flight Sergeant David Hunter had been his instructor, mentor, roommate, and the best tail-gunner in the air force. His loss had shaken him. If they could shoot down David, they could shoot down anyone, no matter how good you were. Now on his way in to Berlin, at the frigid altitude of 18,000 feet, he was beginning to sweat. Nervously, he clapped his hands together hoping to improve their circulation while he peered out into the darkness.

Tail-end Charlie is what they called guys like him. Everyone knew it was the crew position with the highest attrition rate, but he was glad to be in his seat at the rear of the aircraft looking backwards into the night.

He couldn't imagine how horrifying it must be, lying on your belly in the bombardier's blister - or in any position where you could see forward into the sea of flak bursts - watching many of their fellow crews being blown to smithereens and knowing you could very well be next.

Two missions ago on the way into Hamburg, the bombardier had literally pissed his pants due to heavy flak during their bomb-run over the target. When he had tried to get up on the way home, he discovered that the front of his flight suit trousers had frozen to the aluminum skin of the fuselage beneath him.

After the slow climb to altitude, *Oberleutnant* Eugen Mueller levelled the *Ju*88 off at 6,000 metres. It was a cloudless night without a moon, and this far out from the target there was no advantage to flying above or below the well-camouflaged bombers when it came to actually seeing them. They had been told that a moderate-sized bomber force was heading for Berlin, and tonight Mueller would be one of the '*Wilde Sau*' trying to slip into the stream of four-engine heavies as they approached from the west.

As most of the significant cities in Germany had been subjected to area bombing, often several times, they became less important as military targets. Many of the war production industrial sites had been moved to secret underground facilities, which were more difficult to detect, much less successfully damage from the air. Hence, Bomber Command had shifted to smaller numbers of bombers in their night raids and were beginning to apply a more precision-type attack method on strategic targets like rail terminals, ports, and troop concentrations. Some squadrons, still in their night camouflage, had even been assigned to daylight raids, escorted by fighters which were in some cases now based on the continent.

The lower numbers and thinner concentration of bombers at night made the odds of intercepting them smaller. Even though Eugen's crew included *OFw*. Bernt Esche, one of the *Luftwaffe*'s most highly-skilled radar operators, individual enemy aircraft were becoming more difficult to locate. Frustratingly, during this period of limited fuel supplies, his sorties were becoming longer, but with less in the way of results.

The poor-quality fuel was causing his port engine to run roughly, so he opened the throttle a bit and was rewarded when the radial began to rev more smoothly. He turned to Esche, whose face was enclosed by the cowling of the radar set. Despite the cold temperature at this altitude, large beads of perspiration had formed on his jowls and the back of his neck. "Any sign of them Bernt?"

"Nothing." Esche replied. "However, there seems to be something wrong with the screen. It lacks optimum brightness. Perhaps this set is failing."

Feldwebel Jurgen Raul lowered the field glasses from his eyes, hissing. "There is nothing wrong with the set, you fat pig! That stinking sweat oozing out of your pores has covered the screen in slime! You're always sweating, you gutless sack of shit!"

His body was suddenly wracked by a violent coughing fit. Finally, he hacked something up from the bottom of his throat and spat it on the cockpit floor. An infection had settled into his chest weeks ago, but there was no medicine to be had in the dispensary. Nothing but the little pills they gave all aircrew, filled with some chemical that kept them alert. However, back on the ground they also caused you to lie awake for hours in your bunk, unable to fall asleep. The accumulated effects of sleep deprivation were making them all irritable and short-tempered.

Esche lifted his face from the cowling and turned his head. "Yes. By all means cough up your lungs *Maus*. You probably have tuberculosis or some other disgusting little mouse disease, and now you are giving it to us! After we land, I'm going to crush you under my boot like the little rodent you are!"

The last of Eugen's patience had evaporated, and he suddenly exploded. "Shut the fuck up! Both of you, or I'll kill you right now!" His right hand had moved to the handle of the *Luger* strapped on his thigh.

Taken aback by the vehemence of their *Leutnant*'s outburst, and momentarily stunned by the wild-eyed look on the pilot's face, Raul straightened in his seat and silently raised the binoculars to his eyes. Esche, similarly chastened, quickly bent forward to peer into the radar set.

Within a minute, he chirped. "I think I've got something. I'm picking up *H2S* emissions to the left ahead of us. It's about 1,500 metres out."

Eugen, once again focused on the task at hand, grunted with satisfaction. "That's more like it. Let's go gut some fish!"

He gently pushed forward on the yoke of his control column and adjusted the throttles, accelerating the *Ju*88 into a shallow dive which would fly them to a position where they could drift in from the right, below the enemy plane.

As they closed the distance, Raul located the aircraft in his glasses. "This bastard is a Lancaster with a belly still full of bombs, so do not get too close!"

Eugen grunted again. "Don't worry. I can finish off this kind of *schwein* in my sleep."

Cruising above the bomber stream at 7,500 metres, *Hauptmann* Fritz Apfel did not need to remind himself that he loved flying the *Heinkel* 219. He had cut his teeth in the *Bf*110, an aircraft that was practically obsolete as a bomber escort by the time it was seriously tested in the Battle of Britain. It came into its own to some degree as a night-fighter, especially when equipped with the *Schräge Musik* cannons, but although it may have proved relatively effective in that role, it was still not really a pleasure to fly.

However, the *He*219 *Uhu* 'Eagle Owl', with an array of four *Naxos Z* radar antennae protruding from its nose, was one of the most modern designs in the *Luftwaffe* inventory. It had a bubble canopy which sat right on the aircraft's nose, giving its pilot unrivalled forward visibility in flight. This excellent quality also extended to both takeoffs and landings because the tricycle landing gear removed the necessity to peer around a typical tail-dragger's rising nose. It was powered by two *DB*603E V-12 engines, each generating 1,900 hp, and capable of propelling the *Uhu* at nearly six hundred kilometres per hour to a ceiling of 10,000 metres, far above the bomber stream, and into the high-altitude Mosquito's territory. The aircraft was highly manoeuvrable due to its relatively short wings, but because of the resultant high loading factor, pilots had to accustom themselves to its relatively fast landing speed. Despite this, the general consensus among those who flew the *He*219 was very positive, and most agreed that it was the sleek sports car of the night-fighter fleet.

The *Uhu* was lethally armed. In addition to the twin 30mm *Schräge Musik* cannons aft of the cockpit, there was a 30mm cannon in each of the two wing roots. Also, a ventral fairing slung under its belly contained two more 30mm, and two 20mm cannons. Many of the pilots removed the two 30mm cannons in the belly pod to save weight, thus enhancing the *He*219's flying performance, but even that version still possessed utterly destructive power when an enemy was lined up in its sights.

Hauptmann Apfel and his radar man *Oberfeldwebel* Rhienhardt Peitz were arguing the merits of ejector seats - the *He*219 being the first aircraft ever to be equipped with them.

Peitz postulated a theory - having never previously exited an aircraft in flight – favouring the traditional method of bailing out, which required manually opening the canopy, and then climbing out of the cockpit with a parachute strapped to your bottom, while grasping a ripcord to pull when clear of the damaged fighter.

Apfel, on the other hand, knew from experience that canopies sometimes got stuck or jammed, and pilots were sometimes knocked unconscious from contact with wings or tail sections after bailing out, and then were unable to pull their ripcords. He also pointed to the two large propellers spinning on each side of them just behind the cockpit, and then asked Peitz what he thought the odds were of avoiding those in a hurried exit.

The *Hauptmann* was attracted also to the technologically superior aspect of the ejector seat, which automatically threw open the canopy before using explosives to blast both seats upward and out of the cockpit, high above the rotating propellers and the two very solid rudders. After a few seconds, parachutes attached to the seats would automatically deploy, lowering them and their occupants gently to earth.

In the *He*219, the radar operator sat behind the pilot, facing backward. *OFw.* Peitz argued that he found this disorienting in terms of exiting the aircraft in an emergency. "It's fine for you up front where you can see any problems evolving and then anticipate before initiating the ejection, but I can barely see anything from back here. Before I know it, I could find myself and this seat being blasted out into a six hundred kilometre per hour slipstream with shit flowing down the inside of my legs. No, I think I would rather do it all myself."

Apfel laughed. "Really, my dear Peitzy, you worry far too much. If we ever have to bail out, I'll shout: 'We are ejecting! Put your hand over your arse!' and off we'll go!"

Peitz was not amused. "Yes, yes, thank you. You are the soul of consideration. I feel much better now."

He paused a moment. "There is something on my screen. It's about a kilometre ahead of us, and about 2,000 metres below. It's definitely *H2S*."

Fritz opened the throttles, banked left, and then dove at an angle which was forty-five degrees off of the target's flight path. Having descended about 1,000 metres, he gently banked the aircraft to the right, and after a further descent of 1,000 metres levelled off at the same altitude as the bomber.

The *Uhu* underside was painted flat black, while its upper surfaces were covered in a mottled dark grey pattern over a lighter grey background. This made it nearly invisible when viewed at night from almost any angle. As he approached from the Lancaster's eight o'clock position at full speed, it was too late for the bomber crew to react when they finally saw him. The rear and mid-upper turrets had not even begun to rotate in his direction when he thumbed his firing button and a stream of cannon shells illuminated by green tracer flew out from beneath the *He*219, as well as from the wing roots behind him.

As the cannon shells blasted directly into the bomb bay and port wing of the hapless bomber, Apfel snap-rolled left and peeled-off into a high-speed turn a fraction of a second before the bomber, with its heavy bomb load and relatively full fuel tanks, exploded into a gigantic fireball that illuminated the skies for miles around.

Earl had been staring out the rear turret, scanning the black skies directly behind him for any sign of an enemy aircraft creeping up on them, when the huge explosion of a Lancaster about 2,000 feet above his own aircraft, suddenly illuminated the skies around him. To his shock, the flash of light revealed a *Ju*88 with two upwardly pointing cannons, drifting in under his Lancaster from about three hundred feet to his left. Instinctively he punched his left foot pedal rotating the rear turret to its maximum ninety degrees position and squeezed the triggers.

Eugen could now make out the shape of the huge four-engine Lancaster about a hundred metres above, and approximately the same distance to his left. It was flying straight and level, taking no evasive action, and was apparently unaware of his presence. In a manoeuvre that he had successfully completed many times, he synchronized his speed with the bomber and slowly began to drift to his left in order to place himself directly underneath it, from where he would fire his cannons upward. Suddenly, both aircraft were bathed in light from the explosion of another bomber above and ahead of them.

"Shit!" he cursed, but before he could stomp on the rudder pedal and slam the yoke of his control column forward to dive away, he glimpsed the winking of muzzle flashes from the Lancaster's rear turret. The cockpit canopy was instantly shattered by a stream of bullets which tore into him and the other two crew members a second before the *Ju*88 exploded.

Earl continued to fire into the fireball for several seconds before he could force himself to relax his grip on the triggers. He suddenly realized that he was screaming, and stopped. Only then could he hear the excited shouting of his crewmates in the headphones and his own gasping breath, as the bomber sped on through the darkness.

For over ten minutes in the dark night sky, Lieutenant Bradshaw had been patiently circling his Mosquito in an oval pattern about one hundred feet above the ground and approximately seven miles from where his navigator had told him the German airfield was located. He had chosen an area consisting of farmer's fields which were devoid of trees and electricity pylons, hoping to cut the risk of a near-ground collision. To reduce noise and conserve fuel, he had lowered his engine revs to just above stalling speed. Then, in the direction off of his right wing, he saw the airstrip landing lights flicker momentarily before the entire area was plunged once again into darkness.

He rammed both throttles open and cautioned his navigator. "Hang on Tommy. It's time to welcome someone home."

Bradshaw climbed for altitude as he banked right into the wind, and circled around to line up the approach end of the airstrip. He peered ahead of him toward the strip, and suddenly there it was. With angled twin rudders, and the distinctive tricycle landing gear now extended, it was unmistakable – an *He219*!

He pulled in right behind it, and pressed his firing button. The four 20mm cannons in the nose of the Mosquito spat a stream of lead along the top of the *Uhu*'s fuselage, all the way to the wing spar and into the *Schräge Musik* cannons' ammunition bay.

The massive explosion broke the *He219*'s back and blew its wings off.

Hauptmann Fritz Apfel had already extended his flaps and lowered the landing gear when the airstrip's landing lights flickered momentarily to confirm he was correctly on approach. The relatively high landing speed of the *Uhu* could be tricky, and Apfel was mentally reminding himself not to throttle back too far, which would cause the *He219* to stall out, when he felt the impact of the first shell slamming into the aircraft's tail section. He heard Peitz scream, and immediately understood what was happening – and that the aircraft was doomed.

With a fighter pilot's lightning-fast reflexes he punched the ejector button, and the canopy flew off as the two seats were launched explosively upward. With a loud snap, their parachutes popped open and they began to drift earthward. He turned to signal Peitz that the seats had worked perfectly, but to his horror he saw that the radar operator's head was missing.

Apfel felt dizzy, and when his head drooped, he discovered that both of his legs were gone. The last thing he saw was blood spurting from the remains of his femoral arteries as he lost consciousness...

Martin pushed both throttles all the way forward as he accelerated the Mosquito to its maximum speed of 415 miles per hour, briefly catching a glimpse of the burning wreckage in his rear-view mirror. He then refocused all his powers of concentration to race the aircraft for the next two hours at barely a hundred feet above the ground, back to their base in Manston.

The voice of his navigator, pitched high with adrenalin, came through his headphones. "Nice shooting Marty! Scratch one *He*219!"

Bradshaw grinned, and his eyes glistened behind the flight goggles. "As far as I know Tommy, we're not going up again for a few more days. After dinner tonight, I think we should head over to the pub. Maybe we can find some young ladies who will put their heads to work on a physics problem or two."

Continuing, he chuckled sarcastically. "Perhaps an equation concerning expansion factors…"

On The Move

The Gothic Line had been the hardest fought of victories. Defeating some of Germany's best fighting units entrenched in superbly designed defensive positions, had cost them dearly in men as well as tanks. However, there were not enough new men enlisting or being trained to replace the casualties of battle in Italy. Jack was sitting with Captain Bob McLeod in front of their tent inside of the tank *laager*, sharing another liberated bottle of the local vintage. He cursed when he thought of the thousands of 'zombie' soldiers back in Canada who had signed up for the practically unnecessary home defence role, which stipulated no overseas deployment.

McLeod shrugged. "I can understand why a guy who might be older, with a wife and kids, and maybe no one to see to them when he's gone might hold back, but I sure can't fathom some able-bodied single guy seeing all his chums going off to fight, and not joining up. We're talking about the survival of our country and civilization here!"

Jack responded bitterly. "I agree, but I also think it has a lot to do with our gutless politicians being mindful about their own short-term survival. They screwed up the implementation of conscription in Quebec back in 1917, and now they think they have to appease the ignorant anti-war elements there this time."

He paused to take another swig before continuing. "Those feckless backwoods bastards have no idea what the Nazis have in store for them if they win, so they're happy to go fishing while good men die fighting their battles for them. Ironically, Quebec has a long regimental tradition going all the way back to New France. The Vandoos, the Trois Rivieres Regiment, and the Sherbrookes, who have stepped up, actually fight like demons against the Germans."

Staring at the empty replacement roster, he muttered to himself. "When the war is finally over, I wonder if anyone will ask why any of these able-bodied single men who refused to actively defend the country against fascism, should be entitled to any of the benefits of a free society that men like us have actually risked our lives trying to defend?"

McLeod laughed. "Hah! I wouldn't hold your breath waiting for any politician to ask that question – least of all, one up for election!"

Jack's cynical observations on what he considered governmental and cultural cowardice were confirmed, when at the end of September, he had to inform his troop that tank crews would each be reduced by one man, to only four. Thereafter, most crews chose to leave their co-driver / machine gun position vacant, which unfortunately reduced the effectiveness of each tank in its role as infantry support.

In early October, they were moved back to Riccioni, on the Adriatic coast. By now the skies were beginning to collect their first wisps of cloud, while the cooler autumn nights heralded the approach of winter rains, which would slow the fighting as tanks and heavy vehicles bogged down in the mud.

The town had fortunately been spared any severe damage by the surrounding conflict. From higher vantage points, as Jack went on his daily training runs, he observed the colour of the terracotta tiles on the villa rooves alternating between dark rust and a warm russet hue when the sun moved between the variegated cloud patterns now beginning to collect with greater regularity during the day.

It was here that they received their first Fireflies.

British engineers had devised a way to mount a 17-pounder gun in the standard turret of a Sherman tank by rotating the breech onto its side, thus allowing it to fit into a space that had not been designed for it. The resulting tank was still woefully under-armoured compared to the German Panther and Tiger tanks, but it now possessed the best gun of any tank, and for the first time, Sherman crews could win in a one-on-one confrontation against the enemy's steel behemoths.

Initially, until more of them became available, each troop would be equipped with one Firefly, and crews took the opportunity afforded by the break to practice with their 17-pounders and 75mm guns.

Toward the end of the month they spent a week in the line successfully assaulting the Savio River crossing. Then, they were pulled back again to Cervia. Here, they received more new equipment in the form of tanks equipped with 105mm howitzers.

They were mounted in the Ford-built Sherman M4A3 variant, and Jack nodded appreciatively when he noticed it possessed a diesel engine using fuel that was less flammable than the gasoline used in his own multibank, or the standard radial engine.

He noted that aside from the main gun, it was marginally different in appearance from his own tank. The front was sloped slightly less, creating a bit more room in the driver's compartment, and the transmission housing at the front of the tank between the drive wheels was a single cast unit that seemed thicker, and projected further forward than the three-piece unit on his and other earlier models of the Sherman. In addition to providing greater protection, the housing had fewer bolts, so was less time-consuming to remove or service.

Also, the radio compartment had been moved higher up on the back of the turret, and there was also an additional hatch above the loader / operator's position which he knew his own loader and gunner would envy. When a tank began to burn, there were only a few scant seconds for the three turret crewmembers to escape out of the commander's hatch if they hoped to survive. The extra hatch would save lives.

In December, they took Ravenna, but winter had set in and the brief sporadic combat that had characterized the late autumn season petered out even further. In the past year, they had repeatedly hammered the Germans, and more importantly perhaps, had tied down tens of thousands of *Wehrmacht* forces to prevent their deployment in Western Europe, where the numbers of divisions engaged in the struggle on both sides had remained generally equivalent. While the allies now prevailed, several more German divisions in France would have slowed their progress, or perhaps even reversed it.

In early February, they moved to Leghora, where they were loaded onto LSTs - Landing Ship, Tanks - before they sailed to Marseilles. When they arrived, Jack and many of the other young Canadian soldiers marvelled at the shortness of the skirts worn by the local beauties. Unfortunately, he learned, they would have very little time to socialize.

The tanks were immediately loaded onto flatcars, and the men then took seats in the passenger carriages coupled directly behind the sooty locomotives.

Slowly the trains pulled out of the station, gradually gaining speed as they carried their hulking cargo northward. A day-and-a-half later they pulled into the surprisingly pristine city of Roulars, Belgium. They were told that from here, their job would be to fight through the enemy *Panzers* in Holland, and then thrust like a dagger into the heart of Germany.

Having crossed the border into Holland, and about a day short of their destination, Nijmegen, they found themselves low on gasoline, so they pulled up in the late afternoon to wait for the fuel trucks, and set up camp for the night. After everything had been squared away, Jack encountered his gunner Mike Robertson.

Mike's grin was infectious, and as usual aroused Jack's curiosity. "What are you up to now Robertson?"

He took a quick look around to confirm that no one except the crew of *Beowulf* were in listening range, then came closer and lowered his voice to speak. "I walked by the field kitchen and noticed they were scrimping on just about everything except beans and baloney again, so I thought I would sneak back to that farm we passed about a mile back to see if I can scare up some eggs for our crew. I should be back in an hour if it's all right with you."

Jack's stomach was already growling, and he knew that if there were any eggs to be had, Mike would surely find them, so he agreed immediately. "That sounds like one of the better ideas I've heard today. We haven't had a fresh egg for weeks. Just make sure you get the password from the sentry before you head out, eh?"

Mike's grin grew even wider. "Okay. Once I'm out there I'll do my best to see if I can negotiate a five-finger discount!"

Jack shook his head in bemusement as he watched Mike depart, all the while whistling an incoherent tune as he made his way to the edge of their encampment.

Finding that he had a bit of free time on his hands, Jack sauntered over to where he saw the headquarters squadron was situated, hoping to chat with his friend Bob McLeod, who had recently been promoted to the rank of Major and given command of the squadron. He found him peering into the open engine compartment of his Sherman tank.

Jack leant over to see what he was looking at and nudged McLeod gently in the ribs. "What's wrong Bob? Lose your watch?"

"Ha! The damned water pump is shot. We won't have a replacement until the supply trucks arrive along with our fuel."

Straightening up, he motioned to his tent. "What do you say we have a cup of tea? There is not a thing Joe Motorcycle can do until the part gets here."

As they sat in McLeod's tent waiting for the kettle to boil, the Major casually tossed him a chocolate bar. "Try this. I grabbed a whole box of these off the shelf in that half-demolished confectionary I had the tank parked inside of yesterday. They're pretty good."

Jack bit down on the treat and savoured the long-unfamiliar taste. "Thanks Bob, this hits the spot."

McLeod's driver briefly stuck his head inside the tent. "The pump has arrived Major. Joe Motorcycle says he can probably have it installed for you in an hour."

Jack shook his head ruefully. "You know Bob, I feel like an arse, but I can never remember how to say Joe's real name. What is it – Motosato? Motohashi?"

McLeod shook his head and shrugged. "Something like that, I think. I hate to say it, but I'm probably even worse than you when it comes to pronouncing Japanese names."

Jack was puzzled. "He's the best mechanic we've got. When you think of it, we're pretty lucky to have him, considering most of his relatives are probably in one of those internment camps they have out in British Columbia. I wonder how he got past the round-up?"

McLeod thought a moment. "I don't really know, but I suspect he was already in the army and over here before Pearl Harbour. Somebody with a brain that works must have decided he was a lot more valuable to us in Europe than on some onion farm out west."

Jack considered this a moment. "The Japanese military sure didn't do their cousins in North America any favours when they raped Nanking, or raped and bayoneted the nurses on Wake Island,

and in Hong Kong. The brutal way they treat any of our boys who surrender also leaves a pretty sour taste in everyone's mouth too. However, a lot of those internees were born in Canada, and are citizens. I even saw newspaper pictures of some Japanese guys wearing their World War One Canadian Army uniforms as they were being shipped to the camps. When you realize that they were right there with us when we fought at Vimy Ridge and Passchendaele, the idea of taking their property away and interning them like that just doesn't seem right."

McLeod nodded his head. "I read in one of the newspapers that about twenty-five percent of them still had Japanese citizenship though, and I guess some of these people could be sympathizers or potential saboteurs, but you would think that the RCMP could round those guys up and leave the rest alone."

Jack snorted. "Well, one thing I'll bet you can be certain of is that some politicians are playing on fear - or even racism - to make hay, and some other people are glad to be making a lot of money buying their stuff up on the cheap."

McLeod grunted in agreement, as Jack drank up the rest of his brew. He then glanced at his watch, and rose from his chair. "Thanks for the tea, Bob. It's been two hours since Mike went out scavenging for eggs, so he should be back by now. If he was successful, I'll bring a few back for your breakfast."

When Jack got back to *Beowulf,* he immediately encountered Ronnie Corbett, his loader / radio operator. The normally cheerful Manitoulin Islander was looking worried. "He's more than an hour overdue, and it's not like Mike to be that late. Do you think some farmer might have caught him in the act?"

Just then their driver, Tim Irwin, joined them. "I've checked the entire perimeter and no one's seen him. He's still out there."

Jack was concerned, but tried to reassure them. "Let's hope he got caught by the farmer's daughter and she's submitted to his charms, but for now, get some flashlights and borrow one of those universal carriers. If he's not back by then, we'll go out looking for him."

A half hour later, they were nearing the first farm, so they switched off the carrier's shielded headlamp to hide their approach. As they dismounted, Ronnie removed one of the carrier's Bren guns while Tim took one of the on-board .303 rifles. They all wore their side arms, and Jack had taken their .45 cal. Thompson sub-machinegun with him.

The farmhouse, along with a barn and chicken coop were at the end of a lane leading three hundred yards east from the main road through partially forested fields. There were still substantial snow banks in shaded areas, but due to the onset of spring many of the fields were partially bare.

There were no lights on in any of the buildings, so they crept stealthily up the lane, frequently pausing to listen for any sounds of activity. There were none, and when they checked the farmhouse and barn, they were both empty. So was the coop, which was devoid of either chickens or eggs.

Suddenly Tim pointed at two objects on the ground and whispered. "Look at this. It's Mike's beret, and his pistol."

A frost was now beginning to set into the damp earth, but where Mike's beret was lying there were marks on the ground indicating that there had been a struggle.

As they explored the area further, they recognized the distinct German boot prints, which after a rough count, indicated the presence of at least a dozen men. They appeared to have moved off toward the dark shape of another farmstead which was approximately five hundred yards east toward the German lines.

Jack turned to the other two men. "It looks like they've got Mike. They might be holing up in that other farm, and there are a lot of them. However, I think if we get the infantry to surround the place before sun-up, we might be able to convince them to surrender, and maybe get Mike back at the same time."

He pointed behind them, down the lane. "Let's go back to base so we can get the infantry to start moving into position tonight. Then, we can get our troop of tanks ready to come up and support them after the trap has been sprung."

In the grey light of dawn, Jack moved his troop into position behind several squads of infantry. Within minutes, he got a call on his radio. The infantry squad-leader's voice was laconic as he told him they could move up to the next farmhouse which was apparently empty, but also, there was something he needed to see.

The half-frozen fields were still muddy, so he led the troop along a small road that connected the farmsteads. A squad of the Cape Breton Highlanders stood guard around the barn, while five hundred yards further east several more squads had surrounded the next farmstead. As Jack dismounted from *Beowulf*, the Captain who had spoken to him on the radio approached.

Hard lines set in around his mouth as he looked Jack squarely in the eye. "I'm Captain Bill Stewart. We've found your man, but I have to warn you that you're not going to like what you see. C'mon, I'll take you to him – he's over there in the barn."

Jack felt his heart sink. The rest of the crew had now dismounted, and they all followed the infantry Captain into the barn.

Mike was lying upon a section of the straw-covered floor, which was completely saturated in his blood. He had been stripped to the waist and slowly mutilated with knives or bayonets. Several of his fingers were missing, and those remaining had their fingernails torn out. Perhaps worst of all, at the end of this horror he had been decapitated. His head was lying several yards away in a corner of the barn, atop a mound of animal dung. The front teeth were broken, and his skull stared vacantly through gouged, empty sockets.

Jack heard the other crew members gasp. Corbett cursed, and the replacement gunner, Gene Simpson, whispered a shocked "Jesus Christ!"

He found that his own throat was so dry he couldn't utter a word.

His driver, Tim Irwin, began to quietly wail. "Mike. My God, look what they did to Mike."

Stewart was standing beside him as he stared down at the corpse, and Jack dimly realized the infantry Captain was speaking.

In a voice tinged with the bitter contempt of experience, he growled. "Hitler *Jugend*! They're young Nazi fanatics – some of them still teenagers – trained from childhood in master race theory, and to fight to the death."

He explained. "We ran into them before as the *12th SS Panzer Division*, during the first weeks after the Normandy invasion. They tortured and mutilated some of our boys they had captured. It was so bad that a number of our guys, and the 'Vandoos' too, I think, ran amok – crawling out at night against orders, to slit the throats of a lot of these insane fuckers in their foxholes. We assumed they had got the message when the mutilations stopped, but now it seems that they were just saving it up for later."

The Captain paused a moment, then cleared his throat and spat. "Our intelligence people tell us that the *12th SS* were pulled out of the western front after their offensive in the Ardennes failed last December, but a few of them got cut off during the withdrawal. They eventually hooked up with their Dutch *SS* fellow travelers here in Holland. This has their signature written all over it."

Jack's voice had returned, and he replied hoarsely. "I don't think I'll ever understand how someone could do this to another person. One thing's for sure. They don't deserve the right to be called a human being after committing this kind of atrocity. There's no possible redemption for this – none."

He then turned to squarely face the infantry Captain. "Frankly Bill, the only thing I want to do now, is to kill as many of those animals as I can!"

Stewart smiled grimly. "You may get your chance. My boys have got them trapped in the next farmhouse. There also seems to be about fifty Dutch *SS* troops holed up with them – mostly in the big barn next door. Shall we pay the cock-suckers a visit?"

They stepped out of the barn and into the morning light. From there, Jack stared bleakly at the distant farmstead. "I can't wait…"

The four Sherman tanks in Jack's troop pulled themselves up in a semi-circle about two hundred yards in front of the house and barn. They came to a stop just behind where the infantry had deployed in the cover of a raised earthen flood barrier edging the building compound.

A white cloth tied to the end of a broom handle was being waved from one of the bottom-floor windows of the farmhouse, and someone from inside was shouting in accented English that they wanted to surrender.

Jack heard a Canadian infantry Sergeant bark something back in German, and slowly the door of the house opened while a young

German officer slowly emerged. He was accompanied by a boyish-looking regular soldier who had raised the broom and white flag above them.

About half-way across the field the two stopped, and the officer again shouted in broken English that he wanted to negotiate the surrender of all his men. Cautiously, the German-speaking sergeant accompanied by an infantry captain, stood up. With weapons cocked, they walked guardedly toward the two men.

"What the fuck are they doing?" Jack muttered to himself.

There was something in the German officer's demeanour that didn't seem right to Jack as he observed the two parties approach each other. The jaunty cock of his hat seemed almost intentionally arrogant.

He looked up at the surrender flag carried by his subordinate and grinned obsequiously as he slowly pulled a package from his tunic pocket, offering its contents to the two infantry men coming toward him.

His voice held a confident, almost mocking tone when he called out to them. *"Kammerad! Zigaretten?"*

The two Canadians continued to advance cautiously, but when they had got to within fifty feet of them, the smiling German officer suddenly screamed *"Heil* Hitler!" while at the same time he and his subordinate threw themselves face-first onto the ground. Simultaneously, there was the distinctive guttural rip of an *MG42* machine gun firing from the doorway behind him.

Jack saw the two Canadians torn nearly in half by the stream of bullets, and he quickly dropped into the turret, closing the hatch behind him. The infantry immediately returned fire toward the two buildings, where weapons were now firing from every opening. A flurry of bullets pinged and ricocheted off the exterior of the tank, but caused no serious damage to the thickly armoured vehicle. Jack could see through his periscope that the German officer had managed to safely crawl back into the house. However, the other soldier had been felled when the hail of .303 rounds from a Bren gun caught him rising slightly to enter the doorway.

Enraged, Jack screamed orders into the radio. "All tanks open up on the buildings with H.E.! Take no prisoners! Machine-gun any of them that come out or try to surrender!"

The ground shook, and the air was filled with the roar of explosions as the tanks repeatedly rocked backward from the recoil of their 75mm guns. The hail of machinegun bullets ricocheting off the four Shermans subsided dramatically as the tanks rapidly fired round after round of high-explosive shells into the two buildings.

Having moved over to their adjacent machine guns, the tank drivers were pouring a continuous stream of .30 cal. fire into the enemy. For the next several minutes a seemingly endless storm of violent blasts and lethal shrapnel ripped through the house and barn, sending fountains of flaming wood and masonry flying high into the air, as death rained down mercilessly upon the Germans and Dutch Nazis.

In the end, after all the guns had fallen silent, Jack watched from his perch in the turret as infantrymen walked through the smoking ruins with pitiless determination, firing pistol rounds into the heads of the few wounded who had somehow managed to survive.

As Jack eased himself out of the commander's hatch, he saw Captain Stewart, who was also walking amidst the debris, suddenly stop and turn in his direction, motioning at him to come over.

Jack stepped carefully through the broken remains of the house to where Stewart was pointing. "Here's the bastard who suckered us with the surrender flag. He was probably in charge of the guys who did your man too. His legs are busted up pretty good, but he's still breathing."

The German was lying with his back partially propped up against a piece of broken timber. Both of his legs were bent at unnatural angles, and there was a gunshot wound through his lower left arm. He appeared to be not more than twenty years of age, and was no longer wearing his cap. His pale blond hair was dishevelled, and now flecked with clumps of soil and tiny bits of splintered wood.

The young officer regarded them defiantly, while clasping his arm just below the elbow in an attempt to slow the bleeding from his wound. His eyes were still blazing with a fanatical will, as they darted back and forth attempting to read the faces of the two Canadians.

Jack's own face was impassive when he asked. "Do you speak English?"

His eyes were now fixed on Jack, and the German replied cautiously. *"Ja, ein bis –* a little.*"*

Jack's mind was groping to comprehend the insanity of what had been done to Mike, when he asked. "Why did you do that to my man last night?"

With his teeth clenched, the German appeared to wheeze in agony. However, Jack was gripped with revulsion when he realized this totally committed Hitler *Jugend* was actually grinning with contempt.

The German shrugged, and hissed confidently. *"Blut und ehre* is our motto. Blood and honour. When your country has been raped, you sometimes grow indifferent to the suffering of others."

Jack saw him glance at his *Luger* lying on the ground nearby, then growled. "Or maybe you just become a mad dog. Go ahead and make a move for that pistol. I would love for you to try."

The German's grin grew wider. "No, I don't think so. I am unarmed, and under the Geneva Conventions you must take me prisoner and tend to my wounds in one of your own hospitals. You have no choice but to follow the rules."

Jack stepped closer to straddle the officer's chest with his feet. He slid the semi-automatic pistol from his holster and pulled the action back to push a round into the chamber. Slowly, he pointed the gun down to a spot between the German's eyes, which had suddenly grown wide with terror.

Jack's voice came dispassionately from low in his throat. "Not today arsehole. *Heil* Hitler!"

His eyes blazed as the gun roared in his hand. He continued to fire every bullet from the clip into the German's face, reducing his entire skull to a bloody pulp of shattered bone and brain tissue.

When the final click indicated that his gun was empty, Jack's shoulders sagged, and he slowly exhaled. After a few seconds, he turned to look at the infantry captain.

Nonplussed, Stewart shrugged. A hard, thin smile played over his lips, as he observed, acidly. "What could have got into the crazy bastard's mind, going for his gun that way? I saw the whole thing – you had to kill him. Too bad that first bullet did the job, because he definitely deserved to die more than once."

Cruising at 12,000 metres, *Major* Roland Schwartz pushed the control column forward to put his *Me262* into a steep dive. He was travelling a nearly eight hundred kilometres per hour as his *schwarm* closed on the flight of B-17s and their P-51 escorts, approaching their target in the Ruhr.

The skies were cloudless, and at this altitude in the thin air, the sun reflected brightly off the polished aluminum skins of the American aircraft. This had made them easily identifiable as they flew toward his ten o'clock position, 4,000 metres below.

The four jets split into two pairs, as he and the other leader chose their targets. Roland had selected the rearmost bomber, and as he streaked past it his 30mm rounds punched a series of huge gashes between the two engines in the starboard wing, causing it to tear off completely. In his rear-view mirror, he saw the stricken bomber, with flame pouring from its shattered airfoil, roll over and begin its death-spiral to the earth below.

As he pulled up to make a second pass at the bomber formation, he realized that his wingman was no longer there, and he began to scan the skies for any sign of him. It was then that he noticed the pair of P-51s, two kilometres ahead, at his one o'clock location, about 1,000 metres beneath him.

One aircraft was damaged, with the tip of its port wing shorn off. The top portion of its tail-fin was also missing, along with part of the port-side horizontal stabilizer. The cumulative effect of this damage was making the aircraft very difficult to control. He could see that the pilot, escorted by his wingman, was obviously struggling in his attempt to fly it out of Germany.

Roland swiftly dove down upon the unsuspecting aircraft and drifted right until he was directly behind the damaged Mustang. Now at close range, he unleashed a burst of cannon fire that tore into the P-51's rear fuselage, and then through the cockpit. Schwartz grunted with satisfaction as he saw the shattered aircraft explode into a mass of burning fragments.

Ramming the throttle forward, he pulled the *Me262* up and turned left, climbing away at high speed as the escorting American fighter made a futile attempt to follow him. Seeing several other enemy aircraft suddenly appear in the sky, he pointed the jet's nose back toward his base, while accelerating away from the fighters.

As the euphoria from this latest kill receded, he began to brood on how that bastard Schmidt was going to catch bloody hell from him if he didn't have enough of the *Fw*190s up today to protect his landing approach.

Major Joseph Haadland dropped the left wing of his P-51 Mustang slightly to peer out of the cockpit at multiple formations of shiny B-17 Flying Fortresses on his ten o'clock about 5,000 feet below. In the cold thin air at 24,000 feet, each of the four Wright R-1820 engines on every bomber left a white contrail of condensing vapour streaming through the clear morning skies behind it. With the gleaming metallic bombers at the tip, they pointed like a phalanx of long white spears in the direction of today's target in the Ruhr Valley.

Joe was leading the entire squadron at the head of his own 'finger four' quartet of escorting Mustangs. They were equipped with drop-tanks under their wings to make the trip all the way in and back as they flew top-cover, ready to react instantly by taking on any attackers attempting to intercept the American bombers.

These days, the Germans were sending up a mixed assortment of generally late-model aircraft, and they were being flown by pilots possessing wildly variant skill levels. Sometimes the pilots were so inexperienced that they forgot to jettison their drop-tanks before engaging, and they were easy kills. However, you could also find yourself in a dogfight with a veteran pilot who had exceptional flying skills – with sometimes over a hundred victories – and it was not difficult to become his next victim.

The 'wonder weapons' were also a constant threat, but thankfully they did not usually appear in large enough numbers to be decisive in a major engagement. A week earlier Joe had seen one of the *Me*163 *Komets* – a rocket powered fighter – fly into the rearmost formation of a B-17 group at over six hundred miles per hour. In seconds its twin 30mm cannons had ripped two of the Fortresses in half, before it then disappeared into the clouds below.

There was no way for a propeller-driven fighter to catch the *Me*163, and it was virtually impossible to defend against during the powered portion of its flight. However, it did have a very limited fuel capacity, which was a vulnerability the escorts had learned to exploit.

In order to save weight, the *Komet's* designers had eliminated the landing gear. During take-off, it utilized an unattached dolly which dropped behind it. When the fuel expired, a *Me*163 would glide in to land on a single long skid, which it could partially extend from the bottom of its fuselage. While in this unpowered approach, the rocket fighter eventually lost both speed and manoeuvrability, making it a sitting duck when bounced.

The weapon that the escorts feared most was the *Me*262 jet fighter. It used its one hundred mile per hour speed advantage to attack and then outrun escort fighters if it didn't want to dogfight. In addition, the 30mm cannons in its nose were devastating to any bomber when it lined one up at full speed. Few air gunners were able to acquire and properly lead a target diving in on them for a few brief seconds at a speed of six hundred miles per hour.

On rare occasions, you might bounce an unsuspecting *Me*262 pilot, but most frequently kills were achieved on its landing approach. There, it slowed down and also suffered from engines which did not power up quickly, making the jet highly vulnerable to a prop-fighter diving on it at high speed.

Today Haadland saw the jets approaching from two o'clock high and turned his flight directly into them as they began their dive toward the bombers below. He was now on a collision course at a closing speed of nearly 1,000 miles per hour. To his surprise when he pressed his firing button, the Messerschmitt coming directly at him suddenly exploded. He banked violently to avoid the debris, but he felt multiple hard hits on his left wing-tip and tail section.

His wingman, Captain Andrew Levitt, quickly rejoined him at the eight o'clock position, but the news he reported over the radio was not good. "Joe, your left wingtip is gone, but your flaps look okay. I'm more worried about the top part of your tail-fin and rudder which are damaged, and nearly half of your left horizontal stabilizer is gone."

"Haadland replied calmly. "I can feel the plane wanting to roll left Andy, and I'm trying to counter, but it's a struggle. If you can cover me for another twenty minutes until we're over Belgium, I'll feel a bit better about bailing out then."

"Roger that Joe."

Levitt throttled back a bit more and was about to begin scanning the skies above and behind them when he saw the winking of cannon fire suddenly appear in his rear-view mirror. For a fraction of a second, pieces of Haadland's rear fuselage and canopy flew off and then the Mustang exploded. Simultaneously the *Me262* roared past in a high-speed dive as it overshot the Americans. However, before Levitt could attempt to follow, the jet pulled up slightly and banked left before accelerating eastward, where it disappeared into a distant cloudbank.

Jason had just stepped out of the Officer's Mess into the late winter twilight when he heard the telephone ring behind him. He had gone about thirty more paces when another pilot stuck his head out of the door and hollered. "Call for you Jay! It's some American, from Boxted!"

The voice on the other end of the line was restrained and hesitant. "Flight Lieutenant Jason McMurchy?"

Jason was apprehensive. He had been expecting it to be Joe Haadland. "Yes. What can I do for you?"

"It's Major Andrew Levitt here. We haven't met, but Major Haadland told me about you. I'm afraid I have to tell you Joe bought it today. His plane was badly damaged, but we were limping home when a *Me262* got him."

Jason held his breath, and then he asked. "Did you see the insignia on the *Me262*?"

Levitt's voice had also grown tense. "Yeah, I saw. It was our boy, the black boar. He never mixes it up – only picks off stragglers. I've lost count of how many of our guys he's taken out that way. Someday I would dearly love to get on that bastard's six!"

"You'll have to stand in line." Jason's voice had acquired a hard edge.

"As you know, I'm flying out of Evere, Belgium these days, or otherwise I'd drop over to Boxted and pay my respects. Joe was a hell of a good guy – grew up not too far from me, but on the American side of the lake. We were looking forward to doing a little fishing together after this was all over. Now I think I owe it to both him and Charlie Dentine to go trolling for a certain *Me262!*"

Hans and Peter were sitting at the small table in his room adjoining the dispersal hut, sipping their coffee and thanking their luck for having kept David hidden for nearly six weeks. Despite the daily propaganda broadcasts on the radio, it was now fairly common knowledge in the *Luftwaffe* that the eastern front protecting the approaches to Berlin was collapsing. The *Gestapo SS* were now quite arbitrarily executing anyone they suspected of treachery or cowardice.

Peter's anxiety about his sister's safety grew exponentially with every day that passed without any news from her. He had sent three telegrams in the last week urging her to join him here at the airbase, but still there was no response.

He was preparing to walk over to the communications building for the second time today to check for any word from her, when Roland burst through the door, foaming with anger. "Where was the fucking fighter cover when I landed! I saw only one *Langnasse* guarding my approach. Are you intentionally trying to get me and my pilots killed, you incompetent bastard!

Suddenly refocused, Peter remained seated, and calmly replied. "Due to a lack of replacement parts, most of our *Fw*190Ds are not flyable Roland. Perhaps I should tell the pilots to stand on their seats and flap their arms for you. Would that help?"

Roland's face was flushed, and both hands were balled into fists. "If you would just do your damned job and order the proper replacements on time, this wouldn't be a problem. I've a mind to call Göring right now to have you sacked, and then shipped off to a concentration camp, you slacker!"

Peter had pushed his chair back, and he raised his arms to lock the fingers of both hands behind his head. "When you get your Uncle Hermann on the phone, don't forget to remind him that our glorious Führer has personally assured me that a gold-plated set of parts would be manufactured, then hand-delivered today by an assortment of *Nibelungen* river trolls, so there should be nothing to worry about. Especially with the great Roland Schwartz at the controls of a *Wonder Waffen*, we should have the Russians and their allies in the west thoroughly destroyed by the end of this week!"

It was then that the dog-master happened to walk past the open door, where he spied Schwartz and Schmidt glaring at each other. It was well-known that the two aces had a mutual dislike for each other. The *feldwebel* was also still nursing a grievance from the time Peter had stopped him from shooting the Canadian Indian who had killed his lead Alsatian. He had actually turned out to be the bastard's friend! He longed to bring the savage – and Peter – to some grief, but even his brother-in-law in the Interior Ministry had not been able to find out which *Luft Stalag* the Canadian airman had been taken to.

Unable to resist the urge to cause even more trouble for Schmidt, and perhaps exact a modicum of revenge in the process, he thrust his head through the open doorway. "Excuse me *Major*, but some of my men have urged me to ask you about that Canadian we captured in January after he was shot down. How did he first become a friend of yours?"

The unexpected nature of the question caused Peter to pause momentarily, and he was unable to conceal a hint of nervousness in his short laugh, before he responded. "It's a long story. I met him when I was traveling before the war."

The dog-master remained straight-faced, and intentionally appeared to ask his next question quite innocently. "One of our boys loves those stupid cowboy movies and wanted to write a letter to him, but when we checked there is no record of the man in any of the *Luft Stalags*. Do know you which one he went to?"

Peter felt his heart racing but managed to remain calm. "It has slipped my mind."

He hastily added. "But I will find out for you later."

Roland's eyes had narrowed, and he was still seething with anger. "What! First your damned cousin, and now another of the enemy is your friend! And you don't even know which *Luft Stalag* this *schwein* has been taken to! You stink like a rat Schmidt. Where are you hiding him!

Peter was on his feet, with eyes fixed intensely on Roland's. His voice had grown level and cold. "The man was in my custody. I interrogated him, and when I was through, in accordance with the Geneva Conventions, I saw that he was transported to a *Luft Stalag*. I have the paperwork here to prove it!"

He had no idea how much longer this desperate bluff was going to last, but Peter reached into his desk drawer to withdraw the forged documents, glanced at them briefly, and then threw the papers down on the desk in front of Schwartz. "It says right on the first page that he has been taken to the *Stalag Luft* in Military District Eleven, near Hanover!"

Schwartz picked the papers up and began to scrutinize them, growing increasingly more frustrated as he realized they were all in order. When Roland turned to the dog-master, the *feldwebel's* sickly grin suddenly disappeared.

Schwartz exploded. "Fuck you Schmidt! I'm going to call my *Gestapo* contacts right now, and when they find your friend, they will shoot both of you! Then, I'll shit on your rotting corpse, you bloody traitor!"

The dog-master retreated outside, while Schwartz used the back of his hand to wipe away spittle that had accumulated on the corners of his mouth as he glared at Peter. Then, abruptly, he left, slamming the door so hard that it broke the latch.

Nijmegen Salient. March 1945

There was a good reason for calling this part of the world the 'Low Countries', and Jack's troop of four Sherman tanks had spent most of the morning, and half of the afternoon, navigating through muddy water-logged fields, attempting to reach their objective a mile to the east. That slightly raised area, about half a mile square, lay between two patches of forested land, and its drier soils would provide an improved purchase for the tanks and other heavy vehicles. With the assistance of Bailey bridges, they planned to cross the canal bordering it to the east, where they would subsequently push over the Rhine into Germany.

The troop had moved half-way across the clearing when two huge German tanks suddenly roared out from behind a hillock on the edge of the forest to their right and opened fire.

To his horror, Jack saw the first was a massive 50-ton *PzKpFw VI* 'Tiger'. Painted with alternating brown, yellow, and green camouflage, it had been nearly invisible, lurking in its forested lair.

While time slowed down for him as it often seemed to do in the heat of battle, he also noted the tank's coat of *Zimmerit*, a ridged ceramic *appliqué* designed to defeat magnetic mines.

The Germans had chosen the moment for their ambush perfectly, waiting until the troop of four Sherman tanks had reached a point in the open field where they would have no time to retreat for cover.

Jack could see that the Tiger's gun was not pointed at him, but he instinctively crouched lower when it fired its first 88mm round at the closer of the troop's two Fireflies. He winced, as despite the tank's additional externally-welded armour plate, the shell easily pierced the Sherman's hull to make a direct hit on one of the ammunition lockers. Reflexively, he bent even lower in his

319

battened-down turret in reaction to the shock wave that rocked *Beowulf* when the powerful high velocity shells in the other tank immediately detonated, obliterating its entire crew. The blast also sent the turret spinning a hundred feet into the air atop a massive exploding column that erupted through its ring, and also blew open the driver's hatches.

The second German tank, a *PzKpFw V* 'Panther', similarly camouflaged and one of the deadliest tanks on the battlefield, emerged from behind the Tiger. Jack knew from experience that the Panther's long barrelled weapon fired a 75mm armour-piercing shell that was every bit as lethal as the Tiger's 88mm.

The Panther unleashed a round at the second Firefly which was now travelling at top speed toward the lee of another small hillock bordering the forest on the right. Just before the German fired, the Sherman's spinning right track sank into a small depression that caused the tank to lean over about twenty degrees - which saved it. The streaking round tore a sucking vortex through the air as it screamed inches above the turret.

Emerging from the depression levelled the tank again, and the gunner, who had been lining up his 17-pounder on the Tiger, fired a round that caused the Sherman to rock sideways from the force of the recoil. The high-velocity armour-piercing round passed through the side of the German's turret, causing the Tiger to come to a lurching halt before erupting into flames.

The German crew commander struggled desperately to climb out of his hatch but could not overcome the intensity of the fire that now enveloped him completely. His writhing body slid back down into the cauldron as the ammunition suddenly began to cook off. The subsequent effusion of flame stabbed in long roaring jets out of every opening in the turret and hull of the huge tank, and was finally punctuated by a huge explosion that blew the turret out of its ring mount and onto the ground beside the blazing vehicle.

The thick, sloped steel on the front glacis of the *PzKpFw V* was impervious to the Sherman's 75mm armour-piercing rounds, so in a well-practiced manoeuvre the two remaining tanks with their relatively ineffective main guns, split to accelerate in opposite directions. They then began to race at full throttle in an attempt to get into a position on either side - to fire through the Panther's suspension below its sloped sides where the armour was lighter -

or preferably at the rear of the tank where it was possible to make a kill shot.

Jack was speeding to the left, slightly in advance of the other Sherman, *Buffalo,* commanded by Sgt. Bert McAllister - who was circling to the right.

The commander of the Panther knew that his greatest danger lay in the lethal 17-pounder which was capable of penetrating any part of his tank, so he concentrated on lining up the Firefly. They fired simultaneously, and the Canadian's round shattered the German's left track as it tore off the drive sprocket. The German's shell passed through the Firefly's engine, and fragments lethally ricocheted into the crew compartment as flames from the ruptured fuel system ignited the ammunition lockers. The tank instantly brewed up in a series of internal explosions that atomized any surviving crew.

The German tank was now traversing its turret toward *Beowulf,* and Jack was screaming into his radio at the other remaining Sherman. "Bert! Try to get a deflection shot off of his mantlet down through the driver's hatch. If that doesn't work, I'll try going straight in, while you attempt to get behind him!"

In Normandy, the outgunned Canadian tankers had learned that a 75mm AP round could be deflected down off of the rounded bottom half of the Panther's main gun-mantlet, where it could then penetrate the lightly-armoured driver's hatch, knocking out the otherwise nearly invincible German tank. It was a risky shot and required nerves of steel on the part of the Sherman crew.

Ronnie Corbett had already loaded an AP round into the gun's breech, and Gene Simpson, his gunner, stomped the firing button as Jack screamed. "Fire!"

McAllister in the other Sherman fired only a second later. Both rounds hit the lower half of the Panther's gun mantlet but incredibly, deflected upward! While both tanks sped closer Jack swore as he saw the enemy was equipped with a new chin-mantlet. The Germans had cleverly redesigned it with an angled ridge along its bottom to overcome what they learned was possibly the *PzKpFw V's* only vulnerability from the front.

Jack now cursed himself for not recognizing that this Panther lacked a *Zimmerit* coating, which should have alerted him to the fact it was probably one of the late-model *'G'* variants equipped with the new mantlet. Not that it made any difference at this point. They were already committed to the split manoeuvre, and success or failure would be determined in the next few seconds.

The Panther was fitted with a hand-cranked mechanism, making its traverse much slower than that of the Sherman, which rotated its turret utilizing an electric motor. However, the Panther had now nearly lined its gun up on *Beowulf.*

Jack shouted to his gunner. "Gene! Try for that gap near the turret ring! We might be close enough to penetrate!"

He was accustomed to the tank rocking from the main gun's recoil, but this time the roar of the 75mm was accompanied by a deafening blast as the Panther fired a fraction of a second later.

Both Canadian rounds were slightly high and glanced with little effect off of the enemy's turret. However, the German shell tore through the frontal armour just above Tim Irwin's driving position, taking most of his skull with it as it continued into the turret basket. There, it deflected with a deafening clang off of the gun breech, ripping both Simpson and Corbett in half. The projectile continued its path through the firewall, and finally exited as it blasted through the engine cover.

Only Jack's helmet saved him when his head was knocked violently against the inside of the turret by the force of the shell's velocity as it passed through the tank.

Beowulf had come to a complete stop with its main gun now useless. As Jack tried to clear his head, he could smell the strong odour of leaking gasoline. He wiped the dust off of the eye-piece and gazed through his periscope. There, he could see that the German tank was now traversing its gun away from him in an attempt to line up McAllister.

The other Sherman was still a long way from getting into position for an effective shot. It seemed inevitable that the Panther would win in this desperate race between the *PzKpFw V's* turret traverse, and the Canadian tank's full-speed attempt to get around to the German's rear.

Jack unplugged his helmet, and then squeezed past the damaged breech and the shredded remains of his turret crew. He next wriggled through the jagged remnants of the basket into the driver's compartment. Resisting the urge to vomit, he removed Irwin's body and slid into the blood-soaked driver's seat. The engine was still running, so he grabbed hold of the clutch levers to engage both sets of tracks, and then suddenly accelerated the tank toward the immobilized Panther.

The German tank commander was a seasoned veteran. When he first attacked, he had intended to move his Panther to a position behind a small rise of land that would put most of his hull out of sight from the Canadian gunners. This would still allow him to pick off the Sherman tanks in relative safety, as the exposed but very well-armoured front of his turret presented a small and nearly impervious target.

He had been about one tank-length from his intended destination when the 17-pounder had destroyed his drive sprocket, and the Panther had ground to a sudden halt only four metres short of the rise. It was still excellent cover from the front, and as his loader cranked the turret around to the left, it would only be a matter of seconds before he finished off the final Canadian tank. Focused as he was on the next kill, he did not see Jack's tank approaching at full speed from the front.

The German gunner had just acquired his target, and his foot was descending upon the firing button when Jack's tank roared up the slope in front of the Panther. Launching itself over the gap, it crashed headlong into the side of the *PzKpFw V's* turret, dislodging it just as the German gun fired.

A huge column of black mud shot into the air as the German shell blasted directly into the ground only ten metres to the side of the Panther. Simultaneously, the force of the impact ignited the gasoline sloshing on the floor of *Beowulf* causing the Sherman to ignite in a huge fireball which enveloped both tanks, setting off the Panther's ammunition.

Sgt. Bert McAllister, sitting in the turret of *Buffalo,* gasped in awe at the horrific force of the massive explosion. His tank now came to a halt while the entire crew gazed in shock at the blazing conflagration hungrily consuming both of the armoured vehicles. The intensity of the heat forced them to back further away, while the two tanks continued to be rocked by the powerful flaring eruptions of their ammunition.

Soaked in perspiration and profoundly thankful to still be alive, the surviving tank commander used the back of his sleeve to mop the sweat from his brow. Without intending to, he spoke aloud.

"Good grief Jack! Not even you could possibly survive something like that!"

McAllister reflected for a brief moment about the families back in Canada who would be receiving the dreaded telegrams over the next few days – but thankfully not his. Some capricious twist of fate had placed Jack's tank a few feet closer to the Panther as they both raced hell-bent to get behind it, causing the German tank commander to fire at *Beowulf* first.

He slowly surveyed the columns of oily black smoke boiling up into the air from the five burning hulks in the field around him. "Goddamn it," he muttered to himself, before ordering his radio operator to report the loss of three 'B' Squadron tanks and their entire crews.

Prey

Elke Schmidt reached into the pocket of her apron to reassure herself that the telegrams were still there. For a week she had been meaning to reply to Peter, but the speed and intensity of events over that period had been overwhelming. At first, the head matron of the *Isolde* Women's Academy had informed them that due to the proximity of the new front, the classrooms would be converted into medical stations for tending to the growing numbers of wounded German soldiers. In addition, that part of the residence vacated by the younger girls who were being sent home immediately would be changed into hospital recovery wards. Those girls over sixteen years of age were encouraged to stay and work as nurse's helpers but would not be stopped if they expressed a desire to return to their homes further west.

At eighteen, and as a senior girl, Elke could still remember the trepidation she had experienced over Peter's injuries five years earlier. She felt it her duty to stay behind and do what she could. For her, this meant tending to the wounded men who were sacrificing everything to protect them from the depredations of the advancing Russian hordes.

A few days later, she had gone down to the nearby rail station to see the remaining junior girls and some of her classmates off but had been shocked to see the nature of the troops being disembarked from the train and loaded into trucks for the journey east. They had been *Volksturm*, composed mostly of old men and very young boys - some barely in their teens - dressed in their ill-fitting uniforms. All of them carried an assortment of older rifles and a few modern automatic weapons. Most prevalent were the *Panzerfausts*. Every second soldier was carrying one, which could mean only one thing – they were expecting to encounter large numbers of tanks.

Soon the casualties began to arrive. Most suffered from shrapnel wounds as a result of the massive amount of artillery the Russians were bringing to bear on the German defenders. The jagged pieces of metal tended to shred internal organs, making them irreparable in most cases. While the morphine supplies lasted, the best that could be done for these unfortunates was to ease their suffering until they passed away. However, there were also a large number of wounded arriving with severely damaged or completely missing limbs, which required either further amputation or emergency surgery to staunch blood flow and modify the stumps.

Elke often found herself cleaning and dressing these types of wounds, and incredibly, a truck carrying an astonishing quantity of crude prosthetics had arrived within the first few days. As soon as the men had been fitted with the devices and were capable of movement, they were being loaded on trucks and buses which had been seconded for transportation west.

One of the last drivers she had spoken to had been an old man in his late seventies. He had advised her that she should leave with him because he had today heard rumours of an impending collapse to the immediate east of this sector, so the Russians could be expected to break through at any time. Even as he spoke, another shipment of casualties drove in, and reflexively she had returned to the reception area to perform *triage* on the new arrivals.

Prophetically, the old driver's words were confirmed when news came this very afternoon that their position had been flanked both to the north and the south by two Russian tank columns.

As twilight descended, the young women were called together by the chief surgeon who gathered them in a makeshift room that was serving as both his office and a drug storage locker.

His apron was covered in blood, and while slowly removing his surgical gloves he spoke gravely. "Ladies, I have just been informed that we are nearly surrounded and our position here is no longer tenable. The Russians will likely arrive within hours, so I am ordering you to leave immediately. I will remain behind to treat our casualties and expect the Russians will allow me to continue practicing on our men, or theirs, after my capture. However, we know that they have been barbaric with captured German women. Therefore, you must make your way west to Berlin before we are completely cut off. Under no circumstances should you surrender, unless you have no other choice. You must leave now. Good luck to you!"

Quickly returning to her quarters, Elke pushed her long blond hair up under a soft blue hat covered by a light silk scarf which she then tied beneath her chin. She put a small package of biscuits into her purse, and then donned a long grey woollen coat to fend off the night-time cold of early spring. Last, she put on a thicker pair of socks, and then slid her feet back into the sturdy brown leather walking shoes that she had been wearing on the ward for the past ten days.

In complete darkness, she and a half-dozen other young women cautiously made their way through the west gate. They had advanced only a few meters when suddenly mortar shells began to fall on the tree-shrouded lane ahead of them. The force of the first explosions knocked her to the ground. As the barrage dissipated, she slowly rose to her knees, and as her head began to clear Elke realized that all of the other girls had retreated back inside of the academy.

Still determined to make her way west, she staggered to her feet and began to slowly grope her way through the darkness. She stepped carefully over the splintered branches and had only proceeded a few hundred meters when a second more powerful barrage of mixed mortar and artillery rounds now erupted. Cowering in the entrance to a storm drain, she felt the concussion waves rolling over her and saw flashes which intermittently lit up the night, while huge explosions completely enveloped the buildings behind her.

Through the night she often stopped to hide in ditches or behind patches of bare shrubbery as she heard the roar of tank engines moving in the darkness ahead, or on either side of her. If she was in the open, she immediately threw herself to the ground and hoped that by remaining absolutely still, she would go unnoticed until the sounds had grown more distant.

Once she dimly saw the dark shapes of several stationary tanks and trucks a short distance to her right with their engines idling. Unable to discern whether they were German or Russian vehicles, she gave them a wide berth and continued slowly to make her way west.

The first faint rays of dawn found her on the outskirts of Berlin under grey skies smudged with the slowly rising smoke of countless smouldering fires. Most of the buildings had been reduced to rubble by the ceaseless Russian artillery barrages, as well as the blockbuster bombs dropped by the big four-engine bombers flying from bases in Britain.

The scene presented itself as an endless landscape of loose bricks lying in shapeless piles studded with plastered lathe, or charred wood. Reinforced concrete corner supports, often with part of a collapsed wall still attached, poked irregularly upward, sometimes for several floors, amidst the destruction. Otherwise, the whole area was unrecognizable.

Off to her left, Elke saw that a few smaller buildings had partially escaped the onslaught and were still generally intact. As the first raindrops began to fall, she decided to work her way toward them. Bent low, she carefully clambered through a rubble-strewn alleyway to furtively peer through the broken window of a shed, and saw that it was unoccupied. Slipping around its corner to enter, she closed and locked the rough wooden door behind her.

Exhausted by lack of sleep and the night's exertions, she had just reclined on a mound of hay, when suddenly from outside there was a muffled shout followed by a series of unintelligible expletives. Within seconds there was the pounding of bodies against the door, until with a crash of splintering wood it finally burst open.

Major Roland Schwartz was brooding at his desk, seething with anger as he impatiently waited for a return call from the *Gestapo* office in Hanover. With the first ring, his huge hand swept the telephone from its cradle.

He literally barked into the mouthpiece. "Schwartz here!"

The voice at the other end was level, and dispassionate. "It's *Major* Wilhelm Ehrhart, Hanover district *Geheime Staatspolizei* Headquarters Chief. We have been to *Stalag Luft* Eleven, as you requested, and I must inform you that there is no Canadian Air

Force Sergeant by the name of David Hunter being held there. Nor is there any record of him having been registered there on any occasion. We took the time to investigate some of the smaller satellite camps where the prisoners of war are sometimes used as labourers by our local farmers, and the result was the same. There is no record of him. Are you certain he was processed in this sector?"

Roland was elated. *At last he had that bastard Schmidt where he wanted him!* "I am absolutely sure. I held the paperwork in my hands and that is what it says. It can only mean that *Major* Schmidt is harbouring the enemy, and as such is guilty of treason! You must come to arrest him immediately and force him to tell us where he is hiding that enemy airman!"

Ehrhart pushed his wire-rimmed glasses further up the bridge of his thin, beak-like nose, then leant back in his chair and took a slow drag on his cigarette. He exhaled a long stream of tobacco smoke and watched it drift across the neat stacks of meticulously organized paper sitting atop his desk.

The *Gestapo Major* responded calmly. "Yes, there must be no doubt that traitors will be dealt with swiftly and ruthlessly. Once we have got him to confess, and he gives us the Canadian, we will make an example of them both which will impress upon everyone that this kind of weakness and cowardice will not be tolerated. It will take us at least an hour to get there, but believe me, we have methods to extract the information that we want from him in very short order. Will you have any trouble rounding up a firing squad?"

Schwartz was flushed with anticipation as he chortled. "No, but I would love nothing better than to shoot the bastards myself!"

After Schwartz stormed out of the office, Peter had been urgently wracking his brain to come up with some solution to this dilemma. It would only be a very short matter of time before Roland's *Gestapo* contacts discovered that David was not being held as a prisoner of war in any of the regional *Luft Stalags*, and then they would come looking for him. It didn't take a great leap of imagination to guess how the two of them would be treated once they were found out.

The obvious solution was for he and David to flee to the west, where Peter would become a POW. He'd heard the western allies treated their prisoners reasonably well, and surely this war would be over soon. At some point he would eventually be released.

However, all of this was becoming complicated by the fact that he had still heard nothing from his sister Elke.

The most pressing issue at present was to fetch David and flee. Peter surmised however that Schwartz must have alerted the security detail to keep a watch on him, because whenever he stepped outside, he had detected an unusual level of scrutiny.

His hand was forced when Hans appeared, to report that he had seen Schwartz approach the dog-master and ask him to assemble a rifle team. Peter reached into his desk to retrieve a day-pass authorization for the fitter, and forged Roland's signature on it.

He then instructed Hans carefully. "Use the back door and move calmly, then take the *Kübelwagen*, but make sure you aren't followed. After you've got David, return by that access road which connects from the south about half-way toward the end of the runway. I'll be waiting there with the *Storch* to fly the three of us out of here."

David found his time passing slowly in the line shack. The monotony had been broken only three times by Hans, who arrived every two weeks with fresh provisions, and sometimes stayed an hour to question him about his life in Canada...or to describe his dreams of moving there himself when the war was over. He had grown to like the young German, as he gradually deduced that the fitter had never really been an enthusiast for the conflict. Like many youths, he had been swept along in the turbulence of events over which he had only vague knowledge, and no control.

Even though it was out of sight from the road, when they had first arrived at the shack, the three men had used broken pine boughs to sweep the approach clean of any footprints in the snow. Later, to alleviate the boredom, David had taken short excursions deeper into the forest, but he always swept the nearest fifty yards of his trail before re-entering the small building.

At first, when he saw the abundant rabbit trails, he had thought that he might use a bit of the discarded electrical wire he'd seen in the shack to snare them. However, he quickly concluded that building a smoky fire to cook them would reveal his location, so it was out of the question.

One of the things Peter had packed in the original supplies was a hunting knife. David found some lengths of wood, and after doing his daily round of push ups and sit ups, he often whiled away the time by carving. His first effort resulted in a miniature replica of his own canoe. There was the stub of an old lead pencil that he had found in the shack, and he used it to draw a wolf's head fashioned from the outline of Lake Superior on both sides of the prow.

This was followed by a bull-moose carving, which was subsequently modified to a cow when in the latter stages of its execution he accidentally cut off one of the antlers and was left with no choice but to remove the other.

Recently he had completed a strange beast with the head of a bison but the body, tail, and serrated back of a dinosaur. As he gazed at it, he scratched his head and wondered once again what the shaman had been thinking ages ago, when he first painted it on the rock-face near *Agawa* Bay.

Last night he had fallen asleep with the carving on the table next to him, and he had dreamt of fire. Once more he was staring down from his turret at the burning cities. The sickening odour of cremated human flesh was causing him to retch, and now flames were consuming his station at the tail end of the bomber. He released the seat harness, but when he turned to leave, his father was there, pointing to the pictographs which had mysteriously appeared on the doors.

A large horned owl was flapping its wings frantically above them in the smoke-filled turret while his father whispered. "Son, there are some things you do that are so terrible they unleash a *Wendigo* who will come for you and take your spirit..."

David awoke from the nightmare with a start, and then realized that his blankets were tangled about his feet and he was drenched in sweat. A partial moon was shining through the window, and he could see his breath in the cold air. Outside, he heard the low drone of several hundred bombers as they lumbered through the dark skies above him, returning from some target further to the east. The frosted window glass vibrated with their passage, until finally the sound of the engines faded into the night, to be replaced by the distant howl of a wolf...

Fighting to regain consciousness, he wrestled with the arm restraints as something unyielding pushed down on his eyelids, while the seared nerve endings on the back of his hands, and those covering his face and neck, writhed in agony. Sickened by the odour of burnt flesh, he convulsed in horror, as he realized that it was his own.

Near him in the darkness, there were muffled, incoherent sounds, keening with grief.

Amidst this confusion, he struggled to force any kind of sound from his throat *while she cried his name.* Summoning every remaining bit of strength, and despite the excruciating pain, he willed himself to speak...and was woken by the sound of his own voice.

For most of the following morning he was haunted by these unwelcome images. In the early afternoon his thoughts were interrupted by the rapidly approaching sound of the *Kübelwagen*, followed by the screeching of its brakes. Placing the sheathed knife in his pocket, he opened the door to see Hans struggling through the snow near the head of the trail and urgently signalling with his arm that he should quickly come.

As David leapt into the vehicle, Hans slammed the transmission into gear, and they accelerated down the narrow snow-covered road.

He turned to David and breathlessly explained. "The *Gestapo* is on to Peter, and they will arrive at any minute to execute both of you. He is waiting at the airfield with an airplane to take us away!"

They were rounding the last turn onto the airstrip access route, when there was a loud report. The corner of the windscreen to the right of David's head shattered as a bullet passed through it. Turning in his seat, he saw that a black sedan had pulled in behind them and was slowly gaining. One of the pursuers had leaned out of the passenger window to point his *Luger* at them, and now unleashed a volley of shots.

Both Hans and David instinctively ducked lower, but they were rounding a corner causing most of the bullets to pass wide of them, except one which they heard slam into their right-side taillight.

They exited the trees into the clearing surrounding the runway and were relieved to see the *Storch* sitting there with its engine running. Hans pumped the brakes and they slewed sideways across the gravel next to it before finally coming to a halt.

The sedan following them had also skidded to a complete stop. Its passenger, dressed in a black leather trench coat, leapt out of the car. He began to fire at them with his pistol again as they dashed toward the airplane, where Peter was now revving up the engine in preparation for take off.

David heard Hans gasp, and turning, saw him stagger. The young fitter dropped to his knees as blood burst from his mouth and flowed down his chin onto his chest.

His jaws were working, but only a gulping sound issued from his throat. There was a look of disbelief on Hans' face as he struggled unsuccessfully to take a breath. Then, with a final groan, his eyes rolled upward and he fell forward onto the ground.

Both of the *Gestapo* men were now firing their guns while running toward them.

In the cockpit, Peter cursed when he saw Hans fall. Then, David stumbled, nearly colliding with the horizontal stabilizer as he reflexively dodged away from a bullet that struck the tarmac next to his right foot. Two more bullets slammed into the open door of the aircraft as David threw himself into the *Storch*.

Peter released the brakes, then rammed the throttle open, and the tiny aircraft began to accelerate down the runway. Just before they attained takeoff speed, he felt the dull impact of a bullet slamming into the tire on his left main wheel strut. The *Storch* began to yaw left and Peter knew that in a fraction of a second they would be cart-wheeling down the runway, so he immediately dipped his right wing slightly to raise the flattened wheel off of the tarmac. The aircraft maintained its precarious balance on the one wheel for a few seconds more while it continued to gain speed. Yet another bullet ricocheted off the engine cowling, before they finally rose slowly into the air. Once aloft, the small plane gained more speed, and they were soon beyond the range of the guns being fired by the two men on the ground.

While Peter was intently scanning the skies ahead of them, David shouted above the sound of the engine. "Jesus Christ that was close! Those bloody bastards killed Hans! What's your plan now?"

Peter cursed at himself. "Damn it! Hans was a good kid!"

He then glanced out the window at their deflated tire. "I hope you realize that right now I'm flying by the seat of my pants. My only plan is to get us west behind allied lines. Unfortunately, the last thing I saw as we cleared the tree-line was Roland Schwartz running toward his *Me262*!"

Elke sat bolt upright. Her eyes were wide with terror as the door splintered and fell inward, raising a cloud of dust and hay fragments as it landed with a crash on the cold stone floor.

Five Russian soldiers shouting excitedly to each other, rushed into the room. They wore green woollen greatcoats and the distinct soft winter hats that covered both ears and the back of their necks. The crude slip-on leather boots that rose to their knees were worn and covered above he ankles in mud.

As her pupils adjusted to the light, she could see by the crescent shape of their eyes and the high cheek-bones that they were Mongolians. Their raw faces and rough, calloused hands had gone days without a washing, and as they leered at her, she saw that some of them were missing teeth, while most of those remaining were crooked and coated brown with tobacco tar.

The first one approached her, and then gestured to his comrades by grasping at his testicles through the heavy woollen trousers. Gutturally barking his intentions at them, he laughed harshly and grabbed Elke by the collar, pulling his prize to her feet. Next, he pawed at the head-scarf, which fell away allowing the long blond hair beneath it to descend in a soft cascade down her back. This drew an approving gasp of awe from the other four soldiers.

"*Bitte.*" Elke pleaded, but the Mongolian growled and slapped her hard across the face with the back of his hand, causing a small trickle of blood to flow slowly from the corner of her mouth.

She tried to struggle but the man was incredibly strong. He pulled the coat from her, and then threw it down on the mound of hay behind her. In a few short seconds he had ripped the rest of her clothes off and forced her down onto the garments. Quickly, he undid his trousers and was upon her. He forced her legs apart and began to thrust himself between them. She closed her eyes and grit her teeth as she tried to block out the pain and the stench of his breath in her face. The soldier panted lustfully, until groaning with pleasure, he soon climaxed.

Suddenly there were more rough hands pulling the man off, then forcing her down again upon the hay as a second Mongolian climbed atop her, grunting in passion. A third soldier forced himself into her mouth while placing the tip of his dagger to her throat as a warning to comply.

When they had finished, a fourth soldier mounted her, but the wild-eyed Mongol was unable to become physically aroused until he had roughly slapped her face several times, blackening an eye and causing blood to flow from both nostrils. Thrusting excitedly, he climaxed in seconds.

Elke lay there numb with exhaustion, and she nearly slipped into unconsciousness as the last man mounted her. While he grunted above her, she became vaguely aware of a grenade hanging from his tunic.

Finishing, the Mongolian attempted to rise, and Elke mustered the last of her strength to snatch the grenade. He shrieked and grabbed his rifle, pointing the bayonet at her as she pulled the pin and let it roll along the floor into their midst.

She turned aside to avoid the bayonet thrust but felt a stab of pain as the blade entered and passed through her into the hay beneath. Although lying low in the straw, the explosion knocked her unconscious, while the upward force of the blast and shrapnel tore lethally through the Russian soldiers.

When Elke came to, it was dark again. She was shivering from the cold, and the room reeked of blood. The bayonet had passed through her upper leg, missing the femoral artery by only two centimetres, and although the wounds had started to scab over, she tore a piece of cloth from her dress to bandage them.

There was no water in the room, so she desperately urinated into her hand several times and attempted to rinse out as much of the semen as possible. Terrified, she prayed that her menstruation, which was due in a week, would actually arrive.

Every part of her body ached, particularly her bruised and swollen face, but she managed to gather her clothes to get dressed. A broken stock from one of the Russian rifles was lying on the floor, so she used it as a crutch, while beginning to slowly and painfully creep out of the shed.

Limping in the cold darkness, she began again to make her way west.

Still at his desk, Roland was startled when the dog-master burst into his office and breathlessly saluted. *"Major* Schmidt and that damned Canadian have just taken off in the *Storch*!"

"Verdammt! How were they allowed to get away!" Roland demanded as he leapt from behind his desk and barked an order to the *feldwebel.* "Have my fighter prepared to take off immediately!"

The armourers had just finished loading fresh 30mm rounds into the *Me262*'s magazines and were closing the ammunition bay doors when the motorcycle bearing Roland in its sidecar raced into the revetment. It screeched to a halt in front of the crew chief and his subordinate, who was holding the *Major's* parachute. They both snapped crisp salutes.

Schwartz stepped out of the vehicle as the crew chief reported. "The aircraft is fully armed and fuelled *Major*. All systems are in order."

Roland ignored him while quickly sliding into his parachute harness. He then climbed onto the wing to access the cockpit. Pulling on his flying helmet and goggles, he left his oxygen mask dangling, as a rigger securely strapped him into his seat.

"Leave me!" He shouted, while waving off the assistant, and pressing the starter switches for both engines. With a distinct whoosh, they ignited and roared to life. Roland pulled the canopy forward, feeling it lock into the closed position. Then, releasing the brakes, he began to steer the sleek fighter down the access ramp onto the runway. Pointing the *Me262*'s nose down the centre-line of the tarmac, he opened both throttles and was immediately forced against the back of his seat as the massive thrust of the *Jumo*s accelerated the fighter down the airstrip. With a deafening shriek, the thundering fighter shot into the air.

Roland assumed that Peter would try to evade detection by flying at low altitude, so he climbed to only 2,000 metres and began to circle around in a north-westerly direction, which from here was the most direct route to the Dutch border.

He roared down the length of several small river valleys where he thought the nimble little *Storch* might attempt to lower its profile by flying below the tree tops of the surrounding hills, but it was to no avail. Schmidt and the plane had both apparently disappeared.

Roland passed over the edge of the forest, then crossed the Rhine and began to soar over the flatter lowlands, carefully scanning above the crosshatching of irrigation canals. There, he eventually caught sight of the small high-winged monoplane low in the distance. It was circling south toward the Belgian border, so he climbed another 1,000 metres, banked left, and smoothly put the *Me262* into a shallow dive that would place him directly behind Schmidt for a perfect kill shot.

Too late, Peter saw Schwartz's *Me262* swooping down on them in the *Storch*'s rear-view mirror. As the first winks of cannon fire issued from the jet's gun ports, he instinctively banked right, causing most of the tracer to pass under the opposite wing as the Messerschmitt roared by him overhead.

However, as he levelled off, he saw a huge hole torn in the fabric of the aircraft's left wing. The main strut next to it was wobbling loosely where one of the attachments had been shot away.

"That was too close for comfort," David warned. "Damnit! I think he's coming around for another pass!"

'Rhubarbs', Jason thought. Leave it to the British to come up with a term like that to describe something as dangerous and hairy as flying four hundred miles per hour on the deck into blizzards of anti-aircraft fire. All that, to shoot targets that might just as easily blow up in your face, knocking you out of the sky as effectively as a flack burst. Nothing about it was in the least bit related to the leafy green stalks he had seen growing in his mother's garden.

On their second sortie of the day into north-eastern Holland, Jason and his wingman had flown down a length of the Rhine, coming across a string of barges transporting German troops and equipment in retreat from the Canadian advance. As he poured a stream of 20mm cannon fire into one of the barges it erupted in a massive explosion that threw his Spitfire over onto its back, and it had taken every bit of his piloting skill to recover control and then fly up out of it.

His wingman was nowhere to be seen and his radio had been knocked out, so he decided to climb to a safer altitude and head back to base.

Roland throttled down as he reduced speed and then drifted in behind the *Storch*. He thumbed the button on his control column, and was rewarded by a stream of cannon fire that flew out of the jet's nose and directly toward the small monoplane. At the last possible moment, he saw Schmidt bank right, and most of the shells passed under his left wing, except one which tore a hole through the fabric beside the main strut.

Cursing, Roland prepared to bank left into a wide climbing loop that would put him behind the small plane once again.

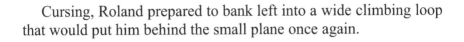

As Jason circled west over the banks of the Rhine, he realized that he was flying over the same sector of Holland that Jack was now fighting in. Out of curiosity he levelled off at 10,000 feet, and between furtive glances into his rear-view mirror, began to search the ground below for any tank formations that he might be able to identify as his brother's.

It was then that he noticed the *Storch* flying at extremely low altitude as it passed over the bright ribbon of a canal. He followed its progress for several seconds before he saw it overtaken at high speed by another aircraft with the unmistakable swept wings of an *Me*262. Incredibly, there was an eruption of bright flashes from the nose of the jet as it fired a stream of 30mm cannon shells at the other German aircraft!

Without trying to solve this bizarre puzzle, Jason pitched his nose down and threw the Spitfire into a high-speed dive that he judged would put him on the tail of the *Me*262.

The air-speed indicator needle had rotated to its maximum point, and as Jason pulled in behind the jet he realized he had misjudged its speed by not taking into account that it had slowed down to make its pass at the *Storch*. Desperately, he squeezed off several rounds from his 20mm guns, but saw no hits as he overshot the Messerschmitt. Keeping his throttle fully open, he rolled right and looped around before leveling out to pull back hard on the control column. This pointed his spinner straight up, while the huge blades dug hungrily into the air and propelled him to higher altitude.

Roland saw a bright stream of tracer fire pass directly over his cockpit, followed almost instantly by the light grey underside of a Mk XIV Spitfire. With a roar, it flashed past him and climbed away to his right. Ramming both throttles open he completed a tight loop intended to bring himself around onto the enemy's tail, and then pointed his nose skyward to follow the Spitfire as it climbed above him.

Peter and David were shocked to see a second aircraft suddenly pass overhead. As it roared by them, they recognized a Spitfire unleashing its stream of 20mm cannon fire, which barely missed the *Me*262 before the allied fighter overshot the jet.

As the Spitfire banked right to climb away, they were both astounded to briefly catch sight of Jason's wolf-head insignia.

As the Spitfire rocketed straight up, Jason felt the gravitational forces pushing down hard upon his chest, but with the greatest effort he twisted his head to peer through the Perspex canopy behind him, where he saw the *Me*262 looping around and climbing in an attempt to get on his tail. Immediately, he rolled the Mk XIV over onto its back and pushed it into high-speed dive, but this time pointed directly at the nose of the German jet. As they closed, he saw the flashing of cannon fire from the Messerschmitt, and simultaneously thumbed his own button, but they were past each other almost instantly.

He quickly pulled up into a banking left turn, while through the rear of his canopy he saw the enemy fighter bank to its left in an identical manoeuvre to bring them back into another head-on trajectory. For the briefest second as the jet was turning, Jason saw the black boar's head insignia on its nose.

Climbing out of his loop, Roland saw the Spitfire reverse course to dive headlong at him, and he felt a stab of fear as a rush of acid curdled in his stomach. Desperately firing his cannons at the oncoming Spitfire, he cursed when the tracers went wide of their mark. As the aircraft flashed past each other, he rolled right and wrenched the jet into another tight loop to get on the Mk XIV's tail. An overwhelming rage consumed him as he recognized the wolf's head insignia on the enemy aircraft's engine cowling while it came around into another head-on manoeuvre.

"I'll kill you both today!" He hissed triumphantly, as he lined up the approaching Spitfire in his sights.

"Come on you bastard!" Jason screamed, as he aimed the Spitfire directly at the enemy's nose and thumbed his firing button. The 20mm tracers leapt out toward the *Me262* just as it began to fire back. This time Jason did not turn, and at the last second the Messerschmitt banked to his left to avoid a collision. As it did so, Jason saw several ragged tears in the aluminum behind the cockpit where he had scored glancing hits along the German's fuselage.

He had just put the Spitfire into a banking turn to come around on the enemy again when suddenly the Griffon coughed, and there was a sharp metallic explosion inside the engine compartment. The propeller feathered uselessly as flames burst out from beneath the cowling.

The cockpit quickly filled with smoke, and more flames began to eat through the firewall under the instrument panel, igniting Jason's trousers. Pulling his feet back off of the rudder pedals, he flipped the release and slid the canopy open. The smoke and heat were becoming unbearable as he fumbled with the harness clasp until it finally opened. Standing on his seat, he prepared to launch himself out of the cockpit, when suddenly the entire aircraft exploded.

As Roland pressed the firing button, he saw the Spitfire's wing cannons winking and realized that this Canadian maniac was not going to turn away! He simultaneously banked right, which caused most of his own bullets to go wide. Then, as he glanced through the rear of his canopy to see which way the enemy was turning, he saw smoke and flame burst from the Mk XIV's engine. Within seconds the airplane completely disintegrated in a huge explosion.

"I win!" He shrieked triumphantly. Roland was about to scan the skies again for the *Storch* when he realized he could not move his left arm. Looking down, he was horrified to see his elbow bone and broken forearm protruding through the flight suit. Further down there was a hole in the aluminum skin of the cockpit next to the bloody exposed flesh of his thigh.

Roland could feel himself going into shock, and as he desperately attempted to bring the jet around in preparation for an emergency landing, the left engine began to smoke, and suddenly flamed-out. As he frantically worked the control column, attempting to fly the *Me262* on its one remaining engine, he heard a rending of wire and metal in the fuselage behind the cockpit – and then the stick went slack.

His chest heaved with the effort as Roland's breath now came in a rapid series of shallow gasps. A cold wave of fear swept through him as he struggled in vain to loosen the canopy release. His right arm went limp, dropping uselessly to his lap as he slumped in his seat, overcome by weakness and loss of blood.

Diving earthward, the last thing he saw through his windscreen was the tall soot-stained smokestack of an electricity-generating station, looming over its colliery. It was surrounded by a wasteland of overburden and dusty piles of coal, studded with the broken limbs of dead trees, clawing skyward. Roland's eyes went wide, and a gurgling scream rose from his throat, as the base of the stack grew suddenly larger, expanding to fill his vision before he and his world disintegrated – sundered in a flash of heat and pain as the *Me*262 became a giant fireball exploding against the massive dark tower of brick.

As both fighter aircraft pulled out of sight behind a cloud bank to the south west, Peter was compelled to refocus his mind on landing the damaged *Storch*. Nervously glancing at the left wing, he saw it was beginning to flap slightly as the loosened strut now failed to completely brace it.

He turned to David. "Make sure you are strapped in tightly. With a blown tire and the wing about to give way at any moment, this landing is going to be tricky."

Searching for some level ground, Peter eventually lined the *Storch* up on a vacant dirt road and throttled down the engine, while reducing their speed as much as he dared without stalling. Gliding in for the final few metres of his approach, he let only the right wheel touch down and used the rudder to keep the aircraft going straight, while banking very slightly to keep the flat left tire off the ground as long as possible. Finally, they had lost so much speed that the left wing dropped, and the flat tire dug into the road.

With a simultaneous screech of rent metal and attachment bolts, the strut tore itself from the wing, causing the left landing gear to collapse entirely. The wingtip then dug into the damp soil, slewing the aircraft sideways as it continued to travel a few more metres along the ground, until coming to a halt in a spray of damp earth and gravel.

They sat silently in the wreckage of the *Storch* for several seconds before either of them could speak.

Peter asked. "Are you okay? We'll have to get out. I think I smell smoke."

David looked around incredulously at the tangled metal and fabric that had once been their airplane. "I think that's coming from the skin that was just worn off my arse. How the hell did we ever survive that landing?"

Peter chuckled. "Are you kidding? I had the whole thing planned, down to the smallest detail!"

"Well next time you had better leave the planning to me. Two hard landings in a row are pushing my luck a little further than this was meant to allow." David muttered, as he reached inside his tunic and pulled out the frayed remains of an eagle feather.

"What is that?" Peter asked, puzzled.

"It might be why I'm still breathing, or it might just be a feather. Either way, I plan to stay on the ground from now on if I can help it."

David placed the remnant back inside his tunic pocket, and then he leaned over to bend back a piece of the instrument panel that was preventing Peter from exiting his seat. After climbing out of the wreckage, they searched the skies for any sign of the other two aircraft, but saw nothing.

"Jason sure picked the perfect time to show up, didn't he? Schwartz would have come around again to nail us for sure if he hadn't." David mused.

Peter nodded in agreement as he remembered the first aerial encounter with his cousin, the previous September. "In my experience, Jason's timing has always been impeccable."

David scanned the skies again. "Well, I hope it's his aim that's impeccable today, especially if he's managed to line up that jet again. Do you think there is any chance that Schwartz could shoot him down?"

Peter considered the question a moment before answering. "The *Me262* is an excellent aircraft, no doubt about that. But even in his Spitfire, I'm pretty sure that Jason can fly circles around Schwartz. Unless Roland uses his extra speed to run away, I'm betting Jason shoots that bastard down!"

For a moment, David raised a hand to his brow as he regarded the sun moving in its westward trajectory across the sky, and then swept his arm to the right where he pointed at a distant rise on the horizon. "We should head north, further into Holland. I think it's our best chance of encountering allied forces."

Peter shook his head and pointed east. "I'm sorry, but I think this is where we have to part ways. If you are careful you should be safe, but I must return to Germany to find my sister. Unless I can find Elke before the Russians arrive, things will not go well for her."

Taken aback, David could only stammer in protest. "But if you are caught, the *Gestapo* will kill you. If you weren't planning to surrender, why did you go to all the trouble of escaping with me?"

Peter shrugged, and then reached into his pocket to remove a shard of scorched black rock, which he placed in David's hand. He smiled, remembering that distant morning on the lake. "Actually, it wasn't my intention to do any of it, until for a second time, you dropped in on me. But you see, there is a mermaid who once told me that she misses her boyfriend, and I think she wants him to bring this back to her."

David took the meteor fragment in his hand, shaking his head. "It's still a while before the ice is off the lake my friend, but I'll try not to disappoint her."

Peter winked, and clapped David on the shoulder. "I'm sure you won't."

He then moved off at a slow jog toward the adjacent forest, turning one more time to wave before disappearing into the trees.

For the rest of the afternoon, David walked cautiously through the fields in a north-westerly direction, constantly checking over his shoulder to see if anyone was following.

Most of the land was either partially flooded or so soggy that he was forced to walk along some of the small dikes separating the farms from the network of canals surrounding them. The higher profile this now presented increased his nervousness because he was not certain he was actually in allied territory.

Cautiously, he came around a copse of trees growing on a small rise, and a sudden flood of relief swept through him as he saw a squadron of Sherman tanks formed up into a defensive *laager*, and preparing to set up for the night.

He was challenged by a sentry, so he called out his name, rank, and squadron designation to reassure the young man. The guard finally relaxed when David got close enough for him to recognize the air force uniform with its Canada patch sewn on the shoulder.

One of the tank commanders approached him, exchanged salutes, and then introduced himself. "Major Bob McLeod, Eighth New Brunswick Hussars. Where the hell did you come from Sergeant?"

"David Hunter, sir. 419 Moose Squadron. It's a long story, starting when I was shot down a month and a half ago - but before I continue, I think there may be a friend of mine in your regiment. Do you know Captain Jack McMurchy?"

McLeod's face dropped before he slowly answered. "Yeah, I know him…"

The Major hesitated, then continued. "I hate to be the one to tell you this Sergeant, but I've just learned over the radio that my good friend Captain McMurchy was killed in action this afternoon, not more than three miles from here."

Olivia thought often of Jason as she went through her usual day at the hospital. They had grown deeply in love in the past year, and while stationed in England, he had made a point of trying to call her nearly every day, or to visit as often as he could get a pass.

However, since November, Jason had been flying out of an RCAF forward base in Evere, Belgium. The limited telephone service there had severely curtailed the frequency of his calls, and now she was forced to endure six or seven days at a time between contacts. She had been expecting to hear from him yesterday, but the phone had sat silently in its cradle for the entire day.

Just after lunch she was paged to report to the head nurse.

Agnes Ramsey was a stocky woman in her mid-fifties. She had lost her youngest son, a merchant mariner, when his ship had been torpedoed in the North Atlantic three years earlier. Soldiering on, she considered it her duty to take charge of the inexperienced young women who had rushed into the profession as a result of the war, but the years and the responsibilities of her job had taken their toll. The short wavy red hair that she kept pinned up beneath her cap had grown mostly grey, and although always a serious woman, the creases now etched deeply into her face attested to her sense of duty. She was standing over her desk and looked up when Olivia entered.

"Yes Agnes. Why did you page me?" Olivia asked.

Agnes' voice was tinged with concern as she answered cautiously. "Olivia, I've just received a call from Jenny Meadows – you remember, she transferred over to the serious burns reconstructive unit at East Grinstead last month. Apparently, they have just admitted a young man to the Canadian Wing there. He is listed on her chart as Jay McMurchy. That's the name of your young man, isn't it dear…?"

Mr. Alexander pulled his car into the lot in front of Queen Victoria Hospital and set the parking brake. He walked around the bonnet of the sedan to open his wife's door, while Mildred assisted Olivia out of the back seat. Arm in arm, the two young ladies mounted the steps into the building's front entrance.

Mrs. Alexander attempted to reassure Olivia, reminding her of Jason's good fortune to survive. "Dear, they are developing new medical miracles every day."

Located in East Grinstead, Sussex, one of the hospital's burn units, led by Dr. Archibald McIndoe, had pioneered methods in reconstructive plastic surgery for the serious burns experienced by some fighter pilots and bomber crew. These were made more devastating by the intensity of fires fed by the oxygen systems in many of the aircraft. As most of the surgical techniques were experimental, the often disfigured patients had proudly utilized a consoling black humour to refer to themselves as 'the guinea pigs'.

Fearing the worst, Mr. Alexander hurried to precede them into the reception area so he could make the first enquiries alone.

Because of their high numerical representation in the Fighter and Bomber Commands, plus their reputation for raucous behaviour, a special wing of the hospital had been set aside for the Canadians, and the Alexander family was directed there.

The wing's charge nurse searched her chart for McMurchy, and then told Olivia that she could find him in the intensive-care section for new arrivals near the end of the corridor. She also informed them that the severest burns were apparently confined to the right side of his face and neck as well as the backs of his hands, but he was now heavily sedated, so they must take pains not to disturb him during her visit.

As they walked down the corridor past the beds of recovering young men, Olivia could not help but be taken aback by the degree of disfigurement that many of them displayed. Some faces appeared to be composed of melted wax, devoid of any eyebrows or hair, with noses much-reduced and lips non-existent. Hands often had fingers missing or fused together - or sometimes withered into boney hook-like claws. She felt an overwhelming dread collecting coldly in her stomach as she entered Jason's room.

She gasped at her first sight of him lying in the bed. His hands were restrained and covered in bandages with only the tips of his fingers protruding, and his entire head was wrapped in gauze bandages, leaving only two small openings over his mouth and nostrils. The gauze around his lips shivered, as breathing came in a shallow series of prolonged wheezes.

Olivia trembled, while Mildred placed an arm around her shoulders and clasped gently as they stared down in silent fear at the tubes and bandages.

A surgeon entered the room carrying a clipboard, but as Olivia turned to him, she was unable to speak. Mr. Alexander stepped forward. "Please tell us Doctor, what is the prognosis for young Lieutenant McMurchy here?"

Momentarily puzzled as he searched his chart, the doctor saw the intensity of the family's concern, so he quickly responded. "Well, it will be touch and go for a while. These burns always induce an element of shock, and we will not know the true extent of the damage until he has stabilized and the bandages are removed. But there seems to be some discrepancy..."

His voice trailed off as a low moaning began to rise through the mouth-opening in the bandages.

Olivia was standing over him now, as tears flowed from her eyes. "Doctor, I think he's coming to! Jason! Jason!" She hoarsely repeated his name.

Now breathing with greater determination, his chest began to rise and fall rapidly as a forced, rasping voice rattled up through the mouth-hole. "Jason? Is my brother here too?"

There was a sudden commotion out in the hallway. A matron was shouting. "Where do you think you're going! You're not allowed!"

Shouting "Get out of my way!" Jason suddenly burst into the room. His disheveled hair and eyebrows were singed, and his trouser bottoms and shoes badly scorched. "I've only just heard! I had to commandeer a bloody Spitfire to get over here! How is he!"

May 14, 1945. Hanover

Peter's eyes slowly scanned the panorama of blackened buildings and rubble-strewn streets that had once been the southern edge of Hanover. In some places, an avenue had been cleared, and occasionally a British jeep or military truck would trundle unhurriedly along it to some more strategic destination further into the remains of the city's centre. Along the route, industrious local survivors were already collecting loose masonry or bricks and stacking them in neat piles beside the road for future use as building material.

He reached up and stroked the unkempt beard which had sprouted from his face over the past six weeks, shocked at the amount of dirt that had accumulated on the back of his chapped hands and under his fingernails. As he smoothed out the creases in his grimy uniform and attempted to kick off some of the mud that caked his once-shiny leather shoes, Peter was overcome by the immensity of the change that had occurred, not only in his surroundings, but also in his own appearance. He was gaunt from hunger, and the food that he had once taken for granted was rarely available. Even a bar of soap seemed like an unattainable luxury from a distant and barely remembered past.

He had spent his days in hiding, and went out only at night to make his way unseen alongside routes that took him further east into Germany. Eventually the allied forces had overtaken him from the west, and later he had actually reached the Russian lines separating him from any possible access to Berlin.

Finally, he had circled south to get near the ruins of his family home in the futile hope that Elke might be there. The entire neighbourhood was deserted, and after he had spent a bleak hour staring again into the ruins of his parent's house, he made his way up the street. Only then did he notice the signs warning of unexploded bombs.

However, he was becoming so emaciated that he could find little strength for additional travel. Therefore, Peter had decided to throw caution to the wind by making his way north to nearby Hanover, where he hoped the British occupiers would at least give him a meal before processing him as a POW.

He was wondering why none of the numerous British vehicles passing on the road had not stopped to apprehend him, when a casual glance into the nearby water-filled ditch left Peter startled by his own reflection. In his present condition he was nearly unrecognizable and now resembled a much older man.

Hunger was driving him now as he moved deeper into the ruined city, where several times he passed groups of celebrating Tommies drinking beer and singing ribald songs with lyrics he vaguely comprehended, but ignored.

One drunken soldier spotted him skirting their group and cursed. "Fucking *Jerry*!" The man then threw an empty beer bottle which missed him by only a few centimetres.

Several blocks further in he came across a bedraggled group of people standing in a line where they were each being fed a bowl of thin soup. The gnawing in his stomach was unbearable, and he had moved forward to take a place at the end of the line, when his eyes were drawn to a figure about a dozen metres ahead of him.

The emaciated woman wore a long grey coat that was covered in filth, and her hair was pushed up under a grimy soft hat which had long-since lost its original shape. Too weak to stand erect, her shoulders were sagging with fatigue, and with a pronounced limp, she slowly shuffled forward. But there was something about the shape of her neck, or the back of her head – something indefinable – that had grasped his attention.

He tentatively approached and touched her lightly upon the arm. Her shoulders cringed reflexively as she slowly turned to look at him. Aside from her dark and sunken cheeks, there were numerous blotches of recently healed, but still slightly redder skin, which even the layer of dirt could not disguise.

Placing his hands upon her shoulders, he couldn't prevent the tears from welling in his eyes as he gazed down at the pitiful condition of his sister.

Trembling, she reached up and cautiously traced a thin finger down the side of his face, unsuccessfully attempting to speak. Finally, with a weak sigh, she leaned slowly forward to place her head upon his chest as Peter wrapped both of his arms around her frail body and drew her nearer.

August 6, 1945. Dawning

David sat on a crate near the end of the long wooden dock bordering *Michipicoten* Harbour, grateful to be once again part of the immense quietude spread out before him. In addition to the soothing lap of the water against the wooden pilings below, the solitary cawing of a crow, echoed *Soto voce* across the surface from a small promontory on the east side of the bay.

He had been home for several weeks but had not yet ventured into town. Although his first days had been characterized by a kind of undirected restless energy, he could now feel himself adjusting to the slower pace of life that one experienced in this relatively isolated little corner of the world.

Things had seemed much different to him before the war. Life had possessed a strong sense of normalcy - as if the whole universe were like this. However, David now felt the uniqueness of this place and how well he fit into it. His frame of reference had acquired a broader new acuity after having travelled half-way around the planet and viewing the shattered Earth from 20,000 feet. Here, on this clear day, the vast distance between himself and what lay beyond the limit of his vision was something that he understood as tangible, while also comforting.

His grandfather was now stooped and wizened. The old man had smiled, and then reassuringly clasped his forearm with a boney hand when David pulled the worn and tattered remnants of the eagle feather from the pocket of his tunic.

Stoic and eternal, his mother had not changed save for a slight greying of her hair. She had been waiting for him at the station when he stepped off of the train. After searching his eyes to confirm that he had returned whole, she pulled him closer, listening to the steady beating of his heart...and then sighed with relief.

After the breakfast his mother served him this morning, David felt that he had time on his hands, so he decided to go down to the water's edge where he could watch the steamship *'Manitou'* arriving from Sault Ste Marie. It was now moored further back along the wharf, and sooty smoke rose lazily from its single tall stack as it disembarked an assortment of passengers and cargo.

In contrast to the pace of his current existence, things had moved very quickly after he rejoined the squadron. There had been several hectic and confusing days during which he submitted a written report of his experiences since having been shot down. He had also gained a new appreciation for hot showers and the abundant food being served in the mess.

After marvelling at his miraculous escape from the burning Lancaster, the squadron commander was solicitous. "Hunter, I think if old Harry Houdini himself was still around, he would be envious of your ability to escape death...and Nazis too! I think this whole show is pretty much over. The unit has been practically stood down, and it is expected that hostilities will cease at any moment. Just a matter of signing a few documents now. There's not really any need for you to be returned to operational duty, so tell you what - I'll personally get your papers processed as soon as possible, and you'll be off on one of the first troop ships back to Canada..."

This week he had talked with O'Brian when the electrician had come down to the harbour to inspect a recent wiring job. Sighting David, the childless shift boss had greeted him like a long-lost son, and later listened, astounded, when David told him of his fiery descent into Germany and subsequent escape. He assured him that there was always an electrician's job waiting for him at the Algoma Ore Division, but David had decided he wanted more time to get himself sorted out before committing to the regimen of full-time employment, or of perhaps furthering other pursuits.

As he now gazed out over the lake, David caught the familiar sight of a commercial fishing boat slowly rounding Lighthouse Point, followed by a massive flock of seagulls wheeling above. Shrieking loudly and diving into the water behind, they fought voraciously to retrieve the innards and small fry being tossed off of the stern.

Momentarily distracted, he looked down and instinctively pulled the toe of his shoe away from a harmless garter snake that had somehow managed to slither this far out toward the end of the dock.

However, as he looked up again, objects slowly began to pull themselves away from the edges of his perspective, while uneasily, he sensed things beginning to drift out of balance. The light was metamorphizing into something different than the timeless waves and photons which had once illuminated his world. Elements of things that had previously seemed solid and sure, now shifted shape to create something that wouldn't take any permanent form - altering their dimensions or dissolving, *to cast weird shadows* - as they were bathed in this strange new light of uncertainty.

His eyes lost their focus as the whirling seabirds assumed the shape of stricken bombers plunging from the skies. While materializing in a mist before him, were the insubstantial forms of countless thousands of young airmen, and behind them, vastly greater numbers of civilians.

These endless ranks of the dead, their youthful faces stamped with an eternal range of expressions – some burning with enthusiasm, others set in grim determination, or palled white with dread – as they had looked that last time climbing into their aircraft to be carried aloft…and never return. While far below, during the last moments of their lives, doomed people looked up at the tiny flashes in the sky, before they too, winked out of existence.

His visions were suddenly interrupted by the clasp of a strong hand upon his shoulder, accompanied by the sound of a once-familiar voice. "Would you take a penny for your thoughts Davey?"

Startled, he stood and wheeled round to grasp the now-extended hand. Before he could stop himself, he blurted the greeting. "Jack! Is that really you?"

The right side of Jack's face and neck bore a slightly reddish hue - the skin smooth, almost shiny - with only the tiniest stubble of hairs protruding from what used to be an eyebrow, and his ear shrunken.

353

"Whoa! Take it a bit easier on my hand there Davey. The skin on the back is still a little tender. What do you think of my new look? I reckon Hollywood should be calling any day now!" Jack affected a rakish grimace and turned to reveal his right profile.

David was grinning with joy at the sight of his friend. "With that mug, you'll have to wait for Boris Karloff to retire! It's great to see you Jack!"

He then stepped back, examining his friend in amazement. "Fifteen minutes after your buddy McLeod told me you had been killed, someone radioed in to tell him that they had discovered you unconscious, about a hundred feet from your tank."

"Yeah, I guess my old troop-mate McAlister will take a long time living down having called that first report in. The last thing I remember is getting out just before everything exploded. After that, I was waking up in the hospital."

David looked again at his friend's freshly healed burns. "You are one lucky son of a bitch – and speaking of luck reminds me, have you heard anything from Jay?"

Jack shook his head. "The crazy bastard signed up for Tiger Force. I think he's getting ready to invade Japan any day now. He'd better not take a shine to any of those Geisha girls, or Olivia will have him drawn and quartered..."

His response was interrupted by the sound of a female voice behind him. "Jack, have you seen that small leather suitcase we loaded yesterday in..."

Her voice trailed off as she suddenly caught sight of David.

"Mildred!" He exclaimed, astonished to experience his second surprise of the day.

She stood beside her large tan-coloured suitcase in a white blouse and khaki jodhpurs. Smiling, she swatted a fly away from her long red hair and laughed. "It's Mrs. McMurchy these days David. When this handsome devil promised to introduce me to the exotic Canadian diet, I couldn't resist!"

She momentarily gnawed at her bottom lip and caught David's eye before asking Jack in *faux* innocence. "Now where did you say that champagne and caviar place was darling? I'm positively famished."

"Uh, it's been temporarily relocated," Jack lied. "But never mind. Once you've had my mom's blueberry pancakes that low-class European fare will never interest you again."

Mildred cocked an eyebrow at David and asked. "Is this true Mr. Hunter? Would you swear to it on a stack of Bibles?"

David appeared to consider the question a moment, and then slowly answered. "No, but if you will forgive the pun, I might very well attest to its truth on a stack of pancakes."

Mildred wrinkled her nose. "Oh Mr. Hunter, that was an awful stretch! You must be out of practice."

Jack interjected. "Don't worry Millie. I have more than a sneaking suspicion that Davey will be dropping by at breakfast time tomorrow, just to confirm. It's a very well-known 'practice' on his part, I can assure you."

David grinned as Mildred leaned forward to peck him on the cheek, and he then responded slyly. "Well, it is actually quite important that they be able to pass the maple syrup test…"

Jack chuckled. "Hah! I've never known them to fail whenever you show up! See you tomorrow when the first one hits the plate!"

They shook hands once more, then David watched them pass out of sight around the end of the wharf.

He reclaimed his seat on the crate and felt the gentle warmth of the summer sun begin to settle over him. A soft cadence of insects buzzing and the tiny liquid song of a nearby warbler filled his ears. While he took a deep breath of the fresh air, his eyes followed the slowly circling path of a large eagle gliding through the cloudless skies above the bay. Beyond the deep greens and striated greys of the shoreline hovering near the periphery of his vision, there stretched a vast, nearly infinite expanse of undulating blue water, invisibly tugging his soul toward a subtle change of colour now delineating the horizon. The lake was calm this morning.

William Myers

Epilogue

September, 1947

Near the edge of town at the west end of *Wawa* Lake, David Hunter stood on the rough-planked dock beside the small office of Timber Wolf Airways. The rocky hills on both sides of the lake were now ablaze in a brilliant pastiche of red, orange, and yellow foliage. The light northerly breeze bore a distinct crispness that signalled the approach of autumn, making him thankful he had worn his jacket.

He turned to Mildred, asking. "Are you sure he said two o'clock? It's half past already."

She turned to look up at Jack. In his arms he held little Ingrid, who had just nodded off, leaving her soft red ringlets spread in a tangle over his left shoulder.

Mildred whispered. "He's right. They're late."

When he smiled, the smooth skin to the right of his lips crinkled slightly, and in a lowered voice, he responded confidently. "Jason could fly the route from Sault Ste Marie with his eyes closed. There is a bit of a headwind blowing today, so that probably slowed him down."

They had just resumed their search of the skies five miles east, above the end of the lake, when they heard the distant snarling of the Noorduyn Norseman's radial engine. David was the first to see the tiny speck, which gradually expanded into the shape of a floatplane as the sound of its approach grew louder.

It slowly descended over the end of the lake, and when it reached a point about half a mile from them, it gently touched

356

down, traveling lightly across the waves until about two hundred yards out, they heard the engine throttle down. The bulky high-winged airplane settled further as its weight pushed the twin floats deeper into the water. With the radial now chugging at minimum revolutions, the Norseman slowly made its way across the light chop to the dock.

At the last second, the engine switched off, and the plane glided silently toward them. It turned sideways, before, with a compressive squeak, finally coming to rest against the old automobile tires that buffered the dock pilings.

Jack was about to lift Ingrid from his shoulder when David said, "Don't worry, I've got it." He then leapt forward and looped two ropes over hitches atop the front and rear of the nearest float, while Jason thrust his head through the now open window.

He smiled down at them, and waved to Olivia, who had just stepped out of the office holding their newborn baby, snugly wrapped in a light blue blanket. "I hope you weren't left waiting too long. There was quite a headwind on our first leg from the Sault. I nearly used up all of our fuel."

Jack nudged Mildred and caught her eye. "What did I tell you, eh? That's my brother."

Jason grinned at Jack and wagged his head toward the rear of the floatplane. Just then, a large cargo door on the side of the aircraft opened. The man stepped cautiously out onto the float and grasped David's hand to help him climb up to the dock. Grinning, they clapped each other on the shoulders. The man raised a hand above his brow to shield his eyes from the sun, and then spying the others waiting, he waved to them.

Mildred caught Jack's eye again, and he nodded his confirmation. "Yeah, that's Peter. Now there will be someone who can actually fly this Norseman when Jason re-enlists."

Peter stepped back down onto the float and leaned toward the door, where he spoke softly to someone inside. The young woman tentatively took his hand as he helped her to climb out, and then assisted her up to the dock. There, David steadied her as he introduced himself.

She wore a long and somewhat threadbare grey woollen coat, while her blond hair was pinned up under a small felt hat. Catching a breath, her pale blue eyes grew ever-wider as she began to take in the boundless natural beauty of these new surroundings. Peter stepped up to gently place one of his arms around her shoulders, while Elke gazed shyly at the others and slowly began to smile.

Glossary of Terms

German

Radar

Freya   Ground–based early warning radar. It eventually became vulnerable to 'chaffe' or myriad aluminum strips called 'window' dropped from allied bombers.

Kammhuber Line   A sting of nearly one thousand *Freya* radar stations along the European coastal approaches to Germany to detect allied bombers. It was named after Colonel (later General) Joseph *Kammhuber,* who was in charge of its construction and deployment.

Lichtenstein SN-2   An earlier version of airborne radar used by night-fighters to detect and intercept allied aircraft. It was highly vulnerable to 'window'.

Naxos Z   Portable radar mounted on night-fighters to detect H2S emissions from allied bombers, facilitating their interception.

German Military Aircraft Designations

German aircraft designations were alpha-numeric. The first two letters of the designer or manufacturer's name prefixed numbers which generally reflected the chronological order of that particular producer's prototype, or introduction of the aircraft into service. A final capital letter, for example an 'E' or 'D' after the aircraft's numerical designation, indicated in alphabetical order, progressive stages of development. They were often used by their pilots as the first letter in a nickname for the aircraft. Some examples include: *Bf*109E *'Emil'*, *Bf*109G *'Gustav'*, *Fw*190D *'Dora'*.

*Bf*108, *Bf*109, *Bf*110.   The two first letters from the manufacture's name *Bayerische Flugzeugwerke* were used for aircraft designed by Willy Messerschmitt before he had taken control of the company.

*Me*163, *Me*262.   The first two letters from his family name were used for aircraft designed by Wilhelm Emil "Willy" *Messerschmitt* after he gained control of the company.

*Do*217.   Uses the first two letters of the manufacturer's name *Dornier Flugzeugwerke*, which was also the family name of the company owner / head designer Claudius *Dornier*.

Fi 156 *'Storch'*.   Uses the first two letters of the manufacturer's name *Fieseler Flugzeugwerke*. The English translation of *'Storch'* is Stork.

*Fw*190A, *Fw*190D.   Uses the two first letters from the manufacture's name *Focke-Wulf* to prefix these designs by the company's head designer Kurt *Tank*. The final higher-performance variant of this design, the *Ta*152, bore the first two letters of his family name.

*He*17, *He*111, *He*219.   Uses the first two letters of the manufacturer's name *Heinkel Flugzeugwerke*, which was also the family name of the company owner / head designer Ernst *Heinkel*. The company was taken away from *Heinkel* by the Nazis in 1942 when it was nationalized, and most of his shares acquired by Hermann Göring.

*Ju*52, *Ju*57, *Ju*88.   Uses the first two letters of the manufacturer's name *Junkers Flugzeugwerke*, which was also the family name of the company owner / head designer Hugo *Junkers*.

German Military Aircraft Engines

German engines used an alpha-numeric designation, with the first letters representing initials for the manufacture's name. The numerical designation usually represented the chronological order of the engine's development, with the final letter indicating in alphabetical sequence any subsequent upgrades in performance. The Germans were the first to use turbojet and rocket engines in combat aircraft. Most commonly however, they used both types of piston engines: the in-line type. (Which was usually, but not always, liquid-cooled, and mounted in an inverted 'V' configuration with the cylinder heads pointing down.), and the radial, air-cooled type.

*As*10c (Inverted V-8, air-cooled.)   Uses the beginning and last letter of the first part of the manufacturer's name *Argus Motoren*.

*BMW*801 (Radial, air-cooled.)   Uses the three first letters of the manufacturer's name. *Bavarian Motor Werke*

*DB*601, *DB*603 (Inverted V-12s, liquid-cooled.)   Uses the two first letters from the manufacturer's name *Daimler-Benz*.

*Jumo*213 (Inverted V-12, liquid-cooled.), *Jumo*004 (Turbojet.)   A contraction formed from the two first letters of the two words in the manufacturer's name *Junkers Motoren*.

German Air Ranks

Oberst	(Br.) Group Captain	(U.S.) Colonel
Major	Squadron Leader	Major
Hauptmann	Flight Lieutenant	Captain
Oberleutnant	Flying Officer	1st Lieutenant
Leutnant	Pilot Officer	2nd Lieutenant

| *Oberfeldwebel* | Flight Sergeant | Technical Sergeant |
| *Feldwebel* | Staff Sergeant | Sergeant |

German Language / Expressions

Air Reichsmarschall   Highest rank held in the W.W. II *Luftwaffe*. There was no generally equivalent rank in the British RAF, or U.S. Army Air Force. It was one rank higher than the top ranking British Marshal of the Air Force, or U.S. General of the Army. It is unlikely that the Russian Chief Marshal of the Soviet Air Forces would have experienced the same degree of autonomy as *Air Reichmarschall* Hermann Göring.

Arschlecker   Arse licker.

Auf wiedersehen   Goodbye.

Bad Weissee   Spa West see. (Spa West view.)   A spa town on Lake Tegernsee, Bavaria. On June 30, 1934, at the Hotel Hanselbauer the *SS* purged (shot dead) the *S.A.* leadership.

Balkencreuz   (Wooden) Beam Cross. The 'black cross' insignia (often outlined in white) used on German aircraft, armoured vehicles, and naval vessels.

Bitte   Please.

Blut und Ehre.   'Blood and Honour'. The Hitler *Jugend* motto.

Condor Legion   Special elements of the *Luftwaffe* sent to Spain to fight on the Nationalist side led by the fascist *Generalissimo* Francisco Franco, against the Republicans during the Spanish civil war.

Dumbkopf   Stupid head.

Ein bis   A little.

Einsatzgruppen   Special squads responsible for rounding up and executing often large numbers of Jews, Communists, or Partisans in conquered territories.

Ersatz   'Synthetic', or 'imitation', when used in the context of replacing an original product with an inferior substitute. (e.g.) *Ersatz* coffee.

Fallschirmjäger   Paratrooper.

Fleidermaus   Flying mouse. A bat.

Flugzeugwerke   Aircraft manufacturer.

Gauleiter   The leader or senior official of the Nazi Party responsible for a specific geographical area or region.

Geheime Staatspolizei – Gestapo   Secret state police.   A para-military police force comprised of Nazis, with nearly unlimited powers to enforce Party policies.

Gott in Himmel   God in Heaven.

Gruppe   Fighter Group.

Gymnasium   The German general equivalent of High School.

Isolde   Name of the Irish Princess heroine in the Wagnerian opera 'Tristan and Isolde'.

Ja   Yes or Yeah.

Jagdgeschwader   Hunter Wing or Fighter Wing.

Jagdverband 44   Was a special fighter unit or 'Jet Fighter Wing' flying the *Me262*.

Jerry   A derogatory slang term used by the allies, generally meaning German combatant, but in some cases any German.

Jugend   Youth.

Kammerad   Comrade.

Kaput   Broken or Finished.

Koenig   King.

Kraut   Abbreviation of *sauerkraut*. A derogatory slang term used by the allies, generally meaning German combatant, but in some cases any German.

Kübelwagen   A light general purpose vehicle produced for the German military by *Volkswagen*. It was the German equivalent of the allied Jeep.

Langnassen-Dora   'Long-nosed Dora'. A nickname for the *Fw*190D, which had an extended engine cowling to accommodate the longer in-line, liquid-cooled *Jumo*213 engine that had replaced the stubbier air-cooled radial engine used by earlier variants.

Leibensraum   'Living room'. The name given by the Nazis to conquered Eastern territories slated for German colonization.

Leica   A German camera brand name.

Lufthansa   The German national airline.

Luftwaffe   The German Air Force.

Luger   A semi-automatic pistol.

Maus   Mouse.

Mein Kampf   'My Plan'. A book written by Adolph Hitler while in prison after his failed Munich Beer Hall Putsch. It described his future plans for Germany if the Nazi Party were to rise to power.

Nachtjagdgeschwader   Night-fighter Squadron.

Nibelungen   Family name of the ancient Burgundian King who was a subject of the Germanic and Norse sagas depicted in Richard Wagner's *Der Ring des Nibelungen* (The Ring of the Nibelungen), his most prodigious operatic creation.

Panzer / PzKpFw   Abbreviated forms of *PanzerkampFwagen*, meaning armoured fighting vehicle.

PzKpFw IV   Medium Tank. It was the most plentiful tank in the *Wehrmacht*. It possessed a 75mm main gun and weighed approximately 30 tons.

PzKpFw V 'Panther'. Main Battle Tank. It was the first German tank design to use sloped armour - in response to the revolutionary Russian T-34 which introduced the concept. It possessed a longer, higher-velocity 75mm main gun, and weighed 45 tons.

PzKpFw VI 'Tiger' and 'King Tiger'.   Heavy Tanks. They used an 88mm high-velocity main gun. The Tiger tank weighed 50 tons. The "King" Tiger tank weighed 70 tons, and featured a longer, higher-velocity main gun. The King Tiger also utilized sloped armour.

Panzerfaust   'Tank fist'. A bazooka-like recoilless infantry weapon, designed to penetrate a tank's armour and set its interior ablaze.

Rotte   A pair of German fighter planes comprised of a leader and wingman. *Rottes* normally flew in pairs to form a four aircraft *Schwarm*.

S.A. (Sturmabteilung)   'Storm Detachment' or 'Assault Division'. The Nazi Party's private 'Brownshirt' army used for security, or to intimidate and assault opponents at rallies or demonstrations before the Nazis achieved political power.

SS., Waffen SS., (Schutzstaffel)   An armed wing of the Nazi Party 'Protective Squadron'. They often enforced Nazi policies and also fought with fanatical zeal. They are considered guilty of having committed many mass atrocities during these activities.

Schadenfreude   Pleasure derived from the misfortune of others.

Schlageter   The family name of a Nazi hero who died resisting reparations to France during the 1920s. The first letter of his name was used to create the gothic "*S*" symbol used on aircraft of *Jagdgeschwader* 26.

Schräge Musik   'Jazz Music'. Twin 30mm cannons firing obliquely upward from behind the cockpit of two-engine German night-fighters into the undersides of allied bombers.

Schwarm   A formation of four German fighter planes composed of two *rottes*, usually flying in a 'finger-four' configuration.

Schwein   Swine. Can mean either pork, or be a derogatory expression.

Schweinhundt   Swine hound. A derogatory expression.

Sieg Heil A Nazi salute used in acknowledgement of orders or senior rank.

Storch   'Stork'. A small short take-off and landing (STOL) aircraft.

Stug III / (*Sturmgeschutz*) III   An armoured, tracked 'tank destroyer' based upon the engine, drive train, chassis, and suspension of the *PzKpFw* III Medium Tank. It possessed a 75mm main gun mounted with its breech completely enclosed in a fixed hull. The gun had good vertical adjustment, but very little lateral movement - and lacked the 360 degrees horizontal movement possessed by similar guns mounted in tank turrets.

Taifun   Typhoon.

Untermensch   A derogatory term meaning 'beneath humanity'.

Verboten   Forbidden.

Verdammt!   'God damn it!'

Volksturm   In the last phase of the war as Germany went on the defensive, a 'people's' defense army made up of older men and young boys - equipped with a mix of available new and older weapons - was deployed in a last-ditch attempt to repel the 'allied invaders'.

Wehrmacht   War makers. The German Army.

Wonder Waffen   'Wonder Weapon'. Scientifically advanced missiles, jets and rocket-powered aircraft developed by the Germans in the latter part of WWII.

Zerstorer   Destroyer. A nickname for the *Bf*110 two-engine fighter plane.

Zigaretten   Cigarette.

Zimmerit   A ceramic barrier applied as a paste to the exterior of a tank's armour, which, when it hardened, prevented magnetic bombs from sticking to it.

Allied

British Military Aircraft Designations

British / Canadian / Australian aircraft were usually given a name preceded by the manufacturer's name. For fighters, this was followed by a Roman numeral 'Mark' (Mk) number. (e.g.) *Supermarine* Spitfire Mk IXb. The numeral normally indicated the chronological stage of development for that particular model of aircraft – usually involving an increase in performance. For heavy bombers, the prefix 'B' preceded the Roman numeral. (e.g.) *Avro* Lancaster B.III. This differed from the German practice of Arabic numerals representing the chronological sequence of a particular company's aircraft as they were introduced to civilian or military service. Upper case letters after the Roman numerals usually indicated a specialized modification like photo-reconnaissance. Whereas, lower case letters following the Roman numerals often reflected a modification to armament.

Avro Anson Mk II. A training aircraft, it was a two-engine bomber with a dorsal turret armed with two machine-guns. It was used extensively in the Commonwealth Air Training Program in Canada to train bomber crews. The Canadian-built Mk II and the British-built Mk III were powered by two American-built *Jacobs* L-6MB R-915 radial engines. All later variants were powered by the *Wright* "Whirlwind" radial, or *Pratt & Whitney* 'Wasp' radial engines.

Avro Lancaster. A four-engine bomber. The B.I variant was powered by R*olls-Royce* Merlin, in-line, liquid-cooled V-12 engines. However, the B.II was powered by *Bristol* Hercules radial, air-cooled engines due to a temporary shortage of Merlin engines. The B.III and Canadian-built B.X were powered by American-built Merlin V-12 engines produced under licence by *Packard Motors*.

DeHavilland Mosquito.   A two-engine fighter and/or bomber constructed of plywood. Hence its nickname 'The Wooden Wonder'. Powered by two *Rolls-Royce Merlin* (or *Packard Merlin* when constructed in Canada) V-12 engines, it is considered the most exceptional aircraft of the war - excelling when configured as either a fighter/night-fighter, or bomber.

DeHavilland DH.82 Tiger Moth.   A training aircraft used for basic training for all pilots of the British Commonwealth. It was a two-cockpit biplane with fixed landing gear. The Mk I model was powered by the *de Havilland* Gypsy III engine, and the Mk II by the *de Havilland* Gypsy Major engine.

Handley-Page Halifax.   A four-engine bomber. The B.I was powered by *Rolls-Royce* Merlin engines. The later B.III version with improved rudders and nose section, was powered by *Bristol* Hercules radial engines.

Hawker Hurricane.   Fighter. Powered by a *Rolls-Royce* Merlin engine.

Hawker Typhoon and Tempest.   Fighters. Powered by a *Napier* Sabre, in-line, liquid-cooled, horizontally-opposed, 24 cylinder engine.

North American Harvard.   A re-named version of the *North American* T-6 Texan training aircraft used to train American military pilots. It was a two-seat, enclosed cockpit, low-wing mono-plane with retractable landing gear, designed to exhibit most of the performance characteristics of then-modern fighter aircraft. It was powered by a *Pratt & Whitney* R-1340 Wasp air-cooled, radial engine. Several thousand were built in Canada for British Commonwealth usage, and along with imported versions manufactured in the U.S., they were re-named Harvard.

Short Stirling.   A four-engine bomber. Powered by *Bristol* Hercules air-cooled radial engines.

Supermarine Spitfire.   Powered by a *Rolls-Royce* Merlin engine. Later variants were powered by the larger displacement, more powerful, in-line, liquid-cooled, V-12, *Rolls-Royce* Griffon engine.

Vickers-Armstrong Wellington.   A two-engine bomber. Powered by *Bristol* Pegasus air-cooled, radial engines.

British Military Aircraft Engines

All British-designed and manufactured fighters were powered by in-line, liquid-cooled piston engines built in a 'V' or horizontally opposed configuration. The exceptions were the relatively rare radial-powered version of the Tempest, and the turbojet-powered Meteor. The Lancaster heavy bomber was normally also powered by V-12 Merlin engines, as was the earliest version of the Halifax bomber. However, the Halifax and Stirling heavy bombers, and the B.II version of the Lancaster, were powered by *Bristol* Hercules air-cooled, radial engines, while the four-engine Sunderland flying boat and twin-engine Wellington bomber were powered by *Bristol* Pegasus radial engines. British engine designations began with the manufacturer's name, and then a generic name. (e.g.) 'Merlin'. This was followed by a Roman numeral which normally indicated its chronological stage of development, but also could indicate a specialized performance capability generally associated with either power or altitude.

Bristol Pegasus.   A 9-cylinder, single-bank, air-cooled radial engine produced by the *Bristol Aeroplane Company*.

Bristol Hercules.   A 14-cylinder, twin-bank, air-cooled radial engine produced by the *Bristol Aeroplane Company*.

De Havilland Gypsy III / Gypsy Major.   A 4-cylinder, in-line, inverted piston, air-cooled engine used to power the *DeHavilland* Tiger Moth trainer. The Gypsy Major engine was a bored-out Gypsy III with slightly greater displacement and power.

Napier Sabre.   An in-line, liquid-cooled aircraft engine, with its 24 cylinders arranged in two "double-decker" banks positioned in a horizontally-opposed configuration.

Power Jets Ltd. W.2. A turbojet engine produced by the designer Frank Whittle's company *Power Jets Ltd.* A pair of W.2s were used to power the *Gloster* Meteor, which was Britain's first operational jet fighter.

Rolls-Royce Merlin. An in-line, liquid cooled, V-12 aircraft engine built in Britain by the *Rolls-Royce* Motor Company.

Packard Merlin. Versions of the Merlin V-12 engine built in America under licence by the *Packard* Motor Company.

Rolls-Royce Griffon. An in-line, liquid-cooled V-12 aircraft engine built by *Rolls-Royce*, with greater displacement and power than the Merlin.

American Military Aircraft Designations

American military aircraft used an alpha-numeric designation employing an alphabetical prefix followed by an Arabic numeral which normally indicated chronologically when the aircraft had entered service relative to other similar types. The aircraft were also given an official name designation which followed the alpha-numeric symbols, and sometimes also an unofficial slang name by its pilots. All U.S. Army Air Force fighter planes bore the prefix 'P' for 'Pursuit', or in the case of Bombers, 'B'. (e.g.) P-51 or B-17. U.S. Navy aircraft used the prefix 'F' for Fighter. (e.g.) F6F. After the war, on September 18, 1947, when the U.S. Army Air Force officially became a separate branch of the armed services – the United States Air Force – all of their subsequent fighter aircraft received an 'F' prefix.

P-38 *'Lightning'*. Built by *Lockheed* Aircraft Ltd. Powered by two *Alison* V-12 engines.

P-47 *'Thunderbolt'*. Built by *Republic* Aircraft Ltd. Powered by the *Pratt & Whitney* R-2800 double Wasp radial engine.

P-51 *'Mustang'*. Built by *North American* Aircraft Ltd. Powered by the *Packard* Merlin V-12 engine.

B-17 *'Flying Fortress'*. Built by *Boeing* Aircraft Ltd. Powered by four *Wright* R-1820 'Cyclone' radial engines.

B-24 *'Liberator'*. Built by *Consolidated* Aircraft Ltd. Powered by four *Pratt & Whitney* R-1830 twin Wasp radial engines.

American Military Aircraft Engines

Except for the Alison V-12 engine, which was used in the (P-38, P-39, and P-40), and the Packard-built version of the Merlin, all American fighter and bomber aircraft used air-cooled radial engines. The manufacturer's name for these engines was normally followed by the prefix 'R' for 'radial', and then Arabic numerals which generally indicated chronologically its development, and increased displacement or power.

Jacobs R-915. A single-bank, 7-cylinder, air-cooled radial engine, used to power the *Avro* Anson Mk II and Mk III two-engine bomber crew trainer.

Packard V-1650-7 Merlin. An American-built version of the two-stage, supercharged *Rolls-Royce* Merlin 66, V-12 engine, which powered the Mk IX Spitfire. The *Packard* V-1650-7 was used to power the P-51D Mustang. *Packard* also built an American version of the Rolls-Royce Merlin XX which normally powered the Lancaster bomber. The *Packard*-built versions were used in the Lancaster B.III and Canadian-built B.X models.

Pratt & Whitney R-1340. A single-bank, 9-cylinder, air-cooled radial engine, used to power the *North American* Harvard and T-6 'Texan' training aircraft.

Pratt & Whitney R-1830. A twin-bank, 14-cylinder, air-cooled radial engine based upon the *P&W* 'Wasp' series, and used to power the B-24 Liberator.

Pratt & Whitney R-2800. A twin-bank, 18-cylinder, double 'Wasp', air-cooled radial engine, used to power the P-47 Thunderbolt.

Wright R-1820 Cyclone. A single-bank, 9-cylinder, air-cooled radial engine, used to power the B-17 Flying Fortress.

Russian Military Aircraft Designations

Russian aircraft designations were alpha-numeric, normally beginning with the first two letters of the designer's family name, or the first letter of his first given and first letter(s) of his family name. This was followed by an Arabic numeral which indicated the chronological stages of that particular aircraft's development.

Polikarpov I-16. Designed by *Nikolai Nikolaevich Polikarpov*, and powered by an *Shvetsov* M-25 radial engine, it was for its time (1933) a revolutionary monoplane fighter featuring an open cockpit and retractable landing gear.

Il-2. (Sturmovik) Designed by *Sergey Vladomirovich Ilyushin*, it was a well-armoured and highly successful ground attack aircraft powered by the *Mikulin AM*-35, V-12 engine. It featured a second crew member in the cockpit operating a rearward-firing machine gun. The *Sturmovic* was produced in higher numbers than any other aircraft in World War Two.

La-5.　　　Designed by *Semyon Lavochkin*, this fighter was largely constructed of wood – a non-strategic material. In later variants (e.g.) the *La*-7, the wood was replaced as greater supplies of strategic alloys became available in the Soviet Union. It was powered by the *Shvetsov ASh*-82 radial engine.

MiG-3.　　A fighter plane designed by *Artem Mikoyan* and *Michail Guerevich*. The contraction of the first letter(s) of their family names *Mikoyan-Guerevich* resulted in '*MiG*'. It was powered by the *Mikulin AM*-35, V-12 engine.

Yak-3.　　A fighter plane designed by *Alexander Sergeyevich Yakolev*, and powered by the *Klimov VK*-107, V-12 engine.

Russian Military Aircraft Engines

Russian aircraft engines used an alpha-numeric designation preceded by the designer's family name, and next, the first letter(s) of the designer's given and family name, followed by an Arabic numeral generally reflecting the chronological stage of that particular engine's development.

M-25.　*Arkady Shvetsov's* version of the *Wright* R-1820 'Cyclone' radial engine, used to power the *Polikarpov* I-16.

Klimov VK-107.　An in-line, liquid-cooled V-12 engine powering the *Yak*-3. It was designed by *Vladimir Klimov*.

Mikulin AM-35.　An in-line, liquid-cooled V-12 engine powering the *MiG*-3 and *Il*-2 *Sturmovik*. It was designed by *Alexander Mikulin*.

Shvetsov ASh-82. A twin-row, air-cooled radial engine based upon the earlier M-25 Russian version of the *Wright* R-1820. Designed by *Arkadiy Shvetsov*, it powered the *La*-5.

Miscellaneous Aviation / Armour Terms

A.P. 'Armour-piercing' ammunition.

Bogey-wheels The wheeled part of a tank's suspension which bears its weight, and runs atop the bottom portion of the vehicle's caterpillar tracks.

'G' forces One 'G' represents the normal force of gravity on an individual. 'Gs' represent multiples of the normal force of gravity on a pilot when performing high-speed, or abrupt alteration of vector manoeuvres in an aircraft.

Glacis An armour plate comprising the front part of a tank's hull.

Glycol A generic liquid aircraft engine coolant.

H2S British ground contour radar capable of cloud penetration and detecting targets in darkness. The unit normally hung in a blister on the bottom of a heavy bomber's fuselage aft of the bomb bay. Its transmissions were detectable by *Naxos Z* sets in German night-fighters.

H.E. 'High-Explosive' ammunition.

Mantlet Armour plate attached to the external base of a tank's main gun to protect the front of the turret where the gun passes through from its interior breech.

Window Thousands of thin strips of aluminum foil that were dropped by allied bombers at night to confuse or defeat the early warning radars of the *Kammhuber Line*.

ABOUT THE AUTHOR

William Myers grew up on the northern shores of the Great Lakes. After a decade with the Royal Canadian Mounted Police, the author spent much of his later career lecturing at police academies, military institutions, and universities abroad. He has also won numerous national awards for his educational video productions. An aviation and military history enthusiast, he now resides near Victoria, British Columbia.

Made in the USA
Middletown, DE
28 January 2022

59906717R00209